CAGED

CAGED

Molly Venzke

a production of

www.traffickinghope.org

ISBN:
ISBN-13: 978-1461065425

LCCN:
2011905682

Book Design:
Cover Concept by Create Space
Cover photos taken by Latasha Haynes Photography
Interior Design by Molly Venzke

Printed in the United States of America

*This book is dedicated
to the millions of children around the world
whose lives have become not their own.*

You are not forgotten.

Please hold on to Life...

We're coming to get you.

CAGED

✤ PROLOGUE ✤

AT THE SIGHT OF HER HUSBAND, she shuddered. Pulling her robe tighter to her gaunt frame, she gathered the collar at her neck and took another glance at him. He sat hunched over his computer, fully engrossed, as he smoked his cigarette and frantically typed away. She thought to ask him if he'd be coming to bed soon, but she resisted the urge. She already knew the answer; she couldn't remember the last time he slept in their bed. And if she were to be honest with herself, she'd admit the deep relief she felt from his absence.

He wasn't the same person she'd married years ago. But then again, neither was she. When they'd met, she was nineteen and still grieving the sudden loss of both her parents. He was a strong, confident, and handsome man who offered her the comfort she so desperately ached for. She fell hard for this man who was over ten years her senior. One year later, she found herself indelibly connected to him as she carried their first baby.

When she showed him the pregnancy test, he didn't even try to hide his disappointment, and he frequently brought up the subject of abortion. She'd hear nothing of it, and convinced herself that he'd warm up to the idea once the baby was born. She was wrong. So much so, when she fell pregnant with their second child, she hid the news from her husband as long as she could, for fear he would force her to abort it. He was furious when he finally found out, and that night was the first time he'd hit her.

It took several years for her inheritance to trickle away, and only in hindsight was she able to see that his manipulation and violence seemed to escalate at the same rate as her financial decline. At first he'd simply berate her and bully her with his words. And somehow, she was mentally able to justify his behavior, even believe she was partially to blame. She allowed him to slowly erode her self-worth so that by the time he was regularly lifting his hand to strike her, she'd lost all sense of perspective. She feared staying with him, and she feared leaving him.

Finally, by the time the last penny from her parents had been spent, she had come to believe she was trapped in the tangles of a life with no exits. Just 34 years old, she'd lost all hope for her own dreams and now lived merely to do her best to give her daughters a shot at a healthy future.

On this uncommonly cold Louisiana night as she watched her husband work, he looked totally unrecognizable to her. The sole source of light in his small office was a blue-ish hue from his monitor, and it made his eyes appear even puffier and more bloodshot than usual. *Does he really look that old*, she thought. *Or is his face just distorted from the light? Good god, do I look as bad?* Through his thin beard, she could make out the long scar across his left cheek-bone as the blue light seemed to give it a slight glow. *He thinks that scruffy beard hides that damn scar. What a fool he is,* she thought bitterly. *The moment I met him, I should've seen that scar as a mark from the universe to run away as quickly as I could.*

"What?!" His voice pierced through the circling cigarette smoke and shot across the room, shocking her out of her thoughts, and almost knocking her over. "What're you lookin' at?"

She knew no answer would be good enough for him. And afraid what the consequences of a wrong response would be, she decided to get out of his space as fast as possible. She scurried down the hall toward her room, stopping first to check that her daughter was safe in bed. She found the young girl sound asleep, tenderly hugging her own nighttime companion, a white fuzzy monkey. The beautiful innocence of her face took the woman's breath away. Quietly, she tiptoed in and sat down on the pink rug next to the girl's mattress. Guilt seemed to swallow her heart as she wished a better future for her daughter. The guilt magnified as she thought about the lifeline this little girl provided. *She's all I have left,* she thought. *If I didn't have her could I even bare to live?*

The woman pulled out a spare blanket and lay on the floor next to her daughter. She found such solace in this room, every toy and book reflecting a much simpler and more naïve time. "Cherish these moments," she whispered more to herself than to the slumbering girl. She began to drift off to sleep, with only the faint sound of her husband tapping out messages on his keyboard.

What in the hell was she looking at? He thought to himself, taking a break from his computer. *Why was she staring at me like that? What does she know?* He searched his mind for the thousandth time to reassure himself that he'd not so much as left a crack open in his plans. *She only knows what I tell her,* he thought, and before he could doubt again, an instant message popped up on his screen. It was from his friend with the username: stableboyz

stableboyz: im tellin u, i know youll be able to get at least 100-150k for the mare

He typed back as username 4mares: how can u be so sure? last time i only got f-ing 50k, and that was way less than what i needed her to go for

stableboyz: this time'll be different. itll be the first of the year, so theyll be wantin to restock their stalls. theyll be lookin for the newest thing. also, this mare is much younger than the one you sold last summer. she'll be in a higher demand. and if you play your cards right, you could get well into the six figures

4mares: why's that

stableboyz: cuz of her age. she'll live a whole lot longer. they're lookin for workhorses that can go the distance and stand the long haul. i guarantee her youth will bring in the big bucks. but you're gonna have to get this one certified. if you'd've listened to me about this for the last one, you prob would've got more for her

4mares: how do i do that

3

stableboyz: my contact there will give you the address of a vet. he'll check her out to make sure she ain't been broken in before. he'll give you the papers you need.

4mares: but why greece? its an f-ing pain in the a**. the cost for gettin her over there, then the money to dress her up, then i gotta train her how to show herself for auction. i dont have that kinda time. plus if i don't get a good net profit, its not worth it. theres gotta be a better place. what do you know about mexico

stableboyz: WTF you crazy if u go down there. u make 1 wrong move, and its all over. they'll f you up down there. i had a friend who tried sellin in mexico city and he came back in a bodybag W/O his head attached. dont even try that, man. its not worth the risk and youll not get close to the same $

4mares: i still think i could make a buck here in the states. i've heard of a large stable and racing operation near portland OR

stableboyz: look, u do what you want. all im sayin is, i've been in the mare biz for years and greece is the best bang for your buck, bottom line. i know the guys to set u up with. i know what trainers are looking for what mares. i dont know nothing about portland, so your on your own there. take it or leave it

Taking a long drag off his Marlboro, the man leaned back in his chair and thought about his last trip to Greece. He hated every minute of it. The prep was grueling, the upfront costs were more than he'd bargained for, and in the end, he barely made back the kind of money he needed. But he only had one mare left to sell, so he had to go where the risk vs. reward would be the most profitable. He really didn't have any other options.

"Son of a bitch!" he cursed under his breath. Greece it is. He went back to his computer.

4mares: i'll take it

AGGIE

❧ 1 ❧

"Dɪs ᴅᴀ ʟᴀsᴛ ᴛɪᴍᴇ I'm gone make dis trek out to Maringouin," Aggie said. "And in da snow at dat! What kinda devil done possessed dis state o' Louisiana and made it snow? And while I'm askin, what ol' black Cajun woman drives herself from Lafayette to da tiny po-dunk town of Maringouin in all dat possessed snow? I'll tell you what kind. A crazy one, dat's what. I swear I'm gone kill myself drivin in all dis snow."

There was no one in the car with her, but Aggie always talked out loud. In her house, in the car, or in the middle of the Olde Tyme Grocery on West Saint Mary Boulevard. Even before Harold died over ten years ago, Aggie's thoughts generally flew right on out, unedited from her mind to her mouth. Only on Sundays, which Aggie called *la jour de Bon Dieu*, the Good Lord's Day, did she practice restraint. And on this late Saturday night, she had at least fifteen minutes until the clock struck midnight and her discipline had to kick in.

"Good ting no one else crazy as me to be out on da roads at dis God-forsaken hour. *Choooh*, it's Mardi Gras weekend, too! Dat's why da streets are bare; all dem heathens still be celebratin da holiday. Da night's still young for dose folks. Well, now I guess it's a good ting Macy *did* call me when she did. A few more hours, and I'd be havin to worry about all dose drunks slidin around tryin to smash into me. Well, all I'm sayin is, I'm not gone do dis again. Dis da last time she gone call me in da middle of da night cryin, needin someone to come save her—*and* her little girls—from dat awful man.

"And she not even making any sense dis time. What she mean 'he done sold em?' Sold what? Ha! What else dat greedy man got to sell, anyway? He already done sold anyting worth of value my girl Macy ever had, he so up to his eyeballs in debt. I told her dat she needed to make dat good-for-nothin get a j-o-b. Den maybe he don't have to hock anyting dat's not nailed down.

"I'll tell you what I'm gone do...I'm gone march in dere and tell dat girl she gettin outta dat house, and dat's just gone be da way it's gone be. I done told her once, I told her a million times, dat boy *canaille* (sly and sneaky) and a cheat. I'm gone pack her up with her li'l baby girl, and she gone come live with Aggie. I'm tellin you, I'm not gone do dis again."

As Aggie turned her '95 Chevrolet off of I-10 east and onto LA-76 west toward Maringouin, she had no idea the irony her words held. This would be the last time she made this drive, but for much different reasons than she ever could have anticipated.

"And I know none a dem roads be cleared. Dis town so small, I bet dey don't even own a plow, or even at da very least, salt da streets. I tank *le Bon Dieu* (the Good Lord) I don't live here. All da poor ol' women like me'll be havin to pour out da entire pantry of Epson Salts all over da sidewalk just so's dey can make it out to da mailbox without breakin a hip."

In truth, even if Aggie did slip and fall, the chances of her breaking a bone were slim. She was strong as an ox for her stout, 5-foot frame, and she only boasted her age so other people would feel compassion and give her assistance. She figured since she'd made it on the planet over 67 years, she might as well use her age to her advantage. Plus, it gave her the opportunity to talk to folks as they carried her groceries, helped mow her lawn, and walked her across the street.

The snow was barely dusting the streets, but for this Cajun woman who could count on her fingers the times she had seen snow, let alone drive in it, there may as well have been ten inches. She slowed down to a crawl as she entered the small town of Maringouin. As she turned onto Landry Drive, gradually making her way to her destination on Lions Ave., she chuckled at the number of families who were out in the snowfall.

"Dose mama's musta woke dem babies right out dere beds just so dey could see dis snow," she said. "Well, I guess I'd pro'bly do da same ting if little Skye and Elle had been sleepin at my house dis night. If da *Bon Dieu* gone bless da South with da snow, ya gotta get out in it, cuz if ya sneeze, ya gone miss it."

Aggie was surprised at how a paper-thin coat of white snow could improve the appearance of the worn-out neighborhood. Blanketing over the thick, mossy patches on the roofs, and trimming the windows and doorframes with a look of cleanliness, the snow offered this particular street a much-needed facelift.

"Too bad da sun's gone come up soon and melt all dis away. Dis house almost looks like a decent place to live." And she pulled into the driveway of a small, one-story home, her wheels sounding pops and crackles over the frozen grass.

Aggie was half expecting to hear chaotic sounds seeping from the house, a party, an argument, or at least a television blaring questionable programming. But there was just a strange, quiet calm. She noticed Jack and Macy's car was gone, and from the lack of tire tracks in the snow, it must have been gone for a while. She breathed a sigh of relief knowing she wasn't going to have to confront Jack. Not only was he conniving, but he was also a brute of a man. There's no way he would allow Macy to pack up and leave, without a fight, that is. And Jack was no stranger to hitting a woman. Macy could attest to that.

Aggie lumbered out of her car, feeling the stiffness of the hour-long drive in her 67-year-old body. "Dis da last time I'm gone do dis," she mumbled under her breath once more. "Aggie, you best be takin it careful *gettin down* out da car, else you slip in all dis snow."

Slowly, she climbed the narrow porch steps, cautious to test each one's sturdiness before trusting it with the fullness of her weight. And once she arrived at the front door, she noticed it was slightly ajar. She entered the house saying, "Girl, what you tinkin keepin dis door open with all dis snow and it being so..."

Her words trailed off as something just did not feel right. What was that smell? Burnt metal? Bleach? Rotten food? Sour alcohol? It was a noxious mixture of it all.

"Macy?" she called out. There was no answer.

The hair began to stand up on the back of her neck as Aggie rushed into Macy's bedroom. She wasn't in her bed, so Aggie checked her bathroom. Vacant. Next, she tried the kitchen, which turned out to be the source of the horrible smells. Covering her mouth with her hand in hopes to keep from gagging, she scanned the wreckage. One end of the kitchen looked like a chemistry lab with glass vials, empty pill bottles, and deeply charred saucer pots. In the sink was a heap of unrecognizable, rotting food, and on the floor tile in the opposite corner, it looked as if someone had vomited...a few days ago. Aggie's heart sank down into her stomach.

"Macy, you in here?"

A soft moan came from the girls' room, and Aggie hurried to respond. When she opened little Elle's bedroom door, she found Macy crumpled on the pink carpet beside Elle's empty bed. Half dressed in a t-shirt and men's boxer shorts, Macy looked as white as the snow falling outside, and the blue hue of her lips brought panic to Aggie's chest.

"Macy girl, Aggie's here," she said as she knelt by her side and tried to cradle her. The stench coming off her body was sickening. "Can you hear me, *Sha* (Dear)? You here?"

Aggie could see Macy's nostrils flaring with each breath; even so, her breathing seemed quite labored. She pulled a blanket off Elle's bed and did her best to wrap Macy's torso with it. Macy let out another soft moan.

"Mama Aggie? Did you come, after all?"

"Aggie's here, *Sha*. Talk to me. Tell me what you done took?"

Aggie could tell Macy was trying to muster up some kind of urgency, but she was barely finding the energy to speak. "Mama Aggie, Jack sold them. Right now. He's selling them. They're gone."

"OK, now, you listen to me right now. You tell Mama Aggie what you done took. And how much of it did you take?"

"I don't know. I don't know. It doesn't matter anymore. They're gone now, and they're not coming back. The god-damned bastard sold them. *(pausing to take breaths)* How could he do that? What kind of person does that? And now we're all gonna rot in hell." And with that Macy lost consciousness.

"Macy! You gotta stay with me, *Sha!*" Aggie started gently patting her cheeks. "Macy, you gotta wake up. You gotta stay with me, and den we'll get back whatever it is Jack done stole. Ain't nothin worth losin yo life over. You hear me? Macy, you gotta keep with me." The old woman attempted to sit Macy up but even as emaciated as she had become, Macy's dead weight and tall body was difficult for Aggie to maneuver.

911! I gotta call 911, she thought, and then realized she had left her cell phone in the car. "Lawd, it's gone take dem too long to get way out here."

Aggie pulled a pillow off the girl's bed, trying to make a comfortable place for Macy to lay. As the old woman gently scooted her onto the makeshift bed, the young woman emerged again into consciousness.

"Mama Aggie. Are you still here?"

"*Bebe*, I'm right next to you."

"There still might be time. I don't know. But there might...you've got to...listen to me, Aggie...I'm all done, Aggie, all done...and I deserve it. I've been a terrible mama to the girls, so blind to everything. I should've seen it; I should've seen it. How could I not have seen it? I deserve to die and go straight to hell."

"Macy, I don't wanna hear you talkin like dat."

"It's ok, Mama. I know I deserve what I get. But not the girls. They don't deserve a single bit of it. I can't even think of the hell they're going through right now. Mama Aggie, please, I'm begging you. Get the girls. Will you promise me to get the girls?"

"You not makin any sense, *Sha*. O' course I'll get 'em. When Skye gets back from her boardin school, I'll get her. And where is Elle? I'll take her home with me right now."

"That's just it, Aggie!" Macy was becoming very agitated. "You don't understand; Skye's not coming home from school! I found out about everything Jack was really doing...Aggie, Skye is not coming home from that school! Oh, god, how could he do it?" and she fell back onto the floor half-moaning, half-crying.

"Macy, you gotta get yourself clear in da head, and tell me what you mean."

"Mama, it's all on his laptop," she whispered "The stupid bastard forgot to take his laptop." And she almost drifted off again, but then she shot up and lunged forward to grab Aggie. Her whole body shook from the effort. Her eyes locked into Aggie's with a desperate intensity. "Aggie, don't you let the police get that laptop. *You* take that. They won't know what to do with that laptop. Do you understand me? *You* gotta take that laptop and use it to get the girls back. Promise me."

"What you talkin about? Why Skye not comin home? Where's Elle? Is she with Jack?"

"Promise me!"

"OK, baby, I promise you. I'll get da girls. I'll take da laptop. Aggie do whatever you need. Don't you worry bout a ting. I gone take care of all of it. Now listen, Macy, I'm gone get my cell phone to call for help. I left it out in da car. I'll be right back, though, so you rest here and Aggie be right back."

"Wait! No, wait, Mama. Take the laptop with you right now. You take that thing out to your car before anyone else can get it. Mama Aggie, you hear me? You've got to take it right now! It's in the kitchen. Give me your word; promise me that you'll take it right now!"

"Yes, girl. I promise I'll take da laptop. Trust me, we'll get all dis worked out as soon as we get you some help."

"Nobody can help me now." Macy whispered as she fell back, and once again, slipped out of consciousness.

✤ 2 ✤

AGGIE KNEW THE MOMENT she came back inside the house, Macy was gone. The absence of life could be felt. And when she approached the door of the girl's room, she saw the proof of it. She'd seen the expression of death many times before, on her mama, both her younger sisters, and on her own husband, Harold, when he died in his sleep over a decade ago. *Funny,* she thought, not yet able to digest the moment in which she stood. *Funny how death looks da same on ever'body. All different faces, but somehow it still looks da same. How dat?* But instead of an answer to her question came the reality of her loss, an engulfing wave of grief so tangible Aggie had to grip onto the doorframe to keep from collapsing under the weight of its rush.

She staggered in toward Macy and fell to her knees beside the dead woman. From deep within her bowels arose a wail of emotion unlike anything Aggie had ever felt, a silent heave of sorrow much too profound to be vocalized, though her mouth was open wide. She wrapped her arms around this woman who was the closest thing she ever had to a daughter. Aggie kissed her hair and her cheeks, and held her body that had not yet grown cold. And she wished she would have waited to go to her car rather than be absent when Macy let out her last breath. Aggie had been in the room when Macy had taken her first breath as a baby; she had aided in her delivery. And now it felt so unjust, that simply by a matter of moments, she had missed her final one.

"Aggie shoulda stayed with you, *Sha.* I'm so sorry you had to go alone. Aggie shoulda been right here with you." Those words paved a way for the tears and the cries to spill forth, and for the next many minutes, Aggie wept as she rocked Macy back and forth.

"Oh, my baby, why you wait so long to call yo Aggie? Why you wait so long?" she whispered to Macy, stroking her hair. "I coulda come here sooner and save you from dis. You know Aggie woulda come to help you. And now how I gone live without my Macy girl?" She rocked and rocked as she groaned in sorrow.

Aggie was unsure how much time had passed when she began to hear the faint sound of sirens in the distance. Instinctively, her grief gave way to her protective nature as she became acutely aware of how unpresentable Macy would appear to the medics. Even in death, Aggie felt obliged to preserve the dignity of this girl she had helped raise.

With great care, she released her embrace and slowly straightened Macy's body across the pink carpet. She found a clean pillow on the bed, placed it under her head and began to smooth down her clothes. As Aggie straightened Macy's shirt, she was shocked at just how bony she had become; even through the white T-shirt, her ribcage could be seen. She covered her body with a blanket, and became determined to do something about the rank smell of vomit in Macy's hair.

She quickly rummaged through the nearby child-sized dresser to find a hairbrush. Taking it into the bathroom, she wet the brush and massaged a bit of shampoo into its bushy bristles. Macy's hair was thin and straight, so it was fairly easy for Aggie to brush out the knots and gather it to one side of her face.

By now, the sirens were quite loud, announcing their arrival to every house along Lions Ave.

"*Bon Dieu,* you'd tink dey'd turn dose tings down. Dey're gonna wake up da whole neighborhood and make dis whole ting a three ring circus."

Aggie walked to the front door to meet the medics and police officers. As the ambulance and cop car pulled into the front yard, their rotating lights seemed to illuminate the entire block as they reflected off the freshly fallen snow. Alternating colors of blue, white, and red streaked in every direction as the men got out and crunched their way toward the house. As she welcomed the officers, she saw that already, the folks who had been out playing in the snow had stopped what they were doing to watch the activity.

"Tank you so much," Aggie greeted. "Tank you for comin so quickly. She right in here." Making sure to close the front door from the outside onlookers, she then escorted the team into the room where Macy's body lay.

The next several minutes seemed surreal to Aggie as the paramedics tried their best to revive Macy. She stood just outside the room and watched them work. There were three of them, one woman and two men. The woman was constantly checking Macy's vitals while one of the men injected something into her arm. The second man began to warm up the defibrillator, and even though several attempts were made to shock Macy's heart back to life, all were futile. Eventually, they stated the inevitable and pronounced her dead on the scene.

A police officer touched Aggie gently on the arm and asked, "Ma'am, I need to ask you some questions, can we sit down in the front room?"

"Yes. Yes, o' course." She replied absentmindedly, keeping her gaze fixed on Macy's face. She could hear her mind telling her body to address the officer, to turn around and start walking toward the front room, but her faculties had grown deaf and dumb. Leaning against the doorframe, she lingered until the medics covered Macy's body with a white sheet. It wasn't until her face was fully hidden under the cloth, that Aggie could manage to peel her eyes away.

"Ma'am?" The officer once again addressed her. He had been waiting, politely giving Aggie a bit more time.

"Yes. Yes. Yes, o' course." Aggie said in a daze. "Questions. O' course, you have questions. Let's go sit in da front room. Would dat be alright?"

Smiling kindly, the young officer nodded and allowed her to lead him. They both began to take a seat, but no sooner had Aggie sat down than she shot back up. Even in her shocked state, she was a Southern Cajun woman through and through, and this DNA offered her the ability to shift into hostess at any given time, regardless of how dire the circumstances might be.

"I'm sorry, sir; where my manners?" Aggie said to the policeman as he sank down into the broken-down sofa. "Can I get you and your fellow officers sometin to eat or drink? You must all be freezin, comin out on a night like dis. And Mardi Gras weekend at dat! Would you like sometin hot to warm your belly? It wouldn't take but a minute. Aggie could look in da kitchen..." and then her words trailed off as she remembered her own revulsion upon entering the kitchen earlier. No, to find anything edible in a wreck like that would be impossible.

"No, no, no, no, no," the officer said as he took her arm in his hands and guided her to rest in the chair opposite the sofa. "Please, ma'am. We're just fine, and you don't need to worry about us at all. It's very late, and I can see you've been through a lot. The EMTs will take good care of...*(trying to be sensitive)* well, of the woman in that room, and I just have a few questions I need to ask you. This isn't going to take very long, and then we'll all be done here. OK?"

Aggie could see this man was trying to be as sensitive as he could. He had caring, dark brown eyes and a smooth, round baby-face, the kind of face that stayed exactly the same from birth to adulthood. She sighed deeply and replied, "Yessir. I want to help in any way I can."

"Wonderful. My name is Officer Mark Landon. Can you give me your full name?"

Aggie: My given name is Agata Prejean, but ever'one calls me Aggie.

Mark: Alright, Miss Aggie, do you live here?

Aggie: Oh no. I live in Lafayette. 311 Bellot Street in North Lafayette.

Mark: Lafayette? How did you get all the way out here tonight?

Aggie: Well, I done drove my car, Officer.

Mark: All the way out here in the snow? You're a brave woman. *He opened up an oblong spiral notebook and began to take notes.* OK. Let's start from the beginning. Can you tell me the name of the victim, and how old is she?

Aggie: Her name's Macy DuMonde. Before she married, it was Macy Bacchus. She only 34 years old, still just a chile.

Mark: And what is your relationship to her?

Aggie: I worked for her parents from, O Lawd, let's see, from 1963, I believe it was, until dey both died in 1995. Paul and Jenny

Bacchus was dere names. Dem's good folks, da Bacchus's ...real good folks.

Mark: How did they die?

Aggie: A horrible car accident. Dey just gone to a birthday party for one a dey friends, and on da way home, dey got in a terrible wreck. Four people died right dere on da road dat night, and one more a few days later in da hospital. It was just heart-wrenchin. Macy girl was just startin her first year at LSU when all dat happened. She got so broken up, she never did finish school.

Mark: So you worked for the Bacchus's. What did you do?

Aggie: *(laughing) Mais*, sir, da only ting a black woman *could* do in da 60s. I's da Bacchus's maid. I tended to da home ever' day for over 30 years. I practically raised little Macy myself; she even call me 'Mama Aggie.' But dey's wonderful folks, the Bacchus's. Dey treated me and Harold like we part of da family; even had us over for ever' single holiday. I didn't know just how much Ms. Bacchus loved me til she died, cuz she put it in her will to pay off Harold and my house *and* my salary for five more years.

Mark: Wow. That was very generous. And who's Harold?

Aggie: Oh. I'm sorry, Harold was my husband. He died in '99, God rest his soul. Can't believe it's already almost 13 years since he went to be with *le Bon Dieu*.

Mark: I'm sorry to hear that, Miss Aggie. *He paused for a moment as he jotted down the facts.* So, Macy...how long had she been using drugs?

Aggie: *(sighing)* At least six or seven years, maybe ten, maybe even more. She met dat awful Jack less'n a year after her parents died, and from da start, I knew he just wanted her money. But she was so broken, she couldn't see straight, and convinced herself dat he loved her.

Mark: Is she still married?

Aggie: Yes. His full name is Jack DuMonde.

Mark: And they had daughters?

Aggie: Yes sir. Dey had two beautiful girls, Elle is 10 and Skye is just 15.

Mark: What do Jack and Macy do for work?

Aggie: Ha! Nothin'! Dat man just hop from job to job while he leach off Macy's inheritance. She used to do secretary work til she had da girls, den she stayed home with dem. But for da last few years, I could tell da money had run dry. At da end of da summer, Jack got into sellin horses, but I don't know too much 'bout dat. It did provide da money for Skye's schoolin' though.

Mark: Do you know where Jack and the girls are right now?

Aggie: Dat's just it. I dunno where he is *or* where Elle is. Last ting Macy say is dat he took her, but I dunno know what she meant by dat.

Mark: Wait. I'm getting confused. Which girl did Jack take?

Aggie: Elle, I tink. *(suddenly remembering)* Oh, Lawd have mercy! I remember now. I know what Macy was talkin about. O' course. How could I forget? Elle is on her trip to see her sissy.

Mark: Where is her sister?

Aggie: Dis last summer, Jack and Macy both decided to send Skye to some kinda art school in Europe. It was 'posed to be a great opportunity, a place where Skye could grow. It was Jack who came up with da idea. Macy was against it at first. She thought it was too far and too long for Skye to be away from home. But den, all Macy wanted was for her girls to wind up better off dan her, so she finally agreed. She'd do anyting for dose girls. Elle'd been missin her sister so much, Jack and Macy gave her a trip to see Skye for a Christmas present. Dat's where dey is, I'm sure of it. Jack is takin Elle over to visit her big sissy.

Mark: Why didn't Macy go with them?

Aggie: Oh Lawd, no. Macy don't fly. She never could get herself over dat silly fear of flyin. I done tell her she shoulda gone with 'em. I don't trust dat Jack as far as I can throw him.

Mark: Do you have any reason to believe there was foul play that might have lead to her death?

Aggie: *(pausing for a moment to think about this question)* I don't know, Officer. She been gone for a while now.

Mark: Gone? Where has she been?

Aggie: No, I mean, gone in her head. She just not been full in reality. She and Jack were *motier foux* (half-crazy) most da time. I mean, don't get me wrong, she a precious girl, and she do da best she know to do. She take excellent care of dem girls, but she just gone. Maybe it was da drugs. Maybe she never got over da death of her folks. I dunno.

Mark: *(writing notes)* Hmm.

Another officer, who had been standing in the room listening, interrupted their conversation.

"Hey, Mark. Check out this picture. What do you make of this?"

"Seriously, Zach? Can you not see I'm working here?" Mark was irritated.

"No, really. You've got to come and look at this picture here on the wall. Did you not notice who these people are?"

Mark went over to look at the photo, and Aggie could see the surprise on his face. She didn't need to get up. She knew this house like the back of her hand, and she knew exactly what was in the frame the men were staring at because she'd hung it there herself. It was a picture of Macy and Jack, shortly before they had been married. The one next to it was one of Macy and the girls, and the one next to that was of Macy and Jack on their honeymoon in Hawaii.

Officer Mark removed the picture from the wall and brought it over to Aggie.

"Miss Aggie, do you know who this man is?"

Aggie's face turned sour. "Yes, I do, and 'cept dat Macy gave birth to two precious girls by dat man, I wish none o' us had ever laid our eyes on him. He a wicked, awful man."

"Miss Aggie," said Mark, sitting back down on the couch. "This man is Richard DuMonde, one of the wealthiest and most influential men in New Orleans. He has a reputation of being one of the most generous philanthropists in Louisiana."

"Dat is *not* who you tink it is. Dat's Jack, Macy's husband, and I've known him since he finally convinced her to marry him over ten years ago. Dey already been livin together for years and had one daughter together. It took her fallin pregnant with her second baby dat finally made her crazy enough to commit to him. I guess he started out nice enough, but it wasn't long before he so drunk all da time, he never knew which way was up. And he da one who got Macy started on all dose drugs. She never shoulda gone and married dat man."

"But this looks exactly like Richard DuMonde. The same dark hair, the same blue eyes, the same face shape...and they even have the same last name. Don't you find that to be a little odd? Even the slightest bit coincidental?" Mark asked. Aggie just shook her head and said matter-of-factly, "I'm telling you, dat's *Jack*."

"Look at this one, Mark," the other officer said, bringing over another picture. "Does Richard DuMonde have a scar on his face? See this pic? It looks like this guy has a scar, pretty distinct, too, like he was sliced right across his cheek. Mr. DuMonde doesn't have that, does he?"

"No...I'm pretty sure he doesn't have a scar," replied Mark. "I went to high school with his son, Wil. He was a great athlete; I swear the guy played almost every sport. It was a huge school, though. We never really ran in the same circles, but I'd see his dad at all the sports events. As far as I can remember, Mr. DuMonde didn't have any major marks on his face, but then again, that was almost 10 years ago. Either way, I'm telling you, this guy is a dead ringer for Wil's dad. It's kinda eerie."

"Did Wil ever mention an uncle, or a cousin, brother, anything?" the officer asked.

"Well, like I said, Wil and I didn't hang around very much, just friends who bumped into each other now and then, so I really didn't know any details about his family," Mark said.

"I'm tellin you, dat *peeshwank* (tiny man) Jack could not be related to nobody like you describin. I'm sure of it. He don't have a speck a righteous blood in his body! Dat boy *canaille* (sly, dishonest)," Aggie announced. She was getting riled, which always brought out the Cajun in her. "Dat *capon* (coward) so full o' da devil, he'd sell his own children just so's to save his-self."

Barely had the words escaped her lips that she heard Macy's pleas ringing in her ears. 'Skye's not coming back home from school. The bastard sold them. Right now, he's selling them,' she had said. 'It's all on his laptop; I found it all out on his laptop.' And then, 'Mama Aggie, please, I'm begging you. You have to get the girls. Please, get the girls.'

A panic gripped Aggie's chest as she tried to make sense of it all. *What could dat mean, 'he sold dem?'* Aggie's mind raced. *Surely, she couldn't've meant dat he sold da girls. How you sell a girl? Who'd sell a girl? Who'd buy a girl? Dis can't be right; you can't do dat sort o' ting in America.* Aggie was having difficulty breathing, and the room seemed to be spinning on an axis, quickly shrinking in on her.

"Miss Aggie! Miss Aggie, are you alright?" Mark's voice sounded a million miles away. "Medic, can you come in here, please?"

Within minutes she awoke, only now she was lying on the sofa, breathing into an oxygen mask, cool compresses on her face. As soon as her eyes opened, the medic began reassuring her that everything was just fine, that she had simply fainted, probably from the trauma of the evening, but suggested that Aggie think about resting here a bit before heading out in the snow again.

"Miss Aggie," Mark said quietly as he knelt down next to the sofa. "I've got enough information from you for now. Can you give me your number so I can call you in the next day or so to get anything else I might need?" He handed her a cool bottle of water as he talked to her.

Aggie took a long drink, halfway wishing it was vodka and that she hadn't decided to support Harold in their early years by going sober with him. She recited her phone numbers to Officer Mark, laid her head back, and closed her eyes.

"We'll be here for quite a while, gathering all the evidence we need," whispered Mark. "You just rest a bit here, Miss Aggie, and I'll wake you up once everyone is heading out. I'll even escort you to Lafayette if you need me to."

Sleep enveloped Aggie as she felt Officer Mark covering her carefully with a heavy blanket.

✟ 3 ✟

"Harold, I wish you was here. I know it's been a long time since you gone, but I'm still mad as hell at you leavin me here all by myself. Now, you hear dat? You just made me curse...on *le jour de Bon Dieu* (the Good Lord's Day) at dat. *Choooh*, I'll probably have to spend two more weeks in Purgatory just for cussin on a Sunday. Well, Hal, I'm tellin you right now, I have half a mind to slap yo face once I get up dere, just cause you left me here by myself for so long. I can see it now: I'll walk through dem pearly gates, check in with St. Peter, slap you upside da head, and den have to go right back down to Purgatory. Well...I'm takin you with me. You hear dat? You're gone go right back down dere with me. And dat's just gone be da way it's gone be."

The first hints of daylight were beginning to glow in the east as Aggie drove along I-10 back towards Lafayette. Still quite groggy from the early morning's events, she was very grateful Officer Mark Landon had kept his promise to escort her back to her hometown. His gesture offered her the luxury of mindlessly following behind the lights of his car, with full confidence she would return safely. The roads were still icy and slick, and Aggie was not at her best.

"Well, at least da snow has passed. I got dat to be tankful for. And, looks like it's gone be sunny today. I bet all dis snow'll be melted by mid-afternoon." Aggie sighed, wanting to keep her conversation going, even if it was simply to give a break from thinking about Macy. "I mighta well just go to early mass dis morning. No sense tryin to go to bed for a bit and *den* get myself ready for church. When I get home, I'll just make myself some *couche-couche* (a Cajun breakfast food of fried cornmeal), get dressed, and head right back on out. It's not my usual mass, so's I'm gone have to get dere early if I'm gone get my pew. Oh Lawd, Aggie's not gone be happy if folks be sittin in my pew. And after da night I just had, I cannot be held responsible for what's gone happen if folks be takin up residence in *my* pew."

She drove in silence for a bit, amusing herself with the scenario of ordering people out of her pew, knowing full well she would never do such a thing. And then, at the first pause in her thoughts, images of Macy began pouring in. Aggie was glad she had her driving to keep her from giving herself fully to the grief.

Losing Macy was so much different from losing her younger sisters, or even her husband. This was her child, maybe not blood-born, but certainly soul-born. And once she and Harold had given up hope of ever having a baby of their own, she allowed her attachment for Macy to burrow deep roots in her heart. Aggie had raised that little girl, changed her diapers, taught her how to go on the potty, kissed her knees when she fell off her bicycle. She was who sat with Macy and helped her with her schoolwork until the tasks grew beyond Aggie's education. Most days, it was Aggie who picked her up from school or cheer leading practice. Aggie even traveled with the family and helped get Macy settled into her LSU dorm room. All of these memories formed a bittersweet montage in Aggie's mind as she drove into Lafayette, silently weeping.

"Lawd, it's just not right to bury a child," she whispered as a prayer. "Dat's not how tings 'posed to go. She shoulda laid me to rest; not me doing it for her. Dat's not da natural order a tings. I shoulda gone first, and den her. Lawd, it's just not right."

Macy's affections for Mama Aggie were wholly reciprocated, especially after the death of her own parents. She deferred to Aggie for everything a daughter would, and often left her girls to stay under Aggie's care for weeks on end, particularly during the summer months or when Macy's drug habit would take a drastic turn for the worst. Aggie was the only grandparent the girls had known, certainly the most stable and trustworthy adult figure, and they all loved her dearly.

As Officer Mark Landon drove into the heart of Lafayette, he pulled over to the side of the road, motioning Aggie to park beside him. Rolling down his window, he asked, "Miss Aggie, do you think you can make it the rest of the way home?"

"Most certainly, Officer Landon," she said. "You've gone far above your call a duty tonight. Tank you for helpin me with ever'thin and for bein so kind. I'm gone be fine da rest of da way."

"Alright, ma'am. If you're sure," he said.

"I'm sure."

"Great, then, I'll be in touch with you in a couple of days. By chance, do you know how long Jack is supposed to be gone?"

"I'm sorry, Officer, I dunno 'xactly when dey left, or when dey comin home," Aggie answered. "I do know da trip was gone take a couple weeks, total."

"OK. If you see or hear from Jack, will you call me immediately?" he asked as he started to roll up his window.

"Yes sir, I will." she said, and began to drive away. Suddenly, she remembered Jack's laptop, the one Macy made her put in her car right before she died. *Bon Dieu, am I committin a crime havin dis ting? Should I turn around and give it to the police?* "No," she answered herself. "Macy specifically told me not to let da police get it. Why would she say dat?"

Her mind began to revolve around her many unanswered questions. With no reasonable answers, she felt a deep pit in her gut, and she promised herself that finding those answers would be the day's priority after she returned from Sunday mass.

I⊤ WAS EARLY THAT SUNDAY EVENING before Aggie woke from her nap. As she opened her eyes, the grogginess gave her a few moments of peace, until the tides of her memory began to come in. The first wave brought in Aggie's precious last minutes with Macy, how she felt in her arms as she rocked her and brushed her hair. The second wave washed in the realization of death's finality. Aggie allowed it to come over her, once again springing forth a fresh stream of tears. She rolled to her side and curled up her body, hugging a pillow as she wept for several moments.

The third wave brought in thoughts entirely different: the laptop, the girls, the fervent pleas from Macy, and a panicky feeling of dread. Almost instantly, Aggie's tears dried and were replaced by a sense of urgency to find out anything she could about whatever Macy was trying to communicate. She jolted out of bed and went in to the kitchen where she had set the laptop and its case. She sat down at the table, trying to decide where to begin. "Girl, what you tink you're gone do with dis ting?" she asked herself as she took all the contents out of its bag. "You dunno how to work one a dem Apple laptop machines. You can't even hook it up to a internet; dey's no wires to hook up. I'll tell you 'xactly what's gone happen...you gone turn dat ting on, get to pokin around on it, and break da ting."

She walked to the stove to put on some tea and sat back down. "Lawd, please show me what I'm 'posed to do." She sat in silence for several minutes until the whistle of the kettle called her back over to the stove.

As she was stirring cream and sugar into her Earl Grey, she decided to go on to her own computer and do a bit of research. A few years back, Macy had given Aggie an old PC and had sat for many hours with Aggie as she taught her how to work it. An amazing world opened to Aggie as she got her DSL connection hooked up and was first introduced to one of her now most favorite friends: Google. Aggie had learned more in the last five years than she had in her entire life, combined. At her every whim, her Google friend could deliver to Aggie any information she wanted...in just 0.28 seconds.

Receiving that computer had been a day of freedom for the old Cajun who only had the opportunity to receive an education until 13 years of age. Then, her father had died, and Aggie's mother was forced to work full time, sometimes even two jobs simultaneously. Aggie would stay home and take care of her youngest sister, Lou-Lou, until Lou-Lou started elementary school. By then Aggie was almost 16, so she got her first job as a maid to ease the financial burden for her mama. It was just after turning 18 that she began the long-term employment as the Bacchus' maid.

While she never second-guessed her choice to go to work, she did regret her lack of education. Ever since Macy showed Aggie how to work the computer, she rarely missed a day to peek through that window to explore the vast and complex frontier outside her state of Louisiana.

"Let's see what Mr. Google can teach me today," she said as she powered up her desktop computer. "I wish I could remember da name o' dat school Skye's gone to. I maybe could call dere and talk with her to make sure she alright and dat Elle got dere safe 'n' sound." With this thought, it dawned on Aggie that she was probably going to have to be the one to tell the girls what happened to their mama. Her heart sank as she imagined how sad they were going to be.

"What's gone to happen to dose girls now? Who's gone watch over 'em? I can't let dat *bon rien* (good-for-nothing) Jack take care of 'em. He'll just ruin 'em. And what'm I gone do if he don't let me see 'em? Well, I done care. MawMaw Aggie is gone have her place in dem girls' lives, and dat's just gone be da way it's gone be." These thoughts fueled her fire to find out what Macy could've been talking about.

After a moment of thinking what words to Google, Aggie decided to simply try "sell a girl." This was the topic of most of her confusion. Almost instantly, her search engine pulled up a page full of youtube videos and various websites addressing "How to sell Girl Scout Cookies."

"Well, now, dat can't be what Macy was talkin about; neither o' dem girls were Girl Scouts. Although, a box o' dem chocolate thin mint cookies'd be nice right now."

She typed in "buy a girl". This time the page was full of various sites: what to buy a girl for her birthday, how to a buy a girl a drink, *and* information about where to buy Girl Scout cookies. Aggie tried "buying and selling a girl" which only brought up a fresh list of results about how to buy *and* sell Girl Scout cookies. "*Bon Dieu,*" she said under her breath. "Dis not gettin me nowhere."

She got the idea to try typing in "buying and selling children". Then, in just 0.28 seconds, she discovered the information jackpot. It was also where she learned a phrase that would alter the course of her life forever: child trafficking.

The minutes turned into hours as a horrified Aggie unearthed site after site offering unimaginable reports, accompanied with pictures and videos, about how children are bought and sold on the black market for the purposes of prostitution, pornography, begging, factory work, and even to serve as soldiers in the frontline of battle. And just when Aggie was beginning to feel a tinge of relief, thinking this child trafficking only took place outside the United States, she ventured onto a new string of sites that focused primarily on how child slavery was occurring this very second in this very country.

"Tree hundred tousand children are believed to be trafficked in da U.S. alone," Aggie read in a whisper, attempting to comprehend the reality of such a sum. "Tree hundred *tousand*?! Tree hundred tousand. Oh, Lawd, have mercy on us all."

Aggie sunk against the back of her chair, stunned. "What kinda person does dat to another person? I just can't believe all dis." And she instantly heard the irony of her own words. Of course she could believe it; this nation had engaged in Negro slavery for many generations and had called it commerce. First hand, Aggie had experienced the residue of this particular form of human trafficking as well as the intense racism still very much alive in her home state of Louisiana. Even now in the new millennia for most folks living in the deep South, this meant carefully structuring social and cultural living within the confines of separatism, favoritism, and racism.

"But what does dis have to do with da girls? Could Macy have meant dat Jack sold Elle and Skye? No. Dat jus' can't be." The thought was unbearable for Aggie and she struggled to keep herself from panicking. The magnitude of what was laid before her began to settle into her heart, making her feel utterly helpless and incapable of taking any action. "And if all dis is true, what can dis ol' black woman do about it?"

Aggie could feel her mind losing its footing, about to slide down a slippery slope of sheer terror, when something on the inside of her began to rise up. The Cajun in her awoke and with steely determination she ordered herself back to sanity. "Now, you listen here, Agata Prejean. You not jus' gone lie down and give up. You not dat woman, never been dat woman. You gone stand up and fight to get dem girls back, whatever dat means. You gone get dem girls safe, even if you gone die tryin', you gone do it!"

The name "Richard DuMonde" popped into her head. "What was all dat talk with the police about Jack lookin like someone named Richard DuMonde? I wonder if dem officers were onto someting?" she said as she googled his name. Aggie gasped at the pictures of this man that now filled the screen. *"Choooh!* It's Jack! It looks jus' like him! How dat?!" For minutes, she sat stunned in disbelief at the resemblance. She had to dig deeper to get to the bottom of it. Although there were many profiles listed about Richard DuMonde, she clicked on her other favorite resource, Wikipedia. She knew they would list a birth date, and possibly, a family history.

"Well, look at dat *lagniappe* (a little something extra)..." said Aggie. "Ol' Jack has a twin brother."

She continued to read the full Wikipedia profile of the man. It included his success in several businesses, as well as an expansive list of generous contributions to the city of New Orleans since the Katrina disaster in 2005. *How can a person look identical on da outside but be 'xactly da opposite on da inside?* Aggie wondered. And for the first time since she received Macy's late night phone call, Aggie began to feel the slightest glimmer of hope.

.

ELLE

 4

ELLE COULDN'T HAVE BEEN HAPPIER. In all of her ten years, she could not remember being able to spend this much time with her daddy. Even when he *was* at home for longer than a few minutes, he was normally much too busy to pay attention to her, let alone play with her. He had work to do on his computer, or he had something important to watch on TV, or he had business to take care of on his cell phone. Many times, Elle would try to sit next to him as he talked and texted away. Being in the same room with him was better than nothing at all. And if she stayed perfectly still, he usually wouldn't yell at her or push her away.

But it had already been three days, and she had been with him almost nonstop. They had flown on the airplane together, walked side by side all throughout the streets of a Greek city that had a name Elle still couldn't pronounce, eaten some delicious new foods together, and met a lot of new people. They hadn't gone to see Skye yet, but her daddy said they'd go to play with her in a few days. Elle didn't care. Even as much as she missed her big sister, she knew they'd visit her soon, as it was the whole purpose of their trip. Right now, she was content to revel in the attention from her father, daring to believe that maybe he loved her at last.

And today was even more special, because he was taking her to buy a very special dress. He had told Elle that since the day they arrived in Greece, almost every person they'd met made a point to mention how beautiful Elle was. It was true that she noticed whenever her daddy introduced her to new people, they always seemed to pay special attention to her, looking her up and down, and talking favorably about her. While she couldn't understand their language, she definitely knew the conversation was primarily about her. Feeling embarrassed by such consideration, Elle wished she knew how to speak Greek, or at least that her father wouldn't speak so softly in the ear of his interpreter. She wanted to know what exactly was being said.

Her daddy told her these Greeks had strongly suggested Elle enter a beauty pageant for young girls that just so happened to be starting in a few days. All she had to do was walk up and down a fashion runway, smiling and wearing a beautiful dress, and she might possibly win all sorts of money and fun prizes. He seemed very eager for her to enter the contest. At first, Elle was hesitant; she'd never done anything like this before, and she'd always felt awkward about her appearance. While she knew she was pretty, as folks always commented on her curly red hair and the single deep-set dimple on her cheek, she was also very petite for her age. All the other boys and girls in her fourth grade class were easily two or three inches taller than she was. They sometimes would tease her about being the "baby of the class."

On the other hand, her daddy had never treated her like this before, so attentive and loving. She certainly didn't want to do anything that might stop how he had been acting toward her. Not wanting to disappoint him, Elle agreed to enter the pageant. And if truth be told, Elle would've probably consented to do almost anything her daddy asked of her.

So today, Elle's dad was taking her on their very first shopping spree together. One of the locals had told him about a special boutique that carried beautiful dresses and matching shoes for young girls. But first, he had told her they needed to make a stop at the doctor's office. It was early morning when Jack and Elle began walking the streets of Thessaloniki, Jack leading the way as he followed some directions he had scribbled on a small piece of paper.

Elle: Daddy, why do we have to go see a doctor? I'm not sick or anything.

Jack: You need to have papers from a doctor to be in the pageant.

Elle: Why?

Jack: That's just how they do things here. The doctor will give us papers that will verify that everything's intact.

Elle: What do you mean, 'intact'?

Jack: That everything is in the right place and as it should be. The better report we get from the doc, the higher the price you'll go for.

Elle: The higher the price?

Jack: *(quickly correcting himself)* Prize. I said prizzzze. The healthier you are, the bigger the prize you will get when you win.

Elle: That's funny; they have different categories for how healthy you are? That's so weird.

Jack: Well, we're in a different country. Who knows why they do what they do here?

Elle: Do you really think I'm going to win?

Jack: *(chuckling)* You just stand there with a big smile, and for sure you are gonna get a big prize.

Elle: But are you sure the other girls won't be older and prettier? I'm only ten, and everyone back at home still teases me that I look like I'm seven or eight.

Jack: Don't worry about it. I know what I'm doing. Trust me, this is a kind of contest where the younger you look, the better the chance you'll bring in the highest score.

Elle smiled broadly at his words. Never before had he expressed such confidence in her ability to do anything well. She looked up at her daddy, but his face was focused forward. Jack seemed to be in a hurry, and Elle had to almost run to keep up.

Elle: How come we haven't met any other kids yet? I haven't even seen any girls my age around here.

Jack: Well, there'll be plenty of girls to meet in the beauty pageant. I'm sure you'll find one of them to be friends with.

Elle: And then, as soon as the contest is over, we'll go and see Skye?

Jack: As soon as the contest is over.

Elle: I can't wait to see Skye! If I win prizes I can bring some for her, too. She'll be so excited to see us.

After walking through the narrow streets for nearly an hour, they came to an archway in the middle of an alley. Elle thought it looked more like an entrance to a cave than a doctor's office, but her dad turned into the opening and waved Elle to follow after him. They walked down a set of musty-smelling stone stairs, stopping at the dark bottom. There was a sole wooden door at the dead end, and by the light of a solitary light bulb, Elle could see there was some lettering in Greek painted on the door. Her father checked the paper he was holding to confirm they had arrived at the correct address.

"This is it," announced Jack.

"Really?" asked Elle as she listened to her voice echo up and down the stairs. "Are you sure, Daddy? It looks kind of old and dirty."

"This is the right place." Jack looked down at his daughter sternly. "Now I want you to listen to me. Whatever the doctor asks you to do, you do."

"What do you mean? What is he going to ask me to do? I'm not going to have to get a shot or anything, am I?"

"I don't know, but what*ever* he asks, I want you to do it. No whinin' or complainin'. Just do what he says. Don't worry, I won't leave you alone with him, because I need to make sure he doesn't try anything fishy, but even if he needs to give you a shot, I want you to just do it, O.K?"

Elle was beginning to feel uneasy. *What did he mean by "fishy?" she thought.* She nodded in agreement to him anyway.

"That's a good girl," said her father, patting her head.

The door creaked open into what looked like a very old basement clinic, and Elle wondered how many people had come here to meet with a doctor. And if they were kids, did they feel as scared as she did? This room was nothing like the bright, sterile clinics her mom or Mama Aggie had taken her to back in Louisiana. There was no friendly lady behind a desk to greet people, no place to sign in, and the six or seven chairs scattered about the waiting area were all haggard and mismatched. There was absolutely nothing hanging on the walls, not even a magazine rack. Elle wondered when the last time those smooth cement walls had been painted. And it was also very quiet; the only sound was a very muffled drone of a radio or television spilling in from some unseen back room.

A short, barrel-chested old man entered the room and looked from Jack to Elle, then back to Jack again. Using the same paper with the address written on it, Jack read off a request in Greek. He stumbled over the language and must have pronounced something incorrectly because the doctor let out a gruff, condescending laugh. But he nodded his head and held out his hand for payment. Jack shuffled through his wallet and counted out the proper amount into the old man's small, fat hand.

After stuffing the bills into his front trouser pocket, he motioned Jack and Elle to follow him into a back room, which was even less fancy than the waiting room. It held one oblong wooden table, one wooden chair, and a small chest of drawers. The doctor pulled open the top drawer and picked out something that resembled a hospital gown. He tossed the thin robe to Jack and motioned for Elle to take off her clothes and put it on.

Jack handed it to Elle. "I think you understood what the doc said."

"Umm...Dad, isn't he going to leave so I can undress?"

"Oh, for chrissake, Elle, he's a f***in doctor. He knows what you look like."

Elle's cheeks flushed bright red, both from embarrassment and from her father's sudden harsh tone, and she felt as if she could throw up. At this, the doctor exploded with another demeaning laugh and motioned for her to get on with it. She turned her back and did her best to remove her shirt and jeans and cover herself with the robe as discretely and quickly as possible.

She obviously wasn't moving fast enough because the doctor briskly crossed the room, picked her up under her armpits and plopped her down on the table. She could smell a stale, sour smell of tobacco on his breath as he bent over to pull a small light out of his pocket. He shined it into her eyes, her ears and her mouth. He seemed to linger as he peered down her throat, and Elle thought it seemed as if he was counting her teeth. His fingers felt all along her neck, and then he motioned for her to lie down. The table was too short for her entire body, only long enough for the span from her head to her knees. When she lay back, her shins and feet dangled toward the floor.

The doctor pulled open her robe and with rough massages, he examined her not-yet-formed breasts. Elle let out gasp as she felt this foreign man touching her with such inconsideration for her modesty. Her eyes filled with tears as he continued downward with his ugly hands poking and prodding into her lower abdomen. After a few agonizing seconds, Elle believed him to have completed his examination as he flipped closed her robe and walked down by her feet still hanging off the table.

She laid her head back and breathed a sigh of relief as a tear trickled out of the corner of her right eye. But she relaxed too soon, because the worst invasion was yet to come. Before she knew what was happening, the doctor spread her knees apart, pulled her underwear to the side and invaded her most private space. She felt a sharp pinch between her legs. She let out a scream, more from shock than from pain, and then he was done.

Elle sprang up to a sitting position and pulled her knees tightly to her chest. Through a haze of tears, she saw the doctor nod his head toward her father as if to approve something. He motioned for Jack to follow him out.

"You can get dressed now," Jack said to Elle, as he left the room.

Alone with her mortification, Elle curled back onto the table and began to cry. *What just happened?* She thought. *Why did he pinch me down there?* Elle could not even begin to make up a possible answer for him to do such a thing. With her mind racing like mad, she tried to understand why they had really come here to this dirty office, what had just happened to her, or worse still, why her dad just sat there and allowed that yucky man to touch her in such a violating way. In her disillusionment, Elle began to wish they'd never come to Greece.

JACK AND ELLE WALKED in silence from the cellar-like doctor's office. By now the young girl's embarrassment had morphed into anger towards her father, and this fueled her steps to the point she had no problem at all keeping up with his brisk pace. Her mind was rehearsing the many words she wished she had the courage to say to him. How she didn't want to be in this stupid beauty contest, how she wanted to see her sister right now, and how she hated the way he didn't even care for her enough to protect her from that fat, disgusting doctor.

And as long as we're being for real, Elle vented internally, *how come you've never cared about me before now? You've never so much as stepped foot in my school when I was in a play or something. And why don't you ever spend time with us? Or even remember our birthdays? And what about the time I saw you hit Mama? Yeah, you didn't know I saw that, did you? Well, I did. I saw it, and I cried all night in my bed, and you never even noticed. I hate you for that.*

At the notion of her mom, Elle almost burst into tears. She had never been this far away from Macy before, and she missed her desperately now. Even during the summer months, when she and Skye would go stay with MawMaw Aggie, her mom was still just a phone call away. Every few days, MawMaw would let them call home so they could connect with their mother.

Elle's homesickness grew all the more with the thought of Aggie. Elle wished her MawMaw had come on this trip with them; *she* wasn't afraid to fly on an airplane and Skye would've given anything to see her. Plus, there was almost nothing bad in the world that MawMaw Aggie couldn't hug away. Whenever Elle was upset, all MawMaw had to do was open up her big arms and Elle would come running. She'd sink into the softness of Aggie's bosom, as she listened to her grandma whisper wonderful things in her ear.

"*Mon Sha* (My Dear)," MawMaw would say. "Why you sad? What you got to be so long in da mouth 'bout? You blessed, *Sha*. You beautiful, you funny, you gots da brightest red hair, *and* you da smartest girl I know. And on top o' dat, Aggie love you more'n life itself." And then she'd kiss Elle's neck until it tickled so much she giggled.

Elle thought she'd give anything for a hug from MawMaw Aggie right now. *MawMaw would never have let that doctor even get close enough to touch me*, she thought. *She'd've whipped the snot out of him!*

"Why're you lookin' at me like that?" Jack's annoyed voice brought Elle back to the streets of Greece. It wasn't until he said something that she realized she had been scowling at him.

Elle didn't answer; she only looked ahead and kept walking. Now, her anger swelled against herself for her inability to speak her thoughts, to stand up for herself.

"Look," said Jack. "If you're gonna give me an f-in attitude, then I can slap your a** right back on a plane to Louisiana and you won't be spending *any* time with your sister. Is that what you want? Here I am, trying to make a great time for you, and what thanks do I get for it? Do you have any idea how much money all this is costing me?"

His words were like a smack in the face, and Elle could feel the guilt rush in as she began to think her daddy was fully justified to say what he did. After all, he had gone completely out of his way to take her to Greece just so she could spend time with her sister. He was giving up at least two weeks of work, and Elle knew very well how important work was to him. Plus, this was by far the most extravagant gift her parents had ever given her. Usually birthdays, and even Christmases, would come and go and the only thing she or Skye would receive was an apology from Macy for the lack of money. Elle could not begin to imagine how much this trip was costing her parents; at the very least, she should be grateful.

"Oh, Daddy, I'm so sorry," she said, her eyes filling with tears. "You're so right! And I *am* very grateful. This is the best present you and Mama have ever given me, and I'm loving every minute of it...I just didn't like that doctor, is all."

"Well, how in the hell was I supposed to know what he needed to do for us to get your papers? It's not like I'm a f***in psychic or anything."

"I know, Daddy. I'm *so* sorry, and I promise I'll be good from now on. Please don't be mad at me. I won't complain about a *thing*, and I'll do my very best to come in first place in the beauty pageant. I'll do whatever it takes to win those prizes for you. Please don't be mad, OK?"

"Now, that's my girl," Jack said, smiling. "That's exactly what Daddy likes to hear. And just in time, too, because we're here."

"Where?"

"This is the store where we're going to buy your dress for the contest." And with that, he walked into the small boutique.

Elle had been so consumed with her own thoughts, she hadn't noticed that all their walking had taken them to a street containing several shops, lined in a row. In fact, she had almost forgotten about the big shopping spree her dad had promised her early that morning. Her childlike joy was restored as she followed in behind him and gazed around at all the beautiful dresses hanging throughout the store.

Elle wondered why everything in Greece seemed so small. The restaurants were small, the streets and cars were small, and this shop was so tiny it could've fit inside Elle's living room. And instead of the racks offering several different sizes of the same dress, like the stores back at home, these only held one dress of each kind, in whatever size that happened to be. *We're gonna have to be pretty lucky to find the right dress,* Elle thought. *I hope when we find the one we like, they have it in my size.*

No one was in the shop, so Jack opened and closed the door again so the dangling bell on the doorknob would sound again. A young woman came out of a back room and kindly said something in Greek to Jack. Elle wasn't sure why, but her Dad seemed surprised to see the lady. He quickly looked around the entire shop, and even craned his neck to try and get a glance into the back room, its door now standing ajar. Jack was looking for someone else to wait on them.

The woman spoke again to him, this time slower and more deliberate. Jack took out the paper he had used to communicate at the doctor's office and read off the one sentence written on it. Unlike the doctor who had laughed at his broken Greek, this woman did not find his words the least bit amusing. Her welcoming smile dissolved into a frown as she crossed her arms and glared at Jack.

A silent moment passed between the two adults, and Elle wondered what was happening. *How come she got such a mean look all of a sudden? Doesn't she know we want to buy a dress from her? She should want to help us.*

But Jack didn't seem to care; he simply repeated his sentence. Finally, the lady spoke back to him, again in Greek, and from her gestures Elle could tell she was asking him where something or somebody was. To answer her, Jack motioned to Elle.

The woman's expression went from disapproval to shock as she looked down at the little girl. Elle thought she'd try to win her approval by giving her an eager smile. The saleswoman's attention returned to Jack. With one eyebrow arched, she locked eyes with him and took a few steps toward him. She leaned nearer in until her face was only a few inches away from Jack's, and then she spit.

Elle gasped and even Jack seemed caught off guard. The woman sprang back, and began yelling loudly, mostly in Greek. But Elle could also hear her attempting to say a few words in English. Her arms were flailing as punctuation marks to her message as she pushed by them so she could fling open her front door. She motioned violently for them to leave, shouting accusations at Jack the entire time.

He paused for a moment to wipe off his cheek, and Elle noticed a very familiar expression on his face. He was going to hit this woman, Elle was sure of it. That's the same look he had on his face that night she saw him beating her mom. Elle tried to ask her dad if they could just leave, but she couldn't make the words come out of her mouth. She felt a pit in her stomach and she squeezed her eyes shut, much too afraid to watch him lash out at this young woman.

It seemed like an eternity as Elle listened for Jack's fist to make contact, when suddenly the lady started yelling "Police! Police!" and then something else in Greek, which Elle assumed was the equivalent to "police". Before Elle knew what was happening, her dad yanked her by the arm out of the dress shop, hoisted her up over his shoulder, and as fast as he could, sped down several streets. He kept looking back to see if anyone was coming after them, and only when he was certain they were not being followed did he set her back down on the narrow street.

Jack flipped open his cell phone and made a call. The person must have picked up almost instantly because Jack began yelling, "What in the hell are you tryin to pull? Are you tryin to f*** me over? Because if you are, I'll kick the s**t out of you, and I won't even think twice about it.....(*Elle could hear the muffled sound of someone on the other end.*) I did! I went to the dress shop you told me to go to, I said the sentence you gave me, and the bitch in there spit at me! *(Elle heard laughter from phone)* Are you playin me? Is this some kinda joke?! Cause I *will* mess you up!"

Jack began pacing back and forth wildly as he listened to the person on the other end of the call. He continued his rant:

"I'm telling you, that's exactly what I did. I went into the store, this little bitch came out, and she—*(the person on the other end interrupted him)*.....I don't know, she was probably about 25 or 26......What?! Well, how in the hell was I supposed to know she wasn't the right person? ....Son of a bitch! I had a feeling she wasn't the right one, but I looked around, and there was nobody else in there. What am I gonna do now? She's already seen me and the girl; it's not like I can just go back in there. She was freakin yelling for the police! .....Is there anyplace else I can go? I still have a few days til the deal. .....OK, I'll call you later." Jack sat down on the ground to catch his breath.

Elle was thoroughly confused at all that had just taken place. Actually, *nothing* that had happened this day made any sense to her 10-year-old mind, and she didn't know what to do other than sit down next to her father. She could tell he was extremely upset, far too angry for her to dare ask any questions. She decided her safest bet was to quietly wait for him to cool down, and then surely he would explain everything to her.

GALEN & SKYE

✞ 6 ✞

GALEN HATED THE BLINDFOLD. He could have managed walking through the streets of Thessaloniki with his hands tied behind his back, but once his friends added the blindfold, Galen was everything but comfortable with the situation. What started out as a light-hearted birthday party hosted by his brother, Nikkos, had now shifted into a bullish prank.

Galen: Come on, guys. You can take the blindfold off now.
Nikkos: Hey, little brother, that's half the fun!
Galen: For all of *you*, maybe, but not for me. Aren't we supposed to be doing what *I* want to do for my birthday?
Nikkos: Trust me, Galen, in a few minutes from now, you'll be doing exactly what you want to be doing. In fact, I'd venture to say there'd be nothing else on the planet you'd rather be doing than what you're about to do.

At this, George and Artimas laughed.

Galen: Can you at least tell me where we are? Or even a hint about where we are going?

Nikkos: I can tell you this; you've never been here before.

George: And it's something you've never done before.

Artimas: *(shocked)* Wait a minute—are you guys serious? This will be Galen's first time?

George: That's what Nikkos said, and he knows him best.

Artimas: Unbelievable. *(to Nikkos)* Is that really true?

Nikkos: Tragic, but true.

Artimas: *(to Galen)* And you're 17 today? That's so embarrassing! What's the matter with you? I think I was 14 when I came here for the first time.

Nikkos: Which is exactly why we're doing this. No brother of mine is going to go through his 17th year without experiencing this at least once.

George: But aren't we paying for the whole night? *(chuckling)* Surely, he'll be able to do it more than once.

Artimas: I still can't digest that the man is 17 and he's still a—

Nikkos: *(interrupting)* Arti, don't give it away; I want this to be a surprise.

Galen: Can someone please tell me what you all are talking about?

Nikkos: Only one more block, and the secret prize'll be revealed.

All the young men laughed, save Galen. The more Nikkos and his friends talked, the more anxious Galen became. And from the sounds of the loud music spilling out from each open doorway they passed, Galen was fairly certain they had come to an area of town he'd never been. Not because he was unaware of it, nor afraid to go to it, but because he felt the behavior of the men who chose to venture into this part of Thessaloniki was beneath him.

Galen considered himself to be a gentleman, a philosopher, an intellect. Standing crammed shoulder to shoulder next to a slew of men in a hot, muggy space as girls in disgustingly skimpy clothing danced and writhed on a metal pole was not Galen's idea of fun. It was base. It was barbaric. It was degrading for both the women *and* the men. Nikkos had repeatedly attempted to sway Galen to join him on his self-indulgent trips into the red light districts of Athens or Thessaloniki, but Galen had always refused.

t>

Galen: Alright, Nikkos, you got me. I know where we are. You finally got me to come with you on one of your sex escapades. You know I hate this kind of stuff.

Nikkos: I told you guys he'd never come here without the blindfold.

Artimas: Why not?! This place is heaven! How can you do anything but love every minute of this place? What's your problem, Galen, do you not like girls or something?

Galen: Of course I like girls.

Artimas: Because if the problem is you don't like girls, I'm sure we could find you something you do like.

George: Yeah. I've never looked around for one for myself, or anything, but I'm sure we could find a *guy* for you to be with.

Artimas: Ha! We sure could! Nikkos, how come you didn't tell us your little brother was not into girls?

Galen: *(angry)* Shut up! You know that's not what I mean. Of course I like girls; I just don't like girls like *this*.

Artimas: *(sarcastic)* But that's what we meant. We could find you the kind of girl you *do* like. Like, how about a guy who is dressed up all nice and pretty so he looks just like a girl?

Indignant, Galen tried to kick one of them, but his blindfold handicap got the better of him. The guys all laughed at his futile attempts.

Nikkos: OK, guys, leave him alone. Besides, we're here.

Galen felt them entering what he assumed was a strip bar. Without his sight, his other senses were heightened, so he was able to feel the thumping bass rhythm of dance music vibrating in his chest. And as they pushed deep into the mass of people, he could smell the foul sweaty men as they cheered for whatever or whoever was on the stage. Yelling over the music, Galen said, "Alright! We're here. You can untie my hands now!" But Nikkos continued pulling him by the arm through the crowd.

Galen could tell they were now on the outskirts of the audience. Nikkos guided him down a hallway farther away from the main room. "OK," said Nikkos. "We're going to be walking up some stairs here in a minute."

Now, Galen had no idea where Nikkos was taking him. The music grew fainter as they ascended the spiral staircase, and once they came to a landing, Galen could only hear the dull, muffled pounding of the music from the lower level. He felt his brother release his arm.

"Good evening," Nikkos said as he took steps away from Galen. "This is my little brother, and for his birthday, my friends and I want to give him a special treat. Can I see your menu?"

Menu? thought Galen. *Are we in a restaurant above the club? This is great! While we eat, it will give me time to talk these guys into getting out of here and moving the party someplace else.*

He felt George and Artimas step forward to where Nikkos was, and he heard them whispering and laughing as they looked through the menu. He couldn't decipher their exact words; he'd just hear a phrase now and then: "Oh! He'd like that." or "No, that's a bit too spicy for Galen."

"I think we've made up our minds," he heard Nikkos say. "How much would this be for the entire night?"

"The *entire* shift?" asked a woman. She sounded about 40 or 50 years old.

The guys burst into laughter. "Yes," said Nikkos. "We want to treat my brother to a whole night of fun. It's his first time here and we want to do it right."

The woman snorted as she giggled, "The full shift will be 200 euros."

Nikkos: What?! Are you joking? We're not going to pay that kind of money. I can get twice as much for half the price in Athens.

Woman: You're not in Athens, Love.

Nikkos: Well, maybe we should take our business elsewhere.

Woman: I run my house just like the others here, and if you want, you can go take a look at their menus. You're going to find the same prices. You want just a hole? Then you go to Athens. You want a night of delicious dessert? You come to Thessaloniki. Your choice.

Artimas: *(interrupting)* We don't need to buy the whole night.

Nikkos: Yes we do. I know my brother. It's going to take him half the night to think about it before he makes his first move.

Artimas: *(laughing)* Then, let's see what else she's got.

Woman: Why don't you tell me how much you want to spend, and I'll give you your options.
Nikkos: I've got 150 euros.
Woman: 150? Well, I have the perfect one for you. Sounds like your brother over there needs someone special, a bit younger. *(giggle-snorting)* One of our more experienced girls would eat him alive. How about this pretty young thing? She's one of our newer girls.
Nikkos: *(after a moment)* I like her. It's a deal.
Woman: Is he going to take off the wrist ties and blindfold? Because if not, there's an extra charge for that.

Galen felt his heart pounding in his chest as he began to understand where his brother had taken him. This was much worse than spending a few hours in a strip club; Nikkos had led him up into an actual brothel. He felt helpless. *What can I do about it now?* He thought. *If I refuse to go in, they'll never let me forget it. They'll call me a coward, and maybe tell my friends that I'm still a virgin, that I don't even like girls. But there's no way I'm going to lower myself to touch a dirty whore who has been with countless men. That's the vilest kind of woman.*

"Brother, we are here!" Nikkos announced. "For your birthday, we have given you the best possible gift. And while you might not thank me for it right now, you'll be singing my praises tomorrow."

Galen felt his wrists being freed and he immediately ripped off his blindfold. It took a bit for his eyes to adjust and to be able to focus on his surroundings. The room was dimly lit by red bulbs, with chairs lining the walls. The woman standing in front of him was an ageless wonder with her thick, pasty make-up and tight polyester clothing; either she was in her 40s and had experienced quite a thorny life, or she was around 70. Galen couldn't decide. He wondered what disgusting secrets she was hiding behind her garishly made-up face.

Looking Galen up and down, the old woman smiled and said, "Follow me, Love."

Galen stood still for a moment contemplating his situation, trying to find a win. *What's the big deal if I just go along with it? They'll never know what really happened back there. I wouldn't even have to touch the whore, and Nikkos would never know the truth. And then I wouldn't have to put up with their constant ridicule.* Resolutely, Galen motioned to the woman to lead the way.

She began to walk down a thin hall when she sensed more than one man following. Turning on her stiletto, she directed her voice to Nikkos. "Are you coming too? Because if so, there's an extra charge for that." Nikkos patted Galen on the back and whispered some last minute brotherly advice in his ear before retreating to George and Artimas. As Galen looked back at the trio, he noticed several other men beginning to wander into the waiting area and peruse the sex menus. He couldn't believe he was now to be classed with such deprivation.

Galen continued to follow the woman. The hallway had periodic industrial lamps hanging from the ceiling, and each door was decorated with a poster of a naked woman in a pornographic pose. They walked past seven or eight doors before reaching the end of the hallway, where there were four final doors. It was noticeably darker at this point, and these doors were different from the previous ones. Each was fastened on the outside with a padlock. The woman rummaged through her pockets and pulled out a ring of keys.

"What are the locks for?" Galen asked. "I'm certainly not doing this if you're going to lock me in there all night."

The woman looked at him as if this was the first time anyone had asked her that question. "Oh, Love, the locks are only for the girls' protection while they rest. You boys got here a little early, so I hadn't had a chance to unlock the rooms yet."

Galen looked at her suspiciously. "If it's to protect your girls, then why is the lock on the outside?"

The woman giggle-snorted and replied. "Well, we wouldn't want our prize girls to get away, would we? Now you stay out here a moment until I'm sure she's ready."

Galen didn't think it was possible to feel any more uncomfortable than he already was, but the sight of those outdoor padlocks did the trick. He couldn't understand why a prostitute would allow herself to be locked inside a room, even if it was for her own protection. What if there was a fire, or a flood or a freak earthquake? It made much more sense to him that the highest level of safety would be achieved from locks fastened on the *inside*.

He heard the woman whispering harshly inside the room. There was silence for a bit and then Galen was pretty sure he heard a slap, followed by a barely audible moan. *Did someone just get hit in there?* he thought.

The woman reemerged, smiling crookedly at him, unaware of the fuchsia lipstick smearing her front teeth. "She's ready for you, Love. Have a wonderful evening." And she motioned him to enter the room.

If he had a guarantee that Nikkos and his friends would be out of sight by now, Galen would have exited the brothel that very moment. But fearing their accusations of failure, he slowly walked into the bedroom.

The first thing Galen noticed was the bars on the window. The room was small and sparse, a chair in the corner, a toilet and sink slightly left of the barred window, a small table next to the bed. And then he saw the girl. She was everything he was not expecting. Not that he knew exactly *what* he was expecting, but whatever that was, she was definitely not it

She seemed dazed as she sat at the edge of the bed, like she wasn't quite awake or tuned into reality. And she was younger than Galen had envisioned. *Much* younger; maybe fourteen or fifteen? That was the age of his sister, Dimitra, and this girl looked similar in stature. He was utterly caught off guard. What was a girl like this doing in a brothel? Shouldn't she be in school?

A blue satin camisole hung from her thin frame, gathering at her waist, so Galen couldn't see if she was wearing anything else below that. Her hair was long and very dark, curling past her shoulders.

He was at a complete loss about what to do next. So he did nothing, but stand there transfixed on the young girl. He could still hear the dull, thumping music from below.

After several moments, the girl looked up at him, and when their eyes locked, Galen's heart began to pound. Never before had he sensed such diverse emotions coming from such a young girl. Her crystal blue eyes pierced him with hatred and scorn, yet at the same time, fear and hopelessness. She was like a caged animal, eyes wildly helpless.

This girl is obviously not in this place because she chose to be, he thought. *And by the look on her face, she certainly doesn't want to do what she thinks I've come here to do. So then...who is she and why is she here, and more importantly, how did she get here?*

Galen dropped his gaze. He couldn't figure out how to feel. Pity for this young girl, who for some unknown reason, was locked in this stifling room? Anger at the people who put her here? Shame for allowing himself to become a part of this degrading business? Maybe none of these. Maybe all of these. Galen wasn't sure.

The girl scooted herself back so her straightened legs could rest on the bed as she leaned her back against the wall. Her eyes had become dull again, and almost robotically, she brushed her hair away from her face and opened her legs. As she exposed herself, Galen could see that indeed she was nude underneath her camisole. His faced flushed at the sight of what he had never seen before, in person at least, and he felt himself becoming aroused.

Disgusted at himself, he quickly turned away and crossed over to the open window. Feeling the crisp, chilly winter air, he held on to one of the vertical bars with one hand and raked through the top of his hair with the other. He brewed over what to do next.

I'm not having sex with that girl, he thought. *It's wrong, and I won't be a part of it. For chrissake, she looks no older than my own sister! And I'd murder the man who would so much as touch Dimitra with a lewd hand. When Nikkos comes here, does he buy girls like this? This young? She can't be here on her own volition; she's got to be a victim of some sort of sick joke.*

I wonder where she's from? And how'd she get here? Where are her parents? Surely someone must be missing her? And why is she locked in the room like this? She's a f***ing prisoner here, forced to do, god only knows what! This is so wrong. It's wrong, and I won't be a part of it. I don't care what kind of s**t I'm going to have to take from Nikkos and his friends; I'm getting out of here.

He walked to the door and began to open it when he had the realization, *If I leave, that old wench certainly isn't going to give me my money back, and as soon as I'm out the door, she's just going to sell this poor girl to somebody else. The least I could do is wait the night out and give her a break.*

Galen quietly shut the door and turned to the girl. For the first time, he noticed the redness of her left cheek. *That sound I heard was someone getting slapped,* he thought. *That old bitch hit her!* Anger burned in his chest.

From the corner of the room, he slid the chair closer to the bed and sat down in it. His eyes were now level with hers, but she refused to make contact. He began to speak softly to her.

"I know this might be different than what you are used to," he said. "But I don't want to do anything to you tonight. Your entire shift was paid for, so you can just rest, or we could just talk, or something..." His words trailed off. He could tell the girl could hear him, but by her blank stare, he wasn't sure she understood what he was saying.

He leaned forward and gently pushed her feet together. Shaking his head 'no', he said, "I don't want to do any of that tonight. But I don't want that woman to bring in anyone else, either. I've paid for your whole shift, so you can just go back to sleep. You look like you could use it." Still, she gave him no response.

Suddenly it dawned on him. "Do you know how to speak Greek?" he asked her. "Are you Greek?"

She seemed confused. He spoke very slowly and asked again, "Do you know how to speak Greek?" No answer. "Do you know any Greek at all?"

Galen could see by the way she had curled up on the bed that she was beginning to become very frightened. He realized this was probably the first time anything like this had ever happened, and she didn't know what to do or how to respond. Also, he was positive this girl couldn't comprehend a word he was saying.

I wonder where she's from? he thought. *How long has she been here, and what horrific things have been done to her? I don't think I even want to know.*

He began to stand up and move toward her. Habitually, she shot up and started to spread her legs again. "No, no, no, no," he said softly, again shaking his head. "None of that tonight." He tugged at her pillow and motioned for her to lie down. Still confused, she obeyed. Then Galen spread out the threadbare blanket over her body and motioned for her to try to go to sleep.

He pushed his chair as far back as he could into the corner. He hoped his distance would help the girl relax. He leaned back in the chair and stretched his legs forward onto the concrete floor. *I may as well try to get comfortable,* he thought. *It's going to be a long night.*

MOLLY VENZKE

❧ 7 ❧

SKYE TRIED TO STOP TREMBLING as she eyed the stranger in the corner of her room. Who was he, and why wasn't he doing anything to her? What was he waiting for? Not one night since her father had sold her into this hellhole had a man come into her room and *not* violated her in some repulsive way. She didn't dare trust this man to be anything different, even if he had motioned for her to go to sleep.

Maybe that's what he's into, Skye thought. *Probably just as soon as I'm asleep, he'll start attacking me. Well, I don't care how long he sits there, I'm not falling for it.*

She laid on her side, careful to keep her eyes glued to his every movement.

He acted as if she wasn't even in the room. He simply stayed leaning back in the chair, focusing his gaze on the ceiling. Skye thought he did seem different from the others, something about the way he looked at her, but there was no way to be absolutely sure. She knew she had no other choice than to stay on guard and watch him like a hawk.

But the longer he sat, and the longer she stared, the harder it was for Skye to fend off the extreme lure of sleep. She tried to remember the last time she slept while it was dark outside, but she couldn't make it out. Had she been here 3 months? 6 months? A year? She had diligently spent every day attempting to forget the day before, that now when she tried to remember, she had no firm memory to grasp onto. She remembered those first torturous nights, too horrifying to ever forget, and then everything else from that point on was a nightmarish blur.

What does it matter anyway? I'm never going to get out of here. The best I can hope for is for someone to kill me. And she scorned herself for the nth time for not having the courage to do it herself. *Maybe tomorrow, I'll find the nerve to finally end it all.*

But then she thought of Elle. The woman who kept her under lock and key barely spoke English, but she certainly knew the vital words and phrases needed to send shivers up her spine. She regularly warned Skye that if she didn't comply with everything she was asked to do, they would go find her family and kill them. And Skye feared that once they saw Elle, maybe they'd bring her back here too. She could never allow that to happen.

In her broken English and thick dialect, the evil witch would giggle-snort as she reassured Skye they knew exactly where she used to live, and the means by which they'd murder her family would be torture. That threat was the only strand of life Skye had to hold on to. Yes, her life here was far below anything her young mind ever could've imagined, but at least she could save her mom and baby sister from a terrible fate. At least there was that. Maybe *only* that. And some nights Skye wasn't sure that even those thoughts were enough to make her endure another encounter with another man.

Skye focused her eyes once again on the man in the corner. She thought it couldn't be possible that he'd come here just to sit in that chair. But by now, he seemed to be asleep. She squinted to make out his breathing. It appeared to be slow and steady, but what if he was faking? What if the moment she fell asleep, he attacked her?

So what? Thought Skye, suddenly defeated. *So what if he's faking. Then he'll just be like the rest, which is what I'm expecting anyway. I don't care anymore, and I'm not going to try and figure it out. It's going to be what it's going to be, and there's nothing I can do about it. Maybe if I dream deep enough, I won't feel him on top of me.*

Surrendering to the rumbles of fatigue sounding inside her head, Skye closed her eyes and allowed herself to slide down into a deep sleep. As she began to dream, images of her Louisiana home flooded her imagination.

"Skye! Wait for me!" yelled Elle. "Skyyyyyyyyyye!"

Skye could feel the intense heat on her skin as she ran recklessly through Audubon Park. Summer in New Orleans made the hot, thick, humid air feel positively three dimensional. Elle tried to keep up with her, but it was no use; Skye was on a mission. She was going to catch that bird. Snowy Egrets were her favorite, and she was determined to use her butterfly net to capture one of the beautiful white birds for her very own.

It was exceptionally hot on this June afternoon, so the New Orleans park was less populated than usual. This allowed Skye to sprint at break-neck speeds, eyes focused on the flight of the bird, and not be concerned with colliding into anyone else. She knew her chances of actually catching an egret were one in a million...but being the eternal optimist, she viewed those odds as a challenge.

The bird darted through the live oak trees, expertly weaving in, out, and around the massive drooping branches that wore their Spanish moss like bundles of scarves. Unaware of the child bird-catcher, he landed on one of the U-shaped branches and sang his song.

Skye had lost sight of him as he had flown so fast through the trees, but now that he had stopped, she was able to spot the back of his white body against the greenish gray moss. Perched on a lower branch, she thought he might possibly be within reach! Skye came to a quick stop, feeling a burn of prickly heat circulating throughout her body as she tried to catch her breath. Perhaps if she was able to sneak toward him, she could capture him in her net?

Her eyes stung from the perspiration dripping from her forehead, and she used her t-shirt to mop her face. She needed to see clearly to be able to snag the egret. Ever so slowly, with her net poised in the air, Skye stalked closer to the bird. He stopped singing, and Skye was unsure whether or not it was because he was aware of her. She froze for a moment, just to be cautious, and waited to hear his song again before advancing.

In just three more steps, the bird might be hers. A thrilled Skye imagined the future with her new pet. She'd buy the most beautiful cage for him, teach him to sit on her shoulder, and she'd let him fly all over the house. And she'd be the only girl in her class who'd ever caught herself a Snowy Egret.

Feeling in full control, she took the last few steps and was about ready to pounce on her prey, when Elle came running from behind.

"Did you get 'em? Did you get 'em?"

And with that, the bird flew out of sight.

Skye collapsed onto the grass. She was so angry with her sister for ruining her chances with the bird, she didn't answer her. By now, Elle had caught up with her and could see the empty net.

"Awww. He got away, didn't he?"

"Ellie, why'd you have to come up behind me yelling like that? I was just about ready to catch him, and you scared him away."

"Really? Oh, I'm so sorry, sissy. I didn't mean to do it." Elle looked at her big sister with tear-brimmed eyes, and Skye couldn't help but soften toward her. Still, she wished Elle would give her some space.

"Look, Elle, for the rest of today, if you see me hunting, could you just leave me alone? I don't want you following me around like a pokey little puppy, scaring all the egrets away. You look around here to find someone to play with who is your own age." And Skye ran back to where MawMaw Aggie was setting up their picnic. She was so thirsty, she felt like she had a mouthful of soggy cotton balls, and there was no cure for that except MawMaw Aggie's homemade lemonade.

Skye: *MawMaw! Did you bring a thermos of your lemonade?*

Aggie: *Now, what you tink, Sha? You tink I lug you girls all da way down to da park in dis heat and leave da lemonade at home? Alohrs pas (Of course not), I might be old, but I'm not senile. Now, where Ellie at?*

Skye: *I don't know.*

Aggie: *What you mean, you don't know? You posed to be keepin a watch out for her.*

Skye: *Well, I'm sure she'll be along soon; she was right behind me. MawMaw, she's been right behind me all day, and it's driving me crazy. Can't she stay with you?*

Aggie: *Aww, Skye-girl, she don't wanna be with Aggie. Dat li'l girl loves you, she tinks you da boss o' ever'ting. So you best keep dat in mind. You da eldest, and you always will be. You need to keep a lookout for her.*

Skye: (*pointing back from where she came*) *There. I see her comin right there. Now can I please have some lemonade? Why's it gotta be so hot already? The summer has just begun.*

Skye plopped herself down on the large picnic blanket and drank her lemonade from the paper Dixie cup Aggie had just given her. It was wonderful to feel the ice cold liquid bathe her empty belly. When she leaned back to ask for a refill, she noticed MawMaw unpacking the basket; she had fixed her famous fried chicken for lunch! Nobody on earth could fry up chicken like MawMaw Aggie. Skye's stomach burned with hunger.

She almost reached for a juicy leg to stuff into her mouth, but she knew better. MawMaw never allowed any eating until everybody had sat down, settled in, and said grace. Skye knew if she tried to grab a piece now, it would only end in a stinging slap on her hand. And then she remembered her words to her sister. She also knew if Elle's feelings got hurt earlier and she came up crying, MawMaw would take her own sweet time fixing the situation. She'd make them sit down and talk it all out to the point of full and complete restoration...which would only prolong the devouring of the juicy chicken. Skye's hunger pangs overshadowed any morsel of pride, and she ran to meet her sister.

Skye: Hey, Ellie, I'm sorry about what I said earlier. I was just frustrated 'cause I had almost caught the little egret in my net when you came up from behind, yelling. And you were so loud, you scared the bird away, and me, too. I got mad, but I'm not anymore.

Elle: Did you mean it when you said I couldn't play with you anymore today?

Skye: Oh, don't worry about that. We can figure all that out later. Aren't you hungry? MawMaw brought her homemade lemonade and fried chicken! And you know MawMaw won't let us eat anything until we've made peace.

Elle: Well, I'm not going to go over there until you say I can play with you.

Skye: Look, Ellie, I promise that we can do something together after we eat. OK?

Elle: You promise?

Skye: Yes.

Elle: Cross your heart, hope to die, stick a needle in your eye?

Skye: All of that. Now, Come on!

Skye took her sister by the hand and marched over to the picnic blanket. As she sat down, she noticed MawMaw squinting her eyes at her. Nothing ever got past MawMaw Aggie. But Skye didn't care. Peace was made, and now there was fried chicken to be eaten. MawMaw dished out the food onto the paper plates, said grace, and gave the nod of approval that it was time to eat.

Skye sank her teeth into the chicken leg, still warm from being in the car. The skin crackled as she bit down, and juice ran down her chin. The salty, spicy Cajun flavors filled her mouth as she ate and ate. She ate one leg, and then another, and then another. MawMaw had brought an entire bucket full of chicken legs!

But no matter how much Skye ate, she could not get full. Her stomach still burned with hunger. She tried to chew faster so her stomach would stop hurting, but nothing seemed to help. Thirsty from the salt, Skye picked up the thermos of lemonade and drank as much as she could. But her tongue still felt dry as a bone as it stuck to the roof of her mouth. Why could she not get full? And how was it possible that her mouth was still so dry?

Skye abruptly awoke, devastated to return to reality. The pains in her stomach were immense and her mouth felt completely parched. *That's why I couldn't get enough,* Skye thought. *It was only a dream.* She sat up in bed, disoriented to be waking up while it was so dark outside. Normally, she slept throughout the day and it was early evening, before the sun had fully set, when the old witch came to wake her.

She thought about getting up so she could pour herself a glass of water when she noticed the sleeping man in the corner. The sight of him startled her, and brought back the earlier events of the night.

She quickly recoiled back under the cover, attempting to be as silent as possible. Why was he still here? What did he want from her? And when was he going to want it?

Skye didn't dare move to get a glass of water; she couldn't risk waking him up. *Maybe if I lay still the entire night, he'll accidentally sleep all the way through, and he'll never have the chance to touch me.* No amount of hunger or thirst would outweigh keeping perfectly quiet, if *that* could be the reward.

She pressed her back against the wall, hoping it would sturdy her from making any noisy movements while she slept. Up and down her spine, she could feel the zingy vibrations of the music from the strip club below. The rhythm quickly lulled her back into sleep. This time her memory took her right in the middle of MawMaw Aggie's kitchen.

Skye loved the zipping sound of MawMaw shuffling cards. They sat across the table from one another, and Skye watched as Aggie expertly split the deck with one hand, shuffled through the two piles, and then made the bridge to collect them back into a deck. Then, with a flick of her wrist, she could deal the cards so swiftly, you barely saw them in flight as each one sailed across the table to its rightful owner. Today's game of Canasta was a dual between MawMaw and Skye because Elle was napping on the couch. Summers with Aggie were the best times of Skye's life.

Aggie: *Now why you tink you gone get yourself one a dem birds?*

Skye: *How can you deal and talk at the same time? I can never make it work. If I talk, then I deal the wrong number. If I count in my head, then I can't talk. How do you do that?*

Aggie: *Mon Sha, MawMaw's been dealin cards since before I could walk. It's just da way it was in my family. My Papa loved to play cards.*

Skye: *I wish I could've met him, your daddy.*

Aggie: *He was a great man. He with le Bon Dieu now, probably up dere beatin the Holy Trinity at Caribbean Stud Poker! Ain't nobody ever beat da man at dat. Now, Skye-girl, answer me dis question: why you tink you gotta get yourself one a dem white birds?*

Skye: *I don't know. I've always wanted a Snowy Egret. They're white and beautiful, and their songs are so pretty.*

Aggie: *It ain't enough to see dem out in da trees? To hear em singin to God ever mornin? Why you want to go and put one in a cage?*

Skye: *So it can be mine. I want to have one for a pet. Haven't you ever wanted to have a pet?*

Aggie: *Well, sure. I had all kinda pets when I was a girl, but only da one's dat are posed to be pets. Dogs, cats. God made dose animals to be pets. But a bird? A bird's not posed to be a pet, Sha. Sure, I know a folks who kept birds as pets, locked em up*

in a cage just so's dey can look at em, but I could never do it.
Just cuz folks do someting, it don't make it right.

Skye: *Why? What would be wrong having a bird as a pet?*

Aggie: *Skye-girl, bird's posed to be free to fly throughout da whole*
entire sky, da's how le Bon Dieu made em. You take away dey
flight, you take away dey very life. It's just not right. 'Sides,
bird's not all dat pretty just sittin in a cage. Choooh, but when
dey's up in da sky with dey's wings outstretched, glidin above
da trees; now dat's beauty at it's best. Ain't nothin like it.

Skye: *I guess...*

Just then, Skye felt an ominous presence behind her. Before she
could turn around, a large hand covered her mouth and a strong arm
wrapped around the front of her chest, lifting her out of the chair.
Aggie hopped up to try and rescue Skye from the intruder.

Skye bit down on the hand over her mouth. As soon as it released,
she screamed for MawMaw Aggie to come and save her. Skye violently
thrashed about trying to break free from the suffocating hold the man
had on her. MawMaw got close enough for Skye to reach around her
neck and she clasped on for dear life. The trio struggled back and forth
for a few moments, but the man was too powerful and was winning the
tug-of-war.

"Noooooo!" yelled Skye as she cried from the depths of her heart.
She determined she would not let go of Aggie for anything. They
would have to cut off her arms her before she let go of Aggie.
"MawMaw Aggie, don't let them take me away!"

Skye held on tightly, weeping and calling out to MawMaw. She
could feel Aggie's arms around her, and surprisingly, the horrible
kidnapper was no longer trying to rip her away. They must have won
the battle. Skye relaxed her grip a bit and melted into MawMaw's
embrace, but could not stop crying. She felt Aggie's hand slowly
stroking the back of her head.

And then she opened her eyes.

Her room. The brothel. The barred windows. The smell of the
building. The thumping of the music.

Who was holding her?!

Skye screamed and shot herself back against the wall. The man, who had been sleeping in the corner, was now kneeling on the side of her bed. So close to her now, and with the morning light beginning to illumine the room, she saw how young he looked. Probably only a few years older than she was. He had been hugging her! *Why?* Skye thought. *Why was he hugging me?!*

Confusion was a mighty whirlpool in her mind. *Was he trying to make me feel better? How did he know I was having a bad dream? Is he going to touch me now?* She pressed herself against the wall, wishing she could melt into it and disappear.

He started saying something to her, but she couldn't understand a word he said. He spoke softly, and he seemed to be kind, but not enough to help her settle down. She sat terrified, pulling the cover around her as tightly as possible. She could not stop shaking.

Just then, they heard the rattling of the doorknob. The witch was back. Skye wondered what was going to happen to her when she found out the man had not gotten what he came here to get.

And then the man did the strangest thing. He stood up, slipped off his shirt and quickly tossed it over on the chair in the corner. Then, he unbuckled his belt and unzipped his pants. He called to the woman, and she entered the room. As they talked, he zipped his pants back up and fastened his belt. He laughed as he stepped over to retrieve his shirt, motioned toward Skye, and said some things that seemed to surprise the old woman.

She nodded with approval and walked over to Skye. As the witch lifted her hand, Skye winced, fully expecting a slap across the face. Instead, she got a pat on the head as the woman continued to converse with the young man. He put his arm around the witch's shoulders and led her out of the room.

Skye could hear the jingling of the keys as the outside locks were being closed, and she listened to their voices fade away as they retreated down the hall.

In her astonishment, all the young girl could do was stare at the closed, locked door.

MOLLY VENZKE

✞ 8 ✞

As GALEN STEPPED OUT OF THE STRIP CLUB, the cool, crisp morning air met his face. It wasn't until then that he realized how stale the air had been inside the brothel. While there had been a small window in the girl's room, the closed door hindered any cross-breeze. He wondered if she was ever allowed to leave the confines of that tiny space and walk about in the fresh open air?

Galen's brother and friends from the night before were not there to greet him, and for this, he was thankful. He felt such a mass of emotions. Combine that with the exhaustion of an entire night faking sleep in an uncomfortable chair, and he honestly didn't know how he would've responded if he saw them. What he did know was, it wouldn't have been good.

Although he was carrying enough money to hail a taxi to drive him home, he chose to walk. At least for the time being, or until he could sort through the events of the previous night. Where was he to go from here? What was he going to do? He knew he couldn't simply walk away from that brothel, wipe the memory of the girl from his mind, and go on with life as he had before. As if nothing inside him had changed. Everything inside him had changed.

At the end of the block, he slowed his stride to wait for an opening in traffic to cross the street. No sooner had he stopped when a young woman called out to him. She was standing a few steps behind him, under the awning of a stone building.

"You look like you could use some comfort," she said. "I'm sure I could take care of you this morning."

Galen ignored her. Without looking, he knew she was a prostitute, and he'd had enough of her kind in the last 12 hours.

"Come on, honey. What better way is there to start off your day? I promise, I'll make it worth your while, baby."

Irritated, he turned to confront her. And for the first time, he saw—really saw—the Thessaloniki red-light district. He had forgotten about his blindfold the night before and how he had only experienced these streets through his other senses. But even if this had not been the case, the light of day exposed the brothels in a starkness that could've never been seen in the dark of night.

In his imagination, Galen had thought the area would look like the kind of places he'd seen in the movies, like Amsterdam, or even like Las Vegas. He expected more lights and neon signs. But here, the brothels just looked like rows of plain, ordinary apartment buildings. And the street he was on almost seemed like the edge of it all, with several railroad tracks and warehouses on the other side. That was when he remembered he had heard the occasional distant sound of train whistles throughout the night.

He noticed all the white light bulbs that were attached to many of the buildings. He knew those lights were to communicate which ones were brothels, and which were open for business. As he scanned the horizon, he couldn't find one building with a light that was *not* illuminated. It disgusted him that places like this keep their doors open 24 hours a day, 7 days a week.

As far back as he could remember, Galen had held the entire class of women who chose this way of life in contempt. Prostitution was a legal profession in Greece, and he had harshly judged them for picking this as their career of choice. There were so many other noble and worthy employments to be had, and yet these women decided to embrace this kind of degrading lifestyle.

So far removed from any woman whom Galen encountered in his normal sphere of relationships, these women were easy for him to categorize into one definitive subculture; 'sub' being the operative word. Certainly, they deserved whatever consequences their profession offered, he had thought. They were the ones who showed up to do the work day after day. They were the ones who chose to dance on a pole, on a lap, or on anything else they needed to in order to pick up the highest cash tips. And at any time, they could have chosen to walk away from this grime and find a more respectable life.

But now, after spending the night in that hole-in-the-wall jail cell, he had been humbled. His frame of reference had been altered, and he could no longer keep the same degree of separation between himself and these women. He had been eyeball to eyeball with one of them, and clearly, she had not chosen this life. The look of pain and terror in her eyes was his proof; that young girl was a victim, quite possibly a slave.

How many of these other people started out like her? He could no longer assume that all these girls volunteered for their position. And for the first time in his life, he thought: *Who would ever choose this as a lifestyle? Wouldn't a woman, if she had any other option, pick anything other than the life of a prostitute? But then, if this is true, how did they get here? Why are they here, and better yet, why don't they just walk away from it? Why do they keep doing it? Not all of them are locked up like the girl I met last night.*

"What's takin' you so long, honey?" the woman asked. Her voice brought Galen's focus back to her, and with a keener awareness, he noticed the hardness of the woman's features. At first glance, she appeared youngish, but a longer look revealed her ragged and worn out features. And in a few decades, she'd probably look just like that old wench at the brothel. A newfound compassion caused him to soften his response.

"No thank you, ma'am. I hope you have a good day." As he began to cross the street, he heard her call back, "You don't know what you're missing, baby!" Galen pretended not to hear, and kept walking forward.

How long would it be until that young girl in the brothel looked like this woman here on the street? He thought. The knot in his stomach tightened to the point of nausea.

"Never," he said. "She will never become that. Not if I can help it."

When he had walked out of the bedroom with the old garish woman, he did his best to relate how pleasing the girl had been to him. How throughout the night, she had been at his beck and call, fulfilling his every whim. He told the woman he came from a wealthy family, and if she would keep the girl well fed and refreshed, he'd personally see to it that each night this girl would be hired for her entire shift.

She seemed surprised, and she joked with him about how much "work" it had taken to finally get the girl to submit. At this, he burned with hatred for this small woman, wanting to lay his own hand of strength and authority all over her pasty, heavily made-up face. But not wanting to ruin his charade, he managed a smile. Then through gritted teeth, he warned her to not beat her anymore, at least not until he was done paying her visits. He made the wench swear to feed her and let her rest. Only then did he promise to come back that evening.

Galen laughed out loud. "What in the hell do I think I'm going to be able to do for this girl?" He was totally unaware he was now talking out loud to himself as he strode down the sidewalks. "My money will only pay for so many nights. And then what? Am I going to just stop showing up? Or, am I going to try to see if I can take her out of that room? Even if I did somehow get her out of there, what would I do with her? It's not like I could take her home with me! What would my mum say? No people I know would take a girl like that in their homes. So, where would she go? How would she live? For chrissake, I don't even know what country the girl is from!"

His frustration brought his pace to a run. Running was always the best escape for Galen, and even though he was not dressed for a workout, his body quickly shifted into his natural jogging rhythm. For the next hour, he was able to lose his thoughts inside the pace of his run.

HOURS LATER, Galen was walking down the street where he lived. He was hoping he would be able to sneak into the back door of his house unnoticed by any of his family. But he had no such luck. Nikkos was waiting for him.

At the sight of his younger brother, Nikkos jumped off the front porch and ran toward Galen. As soon as he was close enough to get a good look at him, he burst out laughing.

Nikkos: My god! You look like hell!

Galen didn't look at him. He kept walking toward the house.

Nikkos: Seriously, brother. You look like she rode you hard and put you away wet!
Galen: I don't want to talk about it.
Nikkos: Why not? You look like you had a great night, and I want to hear all about it! I was starting to get worried that something had happened to you because it's taken you so long to get home. But from the looks of you, *obviously*, she went strong all night *and* morning long!
Galen: Stop it, Nikkos. I said I didn't want to talk about it.
Nikkos: Why not? You should be thanking me! So tell me, did that old bitch make you pay double for the morning, or did she throw that in for good measure? Because, if she gave you the morning too, man, what a great deal! Maybe I'll have to go back there for myself.

That did it. In a flash, Galen had his brother pinned at the neck against a tree. Nikkos, completely caught off-guard by the physical strength of his younger brother, lost his breath.

Galen: Now you listen to me: if I ever find out you went back to that brothel, I will personally rip your balls off. Do you understand me?
Nikkos: What the hell is wrong with you?
Galen: And I don't want you talking about last night. To me, or to anyone else, for that matter.
Nikkos: Why not? It's a monumental occasion.
Galen: *(tightening his grip on Nikkos' neck)* I said what I said. Do you understand? I'm warning you, Nikkos, you stir up the s**t, and you're also gonna stir up the stink.
Nikkos: OK, OK...I get it.
Galen: *(leaning into Nikkos' face)* I want you to give me your word you will *never* go back to that brothel.

Nikkos: Why? What happened last night to make you so crazy?

Galen shoved his arm even deeper into Nikkos' neck. Unable to speak, Nikkos managed to lift his hand up in surrender. Galen released his brother and turned toward the house.

"I don't ever want to talk about this again," he added as he walked away.

Nikkos sat on the ground, leaning against the tree and trying to regain his breath. He'd never seen his brother come undone like this. Galen was the one who always kept a level head, never allowing his emotions to get the better of him. Nikkos couldn't imagine what had happened inside that brothel to cause this change, but at least for the time being, he wasn't about to ask.

⚜ 9 ⚜

SKYE STOOD AT THE WINDOW, watching through the bars as the young man walked away from the brothel. She only allowed her view to be from a steep angle in case he happened to look back and catch her spying on him. *Who was he, and why did he spend the entire night here, just to sit? Who pays to just sit and do nothing?* As he continued out of sight, she moved closer to the window, allowing the fresh air to touch her face.

This was the first sunrise she had seen from her caged room. Normally at this time of the morning, she would've just finished an awful night of violation, and it was usually hours before she was able to coax herself out of the bed. Only a daily tray of lunch was enough motivation for her to come out from under the covers and make contact with the world around her. And some days, not even that.

Her window faced east, and the changing colors of the sky were beautiful. Skye wondered, *How can it be that such an awful place as this would be allowed to see a sunrise like that? If MawMaw Aggie is right about there being a god, how could he let that happen? How could he give something so good to people who do such terrible, horrible things? No one here deserves such a gift. They're only worthy of ugliness and darkness.*

And most definitely maggots in all their food. She almost smiled at the thought of the old witch eating maggots.

Skye was sure MawMaw would have some kind of answer to defend her *"Bon Dieu."* She always had good words to say about him and to explain why he did what he did. Even during the summers, when the girls would stay at Aggie's house, she would tell them the same bedtime story almost every single night. Both Skye and Elle used to snuggle into their pillows and drink in each word. Skye had heard it so many times, she knew it by rote.

"A long time ago, le Bon Dieu created da universe. He made da moon and da stars, da land and da sea, and all da many, many tings dat live in da world. He was very happy, but only for a short while. Den, he became very sad. He had nobody to share all his treasures with.

"He wanted someone to dance with at a fais do-do (Cajun dance party), *someone to play a round of boure'* (old Cajun card game), *someone to share His joie de vivre* (joy of life). *He was very, very lonely. And so, you tink you know what le Bon Dieu did? Da's right! He made Cajuns! Laissez les bons temps rouler! Let the good times roll!*

"And for a long time, he was very happy. Da earth was den full of many people. But den, once again le Bon Dieu became very, very sad. Someting was wrong. Someting was missing! He had an envie, a deep craving in da bottom of his heart. He looked across da earth to and fro, and fro and to. Mias oui, well yes, indeed someting was missing. He could find it nowhere.

"What was le Bon Dieu lookin for? He lookin for da one ting dat was missin from da earth. A beautiful girl with eyes da color of da blue, blue sky and with hair as black as night. He was missin a very special girl who was brave and smart, who loved to dream big dreams, and a girl who always worked hard to take care of others. And so, you tink you know what he did?

"Bon Dieu made la petite fille, a little girl, and he named her Skye because he gave her eyes as clear da blue sky. Now he was finally happy, and he grinned ever'day from ear to ear from da moment she opened her eyes to da minute her head hit her pillow at night. Den he would wait and wait and wait and wait all night long until she opened her eyes da next morning.

"But den, about tree years go by, an even though he so happy with Skye-girl, he starts to feel dat deep envie again. Dere was someting else

dat was missin in da earth! He looked to and fro, and fro and to. Mais oui, someting else just wasn't dere.

"What was le Bon Dieu lookin for dis time? He lookin for da other ting dat was missin from da earth. A curly, red-headed pischouette (little girl) with a face like a porcelain doll. A girl who was soft and tender, and who sang with a voice so soothing dat even Caimon, da famous Cajun alligator, would fall asleep at da sound. And so, you tink you know what he did?

"Bon Dieu made another petite fille, and he named her Elle, because though her eyes were dark, dey could still light up da heart of anyone who looked at 'em. And now he was truly happy. He had Skye and Elle and he grinned from ear to ear from da moment dey both opened dere eyes to the moment dey laid dere heads down on dey pillows at night. And he planned out da great tings dey would do and da wonderful places dey would go. He loved 'em more dan ever'ting...even more dan MawMaw Aggie loved 'em. And ever'one knows dere's nobody on earth who loves Skye and Elle more dan MawMaw Aggie!"

And then, MawMaw would smother them with kisses, sending both girls into peels of laughter.

As Skye stood at the barred window remembering this story, her gut began to churn with anger. From where she was right now, living in this horrid cage, every one of Aggie's words rang totally untrue! How could Aggie have fed her such a bucket of lies? And how could Skye ever have been so foolish as to believe a story as ridiculous as this?

In sudden outrage, Skye grabbed the bars, and with every ounce of strength she possessed, she shook them. But the iron rods were securely fastened, so Skye was the only thing that moved as she violently wrestled with them. She fought with her enemy until all her energy was spent, and she finally slunk to the cement floor. Crumpled in a ball under the window, Skye allowed herself to cry deeper than she had since she'd been locked up in this prison.

In her heart, she cried out for something in the universe to be good, to notice her captivity, and to show her some mercy. But as she scanned the tiny room, her feelings confirmed what she knew to be true. No one here was good. No one cared about her captivity. And no one was going to show mercy. She only had herself, and it was time she took her life in her own hands and figured out a way to end it.

Skye barely finished that thought and the lock on her door began to jiggle. The witch was here. *Why is she coming in here this early?* wondered Skye. *She usually doesn't show up until later. I bet she found out about last night, and she's going to let me have it. That's fine. If she beats me, then I'll just fight back to make her beat me even more, all the way until I'm dead. I'm not afraid to die anymore, it's my only way out.*

As the door opened, Skye stood up to meet her assailant. But this time, the old hag didn't wear an evil frown; she was smiling at her. And she was carrying with her a purse and a little bag. She motioned for Skye to sit down on the bed, the entire time chattering on to Skye, even though the girl couldn't understand a word she said.

She opened the sack and pulled out a doughnut-like thing and gave it to Skye. Skye held it for a moment, not sure what to do with it. Was she asking Skye to hold it for her? But then the woman reached into the bag, took out a second pastry and started to eat that one. Skye was confused about how to act until the woman motioned her and said in English, "You. For to eat."

The witch giggle-snorted at Skye as she hesitantly took a tiny bite out of the doughnut as if it was a foreign object. Then the woman stuffed her entire pastry in her mouth, talking in Greek the entire time, with bits of half-chewed pieces flying every which way. She shook off her hands and took a pretty pink satin dress out of her purse. It was more like a slip than a dress, with thin ribbons for straps and lace along the hem. She motioned for Skye to put it on.

The only piece of clothing Skye had was the blue camisole she was wearing. Everything else had been taken away from her the night she was brought here. And when the cami was dirty, she had to lay naked in her bed until the old hag had brought it back, cleaned. Why was she giving her something else to wear? What was she going to make her do now?

Skye stood up, slipped off the blue camisole and exchanged it for the pink one. It fit her body much nicer, and Skye liked that it was longer. The blue one stopped at her hips; this one covered her to her mid-thigh. The woman clapped in approval and scurried out of the room, leaving the door open.

Skye stared at the open door. The witch had never left the door unlocked and open unless it was time for her shift. Skye could feel the familiar feeling of nausea beginning to engulf her. Maybe because she got to sleep last night she was going to have to make up for it now by working a day shift? Maybe that's why the woman gave her something new to wear while she cleaned the blue camisole.

Skye shuffled over to the bed, resolving that somehow soon, she would find a way to bring this all to a fatal end. She sat herself against the wall, waiting for the witch to return with a new client.

The old woman did return, but when she did, she was alone. She was carrying the usual lunch tray, only this time, it had twice as much food as normal. She motioned to the girl to eat all of the food and then to lay down and sleep. She came close to the girl, patted her on the head, and then quickly left the room.

Skye could not fathom what had come over the woman, or why she was acting so nice to her. What could all of this mean? First, there was the night with a guy who didn't even try to touch her, and now a complete shift in how the witch was treating her. She had even included dessert in her lunch!

But before she could ponder too long, she heard the old woman lock the padlocks outside her door. Skye took a deep sigh of relief, realizing this sound to mean she would not have to work a day shift. So for the time being, she could have solitude, and at that moment, it was really all Skye cared about.

MOLLY VENZKE

AGGIE

✤ 10 ✤

"*Mais, oui.* I got dis one chance to get in da place tonight, and by God, I'm gone get in. Dis outfit is my ticket, and dat's just gone be da way it's gone be."

Aggie took a last look at herself in the mirror. She hadn't worn her old maid uniform since the Bacchus's had died. Once their estate settled, Aggie had been utterly shocked at the generosity of her bosses as they left her a large inheritance, large enough not only for her to retire, but also for Hal and her to pay off their home. For sentimental reasons, even if only to one day show her old work clothes to Skye and Elle, she had kept the uniform wrapped and packed up in her closet all these years.

Her reflection spun Aggie's memory back in time. The crisp, white uniform, a one-piece dress. The thick, dark-beige stockings. The bright white nurse shoes. Her hair smoothed back to the nape of her neck. Every workday, Monday through Friday, this had been Aggie's normal wear. She laughed at the sight of herself.

"*Choooh!* Too bad my face don't look as young as da last time I wore dis. Hal, you remember dis? You was still here da last time I had dis on. How many toilets you tink I scrubbed in dis? How many pots o' gumbo you tink I cooked? And look here, *(pulling at the side of the uniform)* I didn't know I was dat much bigger back den. Looks like ol' Aggie needs to be eatin more pork boudin to fatten her up! Well, it's nothin an apron can't fix."

To make the dress fit better, Aggie tied on her white apron and tucked the material in pleats across her back. She then took out her best wool coat from her closet and bundled herself to make the long drive ahead of her. She stopped for a moment before she opened her front door.

"*Bon Dieu*, dis ain't no time for you not to show up. I'm askin you to walk before dis ol' Cajun woman and make a way for me. Help me save dem girls from dat devil of a man. *Choooh*, Mother Mary, and all dem saints up dere, you hearin' me? I need y'all, too!"

Aggie stepped outside into the cold afternoon and made her way to her car. "Girl," she said to her Chevy as she reached for her seatbelt, "When was da last time I put dis many miles on you, back to back?" Aggie patted the dashboard. "You be a good girl to me today, *Sha*, cuz we gone southeast all da way to White Castle."

Aggie checked the directions she had printed from the google map site: I-10 almost all the way to Baton Rouge, then take Plaquemine exit onto LA 1 South, then drive 18 miles to Nottoway. She checked to make sure her gas tank was full. And finally, she scanned the back seat to make certain she had remembered to bring Jack's laptop, the crucial key that was going to unlock this entire mystery. All was ready, so she backed out of her driveway and began her journey.

Tonight would be the first time Aggie had ever stepped foot on the grounds of the great Nottoway Estate. She'd seen plenty of pictures of the iconic Southern plantation through the years, not to mention she and Hal used to say they'd splurge one of these days and spend a night in the white mansion. But unfortunately, 'one of those days' didn't make it on the schedule before Hal passed away. Aggie never saw the sense in going by herself.

As Aggie was turning her car onto I-10, a glint of light caught her eye. It was the sun reflecting off her anniversary ring as she rotated her steering wheel. Aggie never took that ring off, as it was a constant reminder of her wonderful life with Hal. He had given her the diamond ring on the night of their 30th wedding anniversary, the first diamond he ever gave her, and the last substantial present he had bought for her before he died.

"Well, Hal, I'm finally takin our trip to Nottoway. Although I never thought it'd be in disguise. *Choooh!* Look at yo sweet Agata goin undercover. You didn't know you married yourself a spy all dose years ago, did you, Hal?" And she laughed nervously as she rehearsed her plan for the evening and thought about all she'd learned about the DuMondes in the last twelve hours.

The night prior, Aggie had stayed up until dawn formulating how to get the attention of Richard DuMonde. After reading of his generosity to an array of charities over the last ten years, Aggie thought this man might help her find the girls, if somehow she could just get a moment with him to plead her cause. But a man of his social status would not be the easiest for an old, black, Cajun retired maid to approach. Perhaps if time were not of the essence, and if she was persistent enough, she would be able to manage an appointment with a secretary or someone of the sort. But it was Sunday evening, and Macy had been so urgent. Aggie couldn't risk taking the time to go that route. For all she knew, it was too late already.

As Aggie had sat at her computer, she had decided to direct her research toward Lottie DuMonde thinking maybe she'd be easier than Richard to make contact with. Her full name was Charlotte DuMonde, maiden name, Foster. She was the great-granddaughter of Charles Foster, founder of Foster Energy, and had lived her entire life attending Louisiana's most elite schools and social clubs. The DuMondes only had one son, now an adult, and Lottie spent much of her time working with local charities. In fact, in 2009, Charlotte DuMonde was named "Woman of the Year" by a prominent New Orleans organization.

Wanting to know more about this woman, Aggie had clicked on the link to the article about Lottie receiving that award. As she had read the interview with Lottie, Aggie had begun to get more and more confident this woman would most definitely be willing to help her. In the article, Lottie shared how she'd grown up knowing such prosperity, she had never considered the fact that other people were not also enjoying as blessed a life as hers. She had always taken her wealth, and all the privileges and ease that came with it, for granted. She commented that she was ashamed to admit it, but not until Hurricane Katrina hit New Orleans in 2005 did her eyes become open to the people living every day in lack and need, people who were right under her nose.

Lottie told the story about how an experience during the aftermath of Katrina had altered her life forever. Her maid had been an employee of the DuMonde family for over two decades, and through the years, Lottie had grown very close to her. This maid, her grown daughter, and her twin grandchildren had lived in the 9th Ward. They relied completely on public transportation, so even once the hurricane evacuation orders went forth, this family had no way to properly vacate their house before the storm hit. All four of them were home when the levees broke and the flooding violently coursed through their neighborhood. The waters had swiftly rampaged through their home and had risen to the ceilings. For five days in the unbearable Louisiana summer heat, this family was stranded in their attic, without food or clean water, as they waited for someone to rescue them.

By the time help finally arrived, all four of them were severely dehydrated, especially the 3½ year-old twins. They were taken to a makeshift hospital shelter, where Lottie's maid was then able to contact her. Lottie immediately drove to where her maid's family was being cared for, and ended up staying at the triage for the next several days, 24/7, offering her help in any way she could. Lottie shared how heart-wrenching it was to see so many families who, because they had no means to leave New Orleans, had been caught in the wake of the disaster. In the end, both of her maid's grandchildren were not able to recover, and the precious set of twins died.

Lottie told the interviewer that as she and Richard stood through the double funeral for those two children, who just a few weeks prior had spent the day at the DuMonde's, running around the house and swimming in their pool, they realized how selfishly they'd been living their lives. Up until this point, they'd never really considered how people outside their social sphere managed their lives; they'd simply been focused on building their own dreams and fortunes.

"Not that there is anything wrong with cultivating wealth," Lottie had been quick to point out. "It's just that until this point, Richard and I hadn't learned the true *purpose* for wealth; which we now believe is to help people. We promised each other we'd never become so short-sighted again. Obviously, we can't help everybody, but we *can* help the ones who, for whatever reason, cross our paths."

Then the article went on to give a very impressive list of Lottie's contributions, not only of money but also of hours upon hours of community service to many local organizations designed to equip and empower children and young women.

Both dese folks seem so kind and givin, Aggie had thought. *I just know dey gone help me once dey hear about my girls. I just know it! But how am I gone get to meet 'em? Macy made it sound like dem girls need help today! I don't tink I have da time to go through da proper channels to get to either of 'em.*

She had almost given up on her research, when she found another online newspaper article reporting about an elegant Mardi Gras Ball hosted by the DuMonde's. This piqued Aggie's interest. The event was to be held at the Nottoway Estate, and the guest list included 100 of the most up-and-coming business owners of Southern Louisiana. Richard and his wife, Lottie, had a desire to form a new Mardi Gras Krewe for the following year, with these 100 couples to be invited as charter members. Once established as an official Mardi Gras Krewe, then this fraternity would now have the platform to host their own annual Mardi Gras ball, as well as their own parade. At the very least, the group could showcase their elaborate Mardi Gras float in another krewe's parade.

Aggie chuckled. "Ha! 'Course he gone try to make his own krewe cuz he ain't never gone get into any of dose upper crust krewes. *Choooh*, dose krewes are iron clad; someone gotta die before dere's an openin in ones like da Rex Krewe. You'd tink Lottie's connections were deep enough, though."

Aggie had sat back in her chair, wishing there would be some way for her to get inside that ball. Even if she could just get near the DuMondes for a moment, she could quickly tell Richard about her situation, or maybe even slip a letter to Miss Lottie?

"But what dis ol woman gone wear? Say, by some *cocain* (really big) miracle, I get in, what to do to *pouponer* (to make oneself look nice) so's I won't stick out? Da nicest ting I own, is da black dress I wore for Hal's funeral. Dat won't do at all, at all." She suddenly burst out laughing, "Agata, you a crazy ol' fool! You know you ain't gone get into dat ball; you black! Ain't gone be no black, retired maids like you at dat kinda shindig."

It was as she had gotten up to clean her kitchen before she went to bed, that the idea had come to her. What if she went to the ball as kitchen help? Or as a dishwasher? Even a maid? Would there be any way at all she'd be able to sneak in as part of the extra staff for the event?

"Dat just might work!" she had said. "It's da night before da last day of Mardi Gras and ever'one in da whole state'll be partyin, save the God-fearin folk. Dat Nottoway'd be havin to bring in all kinds of new staff for a Mardi Gras ball like dis."

She'd leaned against her sink as she allowed her mind to begin formulating a plan and said, "I gone get in dere tomorrow, and dat's just gone be da way it's gone be." Just then, her hallway clock stuck 2am. "*Mais oui*, look what time it is; it's already Monday! Dis ol woman gotta get some sleep if I'm gone be good to anyone tomorrow." And as she walked to her bedroom, she prayed, "Lawd, help me lay my head down to sleep, and please, *Mon Dieu*, make a way for your Aggie? You know I need yo help to do dis."

After a few hours of sleep, Aggie had gotten up and had called the Nottoway Estate to verify the staff's arrival time. Aggie had used her best proper Southern English, trying to tone down her Cajun accent, as she spoke in a harried voice, "Hello, I'm calling because I's hired to work for da DuMonde event dis evening, and I've lost my paper dat gave me all da particulars for tonight. I really need dis job, and want to do my best, so can you please help me out? What time do I need to clock in, and what is da uniform I should wear?"

The person on the other end had seemed just as rushed with her time, as she didn't even ask Aggie to verify herself with a name. She had simply told her to be at the mansion by 3pm, that the staff was to wear all white, and without another word, she hung up.

At first, Aggie's heart had sank as she performed a mental scan of her closet. She was sure she had nothing that was *all* white; maybe she could find a blouse, but she was certain she did not have a pair of white pants. And what about the white shoes? She had quickly gone to her closet to see if she owned a pair of white shoes.

"*Gar ici!* (Look here!) My old uniform shoes from when I was da Bacchus' maid, and dey still look white, white. *Mais*, why didn't I think of dat sooner? I'll wear my uniform, da whole ting! It's all white, and it'll make me look like I'm just one of da maids."

Looking at the clock, Aggie had calculated she had almost four hours to get herself ready to leave. If she began driving to Nottoway by 1:30, she was sure she'd arrive before 3, and then hopefully blend in with some of the other staff that'd be walking in. Four hours was just enough time to run over to her salon, get her hair washed and ironed, eat a large lunch, and dress for the event.

Now, as Aggie drove along I-10, she chuckled at the absurdity she found herself in. "I wonder who'll all be in dat place tonight? What you tink, Hal? Dere's gone be more money represented in dat room tonight den either of us have ever imagined. *Choooh!* I bet dey spend more money on da food for da pets than I did for both of us when you still alive. How dis ol' Cajun girl gone act around folks like dat?" Then she burst out laughing. "I'll just have to remember what you always used to say: 'Ain't no matter how much a person makes, dey still sit down to use da toilet.' Dat's what I'll tink about if I start gettin nervous."

At least at this point, Aggie was not nervous at all; she felt happy about how smoothly everything had worked out thus far. But she was also aware that the first part of the day getting ready for the evening was the easy part. The rest of the old woman's plan, once she arrived at the Nottoway Plantation, was much sketchier. While she played out in her mind the many different ways by which she would catch the ear of either Richard or Charlotte DuMonde, she really had no idea what she was about to walk into. Aggie had been to Mardi Gras events before, but she had never experienced a high society event of this caliber.

In addition, she'd never worked a job besides her time as the Bacchus' maid; she didn't know the first thing about how to make herself an effective (and anonymous) part of a systemized staff. She wondered if she would be able to blend in with the rest of the workers. But there was one thing Aggie knew she had going for her; she was a hard-working Cajun woman, very resourceful and scrappy. She knew the odds for success were against her, but she didn't care. If anything, her underdog status only served to fuel her determination. Come hell or high water, she was going to make her case known to the DuMonde family.

⚜

⚜ 11 ⚜

AGGIE PULLED INTO THE ENTRANCE of the Nottoway Plantation off LA 1 South, along with three other cars. Aggie's relief that she was arriving with other staff was immediately squelched as she realized every car was being stopped at the gate. There was a small white building with a side window, much like any check-in point at an upscale country club, and the person inside was talking to each driver, making them show identification before allowing them to enter. Aggie began to panic.

"Hal! Do you see dis, Hal? Dis a *mal pris* (a bad situation)! What to say if dey ask me questions? You know I'm not any good at lyin. I'm gone get myself caught 'fore I even get in. Oooooh, I got the *faiblesse* (I feel like fainting)!"

Aggie tried to regain her composure, as she inched her way up in line. She thought of Macy, of the girls, and knew she could not afford to lose her confidence, at least for their sakes. She took a deep breath, and pulled forward to the man in the window. As she put down her window, she smiled her sweetest Southern smile. She spoke very slowly, as she attempted her best Louisiana—non-Cajun—dialect.

Aggie: Good Afternoon, sir.
Man: Good Afternoon, ma'am. You on staff tonight?
Aggie: Yes, sir. I'm part of da staff for da DuMonde Mardi Gras
        Ball. I was told to arrive by three o'clock.
Man: Yes, ma'am, can I've your name please?
Aggie: Why, sure. It's Agata Prejean. Do you need identification?
Man: Yes, ma'am.

*Aggie handed the man her driver's license. She pretended to be calm,
looking forward as if this was an every-day procedure for her. He paged
through the many pages on his clipboard, and then paged through them
again. Knowing her name was not going to be listed, she tried to distract
him.*

Aggie: Can you please tell me just where to park my car? Of course,
        as staff, I want to make sure the guests have the best
        parking.
Man: *(not seeming to have heard her)* Miss Aggie, your name is not
        on da list for da staff. And I was given very strict orders not
        to let anyone in here tonight dat was not on dis list. I don't
        mean to *faire la misere*—excuse me—I mean, I don't mean to
        cause trouble for you, but-
Aggie: *Dit mon la verite'!* (Tell me the truth!) You cajun, *Sha?*
Man: *Oui, oui! Je reste au Bayou.* (Yes, I live in Golden Meadow)
Aggie: Go to bed! (I don't believe you!) *Mon Defan Nanan reste au
        Bayou.* (My godmother, now deceased, lived in Golden
        Meadow) *Choooh!* It's a small world, isn't it? *J'ai gros couer
        pour le Bayou.* (I have a special place in my heart for Golden
        Meadow.)
Man: I've never wanted to live anywhere else.
Aggie: Dat's Cajun country! Why'd you ever want to move? Listen,
        Sha, I don't know why my name's not on dat list, 'cept maybe
        it's 'cause I just got da call to work tree days ago. I know
        Miss Lottie DuMonde's maid, she a Cajun too, by da way,
        and she heard I needed work. So she gave da
        recommendation for me to Miss Lottie herself. Please, if I
        don't show up tonight, my friend will hear it, and dat'll be
        two Cajuns you gone make da *misere.*
Man: I don't know, Miss Aggie. Dese *Texians* (anyone who doesn't
        talk like a Cajun) run a tight ship. 'Specially tonight, I don't

know why, but dere's a *lot* of extra security. I've never had to be so careful 'bout lettin folks come in here.

Aggie: *Sha*, you tink dis *vielle* (old woman) gone cause trouble for da DuMonde's? What could someone like me do? 'Sides, I'm gone be too busy passin' a mop all night long!

Man: *Alohrs pas!* You a good ol' Cajun woman; I know you'd never cause any trouble. But maybe I should put a call into Wil DuMonde just to make sure? He da point man for da night.

Just then, the driver in the car behind Aggie's impatiently tapped her horn.

Aggie: *Choooh!* You don't want to make ever'one late. If I know anyting about Wil DuMonde, he don't like folks bein late.

Man: Alright, alright! Go on through, but don't talk bout dis to no body.

Aggie: *Merci! Merci! Merci!*

Aggie quickly pulled forward before the man had a chance to change his mind. The road was a straight paved road, with centuries-old trees evenly lining the way on each side, and she wondered when she would actually see a glimpse of the famous mansion. At the end of the road was a large lot, and Aggie parked along a far edge. Because of her extended time with the gatekeeper, the people who had been in the cars ahead of her in line had already gone in to work. So Aggie decided to wait in her car until, hopefully, there would be a small group of employees coming in behind her car that she could walk in with.

"*Mon Dieu, Mon Dieu, Mon Dieu,* I am in dis ting over my head. Once I get in dere, what to say? What to do? I don't know a ting to do! You gotta make a way for dis *vielle* (old woman) and help me to get to a DuMonde tonight."

As she sat in her car, a minivan parked a few spots down from her car. Four women, all dressed in white and obviously employees, unloaded from the car. These women happened to be in their late 40s, and one was easily mid-50s. Aggie breathed a sigh of relief, knowing she wasn't going to be the only older woman working that night. The fear had crossed her mind that if all the other employees were young, she most certainly would stick out of the crowd. Looking at these women, Aggie was sure she'd be able to blend in. Granted, at age 67, she was far their senior, but she also knew she didn't look a day older than 60, if that. With her smooth, shiny, dark-mocha skin, she definitely had a complexion that worked in her favor as she was often mistaken for a woman in her early to mid-50s. Tonight, she knew it was the time to act like it.

"*Mon Dieu*, did you make it so all dem women pulled in here just now?" she said, smiling upwards. "I bet you even made sure to have dat good ol' Cajun boy at the gate, too, didn't you? You on my side tonight, ain't you, *Mon Dieu*? Well, let's just be keepin it dat way, OK?" Suddenly, Aggie felt a deep peace in her heart, and she knew everything was going to work out just fine.

WIL

❊ 12 ❊

WIL STOOD FOR A MOMENT TO TAKE IN THE VIEW. He'd been so 'on task' since the moment he arrived at the Nottoway Plantation, that he hadn't yet given himself the opportunity to broaden his focus beyond his mission at hand. Tonight was going to be a special event for both his mom and dad, and Wil wanted to do whatever was needed to make it be all they wanted it to be. Wil thought it was the least he could do for the man who completely paused his entire life to walk with him, step by step, through his past 6 months of recovery and rehabilitation.

Wil had been serving in Iraq as an E-7 Platoon Sergeant, and considering his age of 26 years, this level of leadership was a substantial achievement. He'd led many missions, most of them with the Army's Special Operation Forces, where he and his team had not only provided discreet reconnaissance to other US security forces, but had also strategized successful dilutions of Al Qaeda operations. He was a high-value asset to the Army, and time and time again, his leadership delivered effects that were disproportionate to the size of his platoon. Wil was born to be a soldier; even as an adolescent, at the slightest whiff of injustice, he could turn defender as easily as he breathed.

And then six months ago, in a matter of a few seconds, his life took a sudden detour. Wil and members of his platoon had made a stop in an Iraqi town they knew to be safe. Across the road, a civilian couple was walking by. Wil saw the man reach into the small bag slung across his chest, and immediately he knew this man was not an ordinary civilian.

Wil's adrenaline had spiked and his senses went into over-drive, causing everything that was happening around him to feel like it had morphed into slow motion. The man pulled out what looked like an old stick grenade, the kind used in World War II, but Wil knew it for what it really was; an armor-piercing grenade, one of the most potent grenade weapons used by Al Qaeda.

Wil had aimed his rifle, and before the grenade's small parachute had time to open upon its descent, he'd already eliminated the man and his friend. But they were not working alone. Wil had heard gunfire all around him as he took out three more of the emerging enemy, and then the grenade had gone off. Explosions were all around Wil, but he thought he'd escaped injury because he felt no pain. Then he felt himself being lifted up and thrown over the shoulder of a fellow soldier and carried to a vehicle. He was placed into the back of an Army truck, and the next thing he knew he had woken up in a military hospital.

Wil's injuries were extensive, and he was in need of expert surgeons. So as soon as he was stable, the Army flew him back to the States for proper care. There he would undergo several surgeries on his left leg, hopefully preventing an amputation, as well as skin grafts for the large wounds he incurred across his upper back. It would be a long rehab, but he was lucky to be alive, as the two men in his platoon who had been next to him had fallen that day.

Wil's father, Richard, had been waiting at the hospital when he arrived, and once Wil was checked in, he rarely left his side. Richard was a man of great influence in Louisiana, both financially and socially. A true entrepreneur with an uncanny intuition for future markets, he would build a company from scratch, lead its growth until it stood head and shoulders above the competition, and then Richard would sell it for an enormous profit. His savvy for business had the Midas touch, as he repeated his formula several times. Since his mid-30s, there had not been a year his name was absent from the Forbes 400 Richest People in America.

But all the money in the world would not have been able to medicate the pain of losing an only child, your only son. Richard understood this. And so, both his social and business calendars had been swiped clean the moment he heard of Wil's injuries. Nothing was more important to him than being with his son throughout his entire rehabilitation. Often, once he was thoroughly mobile, Wil would try to sway his father to return to work; but Richard would hear nothing of the sort. He treasured the concentrated time with his son, a rare commodity for a father and adult child, and he was unwilling to devalue a moment of it by concentrating on business.

"I have top-notch employees that can take care of the businesses, Wil," Richard would say. "Other people can fill in for me there; but only I can be your father. So just be quiet and let me be."

Wil would laugh and shake his head, but then he'd express his extreme gratitude. He knew that without the emotional and physical support his dad was so freely offering, his recovery time would have been doubled. Richard never let Wil give in to depression or self-pity, and would daily motivate him to work his hardest through the hours of painful physical therapy. He would remind Wil that no matter the outcome of this situation, he was born for greatness, and no battle wounds would have the power to thwart his future. These words were food for Wil's soul as he pushed his body to far surpass the expectations of his doctors and therapists.

Now, feeling physically and mentally stronger than ever before, Wil was more than ready to re-enlist and continue his destiny in the military. However, the thing for which he was *not* feeling ready was breaking the news to his mom and dad. While he knew they would fully support him in any career path he chose, he was also aware they would not be happy to hear of his desire to reengage in such a high-risk position. But Wil could not imagine himself doing anything other than this; any other picture he had tried to muster up just looked gray and mundane.

Sensing Wil's restlessness to move on, Richard had been dropping hints to his son about partnering with him in the business of oil and natural gas exploration. He gave his best effort to describe the work as exciting and sexy, and Wil certainly tried to appear interested. But Richard could see past his son's politeness.

Behind Wil's eyes was a fiery vision to conquer opposition, and nothing less than his participation in solving complex, world-changing situations would be able to satisfy his dreams.

As soon as Mardi Gras is over, and we've all settled down, I've got to talk to them about what I want to do next, thought Wil. *I love my dad, but I can't let his fears stop me from doing what I know in my heart I'm supposed to be doing.*

Wil breathed a deep sigh and looked out from the magnificent balcony of Nottoway. Being raised in an affluent family, he'd been around opulence all his life, so there weren't too many houses that could impress Wil. When he was about 8 years old, his parents bought a late-19th century mansion in the famous Garden District of New Orleans, and they still live there today. But even with its 5,000 square feet of bedrooms, sprawling outdoor balconies, library and ballroom, plus a 2-story carriage house, it paled in comparison to the home he was standing in now.

The majestic Nottoway Plantation was more like a blazing white castle that seemed to defy all superlatives. This home had 53,000 square feet of living space, 64 rooms, 6 interior staircases, 12 hand-carved Italian marble fireplaces, and incredibly intricate plasterwork throughout the rooms that boasted 15½ ft. ceilings and 11 ft. doors. The original owner had even installed a bowling alley in the basement of the house for his 11 children. As Wil stood on the main floor outdoor balcony, he felt dwarfed next to the massive 3-story high square columns that served to help hold up the enormous structure. He scanned the property, which in full, encompassed 100s of acres, and wondered what it would've been like to grow up in a place like this.

And I thought I'd grown up with privileges, he thought. *I guess wealth is completely a matter of perspective. What's lavish to one person is lack to another. Hell, just a few, months ago, rich for me meant I would get to keep both my legs! If I'd've lost one, I don't think any amount of wealth would've made me feel rich.*

OK, dude, focus your mind, he reminded himself. *You've got work to do to make tonight great.* And with that, he bounded down the great outdoor granite staircase of the White Castle.

❀13❀

W<small>IL STRODE TO MEET HIS FRIENDS</small> at the Fountain Courtyard, just south of the mansion. He chuckled as he approached the young men, already dressed in their costumes for the evening. As a festive close to the last two days of Mardi Gras, tonight would be an extravagant costume ball, and because the venue was circa 1859, the DuMonde's thought it would be fun to host a *Gone With the Wind* theme. And of course, Richard would dress as Rhett Butler, and Lottie as the famous Scarlett O'Hara.

As he approached the guys, Wil wondered if they felt as odd as he did in his Confederate officer costume. On one hand, he thought it was pretty cool to be accurately dressed in the era of his present surroundings. The existing owners of historic Nottoway had been meticulous to preserve the authenticity of the site, and to walk the exact paths of former young men who had served in the Civil War—in almost the exact same clothes—was a bit eerie. On the other hand, if Wil had lived in Louisiana during this time, would he have worn the uniform of a Confederate? Judging from his values of today, he would've been in great conflict with the ideals for which the South was fighting; but then again, he was a Southerner through and through. It would have torn him up on the inside to have fought against his brother and neighbor. He was glad he'd never have to answer the question.

Weeks ago as Wil had read up on the history of Nottoway, he learned that three sons of John Randolph (the man who built Nottoway) had fought in the Civil War; the eldest son was killed in battle. These very grounds had been occupied from time to time by hundreds of soldiers, from both sides of the war. Now as he briskly walked into the courtyard and saw a dozen of his friends in their Confederate costumes, a sight surely to have been seen by the 1863 soldiers, he felt a strange kindred to these ghosts of the past. As a former American soldier, Wil understood only too well the minds, the passions, and the nightmares of the men who had gone before him.

Using his best commanding voice, Wil yelled, "Atten-tion!"

The guys simultaneously turned to Wil, laughing and greeting him with handshakes and high-fives. The group of a dozen young men, ranging in ages from 20-28, were all close friends of Wil. A few he knew from high school athletics, a couple were close family relatives, and the rest were former fellow Army Rangers.

Matt: Well, I guess it's clear who the man in charge is. Check out that officer's hat! How come your costume is so much better than the rest of ours?

Wil: Because I *am* the man in charge, and besides, who paid for all of your costumes?

Matt: Umm...let's see...your dad?!

Wil: *(laughing heartily)* Ha! Well, you got me there. But at least I didn't cheap out on you and make you wear the $19.99 version with the plastic pants. These costumes are legit. Mine more than yours, though.

Scott: So what's the plan for tonight?

Matt: Yeah, are we gonna get food outta this deal, and more importantly, are there gonna be any single ladies present this evening?

The guys laughed and started teasing Matt about his inability to succeed whenever he asked a girl out on a date.

Wil: Hey, I never said you'd get a date by helping me out, but I can guarantee you'll get a big ol' Southern dinner. Plus, if you want to stay after and hang for beers—and all the leftovers I'm going to steal from the kitchen tonight—I reserved a couple extra rooms in the mansion for us. It's pretty cool, 'cause the guy who built this place actually built separate living quarters for his sons, and those are the rooms I got for us.

Matt: Dude, how cool would that've been to grow up with your own part of the house? Me and my brothers would've torn the place up.

Wil: Well, he did have eleven kids, I guess he had to do something with them all. Wait til you see the inside of this joint. Seriously, the dude spared no expense. In the basement, he even built his kids their own private bowling alley.

Scott: What?! Is it still there? Can we play a couple rounds?

Wil: Are you kidding me? First of all, it's not still there; it's a museum now, but even if it was, do you think they'd let us bowl with 150-year-old balls and pins?

Scott: True that.

Wil: The guy who owns this place would never let us mess around with the antiques; although, I'd be the same way if I was in charge. The only reason we're getting the kind of free access tonight is because, one, he's a friend of my dad's—

Matt: *(interrupting)* Hello?! Who *isn't* a friend of your dad's? He's the epitome of "the guy who knows a guy."

Wil: And two, my dad has the cash to cover anything that might get slightly damaged.

Matt: Ya think?! He's one of the richest guys in Louisiana!

Wil: Dude, you gonna be a smart a** *all* night long? 'Cause I can take ya down right here in front of all these guys.

Matt: Whatever.

Wil: Ok. Let's get serious for a sec. First of all, thanks so much for helping out. My dad and me really, really appreciate it, and realize you could've gone to any one of a thousand Mardi Gras parties tonight, so it's cool you're here.

Matt: Hey, this is just Monday; we'll still be able to make the grand finale of Mardi Gras tomorrow. Which by the way, if any of you guys wanna ride down with me to New Orleans to see all the parades, I got my parent's Expedition. It's gonna be fly.

Wil: That *will* be fun. We'll talk about that after we're done with tonight. Anyway, I gotta fill you all in on what's been happening with my dad over the last few weeks, and why I've asked you guys to be here tonight. I know I'm probably just going overboard, but I don't want to be stupid either.

For the past month or so, my dad's been getting some really bizarre, anonymous emails. Without going into too much detail, whoever's sending them is asking for large amounts of money, along with threats of violence if my dad doesn't pay up. Some of you already know this, but for those of you who don't, my dad has a brother named Jack who basically disappeared off the face of the earth when he was about 20. Dad's tried to get in touch with him over the years, but the guy's a real loser, probably a big drug dealer and into who knows whatever else, and he's never wanted contact. We think the person who's emailing Dad is somehow linked with Jack; probably looking to get back money my uncle owes him. Obviously, all of this is on the D.L., but you need to know this info to be on guard for tonight.

Once the newspapers printed a story about this party tonight, the emails got more frequent. It's been so frustrating because I've been working with one of my dad's FBI friends, and as we've cased out the incoming mail, the email addresses are always different, and look like they're sourcing from public computers in various libraries, so we can't get a handle on any particular location.

I'm almost certain whoever is doing this isn't going to show up tonight, but on all fronts of my parent's social activities, we've been taking extra precautions. And this is where you guys come in. These grounds are so huge, and by no means secure. Anybody could just walk right off of highway 405 over there and come in. So what we've done for tonight is this: First, we've bought out the entire plantation for today and tomorrow; all the rooms, all the venues, and all the tours will only be for the group of about 200 guests who'll be coming tonight. Besides those guests, the only other people who'll be on site will be Nottoway staff.

Last week, all the guests were mailed special gifts to be worn this evening. It's a gold lapel pin that's a doubloon, and it has the crest Dad wants to use as the emblem of the new Mardi Gras Krewe he's going to start.

Scott: Whoa—you're dad's gonna start a new krewe? That is tight! Well, I guess that'll give the Rex Krewe a run for their money.

Matt: Ha! Literally! So who's all coming tonight? And are any of their daughters single?

Scott: Shut it, Matt...don't anger the beast. You might be his oldest friend, but—

Matt: Hey, I'm *family*. Blood runs thicker than water, bro.

Scott: Yeah, and we're gonna see all that blood of yours in a second here if you don't shut your cake-hole.

Wil: *(chuckling at his friends)* I brought one of these gold doubloons for each of you guys.

Wil pulled out an envelope from his outer coat pocket and poured 12 pins into his hand. They were bright 14-karat gold doubloon coins, about an inch and a half in diameter. He passed them out, giving one to each of the guys.

Every person here tonight will have one of these. You guys can pin it on your costume, too. Some of the ladies might be wearing them as necklaces or bracelets, but *everyone* has to have this visible on their person to get in tonight.

Scott: What about the staff? How will we know if they're real staff or not?

Wil: Right. Good question. All the staff has been pre-approved by me, and two weeks ago, they also received one of these pins in the mail, only theirs aren't real gold.

Matt: Are these ones you gave us real gold?

Wil: Yes, Matt, and if I hear you sold yours, I'm gonna kick your a**.

Matt: Wouldn't think of it!

Wil: *(sarcastically)* Riiiight.

Scott: So, do you have specific places you want us to patrol?

Wil: Well, yes and no. Like I said, I really don't think there'll be any action to speak of tonight. The chances that the scumbag who's been emailing my dad would actually have the balls to come here tonight is next to nothing. But because of the nature of the threats, we just can't take any risks. Really, all I need from you guys is to be extra sets of eyes. I'm going to be interfacing with all the staff on many different levels tonight to make sure all goes as planned, so I'm not going to be able to keep track of all the people coming and going. What I need is for all you guys to pair off—

Matt: Dude, if we walk around all night *in pairs* with these light blue costumes, everyone's gonna think we're gay.

Wil: *(to Scott)* I swear, I'm gonna kill him before the night's over.

Scott: No worries, man, I'll hide the body over there in the Mississippi.

Matt: Hey!

Wil: ANYway, as I was saying, I want you to split up, walk around and just keep your eyes and ears open. Before everything starts, I'll give you all radios so we can be in touch throughout the night. Your first priority is to check to make sure everyone you see has one of these doubloons on. And I mean, for the *entire* night. If you notice anyone without the gold pin, politely ask them to show it to you. If they can't produce it, then radio me and I'll come and meet you. Stay with the person until I get there. Otherwise, just stay alert. For you, Matt, that means no booze until the deal is over. And for all my rangers, please remember this isn't some covert op that you have to get all intense about. Tonight's just a party with a bit of heightened security. The last thing my dad wants is for any of the guests to feel something might be up. Does everyone have their cards with the agendas?

As the guys took out small cards from their pockets, Wil continued:

Real quickly, the guests will arrive at 18:00. They'll be greeted and escorted to the main floor of the mansion, which is actually the second floor. They'll get drinks and hors d'oeuvres there, and they're allowed to be in the White Ballroom, the Gentlemen's Study, the formal Dining Room, and the balconies. At 19:00, everyone will be taken to the Randolph Ballroom, and that room is south of the mansion, just a short walk. Everyone'll be seated, and dinner will begin at 19:30. Look for me, and I'll make sure you guys know where to sit. At 21:30, you can see on your card, several things will be happening. Dancing back up in the White Ballroom, poker in the Gentlemen's Study, candlelight tours of the rest of the mansion, and brandy in the dining room. The party will go until exactly 00:00, in true Mardi Gras tradition, and not a minute later. We realize that *technically* it's the night before the end of Mardi Gras, but my parents want to do everything to give the folks a vision of what next year's ball will be like if they do decide to form an official krewe.

I gotta go and meet with the Nottoway staff, but I've already debriefed Scott about everything, so if you have any questions, he can field those. *(to Scott)* Right now, if you walk up to the main front balcony, there's a gal named Suzy who'll be ready to show you and the guys around the entire mansion. She'll be pointing out the rooms we'll be using for tonight, so you'll know if people tonight are starting to stray off the beaten path. You cool?

Scott: As a cuke.

Wil: *(gesturing to Matt)* Make sure he doesn't steal anything.

Matt: Hey!

Laughing, Wil began to stride back to the mansion to meet with the staff, but not before he gave Matt a quick head-lock and pretended that he was going to throw him into the courtyard fountain. All the guys cheered Wil on, and continued to razz Matt after Wil let him go. Before he was out of earshot, Wil yelled over his shoulder, "Oh yeah, and don't forget to have fun! It's going to be a great party!"

MOLLY VENZKE

AGGIE & WIL

❧ 14 ❧

AGGIE HATED LYING. It was the one thing she'd be sure to get a whipping for when she was a little girl. "Da Prejeans never lie," her PaPa would say gently as he'd unhitch his belt. "We may be a lot of tings, but we ain't liars, Agata. I do dis 'cause I love you, *Sha*." And he'd whip her butt with his belt. Never hard enough to leave a lasting mark, but definitely enough to sting and draw tears. Aggie'd crawl up in her PaPa's lap and cry while his big arms engulfed her in a way only a father's arms could. He'd speak softly, right into her ears, telling her how much he loved his girl.

But in this situation, Aggie knew lying would be a necessity...especially now that she'd heard about those gold doubloon pins the staff was required to wear for the party. She had to get herself one of those pins! She wasn't sure how just yet, but she knew she wouldn't last very long inside the mansion without one.

In the parking lot was where Aggie had learned about the doubloons for the first time. Aggie had introduced herself to the women who had gotten out of the minivan, and began a conversation with one of them, the oldest-looking one. Her name was Judy, and as they were walking up to the staff entrance of Nottoway, Judy had given Aggie the run down of the evening.

Judy: How long have you been working here, Aggie? I don't remember ever seeing you at any mansion events.

Aggie: Dat's 'cause dis my first time. I'm a last minute add for da big party tonight. I know Miss Lottie's personal maid, and she told me Miss Lottie was worried about dere not bein enough cleanin staff for da night. I told Bessie, my friend who works for Miss Lottie, dat I'd be happy to help out. So Miss Lottie told Bessie to tell me to show up in my white uniform and get to work!

Judy: Wow, that was mighty lucky for you, wasn't it? I've gotta say, I'm looking forward for tonight. I've heard the DuMondes are great people.

Aggie: Bessie says dey da best she ever worked for.

Judy: So, this is your first time to Nottoway?

Aggie: It sure is. And I know we just met, Judy, but is dere anyway you could show me where to go? I wanna make a good impression, I really need da money. Plus, I gotta live up to Bessie's recommendation.

Judy: Why, I'd be happy to. We all need the extra money, nowadays, don't we? Just stick with me, and you'll be fine.

Aggie: *Mais*, I'm just part of da cleanin crew, *Sha*, so I just wanna stay invisible.

Judy: Ha! I understand. I'll show you what you need to know.

While Judy was leading Aggie into the staff room, Aggie did her very best to not look around at her surroundings like a tourist. She knew she had to act as professional as possible, even though she had never experienced anything remotely close to the grandeur of Nottoway. They entered a woman's staff lounge that had small lockers for all the employees.

Judy: My locker is right over here, and you can just share mine for tonight. You'll want to keep all your stuff in here, and I'll lock it up tight. *After putting her own coat and purse in the locker, she took Aggie's coat and placed it on top of hers. She then took out her gold doubloon pin from her purse.* They're being real sticklers about these doubloons tonight. They told us every staff person has to have one of these pins on their uniform or they'll be sent home. Where's yours? Make sure it's pinned somewhere where it can be easily seen.

Aggie: *(lying)* Uhhh...da pin. Yeah. Bessie told me 'bout dat. I'm posed to get mine from Miss Lottie or Mr. Wil once I see dem. Why we need dose?

Judy: I'm not sure, but you better make sure you get yours right away. We've never had to wear them before; they're just for the DuMonde's event. Everybody was told to make sure we had it on our person at all times. It's pretty unusual; maybe it has something to do with the fact it's Mardi Gras weekend. But then again, I heard the theme of the party tonight was a *Gone With the Wind* deal. These doubloons are Mardi Gras pins. I don't know...I just follow whatever orders I'm given.

Aggie: I'll go get mine right away.

Judy: Great. Now let me show you around.

Aggie: All I need's for you to show me where da cleanin supplies are, so I can get to pushin a mop through dis place.

Judy: *(smiling at her)* Aggie, I don't think you need to worry about living up to your friend's recommendation. You're gonna do just fine.

They walked out of the staff locker room and Judy took her to the several locations of cleaning closets. After Aggie had quickly gathered enough supplies, she asked Judy to show her where the public restrooms were so she could start there. On their way, Judy informed her that Mr. Wil wanted to meet with all the staff at four o'clock sharp in the White Ballroom. There, they would get all the remaining details for the evening's event, and she would not want to be late for that. Aggie thanked Judy for her help and then urged her to go and clock in before her boss thought she was late. Once alone in the bathroom, Aggie closed and locked the door.

This bathroom, like most of the ones Judy had shown her, was a single room bathroom, and Aggie was thankful for the seclusion. She sat down on the toilet and took a deep breath as she attempted to adjust to her surroundings.

"*Mon Dieu, Mon Dieu,*" she whispered. "What has Aggie got herself into dis time? Dis just too much for ol' Aggie to take care of. I'm gone get myself caught and put up in jail, is what I'm gone do! And den, who gone take care a me? And who gone get dem girls?

Oh, *Mon Dieu*, you best hide me tonight, or even better, make one dem gold doubloons appear right now in my ashy black hand!"

She chuckled at herself, trying to order God around like she was fit to be his boss. She knew God would have his way, whatever way that was, and she was just going to be happy with the lot she was given. She took in another deep breath hoping it would calm her down a bit. The peace she had felt in the parking lot was short-lived because from the moment she heard of the doubloon pin, anxiety had set in.

She checked her watch. 3:20. A little over one half hour until she needed to be at the staff meeting with Wil. Without a pin, Aggie knew she needed to stay out of sight, and was hoping she would be able to hide in the bathrooms until then.

Aggie waited until 3:58 to exit her bathroom sanctuary and try to find her way to the White Ballroom. She thought if she was one of the last people to enter the room, she'd be best able to sneak in and hide behind the full staff. Having no idea where the White Ballroom was, she listened for the sound of voices to hopefully guide her in the right direction.

She started back the way Judy had taken her, and luckily, happened to catch sight of a few people walking up a large flight of dark wooden stairs. She sped over to the stairs, not wanting to lose sight of the people. Aggie noticed the simple structure of this particular staircase, concluding it must've been built solely for the purpose of the slaves and servants to move from floor to floor. As the stairs wound upwards, Aggie made sure to leave a safe distance between herself and the other staff. Once at the top, Aggie continued to follow, all the while keeping her head bowed to prevent making eye contact with anyone. She didn't dare venture her eyes away from the floor until she was safe in the White Ballroom.

She watched as the hallway's oriental rug gave way to pure white hardwood floors. Assuming she had reached her destination, she remained crouched down until she found her way to the very back of the room and chose her place behind the largest man she could find. Only then did she feel safe enough to look up. And when she did, the sight before her took her breath away. She'd seen online pictures of the famous Nottoway White Ballroom, but even in their splendor, they didn't compare to the real thing. For the first time since she'd stepped foot onto the plantation, she allowed herself to drink in the view.

Everything around her was stark white: the 15 ½ foot walls, the ceilings with the most intricate plasterwork Aggie had ever seen, the Corinthian columns, the extravagant hand-made archways, the velvet curtains flowing ceiling to floor that framed huge windows, and even the expanse of the hardwoods. The gorgeous wood floors were painted brilliant white and were polished to perfection.

Mon Dieu, Aggie thought. *How many slave girls did it used to take to mop and shine dis floor by hand after a party? I'm glad I wasn't alive den to know dat answer! Choooh, dis da most beautiful ting I ever did see, though. It's like a little piece a heaven itself. I don't tink I'd ever get tired a starin at dis white room, even if I lived here for a hundred years.*

The only color variances from pure white were the gold trimmings accented here and there, and the oil painting of a Civil War-era woman which hung above one of the double fireplaces. The frame of the portrait, the supports of the crystal chandeliers, the frames of the large mirrors, the edges of the white velvet antique couches, and a few other decor items were bright gold. These golden touches only served to accent the regality of this one-of-a-kind White Ballroom. Lost in the breath-taking beauty that surrounded her, Aggie had momentarily forgotten herself and why she had come here. That is, until she heard Wil call the meeting to order.

The sound of his voice caused Aggie's heart to leap in her chest, and she quickly found her place behind the large man she had appointed as the visual barrier between Wil and herself.

Wil was a very handsome young man, tall with dark wavy hair and crystal blue eyes, just like Skye. Aggie was taken aback by the resemblance between these two cousins who had never met each other, never even knew of each other's existence. How much different the girls' lives might have been to have had a relationship with Wil and his parents, people with such a great reputation of strong character. Aggie felt a fire burning on the inside of her, as her passion was renewed to save her girls from whatever danger that evil Jack had put them in.

Aggie listened carefully as Wil outlined the schedule of events for the evening. Here, in this White Ballroom, the costume ball would begin. The guests would arrive around 6pm for pre-dinner drinks and socializing, and precisely at 7:15 Richard and Lottie

DuMonde would welcome and address the crowd, first from inside the White Ballroom and then from the outdoor balcony, for all the rest of the guests. At 7:30pm, the party would move to an onsite location called the Randolph Ballroom for dinner, and then at 9:30, the activities would bring everyone back inside the mansion.

Aggie was fairly certain she'd be able to stay out of sight until 7pm; the staff would be too pre-occupied with their preparation to notice a stray. Then, hopefully right before they addressed their guests, she'd be able to speak to either Richard or Lottie DuMonde. There was no reason to wait until the end of the evening, especially if that meant she would have to try and stay hidden until then.

Wil briefly mentioned the subject of the gold doubloon coins and stressed the importance of wearing them. He introduced a few of his friends, all dressed in Confederate Soldier costumes, and explained they would be helping out with security for the evening. He asked them to be very cooperative with the young men as they worked to verify the authenticity of both guests and staff. Wil then asked if anyone had any questions.

While a few members of the staff were getting their questions answered, Aggie thought this would be a prime opportunity to sneak away. The people were sensing the meeting coming to its close, so they were beginning to rustle around, so Aggie assessed it would be easy for her to slip out and hide somewhere until 6pm. Bending down a bit, she turned to exit.

"Excuse me, ma'am!" Wil's voice called from the front.

Instinct told Aggie to resist the temptation to look back, but she failed to heed the warning. She turned her gaze to the direction of Wil's voice only to find his steely blue eyes focused directly on her. She froze like a statue, unable to move or even think what to do next. With every step Wil took toward her, Aggie knew she needed to be doing something, planning *some*thing, but she was utterly caught off guard and dumbfounded.

"Hello," Wil said as he now stood next to her, his height against her small frame further commanding his authority. And still Aggie stood, silent and motionless, gaping up at his face.

Not understanding her intimidation, Wil tried to soften his approach by holding out his hand. "Hello," he said again. "I'm Wil DuMonde, and I don't believe we've met, which is unusual because I was supposed to have personally met everyone who was working tonight. What's your name?"

Aggie could tell by the look in this young man's eyes, that he probably could smell a lie a mile away. She was going to have to try anyway, "I'm Agata Prejean, and I's just goin to get my doubloon pin. I'm so sorry, Mr. Wil; I didn't put it on yet. I could just run down now and get it and come right back up here. Please don't send me home; I really need da money…"

"Whoa, whoa, whoa," said Wil, laughing. "You're not in trouble, Miss Agata; I just don't remember meeting you. Listen, I'll be here for a few more minutes. You go get your pin, and then come back and talk to me. I promise, I'm not going to send you home."

In a flash, Aggie exited the White Ballroom, with no intention whatsoever to return. She was going to have to hide somewhere no one would ever look, after which she would have exactly one chance to find and make contact with either Richard or Lottie before she was caught.

Wil watched her leave, wondering how he could've spooked the older black woman so badly. At first glance, she didn't seem the type to be easily intimidated. He hoped he'd be able to put her mind at ease once she came back.

He fielded a few more questions from the staff and then dismissed them to their present duties. He thought he'd stay a bit longer to wait for Agata to return, and to talk with some of the staff as they were leaving the ballroom. One of the waitresses came up to him.

Judy: Hello, I'm Judy; we met a few weeks ago, when you came to meet the people who'd be working tonight, but I don't expect you'd remember my name.

Wil: Hi, Judy. I'll admit that I'm not the greatest with names when there's a large number, but I never forget a face. I remember you were sitting on the left-hand side of the room, in the third row. Let's see…4th chair from the right?

Judy: Oh my word! Yes! How in the world did you remember that? That's amazing!

Wil: I don't know how I do that, but I just do. I've always been able to scan a room and later remember the dumbest little things. *(Laughing)* Not that where you were sitting was dumb; I didn't mean that.

Judy: Oh, honey, don't you worry. I didn't take it that way.

Wil: Wow, I'd better get some tact going here before the night begins or I'll have all my parents' guests offended before the first course is served. Like with that woman before. Agata? Do you know her or know why she got so freaked out?

Judy: Actually, that's why I came up to you. I met her on my way in to work this afternoon. She's a sweet, sweet lady, but times have been really tough for her, and she really needs this job tonight to help make ends meet. You probably haven't met her because she told me she was a last minute staff add-on by your mother.

Wil: What? My mother?

Judy: Sure. Aggie said that she's friends with your mom's personal maid, Bessie, and that when Bessie heard your mom talking about how she was worried there wouldn't be enough cleaning staff for tonight, Bessie told your mom about Aggie. Well, your mom, so kind as I've heard her to be, hired her right on the spot, just from Bessie's recommendation!

Wil: That sounds like my mom, but—

Judy: And so Aggie's real nervous about tonight because if she doesn't do well, she's worried Bessie will get in trouble with your mother. Anyway...when she gets back, please go easy on her. She's really a very nice woman, I promise.

Wil: Got it. Thanks, Judy, for all of that info. Now, you'd better go and do what you need to do to prepare for tonight's ball.

Judy: Yes sir.

Wil was now even more puzzled about Agata than he was before. Yes, it was true, the scenario sounded exactly like something his mom would do. She spent her life looking for people she could help. The only problems were: one, his mom had specifically requested to have no part in any of the staffing details for the evening, and two, his mom's personal maid was not named Bessie.

❧ 15 ❧

AFTER DARTING OUT OF THE WHITE BALLROOM, Aggie was not sure where she'd be able to hide for almost three hours until the DuMondes made their opening statements to the guests. She knew the bathrooms were not the option they were before, as 200 guests would be arriving and would certainly notice if one of the doors was locked for that long. She thought about trying to keep inconspicuous in the kitchen because there would be so much activity going on in all the different areas. But then again, even if she would be able to blend in, there was still the issue of the missing doubloon. Certainly, someone would spot she didn't have one, especially since Wil had singled her out at the staff meeting.

Then she had the idea of going outside to her car and laying down on the back seats until it was time to find a DuMonde. *What gone be da best way to get to dat parkin lot from here?* she thought. *I gotta find me a window to try and get my bearings.* She noticed a room that seemed to be empty and stepped into it. It had soft yellow walls lined in white molding, and it contained 3 small pianos and a golden harp in the corner. *Dis must a been da music room,* concluded Aggie.

Dis ain't no place to hide, but it pro'bly won't have anyone in here for a while. At least dey's some big windows for me to see out.

Aggie was thankful for the large marble fireplace that jutted out right next to one of the windows. It provided a little crevice of a corner that she could stand in while she scanned the view outside. Because she was on the second level of the mansion, she was at a vantage point to see quite a bit of the outside lawn. She spotted a strip of a parking lot, but she could not tell if it was the one that held her Chevy. What she did notice, however, were four of the young Confederate Soldiers, part of Wil's security team, walking around the lot. They appeared to be scoping out all the cars, even looking inside the windows of some. Aggie worried they were already on the hunt to find her.

She pressed herself deeper into her corner, hoping she could make herself unseen to any passersby. She was at a complete loss what to do next. *Choooh,* she thought. *Dis place got over 4 dozen rooms in it, dere's gotta be at least one that an old Cajun can hide out in til it's time to find da DuMondes.* She held her breath and listened for any voices or movement outside the room. Once she was sure the hallway was vacant, she left the Music Room in search of a hiding place.

She came to the grand Entrance Hall of Nottoway, and once again had to resist every fiber of her being that wanted to wonder at all the details of this castle Harold and she had always planned to visit. But as she hurried through, she knew there just wasn't time to gawk at the beautiful architecture, or at the antique tables and statues she was passing, or the high white ceilings flaunting their fancy chandeliers. Aggie did take notice, however, of a stairway descending to the lower level of the mansion, and without another thought, she decided to take her chances down the stairs. This would put her on the same level she originally entered with Judy; perhaps she'd be able to find the staff locker room, where they'd left their purses. By now, Aggie was more than willing to squeeze herself into an unused locker for 3 hours, if it meant not being caught and arrested for trespassing.

It was fairly dark and uninviting on the bottom floor, evidently not an area where any festivities were planned for the evening. She heard some kitchen activity happening to her distant left, probably the overflow of catering for the dinner, so Aggie thought it best to move in the opposite direction. She happened by what looked like a small lounge and bar, also dimly lit and vacant for the night. She ventured deeper into the basement of this cavernous mansion, and finally came to a room that served as a small museum for the site.

Aggie sensed this was her spot. It was quiet in the museum, and it was a room set apart. If she kept the door slightly open and listened very carefully, she was sure she'd be able to hear if anyone was approaching. Also, because the only lights in the room were the small ceiling spotlights that shone down on certain exhibits, it was dark and shadowy. She'd easily be able to hide in a corner if someone looked in. Aggie felt this was her best chance to stay out of sight.

She found an old wooden box and moved it to the location in the room that she'd be able to both hear and see most advantageously. And then once again, she sat down to take in some deep breaths. Closing her eyes, she tried to calm herself in the dark solitude of this museum. She encouraged herself that she'd come this far successfully; she couldn't give up now. Only one more thing to accomplish: contact with either Richard or Lottie DuMonde.

Aggie opened her eyes and began to read a large wooden sign in front of her. She happened to have placed her box in front of a display that shared the history of Nottoway and how it was built. A man named John Hampton Randolph, a hugely wealthy plantation owner had decided to build Nottoway in 1855. He hired the then-famous architect Henry Howard to design the mansion, and it took four years to complete the intricately detailed and enormously expensive project.

Aggie read through the list of impressive features for which the home was renowned, including the fact that where she was sitting used to be a bowling alley for the Randolph's eleven children. In addition, the house was finished not only with gas lighting throughout, but also with flushing toilets and running hot and cold water in the bathrooms; all unheard of at that time. *How dis man have so much money?* she thought. *All dat musta cost a fortune!*

She scanned through more of the information until she came to some stats that helped answer her question. At the height of his success, Mr. Randolph owned over 1000 acres of land between two plantations and held over 500 slaves to run his businesses. In fact, the very bricks that made up the 14-inch thick walls of this mansion were handmade and baked by his own slaves. In order to handle that large of a work force, the slave quarters contained a bathhouse, a hospital, and a meeting house used for daycare during the week and church services on Sundays. Mr. Randolph housed the slaves in 42 cabins, whitewashed and set off the ground in case of flooding, with a vegetable plot behind each structure. The cabins had two rooms with a family living in each room.

"Choooh!" whispered Aggie. "What was dat like? To work all day on a mansion like dis and den go home to a cabin where da whole family lived in one room? Lawd, have mercy. How dat kinda ting happen?"

Aggie heard a creak outside the door, and she held her breath. She listened for a few moments, but couldn't hear anything over the sound of her heart pounding in her head. She worried that if someone did look in the room and couldn't see her, surely she'd be discovered anyway, as they'd be able to hear the beating of her heart.

No other sounds. No other people. False alarm.

Aggie let out a deep sigh as the tingles of adrenaline coursed through her body. She picked up her wooden box, moved it back to its original location, and then walked deeper into the museum. There was a very small theatre room used to show a documentary about the estate, and it was pitch black inside. Whether this room was the optimum place for her to see and hear, it certainly was the best place to keep her form hidden from any onlookers. She checked her watch. 4:45pm. Two more hours.

THE OLD BLACK WOMAN SEEMED TO HAVE DISAPPEARED. Wil had waited in the White Ballroom for nearly twenty minutes for her to return, but she never came back. And while this woman appeared to be the last person in the world who'd pose a threat, he just could not take any chances. He wrote down her name, along with the contact information of a friend of his dad's who worked for the Secret Service, and gave it to Scott, the head of his security team. Wil asked him to phone the agent, as many times as needed, until he was able to speak to him personally. Once contact was made, he was to ask the man to acquire any information he could on Agata Prejean.

Now, two hours later, he and his Confederate posse were surveying the growing crowd of guests at Nottoway. Five of the young men had been given descriptions of Agata, and were searching the entire premises to find her and bring her to Wil. At present, no one had been successful in their pursuits. The rest of his team were now watchfully roaming as they expertly dodged the dozens and dozens of large Southern Belle hoop dresses that were now filling the rooms, hallways and balconies. As Wil was performing a habitual scan of the crowd, his mom snuck up beside him.

Lottie: Doesn't this party just take the cake? I love seein all these costumes in this grand mansion. It's like we've truly been taken back in time.

Wil: Hey, Mom! *(When he turned around, it was the first time he'd seen her in her costume. Lottie was wearing an iconic Scarlett O'Hara dress, the green floral dress Scarlett wore to the BBQ in the beginning of the movie.)* Mom, you look amazing! I mean, I've never seen the movie, but you do look just like the pictures I've seen.

Lottie: *(in her best Scarlett voice)* How have I raised you, Wil DuMonde, and you've *never* seen *Gone With the Wind?* Did I completely fail you as a mother?

Wil: *(laughing)* Uhh...mom, it's a chick flick. Don't you remember? Whenever you'd pull out that DVD, it was my cue to go play some hoops.

Lottie: For the last time, sugar, it's not just a chick flick. It's about the Civil War, and it has fightin and killin, not to mention, all of our dear Atlanta burnin to the ground at the hand of those Yankees. *And* it has great heroes in it, like Rhett Butler; he's a real man's man.

Rich: *(interrupting his wife and son's conversation.)* Who's a real man's man? Is your mother talking about me again?

Wil: *(noticing his dad's Rhett Butler costume)* Well, that all depends upon which one of you is asking: you or Rhett Butler. And, she's trying to convince me that *Gone With the Wind* is not a chick flick.

Rich: Ha! Don't try to win that battle with her, son. Just do what I've done all these years; watch the movie with her and act like you're not sleeping.

Lottie: *(to Wil)* Oh, don't let him fool you, sugar. He loves it just as much as I do.

Rich: See? I've got her convinced.

Lottie: Richard! You cry every time Bonnie Bell falls off her horse and—

Rich: Whoa, whoa, whoa! Let's not ruin the ending for him, Lottie. God knows he's going to marry someone just like you who is obsessed with it and makes him watch it every year. Let's at least give him the chance to be surprised. *(whispering to Wil)* And I've never cried during that damn movie.

Lottie: I heard that. *(to Wil)* And yes he has. *Every* time.

Wil: *(laughing)* OK, you guys. Dad, you make a great Rhett Butler. You both look awesome; clearly the best costumes of the night. Anyway, I have an off-the-subject question for you guys. Does the name "Agata Prejean" mean anything to either of you?

Richard and Lottie took a minute to think about it. They both shook their heads.

Rich: No, not that I can think of. Should I know that name?

Wil: Probably not. I'm sure it's nothing. She was just a lady I met earlier tonight at the staff meeting. I wanted to know if either of you knew her.

Rich: Never met her. So, right now it's 6:45. What time are we supposed to greet everyone?

Wil: At 7:15, right here in the White Ballroom, and then again out on the balcony for everyone else.

Just then, Scott entered the back of the ballroom and made eye contact with Wil. From the nod of his head, Wil understood that to mean Scott had gotten the info on Agata Prejean.

Wil: I gotta go and take care of something. I hope you guys are happy with how things are going so far.

Lottie: Oh, Wil, it's beyond my expectation! Thank you so much for all you've done.

Rich: Me, too, Wil. We owe you a huge favor for pulling this off so magnificently.

Wil: Dad, it's me who'll forever owe *you* for all you've done for me these last months. Now go and enjoy yourselves! I gotta go back there and talk to Scott.

Wil quickly strode across the room, anxious to see what Scott had found out about the old, black woman. Scott handed him an ipad.

Wil: Did you read the info? Anything come up on her?

Scott: Actually, no; the files just came to my inbox. Since I was right here, I thought I'd bring them to you.

Wil: Thanks. Let's walk over to somewhere it's quiet. We can go to my parent's room upstairs.

They flew up the velvet carpeted staircase and Wil led them to the door of the Nottoway Master Suite. He unlocked the door, strode in and sat down at the antique rosewood table and chair set. Wil immediately began swiping through the files of information on his ipad. Meanwhile, before sitting, Scott took a minute to look around the large suite that consisted of a main bedroom, a sitting room, and a large modern bathroom.

Scott: Dang! Can you imagine if this was your everyday kind of life? Oh wait...yes, you can. You grew up in the Garden District.

Wil: Dude, my house is nothing like this. We only have 12-foot ceilings; these are all 15 ½.

Scott: *(sarcastically)* Riiiiight, OK. Yeah. That's totally different.

Wil: Plus the square footage of this place is probably 15 of my parents' house.

Scott: Still. That's way more than I can say. I grew up with just me and my mom in a New York ghetto, and I'm pretty sure our ceilings barely cleared 7 feet.

Wil: Whatever. That don't mean a thing. None of that money— my *parent's* money, I should say—could've saved my life over in Iraq. Hell, I wouldn't even be here right now if you hadn't hauled my a** outta that mess and put me on that truck.

Scott: *(joking, as he walked to check out the sitting room)* Speaking of which, I've been meaning to talk to you about that...maybe some kind of monetary compensation from your dad for bringing his only son back to life?

Wil: Hey, I'm already working on it.

Scott: *(surprised, he popped back in the main bedroom)* No way, dude! I was just messin with you. Don't you dare say anything to your dad about that. You'd've done the same for me; that's just what we do.

Wil: Chill out! I've just talked to him about you wanting to get into natural gas exploration; you know that's Dad's newest venture right now, don't you?

Scott: Actually, I didn't. Do you think his company's got a place for me?

Wil: I'm sure he'll make one, if you want it. But we can talk about that later; we've got to get back to the party. Besides, this info on Prejean doesn't tell me a damned thing. She's pretty clean. She was married to a guy named Harold, who died back in the mid-90s, she worked most her life for some folks in Lafayette. Their names were Bacchus, and they also died in the 90s from a car wreck. They left behind a single daughter, named Macy who later married a guy named...*his voice trailed off as he began swiping to new info on the ipad.*

Scott: What?

Wil: *(Under his breath)* No way!

Scott: What?!

Wil: Well, well, well. It looks like this ol' gal isn't that clean after all. Prejean worked for a couple whose daughter eventually married Jack DuMonde, my dad's brother.

Scott: Your dad has a brother?

Wil: A twin.

Scott: He's got a twin?!

Wil: Yeah, that's the uncle I told you about. We think he's the reason Dad's been getting those f-in death threats. I mean, my dad would never say it, but he sounds like a real douche-bag, into drug trafficking and all that goes with it. Dad thinks Jack owes some cartel a ton of money, and they think they'll be able to score the cash from my dad.

Scott: And this old gal works for Jack's wife?

Wil: Well, I don't know about that. All this says is that she worked for his wife's parents until they died. But after working for them for almost 30 years, she had to have had some kind of relationship with the daughter *and* with Jack.

Wil shot up from his chair and pulled the small radio out of his pocket. He used it to communicate with the security team.

"Listen up, guys," Wil ordered. "I need all of you to meet with me asap at the Fountain Courtyard. Whatever you're doing right now, drop it, and be at the fountain in exactly two minutes. Out." *(to Scott)* "Come on, let's go. I don't know what this ol' gal is up to, but I'll tell you one thing: I'm gonna find out. And if she's still onsite, I'm not gonna stop until I find her."

With razor-sharp focus, the two young men quickly made their way to meet the others outside the mansion at the Fountain Courtyard.

MOLLY VENZKE

�֍16✖

AGGIE CHECKED HER WATCH. 7:10. Her heart began to pound harder at each passing moment. *Only a couple more minutes,* she thought. *I'll leave here at 7:15 so dat da DuMondes will already have started talkin. Dat way, all attention will be on dem, and I can hopefully weave my way to dem.*

Her stomach was a churning mess, and her adrenaline was firing so freely, she began to feel a bit light-headed. "Girl, you gotta get yo'self together," she said firmly to herself. "Dis no time to lose it, Agata Prejean. Da girls need you to keep it together. You gone go up dere and get to one a dose DuMondes, and dat's just gone be da way it's gone be."

She took a long deep breath and stood up to try and loosen her body before making her way back upstairs to the White Ballroom. "Hal? You watchin all dis? Can you please go to St. Peter right dis very minute and ask him to send me down some extra angels to carry me through all dis? Lawd, have mercy!"

She exited the Museum and glided down the hallway until she found the stairs she had descended three hours earlier. As she hurried upwards, she could hear the conversation sounds of the large party growing louder and louder. Aggie prayed under her breath that somehow her Bon Dieu would part the waters of this crowd for her to make it to her promised land.

When she topped the stairs, the view stopped her in her tracks. It was the same Entrance Hall she'd walked through when she found the staircase, but now it was filled wall-to-wall with guests dressed in the most beautiful and elaborate costumes Aggie had ever seen. The women were rustling around in their Southern belle dresses, yards and yards of fabrics in every color, accompanied by men dressed in regal Civil-war era suits. She felt as if she was seeing a vision from the past, and wondered if this was really what a mid-1800s ball would've looked like.

Aggie knew she couldn't tarry, however, and she scanned the room to gain perspective. At the moment, there was only one young man dressed as a Confederate soldier in the room, and he was talking to one of the guests. She checked her watch. 7:18. Right now, Richard and Lottie DuMonde were addressing the folks in the White Ballroom, and afterwards, they'd make their way through this Grand Hall to the front balcony.

Aggie spotted a server's tray half-filled with hors d'oeuvres on a nearby table. This was her ticket! She sped over to the table and picked up that tray like it was her best friend. Balancing it on her left hand, she perched the tray up in front of her left collar lapel, precisely the location where the gold doubloon was supposed to be. She began milling amongst the guests, trying to stay closely behind the largest groups possible.

As long as I can stay my eyes on any of dose soldiers of Wil's, I should be able to keep from gettin caught in da next few minutes, Aggie thought. *And den, I'll make my way to Miss Lottie. I'll try her first, cuz bein a woman and a mama, she'll be the best one to understand.*

A large hand landed on her shoulder. Aggie jumped in fright, and in doing so, her silver plated tray tumbled downward, clanking loudly on the hardwood floor. Much of the crowd turned toward the noise as hors d'oeuvres spilled all around her feet. Aggie ducked down as quickly as possible, hoping the young man in the Confederate soldier costume hadn't seen her face.

"I'm so very sorry, ma'am," a man's voice said. "I was just going to ask you for an hors d'oeuvre. Please, let me help you with this."

"No, no, no!" urged Aggie, keeping her face bowed down towards the floor. "I'll get it all cleaned up, sir. You just stay up dere and keep enjoyin yourself. It won't take me but a minute, sir. See? I'm already almost done."

She scurried as fast as she could to pick up each piece of food and to wipe up the floor, the whole time praying under her breath that none of the staff or security would come over and try to help.

Aggie knew she was now going to have to make an exit. Since all the folks surrounding her had seen her tray drop, she couldn't very well stand up like nothing had happened and try to serve more of those hors d'oeuvres. In order to remain in her crouched position, she pretended some of the snacks had spilled farther away so she could scoot herself to the outskirts of the crowd, hopefully completely unnoticed.

To her left, she heard the familiar clinking of kitchen and serving activity. Holding her tray in the position to hide her missing doubloon, she darted into that room. It was filled with over a dozen servers, all dressed in white, busily emptying and refilling their trays of pre-dinner treats. Aggie realized this was a warming kitchen, a room very common in Civil War era mansions, since their main kitchens were usually built adjacent to the main structures. This prevented the entire home being lost if the kitchen caught fire.

As Aggie stood in line behind two other servants, she overheard their conversation:

Woman 1: Did you hear what James was saying?

Woman 2: No. What?

Woman 1: Earlier he was talkin' to one of the security guys, and there's supposed to be someone here tonight who's a threat to the DuMondes.

Woman 2: What?! No, that's just silly. Who'd want to do anything to these people?

Woman 1: Well, from what James could get outta the guy, was that Mr. DuMonde has been gettin death threats from someone. Apparently a brother or somethin owes a ton of money to the mafia, or someone like that. That's why they've got all this security tonight and why they sent out all the gold pins for everyone to wear. I guess they thought someone might show up tonight to try and get the money? I don't know.

Woman 2: Wow. That's crazy! Do they think the mafia dude is one of the guests?

Woman 1: That's just it...it's not a guy. They're lookin for a gal!
Woman 2: Really? Ha! Well, I'm sure one of these women could hide an entire arsenal underneath all those hoop skirts.
Woman 1: James said they're lookin for an older black woman.
Woman 2: Huh. That can't be right. What's an old geezer gonna do to hurt anyone?
Woman 1: I have no idea, but that's what James said the guy said. Besides, nowadays, anyone can do anything if they've got the right gun.

Aggie could feel the room beginning to spin around her. Heat rose in her face and neck, and her heart seemed to be beating out of control. She had to get out of there before these women saw her. She turned on her heel and disappeared back into the massive Entrance Hall. Scrutinizing the crowd to locate any security, she found four of them, but they were all close to the front of the hall near the enormous 11-foot main balcony doors. She could tell by the quieting of the crowd it was almost time for Richard DuMonde to welcome this section of the party.

As the assembly began to face the direction of the mansion's main entrance, Aggie wove her way to the very back of the crowd. She found a trio of tall male guests and hid behind them. Once standing in place, she could feel her knees trembling from anxiety.

Lawd, Lawd, Lawd, thought Aggie. *Dis over my head! Dey tink I'm here to do dese folks harm! What will dey do to me if dey catch me?* She didn't want to know the answer to that question. *And was all dat true about dat peeshwank* (tiny man) *Jack? What kinda money did dat capon* (coward) *steal? He an evil, evil man. I gotta get dis over with before I give myself a heart attack. As soon as Mr. DuMonde is done addressin dese folks, I'm gone make my way to Miss Lottie, or die tryin. Bon Dieu, give me da strenth to do dis without havin a stroke.*

The entire room went silent, and Mr. DuMonde began to greet his guests. Aggie couldn't quite make out the details of his face from her vantage point, but she knew it must be him. Both of the DuMondes were dressed in beautiful costumes, Richard as Rhett Butler and Miss Lottie as Scarlett O'Hara. Aggie smiled at how stunning both of them looked and reassured herself, *Surely, folks like dis will help an ol Cajun woman like me.*

Aggie noticed all eyes in the room were focused on the DuMondes, except for the pairs from the six Confederate soldiers who were facing the crowd. Their eyes were scanning to and fro to examine the guests' faces, no doubt, trying to find hers. The thought made Aggie shudder as she once again crouched over to keep from being seen. Her watch read 7:22. Judy, the woman whom Aggie had met in the parking lot, had told her that dinner was going to begin at 7:30 in a formal dining room located on the grounds, outside the main mansion. Aggie knew it was now or never. She would not be able to keep herself hidden any longer, and certainly wouldn't be able to sneak over to wherever dinner was being served.

As she heard Richard DuMonde giving directions to the crowd about their short walk to the dining room, the "Randolph Ballroom" as he called it, Aggie gathered her courage. She really wanted to exit as fast as she could in the opposite direction, but instead, she thought of Elle and Skye, and her girl, Macy. Nothing mattered more to her than them, and she was the only one who could get them away from that Jack.

She took one last long look at Miss Lottie's dress, Scarlett's flowing light green BBQ dress, and then checked the room to see if she saw any other green dresses. Knowing she would be ducking down on her way to Miss Lottie, she wanted to make sure she found her way to the correct hoop skirt. Aggie noticed only two other dresses of the same color, but they were sewn of dark evergreen velvet. She glanced back at the exact location of Miss Lottie, submerged herself in the crowd, and began threading her way through every opening in the crowd that might lead her to Mrs. DuMonde.

It was difficult for Aggie to keep track of how much distance she'd covered, as she felt lost in the moving sea of guests. However, she didn't dare stand up to look, for every step towards Miss Lottie was also a step toward Wil and his security team. Just then, she spotted the light green dress! In a matter of five or ten steps, Aggie would be able to approach the woman. She held her breath and pushed her way towards the soft, flowing green material. Aggie stretched out her hand and grabbed hold of one of the hoops in the dress.

"Oh!" said a startled Lottie, as she felt herself being pulled to a stop. She turned, expecting to see her dress caught on something, but instead found an old woman on her knees staring up at her.

As their eyes met, Aggie suddenly lost all of her words. She was breathing heavy, not from exertion but from fear, and her face revealed her despair.

"Please excuse me," said Lottie, concerned. "Ma'am, did you fall? Are you OK? Give me your hand, and I'll help you up."

Lottie reached out her hand, and although Aggie took it, she didn't use it to stand. Instead, she gripped onto Lottie's hand with both of hers and pleaded, "Miss Lottie, please. I need your help. Da girls need your help. Please, you and Mr. DuMonde da only ones who can save 'em. I can't do it by myself, Miss Lottie. Please..."

"I'm sorry, I don't understand what you're talking about. Who are you?"

"I know you don't know me, but please, hear me. I know yo family, and dey need yo help! Please, Miss Lottie, you da only one who can help 'em!"

Before anyone could say another word, Aggie felt two strong arms swiftly lift her to her feet. Two Confederates were on either side of her, and Wil was now right next to his mother.

"Mom, I'll take care of this," said Wil. "Guys, can you escort Miss Prejean to the Iris Cottages? I have a room waiting there for her and I'll be right behind you."

"Wait a minute, Wil," said Lottie in a hushed tone. "What are you goin to do with this woman? Obviously she needs help of some kind. And how do you know what her name is?"

"Mom, I said I'd take care of this. You don't need to worry about it, just go on and enjoy the rest of the evening. The party has barely started, and Dad's going to want you with him."

"But Wil-"

"Mom," Wil said firmly. "I've got this. She's just an old woman who needs a bit of help from me. I'll take care of it." He nodded at the guys to escort Aggie out. "Now, Mom, you go and enjoy your dinner in the Randolph Ballroom." He turned and ran to catch up to his team.

Lottie could tell Wil wasn't disclosing the full details about the woman. She followed him to the outside balcony and watched as the men led Aggie down the large outdoor flight of granite steps and across the lawn towards the Iris Cottages.

ELLE

 17

ELLE LIE IN HER HOTEL BED, looking up at the ceiling. Once again, her dad had left her alone in their room for most of the day. She hated sitting around in this foreign place all by herself. In her mind, she counted how many days they'd been away from Louisiana. Tonight was the sixth night without her mom, and Elle was feeling the pangs of it. Jack only let her call home one time, and that was on their layover in New York City, so she hadn't been able to talk with anyone about the things that had been happening. He'd let her send texts, but told her an international cell phone call would be too expensive.

Also, she was feeling very confused about her father. As long as Elle could remember, she hoped and prayed that her dad would spend more time with her, or notice her more, or talk with her more. She remembered how jealous she was last August when Jack took Skye with him on the trip to Europe so that he could enroll her into her new school. Every night, Elle would cry herself to sleep as she imagined the amazing adventures Skye was probably having with their father. Her mom would sleep in her bed with her, stroking her hair, and whisper how much she loved her until Elle fell asleep.

Now that she was on her first big trip with Jack, Elle was very disappointed. Other than the first few days of activity, which included that awful trip to the doctor and the lady who spit on her dad, she had mostly been confined to her hotel room. Jack would bring up breakfast for them in the morning, then maybe they'd leave for a couple hours. But even then, those outings were all about Jack talking to other men, always through an interpreter, and mostly in low tones to keep her from hearing. After that, he'd bring her back to stay in the hotel while he went back out, Elle never knowing exactly what time he would return. The only ways to fill the time were to watch shows on the television, most of which were not in English, or to read the *Little House on the Prairie* books MawMaw had bought for Elle to read on the plane. Normally, Elle would've gobbled up the books, but in this Greek hotel, her mind kept getting distracted by thoughts of her dad.

Elle was beginning to think Jack was not a very nice man at all. Before spending this amount of time with him, she'd been able to make excuses for his outbursts in the home. Maybe he'd just had a bad day? Or, maybe he wasn't feeling well? Since his interactions with her were usually so few and far between, Elle had chosen to believe that he probably acted much better when he was with other people. Rather than blame him for his meanness, Elle had assumed that she was the reason for it. She probably was doing things that irritated him, and if she could just work out how to be the right kind of daughter, then she was sure he'd treat her with more kindness.

But now Elle was seeing that he treated everyone like he treated her and her family, with the exception of some of the men he was trying to impress. And even that attitude could change in a heartbeat if the person didn't give Jack what he wanted. He'd immediately start yelling and swearing at the guy, trying to use his force to get results.

She wondered if this was why MawMaw Aggie never seemed to like Jack. Even when he walked into the room, sometimes Aggie'd just go about with what she'd been doing and never acknowledge his presence. It always surprised Elle because this behavior was completely out of character for her MawMaw. Aggie talked to *everyone*, even to herself, and even to people who had already died, like PawPaw. She could meet a person in line at the check-out and before she'd paid her bill, Aggie would know that person's name, age, job, all of their kid's names *and* their grandkid's names. Aggie loved every person she met. Except Jack.

Elle had never actually heard MawMaw speak badly about her dad, but there were times, late at night, when she would hear MawMaw and Macy talking intensely in the kitchen. Even though they would keep their discussions to whispers, once Elle overheard MawMaw urging Macy to pack up the girls, and for them all to come and live with her. At the time, Elle assumed it was just for a long visit, but now...maybe MawMaw was meaning for them to live with her forever? What did MawMaw know about Jack that Elle didn't?

But if Jack was so bad, then why would he be spending so much money for Skye to go to her special school? And why would he have brought Elle to come and visit? Elle's mom had made it seem like the visit was Jack's idea for a Christmas present, but maybe the truth was that she was the one who had set it up, and was just trying to make Jack look like a good dad?

Nothing made any sense to Elle. She had so many questions that didn't seem to have any answers. She couldn't wait to be with Skye so she could talk with her about all of this. Skye always had the right answers Elle needed, and in just a few more sleeps, she'd be with her at last. Elle wished it could be sooner, that they didn't have to wait until the stupid beauty contest was over on Friday afternoon. She hated that her dad was making her do that. She probably wasn't going to win anything anyway, so what was the point? But it was too late now, because Jack had already bought her the dress.

The day before, he'd gone back to that same store, and apparently had a much better time. He'd come back to the hotel with a beautiful, dark pink satin dress that went all the way to the floor. Elle had never personally worn something so soft and silky before, and she loved the way she looked in it. The dress was fancy with thick satin ribbon straps that tied behind her neck, and a small pink flower right in the middle of her chest that had thin, pale pink ribbons curling down from it. When Elle asked about the lady who'd spit on him, her dad said she hadn't been there that day. Elle thought that lady was lucky, because if Jack had seen her again, he probably would've hit her.

As Elle lie on the bed thinking about the dress, again she could feel the conflict in her heart. If Jack was *all* bad, why would he have bought her such a pretty new dress? Why was he so proud of her as to have her enter a beauty pageant? And why did he believe so much in her that he kept saying he really thought she'd win? She wasn't sure what to believe; who was good, who was bad, or who she could trust.

✦ 18 ✦

ELLE WOKE UP TO her dad loudly stumbling around the hotel room, cursing as he stubbed his toe on something. Bright light poured in as he flung open the curtains. As soon as she stirred, he growled at her.

"Get up! You need to shower and fix yourself up. We're going out today, and I'm gonna take you to see some of the judges for the show on Friday. I want to give you an edge over the other girls, make sure you bring home a big f***in prize. And wear your new dress. They need to be able to recognize you that night." Before Elle could respond, he left the room, still cursing under his breath.

As Elle shook off her grogginess, she began to notice the strong odor of the room. Stale cigarette smoke and a sour, vinegary alcohol smell. It was the same smell that often clung to her father like an invisible coat, but in this small space, it was especially nauseating. She got out of bed and tried to open the old window that looked like it had been painted shut. After quite a bit of effort, she was able to force the old window to open an inch; it wasn't as far as she wished, but it was enough to breathe in some fresh air. She only allowed herself a few moments at the window, however, because she had no idea how long she had to get cleaned up. And she didn't want to face the wrath of her father if she wasn't ready on time.

Elle stepped into the very small shower and looked around for shampoo. The only container she could find was empty, so she decided to skip washing her hair. Her mom had washed it right before they left, so she thought it would be fine. It was an awful shower because the water pressure and temperature kept changing. One minute the stream was strong and hot and the next it was weak and freezing cold. She washed her body as quickly as she could and hopped out.

Elle rolled her eyes when she realized there were no dry towels. The only two the room had Jack had left as wet, crumpled wads in the corner, and she was not about to use one of those. Hoping her dad had left something dry for her, she looked until she found a washcloth on the edge of the sink. She dried herself as best she could and then put on her new pink dress.

The back of the room's front door held a long mirror, and Elle smiled at her reflection. Her soft, curly red hair fell past her shoulders, and the deep pink of the dress made her cheeks appear flushed. She wished her mom was here to see her. Everything about this trip would've been made right if only her mom would've come with them.

Elle heard Jack's key opening the hotel door, and she stood up straight so she could gain her dad's approval for her appearance. The door swung open, Jack threw a brown bag of food on the bed, stormed into the bathroom, and slammed the door shut. He didn't so much as glance at Elle. Dejected, she sat down on the bed and opened the bag of breakfast. Its contents for her were the exact same as they had been for the last few days: one bottle of milk, one bottle of water, one hard roll with butter and honey for breakfast, and one slice of spinach pie for lunch.

She chose the milk first and just as she started pulling off the bottle's tab, Jack burst out of the bathroom. "Why in the hell are you wearing that new dress to eat in? You're going to get food all over it!"

"But you said to get ready and to put on this dress," Elle answered.

"I paid a lot of money for that dress and if you mess it up, little missy, there's gonna be hell to pay."

Elle wasn't sure what to do. Should she keep the dress on, like he asked her to do in the first place, or take if off until she was done eating? She wasn't sure what the right answer was, and she was afraid to make the wrong choice. She sat on the edge of the bed, looking down at her feet.

"Elle!" She nearly jumped out of her skin at his loud command. "Just eat your food, and *don't* get yourself dirty. We're leaving in a few minutes."

Elle covered her lap with a pillow and ever so carefully, and quickly, drank her milk and ate her roll.

ELLE FOUND IT DIFFICULT to keep up with her father as they briskly walked through the streets that to Elle looked more like alleyways. It was quite chilly, and Jack had only allowed her to wear a small, white button-up sweater because he didn't want a coat to cover up the new dress. In addition, he'd bought her a pair of faux-leather, pink ballet flats that were so stiff, they rubbed on the tops of her heels as she walked. Even before they'd met the first judge, her feet were already forming large blisters.

Jack entered a lobby of a small hotel, and began looking around for somebody. Elle saw the man who had been acting as his interpreter since they'd been here, and she nudged her dad to ask if that was who he was looking for. Obviously it was, because Jack ordered Elle to sit down while he crossed over to meet him. They talked briefly, and then Jack motioned for Elle to join them. Just before she'd reached her father and the interpreter man, they both turned to walk ahead of her down a hallway, Elle assumed to one of the hotel rooms.

Although this hotel was quite small, Elle wished they were staying in this one instead of the older, stinky one with the tiny shower. This place smelled much cleaner, and the carpet looked like it was newer. The trio stopped at a door with the number 145 on it. The interpreter knocked on the door. At first, the door was only cracked open, and the person inside spoke in deep whispers to the interpreter. After several exchanges, the door opened wide, and Jack motioned for Elle to walk in front of him into the room.

Inside, there were two men, a large man, who had been the one who opened the door, and a lean man wearing a suit and sitting in an armchair by the window. Elle looked up at the large man as she passed by and noticed his skin was very tan and leathery. She also thought he was the hairiest man she'd ever seen. On his head, he had thick black and gray bushy hair, and his giant arms were coated with the same bushiness. He was wearing a yellow polo shirt, stretched smooth over the massiveness of his chest, and with all three buttons undone, she could see a mound of chest hair spilling out the top. He looked like he could crush a car with his bare hands if he needed to.

The skinny man in the corner had a large glass bowl of purple and green olives placed next to him, and he was continuously popping one after another into his mouth, after which, he'd wash them down with a gulp from an over-sized glass of dark red wine. As he lifted his glass to his lips, Elle noticed his fingernails were perfectly manicured, and in her opinion, too long for a guy. He snapped a finger and motioned to have Elle step closer to him. Elle looked at her dad, who responded by giving her a stern push toward the man.

Elle went to him and stood in front of his chair. She felt awkward as he scrutinized her from head to toe, and then flicked his hand in a circle indicating he wanted her to turn around. She obeyed. After a few seconds, she could feel the man was touching her hair. He ran his fingers through it, taking his time to play with her curls. The light sensation of her hair moving across the back of her neck caused Elle to shudder, and she could hear the man behind her laugh. He tugged on her shoulder to make her face him again. Once their eyes met, he leaned forward until she could feel his hot breath on her face. Nervous, she looked down at her feet, badly wanting to back away. A few long moments passed, and the man finally reclined back in his seat.

He waved his hand again, communicating he was done with her, and Elle quickly walked to stand beside her dad. He went back to his olives and wine, and the apelike man escorted them out to the hallway. Jack, Elle and the interpreter walked back to the hotel lobby in silence.

As they exited the hotel, Jack asked his friend, "How do you think that went?"

"I've never seen him touch a girl's hair like that, so that's good. You want him on your side because he'll be the richest man at the deal," he said in his thick, Greek accent.

"It's that red hair she got from my mother-in-law," Jack said, and then added snidely, "Ha! I guess she's worth something after all. Let's go meet the next one."

Elle wondered who Jack meant with that unkind remark. *Mom is worth something after all, or I'm worth something after all?* she thought. *Or is he talking about my mom's mom?* Either way, Elle thought it was a mean thing to say, and her feelings were hurt. *Certainly, he must be talking about Mom's mom because he wouldn't say that about Mom, or me, right?* She chose to believe Jack would only say that about someone he'd never met, as Macy's mom had already died by the time her parents had gotten together.

"Speed it up, Elle!" yelled Jack.

Elle realized she was several paces behind the two men. She started to run but her heels burned so badly from the new shoes, she almost fell down. She decided she'd rather get her feet dirty than to keep wearing those awful slippers.

"I'm don't want these new shoes to get scuffed," she called to Jack as she stopped to take them off. "I'll put them back on as soon as we get to the next place." Shoes in hand, Elle ran to catch up with the men, and she found it much easier to keep up. She did stay focused on the cement, though, to make sure she didn't step on a piece of glass or any other sharp object that might be scattered on the roads.

Elle wondered how many judges they would be meeting, because her feet were going to be a mess if she had to walk like this all morning and afternoon. The beauty contest was only a couple days away, and if she had terrible blisters, she'd never be able to walk properly on the stage. But she was too afraid to talk about it to Jack. She knew he'd just get mad at her and tell her to suck it up. Elle hoped the hotel they were staying at had band-aids.

MOLLY VENZKE

GALEN & SKYE

✠ 19 ✠

GALEN STOOD OUTSIDE THE BANK CONTEMPLATING as he ran his fingers through his thick hair, a nervous gesture of his that his mom was always trying to get him to stop doing. He was searching his mind for any excuse, even just one, that would convince him not to do what he was about to do. *Am I being impulsive and emotional?* he thought. *Maybe, after not getting much sleep last night, I'm not thinking clearly. If I just wait it out a few more days, I bet this entire idea, which is ridiculous in the first place, will just fade away. I'll forget I ever met her, or after some time passes, realize I made the right choice by not getting involved.*

But then he thought of the ramifications for the girl if he didn't get involved. How many men would be coming into her room, in only a few hours, and begin violating her? For hours on end, the men would pass each other in the hallway, one going in, one going out, and put that girl through god-only-knows what. The thought made Galen want to vomit. *If that was my little sister, Dimitra, I'd personally want to beat the s**t out of every single one of those bastards. All the cousins would gang together, hunt them down, and castrate the whole lot!*

The injustice of the situation burned inside of Galen. He knew he'd never be able to live with a choice of inaction; at least not now that he had seen. He'd never find the way to erase the look of fear and hatred the girl had on her face, an expression all too mature for such a young girl to convey. In addition, now every time he looked at Dimitra, he'd think of the girl and wonder what might've happened to her and if she was ever able to escape from that hellhole. He couldn't just walk away. Now, after being with her for an entire night, Galen felt responsible. He didn't really understand what that meant, or how this situation would end up playing out, but what he *did* know was he couldn't do nothing.

He walked into the bank and looked for someone to help him whom he was absolutely certain didn't know anyone in his family. He couldn't afford for casual gossip to ruin his plan. Galen had told his family he'd taken a short-term, mid-night job to be able to raise the money he needed to buy his first car. This allowed him the latitude to stay out all night, for as many nights as he needed, without his father asking any questions. If somehow, his parents heard he'd been in his bank *withdrawing* a large sum, there would be an avalanche of interrogations, and too many questions Galen had no idea how to answer. After picking a teller he'd never seen before, he walked up and filled out the slips needed to withdraw 1000 euros.

As the woman counted out the money, Galen could feel his stomach begin to churn. In so many ways, this money represented freedom for him. He was the second-born son, and being so, he understood he'd need to be the one accountable for making his dreams for the future come to pass. Nikkos, the first-born, would naturally be offered the option to take over the family furniture business, so his destiny was a no-brainer. *Maybe that's why he lives his life in such a cavalier way*, thought Galen. *He doesn't have to do anything at all to make a financial future for himself; his way has already been paved for him by our father. All he has to do is show up, and not wreck anything, and he'll have the money he needs to make a fine living.*

Galen, of course, would be welcome to work for his family; he'd always have a job waiting there for him. But ownership of the furniture business would never be an option, unless of course, Nikkos extended the invitation. However, Galen didn't care, because much to his father's disdain, he hadn't the slightest interest in buying and selling furniture. Unlike Nikkos, Galen was a visionary, always thinking outside the box of his Greek upbringing, with dreams of college abroad—hopefully in the United States—and desires to travel. He'd even secretly entertained the idea of buying a house and living somewhere outside the country of Greece.

Perhaps it was a blessing in disguise that Galen was the second son because he never could've settled for a position in the furniture company. Had he been first, he probably would've passed on the opportunity to take over the business, which essentially would have completely disregarded both his parents and his culture. Much family drama and resentment, for years on end, would've ensued. But Nikkos, on the other hand, was a perfect match for that course; never once had Galen heard him express any ambitions of his own.

While Galen had never regretted that the universe chose him as the number two son, he did come to realize, at a very young age, that the secondary title also came with a curse. He'd be on his own to finance any vision that involved straying from his family's path. This included college abroad, any entrepreneurial endeavors he might attempt, and all that went with those choices. As a result, Galen had lived a focused and purposeful life; studying to make the highest grades, working every job he could get his hands on, and saving as much money as possible. Every decision he made was with an awareness of his future goals in mind...until today.

Withdrawing such a sum was completely out of character for the conservative, calculated Galen. He looked at the money he was now holding in his hand, knowing it was a precious commodity, every penny a testimony of determination and hard work. To throw it away on an impetuous moment of pity was something Galen knew he'd regret forever. But for reasons he could not yet articulate, he simply couldn't help himself. He neatly folded the sum of bills into his wallet, and exited the bank to hail a cab.

Galen had to swallow his pride when he first got into the cab and read off his destination. The cab-driver, clearly familiar with the area, had started to snicker and tease Galen about what kind of girl he'd be having tonight. Trying to ignore his jests, he simply sat back and asked the man to drive. He hated that someone thought he was going to engage in such filth, even if it was only a guy he'd probably never meet again. The driver had taken the hint, and hadn't said another word.

What in the world am I trying to prove? Galen thought. *Where is all of this going to take me? It's not like I have an endless supply of money...even if I drain my entire savings on this girl, then what? If somehow I'm able to get her out of there, where will she go? She can't even speak any Greek! And when eventually my parents find out my money is gone, what in the hell am I going to tell them?* "Oh, yeah. I used to have all that money, but I spent it all on a prostitute. But don't worry, Pop! I never had sex with her; I just sat there all night and talked with her." Galen had to chuckle at how ridiculous that sounded.

Galen's thoughts went around and around, analyzing every angle of the situation he had put himself in, until the cab began to slow down, and he knew he had reached the brothel. As he paid the fare, he avoided eye contact with the driver to spare himself from the man's cheesy grin, and quickly hopped out of the car.

As he stood on the road outside the strip club, he noticed how much more activity was going on than when he'd left the place earlier this morning. Every corner had several girls standing around, talking to the men as they passed by. Some of the women were leaning into cars; Galen assumed they were trying to make a deal. He stood and watched one of the girls as she obviously sweet-talked the man into choosing her, because the car door opened, she disappeared inside, and they drove off.

How does that woman know that guy isn't going to do something terrible to her, maybe even kill her? She has no idea what kind of person she just left with! Galen was dumbfounded as the reality of the profession, along with its potential dangers, began to sink in. Then he noticed one of the prostitutes had spotted him, and was walking his way. Before she had a chance to approach him, he turned and entered the strip club foyer.

Two large men greeted him and made him pay the entrance fee required to go deeper into the club. Once inside, Galen was now able to see for the first time, the club in full swing. Last night he'd been blindfolded, so he'd only heard the sound of the music and smelled the sour alcohol coming off all the men. Tonight, he could see the room was large and dark, with most of its illumination coming from the flashing lights on the stages, of which there were three: a large center one and two smaller off-shoots. Several young girls were dancing throughout these stages, some on poles, some on higher platforms, and some bending over to tease the dozens of men who lined the edges. Then throughout the room, girls in various phases of nakedness roamed about with trays, a few more were sexually poised on small tables, while others could be seen writhing up against the men standing against the walls. Galen didn't even want to know what was happening in the far corners that were too dark to see into.

He closed his eyes to try and recall which direction Nikkos had gone to find the upstairs brothel. He'd been so tired and emotional when he left early that morning, he'd forgotten to take note of his exit. If his memory served him correctly, they had walked into the crowd and then around to the right. Galen opened his eyes, acted like he knew exactly what he was doing, and weaved his way through the crowd and over to the right. Once on the edges of the bar, he saw a dimly lit hallway with a red painted spiral staircase at the end. This was the right way.

His heart began to pound in his chest as he circled up the red iron staircase. Nervous adrenaline coursed through his veins, and he felt his face, armpits and hands begin to sweat. Everything inside him wanted to turn back and forget the entire plan, but he couldn't seem to turn himself around. His legs were resolute to make it to the top of the stairs.

The little fat woman he'd met that morning appeared to be waiting for him, because as soon as he emerged to the second floor, she was right there to welcome him, lipstick-smeared teeth and all.

"Ooooh, Love!" she sang to him. "I've been waiting for you, and so has your girl!" And she giggled wickedly at him. "I've made sure she's nice and fresh for you. I even dressed her extra pretty for your entire night; you're still paying for the entire night, right?"

Galen wanted to smack the woman's grin right off her face, but he knew he had to play along with her. "Yes," he said. "And are you sure you did that? Because I'm not going to be paying the full price for her if you've had her working all day, too. I like my girls to be awake and ready to please while I'm with them." Galen gritted his teeth in disgust at his own loathsome words.

The old hag squinted her eyes and looked at him sideways. "But last night, your friend said this was your first time."

Galen had forgotten Nikkos had told her this. He tried to laugh it off, "Ha! Oh yes," he said. "*That.* That was just my brother trying to make you feel sorry for me and maybe even get a bargain from you...He's such a lying bastard. No, last night was *definitely* not my first time." Galen stopped for a second to see if the woman was believing his story. He thought she seemed to be buying it.

Running his fingers through his hair, he continued, "It was my first time here, though, and I'm looking for somewhere new to go. I'm tired of the spoiled whores I'd been having at my old place. I want something younger *and* fresher. So you better not be trying to pull a fast one on me, giving me the stale leftovers from the day."

The woman quickly answered, "Oh no, no, no. Your girl has been resting all day, just like you asked. Will it just be you tonight? I thought you said you would be bringing some others with you."

Wanting to distract her, Galen pulled out the large wad of money he had just withdrawn from his bank account. "Don't you worry," he said while counting out the bills. "I've got lots of friends who I can bring, but first, I want to make sure I can trust you. My guys are like me; they'll want to buy all-night shifts; we like to train our girls to do what we like, if you know what I mean."

"Yes, yes, I do, Love," giggle-snorted the old woman.

"But, before my friends dole out tons of cash like this, I need to make sure you're going to make good on your promise to have fresh girls."

"Oh, I will, Love!" she promised. "For you and your boys, I will!"

"Well, let's just see how this week goes. *If* you follow through, then by the weekend, you'll be a very happy woman. I'll bring a dozen others with me."

"I will, I will. Don't you even doubt it, Love."

"Great. Then let's get started. Where is she?"

The woman picked up her large ring of keys. "Oh, she's in the very same room as last night. I don't like to move the girls around from room to room once I buy them."

Galen felt his stomach churn at her words. Had he heard her right? Had she said 'once I *buy* them'? He realized he was stepping into dangerous ground by asking, but he needed to know. "What do you mean, 'buy them?'"

For a split second, the woman seemed shaken, but almost as quickly as the worry appeared on her face, she masked it with a lipstick-smeared, toothy smile.

"Oh, Love!" she said condescendingly. "I just meant after I buy all the things the girls need to keep themselves nice and comfortable. I want them to stay with me as long as possible."

Galen bit his lip to stop himself from saying anything further to the woman. He wanted to belittle her with ugly words, to accuse her of harboring illegal aliens and forcing them to engage in prostitution. He wanted to threaten to turn her into the authorities. But he kept his mouth shut. He knew he needed the woman to think he was on her side, else she refuse his patronage.

"Whatever," he said. "I really don't care what you have to do, as long as the girls are ready to go when I get here. I'm looking to find a new place to frequent, and I'm hoping this'll be the place."

"Yes, yes, yes, Love! I'll make sure of it!"

The woman unlocked the padlock outside the girl's room, and as she did the night before, she went in first to prepare the room. Galen wiped his hands on his jeans and wondered why he felt so nervous to spend another evening with the young girl.

❧ 20 ❧

SKYE WAS COMPLETELY DISOREINTED when she heard the jingling sounds of the keys and padlock. She had slept almost the entire day, waking up only to eat the lunch the witch had brought earlier. Combine those hours of sleep with the sleep she'd had the night before when the guy had just sat in the chair, and Skye felt very groggy and upside down. Her body was not used to so many consecutive hours of deep slumber. It made her feel strangely alert, yet at the same time, more exhausted than she'd ever felt in her life.

She tried to blink through her haze to discern the mood of the witch. Earlier, when she'd brought the lunch, the old hag was nice again, just like she'd been in the morning when she'd brought the doughnut. In addition, the lunch was not the usual crusty, thin sandwich; it was a bowl of warm soup and hearty bread. Then, the woman wouldn't leave until Skye had eaten the entire tray of food and had gotten back into bed for more rest. Skye could not imagine why she was acting this way, or how long it would last, so she knew she had to stay on her guard.

As Skye squinted to focus on the witch, she saw her smiling at her as she hobbled over to her bed. Alarmed at the quick approach,

Skye tried to wrap as much of her body in the covers as possible in case the witch was coming over to strike her. But instead, Skye heard the woman giggle-snort and talk to her with an awful sing-songy lilt. She pulled the covers off Skye, gestured for her to sit on the edge of the bed, and then fingered through her long, curly hair in an attempt to make it look fixed. The witch pinched her cheeks the way Skye had seen actresses do in the movies when they were trying to blush their cheeks. And then she hobbled back out.

Skye could not understand what possibly could have caused such a change in the ugly old woman. But it really didn't matter to her because a new night had begun. A new night of terrible things would soon be happening to her and no amount of niceness from that witch could make it any less unbearable. On her bed, Skye pushed herself back against the wall and stared off into the distance to await her first visitor.

She didn't bother to look up when the man came in, nor when she could tell the witch was trying to get her attention. It didn't matter who it was; in fact, Skye generally tried to avoid eye contact with every visitor so she'd never have those wretched faces burned in her memory. She heard the witch leave the room and close the door. Then she waited for the man to speak, or to come over to her bed.

The first one of the evening was always the worst because he broke the hours of solitude she'd have during the day, her only relief from the horrors she'd face each night. She closed her eyes as she sensed the person in her room was moving about, and her heart began to pound in her chest. The seconds seemed like hours as she sat on her bed waiting. And as her heartbeat ticked past the moments, still nothing was happening. The man had not approached her yet. Finally, unable to take the suspense, she focused her eyes and wildly looked around the room.

She gasped in surprise. It was the young man who had just left her room that morning. What was he doing here? Why was he back? Has he come to get what he didn't get last night? Questions swirled in Skye's head as she stared at the man.

He seemed nervous and uncertain, standing awkwardly with his hand on his head and his mouth open, as if he wanted to say something but didn't have the words. Then, he did the very same thing as he'd done the night before. He motioned to Skye that he didn't want to touch her and that she should lay back down and go to sleep. And once again, he pushed the chair as far back into the corner as he could, faced it toward the barred window, and sat down. He leaned back, stretched his long legs forward, and tried to make himself comfortable.

Skye was dumbfounded. She could not understand what was happening, why the witch was being so nice, why the guy was back in her room, or why he was paying money to just sit in that chair all night. She didn't know what to do, or how to act, or even how to feel about all that was happening. She wanted to believe this guy was not here to violate her, but after what she'd experienced during the last months, Skye had come to believe there was no one left in the world, except MawMaw Aggie, her mom and her sister, who was *not* out to hurt her. She sunk down onto her pillow and began to cry softly as she thought of her family.

For a long time, Skye kept her teary eyes on the young man in the chair. But the fatigue from her time at the brothel was pressing heavily upon her. It was as if the last many hours of consecutive sleep had allowed a crack to form in the dam of her defenses, and now the exhaustion was tumbling out and engulfing her. As hard as she fought to keep sleep at bay so that nothing could suddenly surprise her, she finally relented. Once again, she fell into a deeper sleep than she'd experienced in many months.

Galen could hear the girl crying. Her woeful sounds made him so wrought up inside, he thought he might explode. His nature was to offer comfort or to provide justice, and he felt utterly helpless to accomplish either. He couldn't go over to her and try to console her; last night when he attempted that she freaked out. And he had no idea how to defend her or bring her situation to any kind of resolution. As he listened to her sobs, his own eyes burned with tears of indignation and sorrow.

At length, her crying stopped, and she became quiet. From the occasional sounds of her movement, Galen could tell she was awake, and he wondered what she was doing. He didn't dare turn his head to see. He thought he could feel a tangible tension in the air, as if both were waiting on pins and needles for the other to make the first move. But as the minutes passed, peace seemed to settle into the small room, and he was convinced the girl had fallen asleep.

He waited at least an hour before he turned his body to look at the girl. As he did, his jacket fell to the concrete floor with a rustling and clinking that seemed deafening to Galen. But the girl did not so much as twitch at the sound, convincing him she indeed was deeply asleep. He carefully turned his chair so he could get a better look at her face. Maybe if he stared long enough, he'd be able to figure out what country she was from?

She really is a beautiful young girl, he thought. *Such smooth white skin, and long, dark curly hair. I wonder how old she is? Her face looks like a little kid, but her figure seems to put her about 15 or 16? I've heard a lot of the prostitutes here come from Russia, but she doesn't have that classic, Slavic face and eyes. Maybe she's French? Or Italian? But if she was, wouldn't she know even just a little bit of Greek?* And then he chuckled to himself. *This is ridiculous! Like I'm going to be able to make out her nationality by sitting here and gawking at her.*

But he didn't want to stop looking at her. Last night, she had on a blue nightgown that looked almost like a tank top, but tonight she had a pretty satin pink nightgown. The blue one against her skin made her look gaunt and pale, but this pink one brought out a little bit of a healthier glow. Or did she just have make up on? Or was he simply noticing more about her? Galen couldn't tell.

She seemed so delicate as she lay there, and the longer he watched her sleeping the stronger his passion grew to protect her. To help her. To get her out of here. Never again would a man touch her, mistreat her or make her degrade herself at his command. He was sure he would kill the man who tried. Galen felt his cheeks flush with emotion for this nameless girl as he once again scoured his mind for a reasonable plan of escape.

The plan had to be flawless, and not without extreme luck from the gods. He rehearsed in his mind the different ways in which he could sneak her past the old woman, but he wasn't sure how he'd make it past those guards in the foyer. And then he thought of what might happen to the girl if his attempt to rescue her failed. She'd probably be beaten senseless, and he certainly would never be able to see her again. Those concerns were very sobering for Galen. *Whatever I do, it's going to have to be watertight or the retribution for both of us will be hell.*

He took a deep sigh. The last two days of sleeplessness were taking their toll as he could feel his head begin to swim in the waves of fatigue. He closed his eyes, and fell asleep to the vibrating rhythm of music seeping in from the strip club below.

MOLLY VENZKE

❧ 21 ❧

SKYE AWOKE TO THE SOUND OF KNOCKING. *It must be time to get up for school,* she thought as she sensed the morning light through her closed eyelids. *What day is it? Do I have school today? I can't remember going yesterday, so I'm sure it must be a school day. Did I do my homework? Man, I still feel so tired, I wonder if Mom'll let me stay home from school today.*

She felt someone gently shaking her shoulder to wake her up as the rapping on the door sounded again. Then she heard a male voice quietly saying something undecipherable. *Is my dad in my room?* Skye thought. She shot up in bed and opened her eyes.

Reality. The brothel. Her room. Hell.

More than anything else in the world, Skye wanted to slip back into the freedom of her unconscious imagination. But she also knew the bitter price the witch would make her pay if she didn't obey. She shook off her grogginess, sat up, and looked around the room.

The young man was next to her, and he was the one who'd shaken her out of her sleep. He was shirtless with his jeans unfastened. *Why is he undressed? Did he have sex with me last night?* She searched her mind to try and recollect. *I only remember him sitting in that chair and then I fell asleep. Could I have slept through it? My body doesn't feel like anything happened, but maybe I was drugged?*

145

And then she remembered the morning before, how as soon as the witch came to the door, he had quickly pulled off his shirt and belt and had undone his jeans...only to put it all back on once the woman came into the room.

Sure enough, as soon as the witch peeked in, the man stood up to button his jeans and throw on his shirt. He began to talk with the witch, and they both began to laugh.

Why does he change so much when she comes in? When she's here, he's ugly and acts like the other men who come in here, but then as soon as she's gone, his eyes turn soft and he doesn't try to touch me. Skye couldn't figure out the young man or what his motives could possibly be.

He put his arm around the shoulders of the witch, and escorted her out of the room, talking to her the entire time. As they were about to exit the room, he let the witch go into the hallway before him, and as he closed the door, he turned around and made eye contact with Skye. It was a very intentional gaze, long and deliberate. And then he was gone.

What was that? Why did he look at me like that? Was he trying to tell me something, or was he just pitying me, or...what? Who is he and why is he coming here? He seems to be nice, like he cares about me. Skye shook her head. *No. That's not true. It can't be true. Nobody here is good, and nobody here cares about me. I cannot trust him, or anybody else who comes into a place like this.*

She fell back onto her bed, and covered herself with the sheet. The first rays of sunshine were beginning to break through her barred window, and Skye looked at the shadows of the bars on her ceiling. On a sunny morning, this grid silhouette served as her only means to mark the passage of time. Each morning, she'd desperately watch for it because its presence signified a near-end to her shift. An eternity would pass as she followed the shadow-clock's painstakingly slow movement to the middle of the ceiling. But once there, Skye would begin to feel relief knowing at any moment, it would be time for the witch to knock on the door, make the last man leave, and then lock the outside padlock.

The next marker was when the shadow passed by the corner where the ceiling and wall met, and climbed halfway down the wall. On some days, this was when the witch would come back with a tray of food for the day and check the room for cleaning needs. On the days she didn't arrive at this time, then Skye knew she would have to wait for food until the grid slid down the entire wall and crept to the center of the concrete floor. In Skye's depressed state, she hadn't cared to figure out if there was a pattern to the times and days so she never knew what to expect from day to day.

But on this day, Skye was startled by the witch's early entrance. The shadow hadn't had a chance to so much as touch the corner of the ceiling before she came back. And like the morning before, when she hobbled into the room, she wore that same repulsive lipstick-smeared grin as she approached Skye and patted her on her head. She also had a small cup and a bag with a fresh pastry in it. She spoke to Skye, motioning her to eat and drink what she'd brought, and then she left the room. Skye heard the padlock close and the jingly sound of the keys grow faint as the witch's heels clicked down the hall.

Skye picked up the small cup and felt its warmth. She peeled off the lid, and smelled the wonderful aroma of chocolate. Had the witch actually gotten her a hot cocoa? Skye's head was spinning, not able to comprehend the kind gesture or the motive behind it. She knew this woman was pure evil, so it was impossible the witch was doing any of this out of the kindness of her heart. Skye was sure she didn't even have one of those.

All of this had to be because of that guy. The witch's transformation had to be because of the guy who had sat in her room the last two nights. How was he making the witch act like this? Did he know something bad about her? Was he threatening her? Or was he just paying her more? And even more confusing...Why was he doing all of this? Surely it was only a matter of time before Skye had to return these favors.

She had no answers. But she did have a hot drink in her hand, and when she took her first sip, it was like heaven in a cup. It tasted almost as good as the homemade hot cocoas MawMaw Aggie used to make for them, and the girl's sensory recall transported her back into the security of MawMaw Aggie's beautiful sage and butter-yellow painted kitchen.

"*Choooh!* Dat Starbucks ain't got nuttin' on dis ol' Cajun woman," MawMaw would say as she carried the tray to the round wooden table. "Starbucks wish dey knew Aggie's secret to da perfect hot cocoa! And dose tings dey try to pass off as pralines are a disgrace! Dose wouldn't melt in da mouth of a fire-spittin dragon. *Mais non, non, non!* But Aggie's pralines, now, dat's a whole 'notha story, ain't it, *Sha?*" And she'd set down the tray of cocoa and homemade pralines. Skye and Elle would wiggle in their seats waiting for MawMaw to give them the cue to dive in.

Skye closed her eyes and reveled in the sweet memory of Aggie, trying to recall every detail of her house. Perhaps if she concentrated hard enough, she'd somehow be transported back in time, before any of this nightmare began. She could feel the warm drink hitting the bottom of her empty stomach, just like those early mornings at MawMaw's. She visualized the smooth wooden kitchen cabinets, painted butter-yellow, and their metal knobs molded like daisies. And the light green walls. And the window above the sink with the yellow and sage striped curtains. And the bright green ceramic frog that always sat to the left of the sink, his mouth wide open to serve as a holder for Aggie's S.O.S. pads.

The ache in Skye's heart for MawMaw Aggie grew unbearable, too much for her to contain. She let out a deep groan as she hurled the cup across the room, hot chocolate exploding in the corner where the young man had sat in the chair all night. Surprised at the volume of her outburst, she snapped back into survival mode, fearing the mess would anger the witch, perhaps enough to invoke a beating.

Skye scanned the room for something to clean up the chocolate, and remembered the small pile of tattered rags underneath the nightstand. Moving quickly, she grabbed the old towels and mopped up the floor and ceiling. While it was highly unlikely the witch would come back to check on her so soon, Skye didn't want to take any chances. Unfortunately, some of the liquid had run under the chair and into the corner, so she scooted it over to clean every last bit.

As she was down on all fours, examining the concrete for anything she missed, her eye caught a glimmer coming from the opposite corner of the room. *What is that?* she wondered, and she crawled over to see the source of the sparkle.

She reached out to grab the item and the moment she touched it, she knew what it was. Wholly astonished, she sat frozen to the concrete staring at the small broken bracelet gathered in the palm of her hand. Several moments passed as the motionless girl's eyes stayed fixed on the silver treasure, all the while dropping steady tears on the charms as if to wash away the dust. It was the charm bracelet MawMaw had specially designed for Skye's thirteenth birthday.

The dainty bracelet consisted of sterling silver links and three handcrafted charms. The center charm was an ornately wired, round birdcage. The charm to the left was a sterling silver heart, hammered for texture, and the charm to the right was a small bird with her wings open in flight.

"You see dat birdcage? It's beautiful, but it's empty, just as a birdcage should be," Aggie had said. "And dis petite bird? Dat's your pet egret you've always wanted to catch, *Sha*. She's flyin free, never ever to be put inside any kinda cage. Dat's you, Skye. You a beautiful bird dat *le Bon Dieu* put on dis earth to fly da open sky with your dreams. You can't never let yo'self be caught in any cage, you hear me? You a bird, *Sha*. And you gone soar up as high as your dreams can take you. And dis heart? Why, dat's MawMaw's heart dat'll always be with you no matter where dose dreams take you. No matter how high, no matter how far, Aggie's love'll always be with you, *Sha*." Aggie had latched the bracelet on Skye's wrist and hugged her long and tight. Skye had whispered her vow to never, ever take the bracelet off.

Over and over, Skye replayed this scene with Aggie, as she scooted to her bed. She had no idea how the bracelet ended up hidden in the corner under a covering of dust. All of her personal belongings had been stripped from her that first night in the brothel. And while many of the details of those first 72 hours were hazy, she did remember trying to fight off her attackers in the beginning. Perhaps in the violence of it all, the bracelet had been ripped away and forgotten.

Many links had been torn off, so there was no way to put it on her wrist. But then again, now that Skye had this in her possession again, she wouldn't have worn it anyway for fear the witch would notice and steal it away forever. No, she would be very vigilant to keep this precious memento safely hidden from any person who came into her room from now on.

Clutching the silver charms to her heart, Skye curled up in her bed, heart aching, and she cried herself to sleep.

THE DUMONDES

⚜ 22 ⚜

LOTTIE WATCHED FROM THE HUGE OUTDOOR BALCONY of Nottoway as Wil and his two security guards walked the woman toward the Iris Cottages. She felt her husband's arm encircle her waist. "What was that all about?" Richard asked.

"Well, I'm still not sure," she answered, "but Wil was definitely not tellin me the whole truth about that ol' woman."

"Well, one thing we know about our son is that he's fully capable to deal with almost any circumstance. He'll take care of it, Lottie. Now let's go to the Randolph and eat. I can't wait to see what Max prepared. There might be bigger Mardi Gras Balls going on tonight, but none of them have the best chef in Louisiana. Did I tell you Max was offered to be head chef at the Rex Krewe's ball tomorrow tonight? It won't be long until our own krewe is neck and neck with them, competing for the best floats in the Mardi Gras Parades."

Lottie wasn't listening. "Are you sure I shouldn't go and check on her? Richard, you didn't see the look in that poor woman's eyes. It was so desperate, like something just terrible was about to happen to her."

"Charlotte, Wil can handle whatever she needs. He's perfectly capable. Now please, come with me and let's go join our guests in the Randolph. The waiters won't start serving food until we're seated."

"You're right," she said, trying to convince herself. "I know you're right."

Taking one final glance toward the cottages, Lottie smiled up at Richard and took his arm. She loved being escorted by her tall husband, even more today than when they'd first fallen in love as teenagers. He was home for her; strong, secure, loving. It was a chilly winter night and before Lottie could give the slightest shiver, Richard instinctively pulled her to his side and covered her with his jacket.

"I love you, Richard," Lottie said as they walked down the curved granite staircase.

"I love you more, babe. And after dinner, I'm looking forward to dancing in the White Ballroom with the most beautiful woman here. I want everyone to see what a lucky man I am."

"You don't think anyone will snicker at this 46-year-old woman dressed as the young Scarlett O'Hara?"

"Nope. They'll just be jealous of you because you look better than a thousand Scarletts put together...not to mention that you're on the arm of such a dashing Rhett Butler."

Lottie laughed. "Your humility is really something to be proud of."

"And so is your wit," Richard said, chuckling. They walked under a live oak and stopped to look at the maze of branches swirling above them.

"I wish we had one of these on our property," said Lottie. "As a girl, I used to climb up and down the ones on my Granddaddy's estate. It drove my momma crazy that her Southern Belle daughter had skinned up knees every time I'd come home."

"You think anyone'd notice if I dug this one up and hauled it away? Or better yet, how much trouble do you think we'd get into if I carved our names in this trunk?" Richard started checking his pockets for an army knife.

"Richard! Don't you dare! This is an historic monument. You'll go to jail, and then I'd never be able to face my momma again. Every Sunday brunch, she'll look at me through her little rhinestone glasses and say, 'Sooo, Lottie-baby...How's that convict husband of yours?' And I'll have to eat crow as she sits there with that smug look on her face."

"Ha! They never did think I'd amount to much, did they?"

"Oh, you know I never cared one iota what Momma and Daddy thought about you. Still don't. Although you've certainly showed them that they were wrong, and Daddy'd be the first one to admit it. He loves you like his own son, you know that, right?"

"Has he finally approved of me after all these years?" he joked. "Well, I don't blame him for holding the bar so high for me. If we had a daughter, I'd be just as protective of her. Nothing but the world's best would've been acceptable for her." They walked for a moment in silence, both knowing the thoughts of the other. Richard and Lottie had given birth to a baby girl over 15 years prior, but she was a premie, and she only lived five days. The sting of her vacancy was still often felt deeply by them both. Richard's arm tightened around Lottie, and he began to lead her away, as much toward the dinner hall as away from the reminiscence of their baby-girl's death.

His face turned sour. "Besides, I certainly wouldn't want to get myself arrested; they'd probably stick my mug shot right next to Jack's."

"Richard DuMonde, don't you ever compare yourself to that brother of yours. Yes, you might look alike, but it stops there."

Richard sighed as they continued walking toward the Randolph Ballroom. The thought of Jack always brought heaviness to his heart. As children, the two boys were inseparable and the best of friends. It wasn't until their late teens that their paths began to split as Richard grew more responsible and focused, and Jack became everything opposite. Always conniving and looking for a fast buck, Jack was out for himself, willing to do whatever he needed to make his fortune. For many years, Richard had tried to bend Jack's direction, to convince him to build a more disciplined life, but his efforts were ineffective.

Shortly after high school, Jack disappeared out of Richard's life. Once, early in Richard and Lottie's marriage, a cop had shown up on their front porch, trying to gain information on Jack's whereabouts. Another time, Richard had caught wind of a marriage between Jack and a girl with a more-than-modest inheritance. But after these incidences over 15 years ago, Jack seemed to have completely fallen off the grid, and Richard often wondered if his brother was still alive. Then the threatening emails began to surface, demanding the repayment of a very large sum, or else there would be harmful measures taken. Jack was definitely alive, and obviously, as slippery as ever.

Richard and Lottie were now standing at the entrance of the Randolph Ballroom.

"Alright, Richard," Lottie said. "Enough with the long faces, and I mean to say that to the both of us. We are at a gorgeous Mardi Gras Ball, and we can't very well be proper hosts if we're actin so sullen. Let's go in there and turn on the DuMonde charm!"

When they entered the elegant dining hall, all the guests began applauding. Richard quickly went over to a microphone, and motioning for them to stop clapping, he said, "Please, please. We're not a bride and groom, for heaven's sake. Or are you all just cheering because, finally, you can start to eat?" The room laughed. "Sorry for taking so long and causing the delay. Lottie and I couldn't help ourselves from side-steppin under the balcony of live oaks, and I have to admit, I could not make out who was more beautiful, my wife, Charlotte, or these incredible Nottoway grounds. However, after about a half-a-second, I was sure as ever that one thousand Nottoways all put together could never stand up to my Lottie."

"Richard!" Lottie exclaimed, blushing as she playfully hit his arm.

"My wife, ever the picture of modesty." Richard said as he put his arm around Lottie's waist and bent to kiss her on the cheek. "But without further adieu, let's get dinner started. I'm excited to introduce to you our chef for the evening, Maxwell Toussaint. He's the finest chef in New Orleans, and we are honored to have snatched him up for *our* Mardi Gras Ball."

The crowd applauded as Max took the microphone and began announcing the menu for the evening. The feast would begin with more appetizers of Shrimp Remoulande and Crawfish Beignets followed by Chicken and Tasso Gumbo. The salad would be a simple Plantation Salad, and the entrees would be a choice of either a classic Filet Mignon or Max's signature dish: Boudin Stuffed Chicken Roulade. Dessert and after dinner drinks would be served later, once the party had returned to the main Nottoway mansion.

The DuMonde's table of honor was on a platform, slightly elevated above the other guests, and as Lottie took her seat, she read the room. Most of these 200 people were constituents of Richard; only about a dozen of the women did she know well. And even those women were a bit difficult to recognize in their Southern Belle costumes. But Lottie was well-bred to feel at ease, even in a room full of the most wealthy and elite.

However on this night, she was unable to set aside her anxiety. But it wasn't because she was hosting a party for many of the most prestigious and successful men and women of Louisiana; it was because of the old woman who had caught hold of her dress. Lottie could not stop thinking about her.

Who was that lady and what was she trying to tell me about her girls, thought Lottie. *She looked so desperate, like she was facing a life-or-death situation. But why did she come here? And how did she get past Wil's security? She said Richard and I were the only ones who could help her save her girls...why would she think that? And save them from what? Did she come here just because we have money? It seemed so much more than that...And I thought she said something about knowing my family. What did she mean by that?*

Lottie fully trusted Wil would take care of the woman properly, but she couldn't help but think, *What if she didn't tell him what was really troubling her? The expression on her face was so vulnerable and helpless, what if she needed a woman to share her story with? What if she was too afraid to talk with someone like Wil?*

"You're not eating your food," Richard whispered in her ear.

"Oh, I'm sorry," Lottie said. "I was just lost in thought for a moment. But honey, I've got to say, Max outdid himself with this gumbo. It's simply to die for!"

"Yes, he did, but I can tell you're just humoring me. You haven't even taken one bite out of your bowl."

Lottie looked at her husband, feeling like she'd just been caught. Laughing, she said, "How is it that you know me so well?"

"Twenty-seven years of marriage is how. You're still thinking about that woman who pulled on your dress, aren't you?" Richard asked.

"Mmm." she answered, and she took a spoonful of her soup.

"I promise you, babe, Wil's got it covered. Please, you don't need to give it another thought."

"Yes, yes, yes. Not another thought. I promise."

Lottie sighed and dipped her spoon back into her gumbo. But before she could raise it up again, Richard gently put his hand on top of hers. Lottie looked up at him.

"There's only one problem, Lottie, and that is this: *I* won't be able to stop thinking about her. I'm worried sick about that old lady and I probably won't be able to eat another bite of this delicious food—that I'm paying an arm and a leg for by the way—unless you personally go and check on her."

"Richard..." Lottie said, cocking her head to one side. She knew he was fibbing, and she loved him for it. He was giving her his permission to leave the party.

"I'm serious, Lottie," he continued with his ruse. "I've got all this food sitting here, and I'm so worried right now, that it all just tastes like rubber. Will you please, do me a huge favor and go find out what that woman needs so I can finally enjoy my food?"

She smiled and kissed his cheek. "Thank you so much, and I promise I won't be long. I'll just run there and find out what the problem is, and I'll be right back."

"Take whatever time you need, Lottie. Really. This is only a party, and if that woman truly needs our help, we'd feel awful that we ignored her just so we could enjoy our filet mignon."

"Thank you, thank you, thank you. I'll be back before you know it."

Lottie slipped out of the ballroom and walked as fast as she could toward the Iris Cottages. She felt foolish as she lifted the lower hoops on her dress so she wouldn't trip and fall. "Could this look any more dramatic?" she said aloud and looked around her to see if anyone was witnessing her trot awkwardly across the lawn in her Scarlett costume. "How did these women ever make it through one day in dresses like this?"

At a glance, Lottie knew which one of the cottages was being used to house the woman because four of Wil's Confederates were hanging out on the porch. The white wooden cottages were built two per structure, sharing a common front porch and decorated with classic white, Southern rocking chairs. As soon as she approached the porch, the four men stood to greet her.

"Listen, boys, I need to talk to Wil, and I need it to be right away. Which side of this cottage is he in?"

"I'll fetch him, Miss Lottie," said one of the guys, and he promptly disappeared into cottage #17. Seconds later, Wil came out.

Wil: Mom, what are you doing here? Why aren't you with Dad at dinner?

Lottie: Listen, Wil. I need to talk to that woman in there.

Wil: That's crazy. You don't even know who she is, or why she's here.

Lottie: And you do?

Wil: Well, not fully. Yet. She knows Jack, though, and I'm sure she's connected with those emails Dad's been getting. She's very close with Jack's wife, Macy, and she keeps talking about their daughters. I've barely had any time with her, Mom, but if you'll just go back to the party, I'll get all her information, and I'll come and tell you.

Lottie: No. I want to talk to her myself. *She started toward the door, but Wil stopped her.*

Wil: I'm sorry, Mom, I can't let you do that. She could be dangerous.

Lottie: Do you honestly think that poor old woman in there is here to cause me harm? Or anyone else for that matter? I saw the look in her eyes, Wil. Have you taken a moment to do that? I don't think so, because if you would have, you'd have seen she is in desperate need of some sort, and I'm going to find out what it is.

Wil: Mom—

Lottie: *(to the other guys)* Listen boys, we need your help over there in the Randolph Ballroom, and if you can't find anythin to do, why then, you just sit yourself down and eat a delicious dinner. I promise it'll be some of the best food you've ever tasted. Wil can stay with me and help me out with this woman. Better yet, can one of you be so kind as to ask a Nottoway waiter to bring three full meals to this cottage? I'm sure the lady in there could use a bite to eat as well.

Wil nodded to the four young men, giving them permission to follow his mother's orders. Lottie laughed as they almost sprinted towards the Randolph. "Well, we didn't need to tell them twice," she said. "They must be hungry."

"Mom, they're guys. They're always hungry. Now, why are you so concerned about this lady in there?"

"I don't know, Wil, but there's somethin special about her that I can't quite put my finger on. Please, let me go in by myself and speak with her. I have a feelin in my gut that she needs to talk to a woman...alone."

Wil thought for a moment and then said. "Alright. I guess if there's one thing I've learned being your son is that your hunches are almost always dead on. But listen to me, Mom; I'll be right out here on this porch. If I hear even the slightest weird sound, I'm coming in."

Lottie chuckled, "You're almost more protective of me than your father. And I love you for it, Wil."

Lottie slowly opened the door into the cottage. Inside, Lottie could see the woman sitting at a wooden table and she jumped a bit when she heard the door. But as soon as her eyes met Lottie's, she seemed to melt in relief.

The cottage room had a crisp feel with soft, light green walls and two wooden beds with curved white antique headboards and all-white bedding. The floor was a dark espresso hardwood, a nice contrast to the pastel colors of the rest of the room. In the corner of the cottage was a small dark wood kitchen table with simple plantation-style chairs. This was where the black woman sat, and she appeared to be waiting to speak until Lottie directed her.

Lottie managed to sit down at the table, adjusting the hoops on her dress so she could get as close to her as possible. Reaching across the table and taking hold of both the woman's hands, she looked with great compassion into her eyes and said, "Please don't be afraid, ma'am. I'm Lottie DuMonde, and I'm so glad you've come here tonight. I want to help you with whatever it is that you need."

The black woman's head crumbled forward onto her arms and she began to sob. Lottie scooted her chair next to hers, put her arms around her, and held her tightly as her back shook with her cries. Although not a word of her troubles had yet been uttered, Lottie could feel the depth of this woman's grief, and her eyes also began to swell with tears. She could sense this was a holy moment. Right now they were strangers, but Lottie knew that by the end of this night, their souls would have become knitted together.

AGGIE

✤23✤

Aggie awoke to a soft rapping on her door. Her eyes opened, and it took her a moment to get her bearings. Scenes from the previous evening downloaded quickly in her mind as she sat up in her bed. How terribly nervous she had been. How incredibly beautiful all the guests looked in majestic Nottoway. How she'd been caught by Wil, and escorted to the cottage. How Miss Lottie had come to her rescue, had cried with her, and had sat for two hours with her as Aggie shared her story.

Aggie looked around this quaint cottage room. The morning light was spilling in through the corner windows and illuminating the room with a nice warm glow. There couldn't have been a more perfect room for her to have slept in since the soft green painted walls and dark hardwood floors reminded her of her own kitchen and bedroom. She wondered if all the cottage rooms were decorated just like this one, or had she just gotten this particular one by accident?

The knocking at the door sounded again.

"Miss Aggie, it's Lottie."

Aggie, still dressed in her white uniform from the night before, got up and answered the door. Lottie was standing on the porch with a small tray of coffee and food, along with three large shopping bags looped around her forearms.

"Lawd have mercy, *Sha*. Come in here, and let me help you with dose tings."

Aggie took the silver tray from Lottie and carried it over to the small wooden table in the sitting area by the windows.

Lottie set the shopping bags down on the bed that Aggie had slept in, and then took off the scarf she had around her neck.

"Good morning, Miss Aggie. Can you believe this cold spell we've been havin? It's so strange! Why, I almost cried the other mornin when I woke up and saw snow on the ground. I'd *just* planted some spring flowers, and now I don't think they're goin to make it. It's crazy. Did you sleep well? I hope you were able to sleep after all the fuss last night. Was your bed comfortable?"

"*Oui, oui*, Miss Lottie. Don't worry 'bout a ting; ever'ting was just right. I'm gone have some dis hot coffee, can I pour you a cup?"

"Please, Miss Aggie, just call me Lottie, or Charlotte, whichever you prefer. And, yes, I've already had some coffee, but you feel free to serve yourself. Once again, I am so very sorry about how Wil treated you last night—"

"*Mais, non, non, non*," Aggie interrupted. "Wil a good young man. He just lookin out for his mama. 'Sides, he was very respectful to dis ol' Cajun woman."

Lottie smiled. "He really is a wonderful son to Richard and me. Look, Miss Aggie, we've obviously got some things to talk about." She took Aggie's hand and led her to sit on the side of the bed. Then she sat next to her and looked solemnly into her eyes.

"Honey, I'm not goin to beat around the bush with you; we've got a lot to accomplish today. After you told me your story last night, Wil and one of his army buddies, Scott, took that laptop from your car. Scottie specializes in computer hackin and all that kind of stuff I'll never understand, and they were up the entire night gettin information about Jack...and the terrible things he's gotten those girls into."

Aggie noticed Lottie's chin was starting to quiver, and she stopped talking in order to regain her composure. She cleared her throat and began talking again, this time slower and more deliberately.

"I've gotta warn you, Miss Aggie, the details Wil and Scott have uncovered are probably worse than you originally thought, and it's not goin to be easy to hear. But I want you to know, and I give you my solemn word about this, we *all* are goin to do everything in our power to get those girls back to the U.S.

"You don't know this yet, but my Wil was a tremendous asset to our government when he served in the Special Forces. He's just like his daddy, with a work ethic like no other, and he rose up in the ranks very quickly. The only reason Wil is home now is because several months ago, he was severely injured in a terrible Al Qaeda attack. He almost died."

"Oh, Miss Lottie," Aggie said. "I'm so sorry. Dat musta been awful for you and Mr. Dumonde."

"Yes; it was a very stressful time for all of us, to say the least. But the reason I'm tellin you this is because I want you to know that if anyone can come up with a strategy to bring back both Skye and Elle, it's Wil. He's an expert in this sort of thing. In addition, my husband *and* my daddy have connections with top government officials, and when it comes to family, they'll have no problem usin their influence to get done whatever they need done. Miss Aggie, are you alright with that?"

Aggie nodded her head.

"Good." Lottie said as she looked at her watch. "Right now, it's almost a quarter past seven. What we'd like to do is for you to come and join us up in our suite so we can talk about...well, all that's goin on. We'd like to start right at 8:00, do you think you can be ready by then?"

Aggie smiled, a little sheepishly, and glanced down at her white uniform. "*Mais oui*, I don't got much to do to get ready."

Lottie's eyebrows sprang up. "Oh, I almost forgot! I knew you hadn't expected to stay overnight, so I took the liberty to buy you a couple things, I hope you don't mind. Everything is in those three bags."

"*Choooh!* Miss Lottie, you didn't have to do dat—"

"Remember, it's *just* Lottie, and it was nothing."

Suddenly curious, she asked, "How you know what size to buy?"

Lottie laughed and said, "Oh, honey, it's a god-given gift of mine. I just got a knack for it; with one look up and down, I can tell you the size of any woman, her garments, her undergarment, *and* her shoe size, give or take a ½ size. Besides, all these things are from Chico's, and their active wear is nice and stretchy, so it's easy to size. I hope you like everything I got, or I should say, that my assistant got. She was up at the crack of dawn making her friend, who's the manager at the Baton Rouge Chico's, open her store so we could get these for you before you woke up."

Aggie wasn't sure how to accept such a generous gift. She said softly, "I don't know what to say, Miss Lottie."

"Please trust me, Miss Aggie, after all you've been through, it's the very, very least I could do. Now you gotta get yourself freshened up before our meeting at 8. Neither Richard nor Wil know how to act if someone's late to one of their meetins. That tray over there has fresh coffee and water, along with a full breakfast. We'll only have fruit and snacks at the meetin, so please have your fill before you come. I'll see you then."

Lottie leaned over to give Aggie a hug. "You're not alone, Aggie; we're in this together now." Then she waved and exited the room.

Aggie poured herself a cup of coffee and sat down to try and comprehend the good fortune that was coming her way. "*Bon Dieu,* I don't know how to tank you for settin up dis meetin with da DuMondes. *Merci, merci, merci.* Dis all beyond what I ever could've asked. I gotta believe you have dis ting in da palm o' yo hand and you gone help us get dose girls back home safe."

She took a long drink of coffee and thought of Lottie's words, 'Miss Aggie, the details are probably much worse than you originally thought.'

Lawd have mercy, I hope I have da strenth to hear it all. I cannot bear to tink dose girls have been brought to harm. And I swear, I'll kill dat Jack if he's to blame for it all.

She shuddered at the truth of that thought. Never before had she felt an honest desire to take away a human life; it went against everything she'd ever confessed to believe. But if Jack truly had brought evil upon her Skye and Elle, Aggie would not think twice about breaking the 6th Commandment.

Aggie finished her coffee and breakfast, washed up, and then emptied out the Chico's bags. Aggie was shocked at how many items Lottie had purchased for her. There were three active wear suits, one black, one purple, and one gray. All the pants were the same style but each corresponding jacket was designed differently. Six matching shirts, three short-sleeved and three long. Three beautifully patterned scarves. A very nice black leather purse paired with a pair of black leather clogs that fit Aggie's feet perfectly. And just as Lottie had said, everything, including the undergarments were sized correctly.

"*Choooh!* Hal, you not gone recognize yo Aggie in dese clothes. Dat woman gone and spent over a tousand dollars on dis ol Cajun like it was nuttin. And ever' single one a dese garments is 'xactly what I'd pick for myself. Ha! Only it'd all be from Lafayette at da Acadia Mall TJ Maxx...and it pro'bly wouldn't be Chico's."

Aggie selected the black outfit with the light blue shirt, and as she dressed, she tried to think of the last time in her life, if there ever was one, when each item on her body was brand new. She couldn't think of one and wondered if this was an every day occurrence for Lottie DuMonde. Checking the clock, Aggie realized she only had 10 minutes to make it to the meeting on time. She grabbed a scarf to wrap around her shoulders and left the cottage.

As she stood on the porch, Aggie took a moment to take in the magnificent view of the white Nottoway Mansion. She'd always read Nottoway was the largest antebellum mansion in the entire South, and from her vantage point, she believed it to also be the most beautiful. *And dis mornin, I'm enterin as a guest, not a servant or even a tourist,* she thought. *If only dis was because of a happier occasion.* The chilly morning air caused Aggie to tighten her scarf-turned-shawl around her shoulders, and she walked briskly around the Iris Pond toward the enormous historic home.

Aggie had forgotten to ask Lottie where to enter the mansion, so she decided her best bet would be to go through the huge front doors. Because Nottoway now functioned as a full-service bed and breakfast, at the very least, there ought to be a receptionist at a front desk. The door was unlocked, and sure enough, Aggie was greeted by a young woman dressed in a sharp suit.

"Good morning, you must be Mrs. Prejean," she said. "It's so nice to meet you. I'm Rebecca, Mrs. DuMonde's personal assistant. I'm here to show you to the DuMonde's suite."

"Rebecca, are you da one who got up so early to go and buy all dese clothes?"

"Oh yes! Don't you worry about that, Mrs. Prejean, I live for that kind of stuff! Plus, the manager of that Chico's is my mom's bestie; they went to high school together. She lets us in after hours—or before hours, in this case—all the time."

"Well, tank you very much, *Sha.*"

"Are you Cajun?" Rebecca asked.

"To da bone."

"Oh, that's so cool! My finance's granddaddy, Mr. Floyd; he's a Cajun, too. He lives in Lafayette and absolutely *lives* for Mardi Gras every year, so you know he was in heaven for the last several days."

"Honeychile, did you know I'm from Lafayette?"

"Are you serious? I cannot wait to tell Greyson, that's my fiance's name. Where do you live?"

"North Lafayette, on Bellot Street."

"Did you get out to any of the parades this past weekend? Lafayette gets almost as insane as New Orleans during Mardi Gras weekend!"

"When my husband, Hal, was alive, we never missed a parade, not even one. But dis year, I wasn't able to get out dere."

"Oh, you sure missed a good one! Greyson's granddaddy is a member of two or three krewes, and is one of the only people to ever have been named King of Lafayette's Mardi Gras Parade *twice.*"

"Go to bed, *Sha!*" exclaimed Aggie. "Mardi Gras King *twice?* Dat's unheard of."

"I know, and Mr. Floyd is not shy to tell you all about it, too. He is the oldest living float rider in Lafayette, and he *loves* to throw on the floats during the parades: beads, doubloons, coins, candy, whatever. Mr. Floyd claims that he can pick a target over 30 ft away, throw the Mardi Gras beads, and hit his bull's eye every single time." *She stops walking.* "Oh, look! We're already at their room, and I've talked the entire way. I'm so sorry, Mrs. Prejean. *(whispering)* I kinda do that a lot. So anyway, this is the master suite, and it's where Mr. and Mrs. DuMonde stayed last night; it's the actual bedroom of the people who lived here back in the Civil War days. Isn't that so cool? And all the furniture is the original! If you look closely, the posts of the bed are totally hollow, supposedly where the Randolph's would hide away treasures during the war."

The door of the bedroom opened; it was Lottie.

"I thought I heard your voice out here, Rebecca," said Lottie.

"I'm sorry, Mrs. DuMonde, you know me, I got to talking to this nice lady—"

"I know, Rebecca, bless your heart. You do love your words, don't you, sugar?" Lottie said. She looked to Aggie. "I'm so glad you're here, Miss Aggie; we've got some nice warm coffee and fresh beignets waitin for you. Thank you so much, Rebecca, I'll text you if I need you for anything else."

"Yes, ma'am. Nice meeting you, Mrs. Prejean," said Rebecca as she left the room.

"Please come on in, Miss Aggie, and make yourself at home."

Lottie led Aggie into the Master Suite. It was a beautiful room with slate blue painted walls fully trimmed in white. The high ceilings were dressed with dazzling white plasterwork and had an elegant crystal chandelier hanging down the center. All the furniture was a rich rosewood, including an oblong table set to serve five that seemed too big to have been part of the normal bedroom set-up. Aggie assumed it had been moved in the suite just for this meeting.

"You look beautiful in your new outfit, Miss Aggie. Do you like them?"

"Oh, Miss Lottie, you bought me too much! Dis ol woman don't need dat many clothes."

"Please listen to me, Aggie. God has blessed my family with more money than we could ever need...what good is it if I can't do things like this? Please accept it all as a personal gift from me, and as my thanks for you takin the courage to come all this way and open up your life to Richard and me. Please."

"Tank you, Miss Lottie."

Lottie gestured to an armchair for Aggie to have a seat. "Rich, Wil and Scott are in the sittin room workin on your laptop," Lottie said as she sat across from Aggie, instinctively crossing her legs at the ankles and placing her hands formally in her lap. She would've seemed completely composed were it not for her thumbs that kept nervously crossing over each other. "Scott is Wil's SOF buddy, and he's the one I told you about who can do just about anything with a computer."

"What's SOF?" Aggie asked. She could sense the tension in the room, and felt her heart beating more rapidly than usual.

"Oh, SOF. That means Special Operations Forces. Scott served with Wil during his last deployment in Iraq, and in fact was responsible for saving Wil's life. He's a Yankee, but we love him." She tried to squeeze out a laugh, but only managed an awkward chuckle. After a moment of thick silence, Lottie stood and called to the men, announcing Aggie's presence.

Wil and Scott emerged from the connecting room first, Wil immediately coming over to Aggie and taking her hand. "Good morning, Miss Aggie. I'm so sorry, if we got off on the wrong foot last night. I'm glad you came here and that my mom got to spend so much time with you..." Wil's voice trailed off because he could tell Aggie wasn't listening to a word he was saying. She was too distracted looking up at something past his face, and she now had an expression of shock, like she was facing a ghost.

Wil turned to see what she could possibly be staring at, but he only saw his dad standing behind him.

Lottie was the first to figure it out. "Miss Aggie," she said, "Does Richard still look *that* much like Jack?"

Aggie seemed in a trance as she stood to greet him. "Sorry...I'm so sorry," she whispered, her eyes still hanging on Richard's face. "It's not right to stare, but I just cannot stop. Mr. DuMonde...you da spittin image of dat Jack. Da black hair, da blue eyes, da mouth..." She stopped for a moment trying to absorb the likeness. "I mean, I saw da pictures on da computer, but I had no idea dat eyeball to eyeball you'd look so much like dat man."

"Miss Aggie," said Richard gently, "I cannot tell you how grateful I am you came to find both Lottie and me." He slowly stepped toward her and reached out both his hands to take hers. His voice cracked with emotion as he said, "I don't know how I can possibly apologize for the pain my brother has caused you and your family. I knew Jack had gone down a terrible road, but not until last night did I know the depths of his wicked life. And how many people he's hurt."

Aggie's eyes, still gaping, filled with tears. Suddenly aware of his towering height, he bent down a bit towards her and said, "I promise you, Miss Aggie, I'm nothing like Jack, and I will do everything in my power, I'll use all my influences, I'll pay any amount of money, I'll do anything I need to, to get your girls back to safety. Lottie, Wil and I are committed to you, Miss Aggie, and we won't give up until we've got them back home."

Beginning to weep, she almost lost her balance, but Richard was right there to catch her. His long arms swallowed her up, and for a moment he comforted Aggie. Lottie slid over to take Aggie from his arms and lead her to her seat at the table, speaking loving encouragement the whole time.

Once Aggie was seated, Lottie picked up the coffee server from the center of the table and filled Aggie's cup. She then turned to the others.

"We've got so much to discuss, how about we get started?" Lottie said. "But first, let's take a few moments to enjoy some coffee and beignets before they get cold. That'll give us a bit of time to get better acquainted with each other."

As they approached the table, Lottie had a specific agenda for their seating. Richard sat at the head, Lottie to his left and Aggie had been seated to his right. She asked Wil to sit next to herself and for Scott to sit next to Aggie. Once seated, the two Nottoway waiters immediately began pouring coffee and uncovering the piping hot beignets.

MOLLY VENZKE

�֍24֍

F OR TWENTY MINUTES, THE FIVE SAT at the oblong table chatting and giving further introductions. How Hal and Aggie had met, how Richard and Lottie had met, what schools Wil had attended, Scott and Wil's time serving together in the Special Forces. And then, as if some unseen, unheard alarm had sounded, the conversation reached a lull and an uncomfortable silence blanketed the room.

Aggie saw Richard nod towards Lottie, an obvious cue that it was time to delve into the information they'd found about Jack. Lottie asked the waiters to clear the dishes from the table and to leave behind fresh carafes of coffee and water. The last server placed a new basket of hot beignets next to the drinks before checking with Lottie to see if there would be anything else they needed. Lottie excused the waiter and watched as he exited their room. She waited until he was completely gone to speak.

"Miss Aggie," said Lottie slowly as she picked at the corner of the cloth napkin she'd just neatly folded, "we need to fill you in on what the boys have found out about your girls. I know I told you this earlier in your cottage, but please let me reiterate. The facts you are about to hear are grave, very grave indeed. But even as you listen, *please* keep in mind that you are in the best possible hands. We *will* find those girls, and we *will* get them back safe."

Aggie nodded her head and felt her chest begin to tighten from panic.

"Wil," said Lottie. "Can you please tell us, startin from the beginnin, everythin you and Scott got from that laptop?"

"Yes, ma'am," he said. He looked diagonally across the table at Aggie. "Miss Aggie, last night when I was asking you questions about Jack, you told me that he had recently gotten into the business of buying and selling horses."

"Dat's right. Dat's when tings began to turn around for dem with money. It was how Macy and Jack were able to send Skye to dat school in Europe."

"Right." Wil pressed his lips together, taking a moment to find the right words. "Miss Aggie, The first thing you need to know is that Jack has never been in the business of buying and selling horses. He might have used words to make you believe that he was, but the truth is, that was all code to cover what he was really doing."

"What was dat *peeshwank* really doin? Ain't nuttin gone surprise dis old Cajun woman."

"What he was really into was the buying and selling of girls."

"Well now, dat night I found Macy, she was tryin to tell me somethin 'bout how he was doin dat. Before I came here, I did some research on Google, but I don't tink I really understand what all dat means."

"Maybe you've heard the term being thrown around on the news these last few years, or maybe you even saw that movie called *Taken*? What Jack was really doing is called human trafficking, sex trafficking in this case, and it goes on all over the world. Probably has been going on from the beginning of time. Basically, what happens is, a girl is sold to someone, and that someone uses her to make money by forcing her into prostitution, pornography, and the like. You don't have to think too hard to imagine the horrors these girls face."

"Lawd have mercy," Aggie whispered as she leaned back into her seat. "Dat Jack got da devil in him to do such a ting...even if it was to try and send Skye to dat school. Macy would never've gone along with someting like dis, if she knew. *Mais*, Skye don't need to be dere if *dat's* how it's bein paid!"

Wil looked at his mom, concerned about how to proceed. Aggie wasn't connecting the dots of information, and he didn't want to have to be the one to look in this woman's eyes and tell her the full truth. Lottie returned his look with an ever-so-slight nod of the head, indicating that he could pass the baton to her.

Seeing this nonverbal exchange, Aggie shifted her focus to Lottie. "What, Miss Lottie? What he not tellin me?"

Lottie's chin began to quiver as she tearfully looked back at Aggie. Richard's hand slid over and warmly rested on Aggie's. "What, Mr. DuMonde? What ya'll know dat ya'll not sayin to me?" Aggie was getting agitated.

"Aggie, dear" said Lottie softly. "Skye is not goin to a school in Europe. Honey, can't you see? Jack never sent her to a school...he took her over to Greece and...well, honey...we believe that Jack took her to Greece and sold her."

Aggie's response was swift. "Dat's just not true. Miss Lottie, dat's an awful ting to say. I know Jack's bad, but he'd never sell his own flesh and blood, his own little girl, like dat."

"Aggie, listen—" Lottie whispered, barely keeping herself together.

"No!" Aggie insisted. "*You* listen. You wrong! Dat bastard did *not* sell my Skye! 'Sides, Macy would get emails all da time from Skye tellin her how happy she was in dat school. Her school wasn't even in Greece, it was in London or sometin like dat. I saw da emails with my very own eyes. You wrong, Miss Lottie!"

Wil interjected slowly, "Miss Aggie, Scott found those emails from Skye. They were generated from this laptop, the very one Macy gave to you. Skye didn't send them; Jack did. He had made a fake email account and he was the one who actually wrote and sent those email letters. Miss Aggie, if you'd like, Scott can pull them up on the computer right now and show them to you."

Aggie didn't answer; she was too dumbfounded. She simply sat in her chair, eyes focused on the table, head wagging back and forth. After a few moments, Lottie spoke.

Lottie: Honey, I'm so sorry to say this, but there's still more for you to hear. Are you doin ok? Do we need to stop for a bit, or can we keep movin on?

Aggie: *(under her breath)* I'm gone kill dat Jack.

Lottie: Excuse me, Miss Aggie?

Aggie: *(louder)* I said, I'm gone *kill* dat Jack!

Wil: I promise you, Miss Aggie, Jack will pay for what he's done. I'll see to that.

Aggie: So what you're tellin me is dat Skye has been workin in a brothel all dis time? What a *petite fille (little girl)* like her gone do in a place like dat? Cook and feed da hookers? Clean da rooms? What?

Lottie: We're not goin to know exactly what she's been doin until we rescue her, Aggie. We can hope for the best, but truthfully, she's been gone for almost 7 months now, so we're also goin to have to prepare ourselves for the worst.

Aggie: What you mean by dat?

Lottie: *(slowly)* It's very possible, Miss Aggie, in fact most likely, that they've been forcin Skye to...*her voice trailed off, unable to say the words.*

Aggie just sat there continuing to shake her head.

Aggie: No. *(pause)* No. *(pause) Main non,* why Jack take Elle, den? Can you tell me dat? He took Elle to go and visit Skye, so she *can't* be in one a dose brothels. If Skye done been sold, den why he spend all dat money to take Elle on da trip with him?

Rich: Miss Aggie, my brother has been lying to you all. He's not taking little Elle over to Greece with him to visit Skye. He's taking her there so that he can sell her too.

Aggie: *(exploding)* What?! What's wrong with you people? Ya'll *motier foux (half crazy),* sayin sometin like dat! She just 10 years old! Who gone buy a tiny 10 year old?! What you gone do with a 10 year old? Dis crazy! Ya'll crazy! None o' dis is true. Miss Lottie, why you bring me here to listen to all dis? I thought you a nice woman, actin like you care bout me, buyin me all dese fancy clothes, but dis whole ting is just to torment me! Why ya'll gone do dis to me? Lawd, Lawd, Lawd! *I got da Mal au Couer (I need to vomit)!*

Aggie looked frantically around the room looking for a toilet. She ran to the bathroom and slammed the door.

The rest sat at the table in silence for several moments. Lottie, with tears streaming down her face, looked over at her husband.

She could see he also was struggling not to break down. "I cannot fathom how difficult this all must be for that woman," he said, choking back tears. "She's finding out, all in a matter of a couple days, that everyone she's held dear has been taken from her. And worse, that those two young girls are being terribly abused in the worst way possible."

After a few more minutes passed, Lottie said, "It sounds like she's gotten quiet in there. I'll go and see if there is anything I can do to help her." She poured a glass of water for Aggie, walked over to the bathroom, and tapped lightly on the door. "Miss Aggie?" Lottie could hear the woman crying. "Miss Aggie, I've brought some nice cool water for you, may I come in for a bit?"

Lottie waited, but Aggie did not answer. Lottie made the executive choice to go in anyway, and she slowly opened the door. "Miss Aggie?" she barely whispered as she entered.

Aggie was sitting on a closed toilet, elbows in her lap, and head buried in her hands. She didn't look up when Lottie came in, but she did acknowledge her by softly saying, "I'm so sorry, Miss Lottie, I don't usually raise my voice to folks like dat."

"Don't you even think about apologizin to me, Miss Aggie," Lottie said as she came and sat at her feet. "I cannot imagine what it must be like to be hearin this kind of information. If my babygirl was here, I think I'd just die on the spot to know she was trapped in a world like that."

"What you mean, 'if my babygirl was here?' You and Mr. DuMonde got a daughter, too? I thought you only had Wil."

Lottie sighed and dropped her eyes from Aggie's. "We did have a daughter, a precious little babygirl named Evelyn Rose. After Richard and I had Wil, we tried and tried to have another baby but we couldn't seem to make it work. After almost 10 years of tryin, I finally fell pregnant with a little girl. But she didn't make it. She was born way too early, and she lived for only 5 days. I don't think a day goes by that I don't think about my girl and what she would've been like. If little Evie was alive, she'd be turnin 16 this year; just a little older than your Skye."

"Ooh, honeychile, dat so sad. I'm sorry you had to go through dat. Dey's nuttin like losin a baby...nuttin else dat can cut dat deep. Harold and I tried and tried, too. For years. But nuttin ever took; I just couldn't hold any dem babies in past da first ten weeks. But Macy was my girl, 'specially after her own folks died, and dose girls of hers are my grandkids. Dey not my flesh and blood, but dey's still my girls."

"Yes, I can see that." Lottie reached up and laid her hand on Aggie's knee. "Sometimes the truest family is not blood-born, Miss Aggie, it's heart-born."

"Dat's true, Miss Lottie. You know dat's true."

"Listen, honey, I do want you to hear a glimmer of light about everything. Elle has not been sold *yet*; the auction is not until this Friday afternoon, so there is still time to keep her safe. Scott found many of the details on Jack's laptop, and from readin all his emails, they have a pretty good idea about where in Greece they are and who it is they're lookin for. It's a city called Thessaloniki, and apparently, there is a huge market for girls there."

Aggie took a long drink of water. "Is dat why Jack went all da way over dere?" she asked.

"Wil thinks Greece was just where Jack happened to know someone. It's where he went when he took Skye out of the country, and the emails show he has a friend who knows exactly how to connect him with the right people there. Also, I think I need to tell you that after this trip with Elle, Jack was probably never comin back here again. He mentioned in one email that after he got all his money from...well, from takin Elle over there, he wasn't comin back to the States."

"He just gone leave Macy for dead, wasn't he? After he done used all da money her folks left her, he just gone leave her for dead. He da devil's chile for sure, dat Jack."

"But listen, Aggie, Wil's formulating a plan. Because of the info Jack left in his emails, he's almost 100% sure he'll be able to get to Elle before she disappears. I'm sure it was an oversight for Jack to have left that laptop behind, but still, I'm very surprised at how much detailed information the boys were able to find. Jack didn't delete any of his emails, and many of them are very incriminating; not just about the things he's doing with the girls, but other illegal activities as well."

"Mais, dat *peeshwank* ne'er been da brightest bulb in da bunch. What about my Skye girl?"

Lottie exhaled a long breath. "That's a little more complicated. As far as Skye goes, Wil's goin to do his best to find her in the next few days. He's got some leads, but I can't lie to you; it's still gonna be like tryin to find a needle in a haystack. But even if he doesn't find her while he's there, we won't lose hope...we'll not give up tryin until we do."

"How dat?" Aggie said exasperated. "Even if he do find da girls, how in da world we gone get dem back, all da way from Greece?"

Lottie just smiled at her. "Look at me, Aggie. This is what Wil *does*. In all his years with the SOF, he has strategized dozens of top secret rescue missions in much more dangerous places than Greece. If anyone can do it, it's Wil. We're all goin to be leavin this afternoon on the company jet, and we'll arrive in Greece on Wednesday afternoon. That'll give Wil over 48 hours to put his plan to action."

"Who dat leavin tonight?"

"You, me, Wil and Scott. Once we're in Greece, you and I will check into a hotel, and basically just wait out those two days before we meet back up with Wil. He'll give us the exact time and place to pick up him *and* the girls, and we'll fly right back."

"I can't go with you, Miss Lottie, I don't have a passport. I ain't never been outta United States."

"You *have* to go with us, Miss Aggie. You're the only one those girls know, and they're goin to be in such a state...Honey, you *have* to be in that car when Wil brings them to us; I'm sure you can see that. Elle and Skye are goin to need you from here on out. Don't worry about the passport; that's just a minor detail, and my husband is already workin on it. Jack's not the only one who has connections, and Richard's are far more powerful and influential...not to mention, on the right side of the law. Trust me, you'll have a passport *and* a visa by the time we leave. Scott will be stayin with us the entire time, just in case we need him, and Richard will remain in the States takin care of things here."

"My head's spinnin with all dis."

"You'll have time on the flight to digest it all, but right now, we're on quite a tight time frame. I've arranged for a driver to take you back to your house in Lafayette to pack for the trip. You need to take the time in the car to make a list of any essentials you need to take: medications, vitamins, personal items, and the like. We'll be back by Saturday evening, so you don't need to pack too much, and that girl you met before who showed you to this room, Rebecca; she has a new suitcase for you to use. Also, last night when we talked, you said that the girls would often stay with you, am I rememberin that correctly?"

"*Mais oui.* Dey stay with MawMaw Aggie for weeks on end."

"So then, I'm assuming you have some of their clothes at your house?" Aggie nodded. "Perfect. Please make sure to grab a few outfits for both Skye and Elle. We're just not certain what kind of state they'll be in when we get them, and we'll want to make sure they are as comfortable as possible. Can you do that, too?"

"How you tink of all dese details? I'd never tink about doin dat."

"Oh, honey, I don't know. I just do, that's all."

"Miss Lottie, how'll I ever tank you for all dis? For all dat Mr. DuMonde and Wil are gone do?"

"Aggie, dear, we're family now, and that means from this moment on, we're all in this thing together. Do you understand that? We're *family*. We'll see this thing through to the end, and then Richard and I are gonna help you give both Skye and Elle the kind of life Macy always dreamed she could."

Aggie took a deep breath and mustered a hint of a smile to Lottie.

"Miss Lottie, I'm so sorry I called you crazy."

"Ha!" said Lottie as she stood to help Aggie stand. "I promise you, honey, I've been called worse."

The two women embraced each other for several breaths.

"We're in this together," whispered Lottie.

"We in dis together," Aggie whispered back.

THE DUMONDES

✦ 25 ✦

"Now listen very carefully, Rebecca," Lottie instructed her personal assistant. "You need to take care of anything Ms. Prejean might need. Is the driver here, yet?"

"Yes, ma'am, and I've already had all of Mrs. Prejean's belongings loaded and packed into the car. He's all ready to drive her to Lafayette."

"Good. I want you to call Ms. Prejean every hour, on the hour, to check in and see if she's thought of items she needs for you to pick up and bring to the airport. Also, make sure you are closely in touch with the driver. Did they send us Thomas today?"

"Yes, ma'am, and I have his personal cell number in my phone."

"Wonderful." Then Lottie looked at Aggie. "You're goin to like Thomas. He's one of the best drivers we've got. He likes to chat, but, honey, if you need yourself some quiet time, he's more than happy to give it to you. All you need to do is speak up."

Back to Rebecca, Lottie said, "Did you make sure the car had plenty of food and drinks for Ms. Prejean?"

"Yes, ma'am. Fully stocked."

"Excellent. Miss Aggie, the weather in Greece this time of year is much chillier than what we Southerners are used to—oh, what am I talkin about?—it's been downright freezin here the last week or so! If you pack all the clothes I had Rebecca pick up for you this mornin, along with a nice, warm overcoat, I think you'll be just fine.

"Now, it's just about 9 o'clock right now. You should get to your home by 10:30. Do you think you'll need more than an hour to pack up everything for you and the girls?"

"Dat should be just fine," Aggie said.

"Great. Rebecca, you need to make sure to tell Thomas that he *must* have the car packed and ready to leave Ms. Prejean's home no later than 11:30. Our flight leaves New Orleans at 3:05, and it's going to take about 2½ hours to drive from Lafayette to the airport. Tell him to park in his usual spot at the airport and to escort Ms. Prejean through the terminal, all the way to our jet. Do you have any questions?"

"No, ma'am," Rebecca answered. "I'll text you if anything comes up."

"Good girl." Lottie stepped close to Aggie and put her hand on her shoulder. "Listen, honey, please do not hesitate to call me or Rebecca if you need anything in the next few hours. Otherwise, I'll be at the airport waiting for you." Lottie could see an overwhelmed look on Aggie's face. She moved her hand from Aggie's shoulder to her cheek. "You look at me, Miss Aggie. We're gonna get your girls back. In just two days, you're gonna be snugglin with your grandchildren, one on each side."

Aggie nodded, tears filling her eyes. "Tank you, Miss Lottie."

Lottie gave Aggie a hug, whispered her love for her, and then escorted her toward the door. "You've got to get on the road, honey. Rebecca will take you to the car."

Lottie led the two women out of the room and closed the door softly behind them. Her hand still up on the door frame, she sighed heavily before leaning her head forward to rest against the wooden frame. Only when she was certain Rebecca and Aggie were out of earshot did she allow herself, for the first time since she'd heard the news, to fully release her emotions.

The instant Richard saw his wife's shoulders shaking from her sobs, he arose from the table and was right behind her. His strong arms encircled her, and she clutched onto his arm as he pulled her back against his chest. For moments, they stood embracing, Lottie weeping, Richard softly stroking her hair.

"I just have no words," she whispered in between sobs. "No words to describe how I'm feeling right now. So sad, and scared, and angry."

"I know, Baby," Richard whispered back. "Me, too."

"How could someone do such a wicked thing? To his own flesh and blood? Honey, those girls are just *babies*! It's unthinkable what kind of a person could do something like this."

Having no answers, Richard simply held her tighter and kissed the top of her head.

Both Wil and Scott were still at the table. Scott, sensing the family needed privacy, quietly motioned to Wil that he was going to go back into the sitting room to work more on Jack's laptop. Wil nodded, and Scott exited, silently closing the door behind him.

"Baby, let's go sit down." Richard led Lottie over to the antique loveseat and sat her down next to him. She brought her knees into her chest and melted into him.

Wil grabbed a box of tissues, came over to his parents, and sat down in the rosewood armchair opposite the loveseat. He passed a few tissues to his dad, who slipped them to Lottie. The three sat quietly for several minutes. Finally, Lottie sat up and broke the silence.

"There," she said as she carefully wiped her eyes with the corner of the tissue. "I'm all done with that. Well, for now, at least. We don't have time for me to sit here and cry the day away while those girls are over there needin to be rescued. What needs to be done?"

Richard laughed at the sudden composure of his wife.

"What?" she asked him. "What are you laughin at, Mr. DuMonde?"

"You," he said as he caressed her cheek. "You're a 'Steel Magnolia' through and through."

Lottie smiled up at her husband. "Yes...well...I just can't help it. It's how my mama raised me. She'd always say, 'There's no time for blubberin when there's work to be done!' Now, what time is check out today?"

"We've actually reserved all these rooms until tomorrow, remember?" Richard answered. "So we can take our time and leave whenever we're ready."

"I'm actually going to check out in just a few minutes," said Wil. "I've got to be in Baton Rouge by 10am to meet with some folks who'll be able to give me some insight into the business of sex trafficking."

"Who are you meeting with?" Richard asked.

"Well, interestingly enough, when Scott and I were Googling about human trafficking in Greece, we came across an organization located right in Thessaloniki that is working to rescue as many girls as they can from forced prostitution. It's called A21, and from their website, it looks like they're doing some really amazing work. I'm sure they could be a huge resource for us to be able to draw some intelligence about the in's and out's of the business there.

"Then, as we dug deeper, we found the A21 Campaign has many org's that help sponsor them, and one of them is right here in Baton Rouge. It's called Trafficking Hope."

"Trafficking Hope. Why does that sound familiar to me?" asked Lottie.

"Remember a couple years ago, when I came home in between missions and I asked you about those big highway billboards about sex slavery? They'd just gone up and had that black and white picture of the young girl on it, and there were these stats printed on it that had to do with prostitution and sex trafficking in Louisiana. Do you remember what I'm talking about?"

"Yes, I do remember seein those. There was one up on the way to my spa," she said. "Wow. I'm ashamed to admit it now, but I probably saw that thing a few dozen times, and never *really* thought about what it meant."

"Well, this is them. They're pretty involved with what's happening here in Louisiana, and most importantly for us at this moment, they are linked with the A21 Campaign. I left an urgent message late last night, or should I say early this morning, on their hotline. I gotta tell you, I'm pretty impressed at how quickly they responded. I got a call from a gal first thing this morning and she set up a meeting with me and some of their folks today at 10.

"I'm hoping they'll be able to help me get a better idea of this whole network, as well as give me the contact info for who I need to talk to at the A21 org in Thessaloniki. We're only going to have 48 hours to complete our mission once we get there; I need to connect with as many sources as possible, extract as much info as I can, between now and when we touch down in Greece."

"OK, now, forgive me for askin this, maybe I'm just bein a mama, but I'm sorry, I just need to ask it. Why are we not using our FBI, or our embassy there, or even the Greek police force to find the girls?" Lottie asked. "I mean, for all you know, Wil, you might be steppin into a hornet's nest."

"Mom—" Wil was irritated.

"Well, I'm just sayin. You have no idea the kind of danger you're puttin yourself into."

"For chrissake, Mom, what do you think I've been doin for the last 8 years in the SOF? Playin desert Lazer Tag with a bunch of my buddies?"

"Listen, Son," Richard said sternly. "Don't talk to your mother like that."

"Well, seriously, Dad. I've been face to face with some of the most dangerous Al Qaeda there is and lived to talk about it. Do you honestly think I won't be able to handle a few brothel owners in Greece?"

"First of all, Wil," Richard said, "you don't need to remind us of your resume. Let's not forget I personally nursed you back from the grave from your last mission. And second, let's not downplay the situation here. You're *not* just dealing with a few rinky-dink whorehouses. You know just as well as I do from all the info we've gathered these last several hours, that this trafficking deal is a very sophisticated operation. So you can't be naive to the reality of what you're signing up for."

"Yes, sir," Wil said quietly, looking down at his feet. "I wasn't trying to downplay anything; I'm fully aware what I'm getting into. And, I'm sorry, Mom. I shouldn't have raised my voice at you."

"We love you, Wil; you're our *only* son," Lottie said. "It's not that I don't think you're capable; I know you are more than. But I'm also a mama, so naturally, regardless of how experienced or skilled you might be in this sort of thing, I'm still goin to be worried sick about my son's safety."

"Alright. I get it, Mom. Listen to me." Wil looked back up from the floor and into his mother's eyes. "One thing I've been thinking all night is, what if this was Evie? What if Evie had lived, and been my little sister, and what if she disappeared, and we found out this had happened to her? Do you think that I'd care for even a half of a millisecond about what might happen to me if it was in my power to save her from those bastards?

"Dad, I understand the risk. So do you. And yes, Mom, it's probably going to be dangerous. I may even be risking my life. But how could I live with myself if I passed on this opportunity to help these two girls, who happened to be my own cousins, when I know in my heart I can do this?

"We don't have the time to get our FBI involved. Elle is going to be sold *this* Friday, and by the time we'd talk to our guys here, and they'd get the people mobilized on a mission, it will be too late. Elle will have been sold, and long gone. The American Embassy in Greece isn't going to be able to do anything for us, either, with this kind of time frame. And as far as the Greek police go, Aeton says we just don't have the time to know which of those cops are on the up and up. There's so much corruption in the system, some of the police over there are just as involved as the traffickers."

"Who's Aeton?" asked Richard.

"That's the guy I told you about, my SOF friend in Greece."

"Oh, right, right, right. Got it."

"Wait a minute," said Lottie. "Can you fill *me* in on who Aeton is?"

"Aeton was in the Greek military, a member of their ETA, which essentially is equivalent to our SOF. These guys are the real deal, total machines. Back in March of 2004, about 400 of us SOFs were stationed in Athens to help train some of their ETA forces for the upcoming summer Olympics. Not sure if you remember this, but that was going to be the first summer Olympics since 9/11, and there were fears—internationally, actually—that Bin Laden was planning on using the Olympics in Athens as a platform for his terrorist agenda. We set up a ton of special high-end surveillance systems for them, and helped them all get ready for the event.

"Aeton's platoon and my platoon worked side by side for several weeks, and we became good friends. He left the service last year, and has since gotten married and had a kid. But he's still pretty involved with training the younger guys over there. Anyway, he's going to meet me in Thessaloniki as soon as we land. Really, there'd be no way I'd be able to do this without him. He'll serve as my interpreter, definitely get me into places I'd never be able to find myself, *and* he'll provide the weapons we might need, the stuff I'd never get past airport security."

"Well, now, that's the best piece of news I've heard yet," said Lottie. "I was hopin you'd be packin plenty of heat to take care of those horrible people. You have my permission to shoot every single one of them in the—well, where it would hurt the most."

Wil chuckled a bit. "We'll do whatever we need to do to get the girls. But nothing more. I don't want to cause too much of a commotion so our exit can stay as clean as possible."

"I'm really glad Aeton will be there to help. You make sure you let him know he will be very well compensated for his trouble," said Richard.

"To tell you the truth, Dad," said Wil, smiling. "I kinda already promised him that."

"Good job," Lottie said. "You think just like your father."

Checking his watch, Wil said. "I've really got to head out if I'm going to make it to my 10 o'clock." He called over in the direction of the sitting room. "Hey, Scott! We've got to get to our meeting."

"Oh dear!" said Lottie, standing up to face Scott as he emerged from the side room. "I almost forgot you were in there! How rude of us to be banterin, leavin you cooped up in that sittin room."

"Mrs. DuMonde, you don't need to apologize," said Scott, Jack's laptop in hand. "I knew you guys needed your time to work things out. And as far as what we'll be doing in Greece, don't you worry about a thing, ma'am. Thanks to Jack's loose-lipped emails about where and when the auction will take place, at least half of this mission will be very straight-forward."

"Yes, and thank you for saying that," Lottie said. "After all this is over, I want to make sure and meet your mama. She raised herself a mighty fine young man."

"She'd love to meet you, too, Mrs. DuMonde."

"Come on, Scott, we've gotta go," said Wil, halfway out the hotel room door. "Mom, if we don't see you back at the house getting packed up, then we'll meet you at the airport."

Richard and Lottie watched as the two young men hurried off. Lottie looked down at her husband, still sitting on the loveseat. "Sugar, are you sure we're goin about this the right way?" she asked.

He pulled her down on his lap and hugged her. "I don't know, Babe," he said. "I hope so. I'm not sure we have any other options. One thing is certain, though, and that is this: we've got to try our best to undo the harm that brother of mine has caused."

ELLE

✦ 26 ✦

SOMETHING WAS NOT RIGHT about the beauty contest. At first, Elle assumed that since this pageant was being held in a foreign country, they just did things differently here. But after the past two days of walking all over the city to meet the judges, as well as overhearing Jack's remarks along the way, Elle was beginning to dread having to take part in the event.

First of all, there were more judges for this pageant than Elle had ever seen. The American beauty pageants that she'd watched on television usually had only four or five judges, but this one had at least ten. And that was only the number of judges they were able to meet. Jack told Elle that on the day of the contest, there would be many more judges, probably another dozen or so. That seemed like way too many for something like this. Especially since all the girls had to do was stand on the stage, walk down and back on a little runway, and smile. Apparently none of the contestants needed to talk, to change clothes, to perform a talent, or anything else that was normally done; all they had to do was stand there. Why in the world did there need to be so many judges?

In addition, Elle didn't like any of the judges they had met. It seemed odd to her that almost all of them were men, most of whom spoke in a foreign language and looked at her in an unusual way. Every single one of them made her feel squeamish and uncomfortable. Only one of them was a woman, and she looked like the last person on earth who should be judging a beauty pageant. She was short and stocky, she wore way too much make-up, and her clothes were so tight, Elle could make out every bulge, dimple and pantyline. She had hobbled over on her high, pointy heels to look closely at Elle's face, and when she did, Elle could see that her gross red lipstick had smeared all over her front teeth. And she kept patting Elle on the top of her head like she was a puppy, while she talked in an awful sing-songy way. Even Jack appeared to not like her for some reason, but he had to be nice to her because she happened to own the venue where the contest was taking place.

It was first thing in the morning on the second day of judge-meeting when Elle, her father, and the interpreter had arrived at this woman's performance space. It was weird to Elle because as they had entered the front doors, they passed by a dozen men who were being ushered out. The men looked like they were drunk and acted quite surprised to see the daylight. Elle wondered what they'd been doing in the warehouse-turned-theatre all night.

The interpreter had talked briefly with the big man who guarded the entrance, and after a few sentences, they were given admittance. As they walked in, Elle had heard the interpreter tell Jack that this place only closed down one hour every morning in order to be cleaned, so they didn't have much time to meet the owner before it re-opened.

The entire structure was one spacious main room, lit with strips of fluorescent lights mounted high up on the ceiling. Below those house lights, Elle could see a black grid of stage lights, now turned off, and all of them looked to be focused on the stage areas. She wondered why, even with all the strips of lights illuminated, it still looked so dim in the room, but then she noticed everything was painted black. The walls, the cement floor, the ceiling, and even all the tables and chairs were black. In addition, there were no windows anywhere to be seen. *No wonder those men who were being pushed outside were blinded by the sun,* Elle had thought.

The only other person who was present in the room was an older, hunched-back man who was mopping the floor. The interpreter called to him in another language, and in response, the older man had dropped his mop, shuffling off to go get something. The sounds of the mop's handle hitting the concrete echo-ed through the space.

"He's going to get the old hag," the interpreter had said. "She'll show your girl what she's supposed to do on Friday afternoon. She owns this joint, you know, and then another one a couple blocks over that is much larger than this one. This is just a show club, but the other place she runs is a full service deal. It has everything a guy would want, a huge club, lots of side rooms, and a ton of girls upstairs for whatever you'd like to do."

Elle had wondered what the interpreter meant by that.

"Yeah, yeah, yeah. I've met the bitch before, remember? This is where I came the last time I was here," Jack had answered.

The interpreter thought for a second. "That's right," he said. "And wasn't she the one who actually bought your—"

Jack quickly interrupted with a loud clearing of his throat. "Yeah, but let's not talk about that right now." He had looked over at Elle to see if she'd been listening.

"Got it," the interpreter had said, obviously understanding something Elle did not.

The hunched-back man had returned and hollered something back to the interpreter, after which he picked up his mop and resumed swishing it across the floor. Shortly thereafter, the short, stocky woman came tottering in, her heels clicking on the concrete. She seemed happy to see them, as she over-projected her words to them. Even close up, she had felt it necessary to talk in what MawMaw Aggie would've called her "outside voice."

For several minutes, Jack, the interpreter, and the old woman had talked. Elle wished she understood whatever language the old woman spoke because while her father only talked in low tones, this woman was loud and clear. Perhaps she could've offered Elle some clarity about what exactly this beauty pageant was.

Jack had come back over to where Elle was standing and told her that the old woman was going to take her up on the stage and give her instructions about what she was supposed to do during the contest. He was very firm with Elle, warning her that she had better comply and do whatever the old woman asked of her. He reminded her that not only was this woman one of the judges, but also she owned this place, so Elle needed to do her best to impress her. The intensity of his direction had scared her. The last time he'd said this was days ago when they'd gone to visit that awful doctor. Elle prayed to god that the ugly woman would not ask her to do anything she didn't want to do *or* touch her the way that doctor had.

But everything had turned out alright. The woman had communicated with Elle through the interpreter, sing-songing the entire time, and the only thing she'd done was take Elle up on the stage and show her where she was to stand and walk. The stage was shaped like a "U", with long narrow, curved runways extending from the large center part. She had instructed Elle that on the night of the pageant, Elle was to wait until her number was called, go and stand at the top of the "U" for a few seconds, then walk up and down each of the runways, right first, then left. She then needed to stand again in the center until she was motioned to leave.

In the middle of the black stage wall, there was a door that served as an entrance and exit to the performing space. The woman had told her that there was a room behind that door where Elle would wait with the other contestants until it was her turn to go.

And that was it. The lipstick-smeared old woman had patted her on the head, said a few more words to the men, waved her fat, wobbly arm with motions that it was time for them to leave, and then had hobbled off in the same direction from which she came.

Now, as Elle sat alone in the hotel room, once again brooding over the details of their stay, from the time they'd arrived until this moment, she felt a foreboding in her heart that had not been there before. She knew she couldn't deny the fact anymore that something was very wrong. But what exactly that 'something' was, she didn't know.

The one thing she was certain of, if she was truly honest with herself, was that since they'd left Louisiana, she hadn't felt safe. Her dad was turning out to be someone she did not like at all, definitely not someone she could trust. And the people they'd met hadn't made her feel good on the inside either. Sure, many of them had been complimentary, but not in a way that made Elle feel comfortable. Again, she didn't know why, she just knew they seemed sneaky somehow, or like they all knew a secret that she didn't...and they weren't about to let her in on it.

But what can I do? I know I can't talk to Dad, she thought. *Even if I felt like I could, what would I say? I'm not even sure what is wrong, or why I feel so scared.*

The only thought that brought relief was the image of seeing Skye again, and that was going to happen in just a few more days. She couldn't wait to jump into her arms and hug her. She imagined she'd probably cry like a baby and embarrass Skye in front of her school friends, if they were there, but Elle didn't care. Just thinking about it now made Elle want to cry. But instead, she chose to comfort herself with the thoughts of being with her big sister again. They'd talk about all the wonderful things Skye had been up to at her new school, they'd go see all the fun places she and her friends hung out, and they'd laugh and have fun just like they used to.

All Elle had to do was make it through the next couple days. And then she'd be with Skye, and everything would be OK.

MOLLY VENZKE

GALEN & SKYE

✞ 27 ✞

GALEN WAS DETERMINED TO GET THE GIRL TO TALK. This would be his fourth night with her, and there was just no way he was going to be able to sustain these all-night meetings. Not only was he exhausted, but more importantly, he was running out of money. The evening before, he had had every intention of trying to communicate with her, but his fatigue had gotten the best of him. Once he was escorted to her room, he'd made the choice to give the girl a bit of time to adjust to his presence, so he'd sat down in his usual chair for a while.

He waited too long, however, because he'd fallen asleep and before he knew it, morning had come and the ugly, fat, lipstick-smeared wench was knocking on the door. Galen hated that bitch. The sound of her knocking startled him so much, he nearly fell out of the chair and blew his cover. As the old woman had opened the door, Galen played it off like he'd simply lost his balance while tying his shoe, and he was fairly certain she'd bought the facade. And because it had all happened so quickly, Galen barely had the time to check to see if the girl was even awake. Luckily, she was sitting up in her bed, once again giving him a bewildered look. He'd left that morning feeling totally defeated that absolutely no progress had been made to help that girl.

Galen was now in the taxi, on his way to the brothel, and was feeling the pressure of time. He was worried the old woman was going to catch on, and he couldn't afford that. *What in the hell would that ugly whore do if she found me out?* he thought. *I wouldn't put anything past her, seeing as she sells girls like slaves. If she feels no remorse about doing that, then torture or murder can't be beneath her either! Somehow, I've got to get that girl to talk to me, or at the very least, communicate with me through hand motions or something. And it has to be tonight.*

Galen hadn't worked out exactly how he was going to get her out of there, or what he was going to do with her once he did, but at the very least, he needed to get some information from her. Maybe once he knew a bit about her story, the exact strategy would fall into place.

The girl still didn't trust him, which Galen completely understood, so this night, he decided to do everything he could to help her relax, and hopefully, talk. The best way he knew to do this was through food. Not to mention, the girl appeared way too skinny; he thought she'd probably not had a good meal since she'd been there.

That morning before he was leaving for school, Galen had asked his mum to cook a bunch of extra food for him to eat while he was working his so-called "night-shift" job. And to really get her to show off, he'd told her one of his workmates was a German who'd been mouthing off about his disappointment with Greek cuisine. Galen knew those comments would spur his mum to cook her best dishes, because nobody could make Greek food as good as she did; everyone in town knew that. And anyone who didn't, his mum would be on a mission to convince them of this undeniable truth. Galen was sure if he could just get this girl to eat some of his mum's dishes, she'd realize he was not there to harm her, maybe even start to trust him.

True to form, his mum had packed an ample amount of *spanakopites* (baked spinach and feta cheese puffs), *moussaka* (the national dish of Greece), and *koulouria*, her melt-in-your-mouth butter cookies. She'd timed it out so the food would be coming fresh out of the oven right at the time Galen had to leave, and she'd put the food in individual plastic boxes, servings for both Galen and his

German workmate. And in an effort to keep the meal warm for as long as possible, she'd enveloped them in copious amounts of aluminum foil.

Galen then wrapped the packaged meal in a small fleece blanket and put the whole thing in his orange backpack. He thought it best to try and keep the food's smell contained so that once he'd entered the brothel, the old woman didn't get suspicious, or ask why he was bringing in so much food.

He also decided to pack a small, folded map of the entirety of Europe. He hoped that even if he could simply get the girl to point to the country from which she came, he'd be able to start formulating a way to get her back home to her family. *I wonder if she has any family to speak of?* he thought. *Have they been looking for her this entire time, wondering if she is dead or alive? I can't even imagine what it would be like to have my sister lost like that. Mum would die from worry, and Pop would be unbearable to live with.*

Galen felt his taxi come to a sudden halt, and he knew he'd arrived at the brothel. He checked his watch and was surprised to see he was almost fifteen minutes late! He paid the driver, grabbed his backpack, and started into the club. By this time, the bouncers recognized him as a frequenter and let him right into the building without having to pay the entrance fee. He quickly pushed his way through the crowded room toward the red iron spiral staircase, and bounded up two steps at a time in hopes he would get to the brothel entrance before the old woman let anyone else into the girl's room.

When he got to the second floor and saw the waiting room was vacant, his chest began to feel tight. He could hear the hobbling clicks of the old woman's heels going down the hallway, talking to someone, most assuredly a customer. He wanted to run down the hall to make sure the wench didn't let that man get to his girl, but he knew he couldn't appear as if he cared that much. He paced back and forth, feeling like he was going to jump out of his skin as he waited for the owner to come back.

The minutes stretched on, feeling more like hours, until finally, Galen chose to sit down in one of the waiting chairs. The orange backpack full of food was getting heavy, not to mention, the heat from its contents was beginning to bore into his back. He slouched over, head in his hands, and felt his perspiration slide across his face and drip off his nose. He was completely unaware of how hot he'd gotten, running through the club and up the stairs.

For chrissake, I bet I look awful! he thought. He scanned the room looking for a mirror or anything reflective for him to use so he could check himself out. There was nothing of the sort on the old, cracked walls, just random cardboard posters of naked girls. *I bet with all that makeup she heaps on her face the old wench has a mirror in her desk.* And for an instant, Galen considered rifling through her drawers, but knew he could not risk getting caught. Instead, he simply wiped his face off with his shirtsleeves and ran his fingers through his hair.

"Ooooh, it's you, Love!" the old woman said in her grating voice as soon as she reappeared from the hallway. "I wasn't sure you'd be coming here again tonight."

Galen: *(standing quickly)* Why would you think that? I told you this morning I'd be back tonight, didn't you hear me? You didn't give my girl to someone else, did you? Because if you did—

Woman: *(interrupting)* Now, now, now, calm yourself down, Love, I promised you I'd keep your girl for you. *But* I might not continue being so nice to you if you don't come through on your end of the bargain.

Galen: What do you mean, my end of the bargain?

Woman: You promised me that you'd be bringing in business with you, if I kept your girl nice for you. Tonight it's your fourth time here, and I still don't see any of your so-called big spenders.

Galen: *(trying to laugh it off)* You don't need to worry about that at all! What I said was that I needed to know I could trust you to have the right kind of girls ready for us. And I think it's safe to say that you've proven yourself worthy. Believe me, I've been talking this place up to all my buddies. In fact, this very weekend, I have about a dozen guys planning to come with me. Is *that* enough for you? Or should I say, are you sure you can even handle that many? I mean, this place *is* kind of small.

The garish woman did not take kindly to his condescension. She suddenly became serious, almost ominous, as she looked steadily up into Galen's eyes. Her piercing gaze was filled with such evil, Galen felt a chill run through his body. Never before had he looked into the soul of one so filled with steely darkness.

Woman: *(cocking one eyebrow)* Don't insult me, my sweet boy. You've been so smitten with your little piece of a** in there that you haven't even looked around at all this club has to offer. There's two more areas just like this in here; one on the other end of the club, and another underneath in the basement. Love, I've got more than enough pleasure for *three* dozen of your tiny little man-boys...and then some. And, I might add, this place of heaven is only *one* of the clubs I own on this strip.

Galen: Wow. I'm sorry, I didn't know that.

Woman: And another thing, *all* of my girls are just as pretty as your tight little whore in there, so you don't need to get yourself in a rut. I've even got some who are younger than her...not that you'll ever have one of them. *(giggle-snorting)* Those girls are way out of *your* price range, boy. I keep them saved for my very special clients, the kind that lose more money than *you're* spending each night in the time it takes them to piss.

Galen sensed his cheeks flushing at the intense arrogance being thrown up by this short, fat old broad. He was beginning to understand just how out-of-his-league he was, in the bowels of this shady underworld. Fear began to stew in his gut.

Woman: Now, now, little man, don't let yourself get down about it, if you get my meaning. *(patting his chest and smiling at her own wit)* I'm sure that once you're all grown, you'll be able to enjoy the creme de la creme, too. For now, you've got a pretty little girl waiting for you to have your way with, all night long...you're paying for the entire shift, right?

Galen: *(attempting to hide his uneasiness)* Yes, I am. Wouldn't want it any other way, if *you* get my meaning. Let me go get my bag, and I'll be ready to go.

Woman: *(noticing the orange backpack)* What do you have there, boy? Are you thinking of trying something kinky? Because if you are, there's an extra charge for that.

Galen: No, I'm not into weird. I gotta be somewhere in the morning, so I brought my stuff with me.

Woman: Fine, fine. *Other men were now starting to enter the brothel, causing her to lose interest in Galen. She waved her arm at him to go down the hallway.* You know the way, Love, I've already unlocked her door many minutes ago. I can't be bothered with you; I've got these gentlemen to take care of. Give me your money and be on your way.

Galen was a bit taken aback that she wasn't going to escort him down to the girl's room, but he welcomed her absence as he grabbed his backpack, handed her his cash, and started down the narrow hallway. The old hag was far shrewder and more calculating than he'd given her credit, and she was not going to buy his lies for much longer. He had to get the girl to talk, and it had to be tonight.

❦ 28 ❦

THE WITCH HAD ONCE AGAIN LEFT the door slightly ajar. Skye studied the two inch opening, desperately wishing she could walk through it and break free. It would take about three steps for Skye to leave her jail cell, but in her heart, she knew it might as well be three million. She'd only be caught, thrown back inside, and whipped or beaten for her audacity to escape.

And now, her imprisonment was worse than ever. With the clarity of mind these last few days of rest had given her, Skye's consciousness of her situation had only become more vivid. Before the guy who only sat in the chair had started coming, at least her fatigue and pain would sometimes give her the gift of delirium to make it through the horror of each night. Not that she would trade the last few days of peace for anything in the world, but now that she'd experienced them, how was she to endure this place once the guy stopped coming? Certainly, his visits would stop soon, and then what? She'd have to go back to servicing dozens of men a night...only this time with a sharper awareness of their sour odors and their hideous hands.

The thought was unbearable. *No,* Skye vowed. *I'm not going to do it anymore. I've got to find a way to end this.* She looked around her room to see what her choices would be if she could finally muster up enough courage for suicide. There were no sharp objects at her disposal, and the witch surely never brought anything like that in with her meals. So unless she could figure out a way to make a knife, cutting herself was not an option.

There is a lamp here that's plugged into the wall. If I broke the bulb, would it be sharp enough to cut me? Or, I could try to electrocute myself. But the thought of that option made Skye shudder, and she doubted she would ever have the guts to actually do something like that. *Besides, what if there wasn't enough electricity and it didn't work all the way? That would be worse than dying.*

She glanced down at her bed. *Maybe I could tear my sheets somehow and make a rope to hang myself?* And she looked up at the ceiling to see if there was any kind of hook or bar that could support her weight. But the ceiling was smooth, and had nothing at all that would work. She then noticed the bars on the window. *Those would be strong enough,* she thought, *if they are high enough.*

Skye walked over to the window to get a closer look. At the tops and bottoms of the bars, there was about one inch of each bar that jutted out horizontally before the metal curved to its vertical length. *If I was able to secure the rope just right at the top so it doesn't slip down as my weight drops, this just might work.*

She felt the top of the bar to find out how slippery it was. Because the bars were so old and rusted, they felt very rough and prickly. She was pretty convinced there was enough texture for the sheet to stay in place. *It's not that very high up, so the noose part can't be very long, but if I make it just right...*

Skye was surprised at herself; how resolute and calm she was as she stood there, planning out her own death. She looked down at her charm bracelet that she still clutched in her hand. She replayed Aggie's words in her mind once again:

"You see dat birdcage? It's beautiful, but it's empty, just as a birdcage should be," Aggie had said. "And dis petite bird? Dat's your pet egret you've always wanted to catch, Sha. She's flyin free, never ever to be put inside any kinda cage. Dat's you, Skye-girl. You a beautiful bird dat le Bon Dieu put on dis earth to fly da open sky with your dreams. You can't never let yo'self be caught in

any cage, you hear me? You a bird, Sha. And you gone soar up as high as your dreams can take you.

While deep down she knew MawMaw never meant for her to interpret the bracelet like this, she felt killing herself would be the only way she'd ever be able to experience the freedom of that little silver bird. And isn't that what MawMaw would want for her anyway? She'd said it herself: Skye was never meant to be put inside any kind of cage.

Tomorrow, Skye promised herself. *As soon as this night's over with, and I'm locked back in my room, I'm going to do it.*

Skye heard the door creak open and she turned to see who it was. It was the guy who'd been coming the last few nights, but oddly, the witch was not with him. Plus, he'd brought what looked like an orange bookbag with him. *What is that?* she thought. *Is he going to sit in here all night and read?! This is getting really weird.*

She crossed over to her bed, slipped her bracelet under her pillow, and sat down, waiting to see whether or not this guy was finally going to make his move. Either way, it didn't matter to her. She already was feeling a power of freedom, knowing that this hell would soon be coming to an end.

The girl was different tonight; Galen noticed it immediately. Her countenance had a calm that he'd not seen these last few nights, and when she looked at him, she actually held eye contact for longer than a moment. He wondered if she had decided to trust him at last?

He set down his backpack and sat in his chair. He was still feeling the sting of the brothel owner's words; the words that to Galen, seemed much more like a veiled threat than idle chatter. *I wonder if that old bitch is on to me?* he thought. He slouched over as he ran his fingers through his hair once again. His stomach rumbled with hunger, as he hadn't had the time to eat before he'd left. He looked back at the girl.

Why does she seem so different? he wondered. *Usually, she lays on her bed trembling, keeping her eyes glued to me like a hawk, at least until she falls asleep. She's just sitting there picking the threads at the edge of her sheet. Maybe she's finally feeling comfortable with me? Well, as comfortable as is possible in a place like this.*

He thought now was as good a time as ever to talk to her.

"Listen," he said in a low voice. "I know you don't understand what I'm saying right now, but I'm going to talk to you anyway. We've got to find a way to get you out of this place. I'm not going to be able to keep coming and staying here all night long. So you've got to help me out and tell me where you're from."

The girl looked at him while he was talking, and she didn't seem to be getting afraid at his words, so Galen took that as a good sign. Granted, the look on her face wasn't the most inviting, but at least she wasn't curled up in a ball, frightened. He wondered what she'd do if he approached her.

But when he stood up and faced her, he saw her jump a bit and push herself slowly against the wall. He definitely did not have her trust yet. *Maybe once I give her the food, she'll realize I'm on her side, that I'm truly not going to do anything to harm her.* He picked up his backpack and started to unpack it.

"I brought you some food. You look like you could use a good meal." Galen felt silly talking to a girl who couldn't understand a word he said, but he thought that if he spoke with a gentle tone, she'd feel more comfortable to try and communicate back. "I had my mum make us some food; it's really good Greek food. Nobody cooks better than my mum, and I know you'll like it. You've probably not had anything good to eat in this place."

He took the container of the *spanakopites* over to the girl and tried to hand it to her. She just squinted her eyes at him, obviously perplexed, and wouldn't reach out to receive his gift. Galen sighed in frustration.

"OK, I get it. You probably never had a guy come in here and offer you a home-cooked meal. Maybe if you see me eat it, you'll know it's safe. This right here is *spanakopites*, and you'll love them. They're little puffy pastries with spinach and feta." He set down the container, along with a fork and napkin, on the edge of her bed. Then we went back to get the rest.

"This is *moussaka*. It's kind of a mixture of eggplant and meat and noodles, something like an Italian lasagna, but far better. It's pretty much known as the national food of Greece. And this little bag has my mum's famous *koulouria*. It's her own secret recipe, and these cookies will melt in your mouth." And with that, he popped one in his mouth and said, "mmmmmm," hoping that his response would give her the impetus to try one.

No luck. The girl just sat there looking at the food, showing no desire to eat any of it.

"Well, I'm hungry," said a disappointed Galen, "so I'm going to eat before it gets colder than it already is." And he sat down in his chair and started to eat his food. He could sense her eyes on him, which caused him to feel hyper-aware of himself, so he shifted his posture so that his profile was to her. *I guess I was wrong. She doesn't trust me any more than she did three days ago,* he thought.

Many uncomfortable minutes passed as Galen ate his meal, all the while strategizing what to do next. *I can't let the night get away from me, like I did last night. I'm just going to have to confront her and try to convince her to tell me where she's from.*

Skye was utterly confused. *Who is this guy and why is he bringing me food? Why would he do something like that; he doesn't even know me? Does he feel guilty about what he's about to make me do, and so he's giving me some kind of peace offering first? Well, good. Let him feel guilty. I'm not going to eat a single bite of that, no matter how good it smells. All that will do is make him think he's done me a favor and that now I owe him one.*

She tried to distract herself away from the man by focusing her energies on pulling apart the edge of her sheet. She knew once she got a good rip going, it would be easy to tear the material down the length of the sheet into thin enough strips to make a rope. *If I can manage to make tears all along the end of this, about two inches apart, then once the witch leaves me alone for the day tomorrow, it'll take no time at all to shred this sucker to pieces.* Impatient for progress, Skye began using her teeth to bite through the hem.

The guy had finished eating, and was rustling through his orange backpack. He pulled out a little brochure and began to unfold it. Skye realized it was actually a map of some kind. As soon as he had it open, he walked over to her bed.

Oh, dear god, this is going to be it. He's finally got his nerve. Skye stopped chewing on her sheet and sat frozen on her bed. Empowered by the confidence that this was going to be her last night in the brothel, she began contemplating whether or not she should fight him off. *No*, she decided. *Just go along with whatever he wants. The last thing you want right now is to anger the witch.*

She closed her eyes, took a deep breath, and waited for the guy to touch her. She heard the sound of him moving the food containers onto the floor, no doubt to make room for himself next to her. But instead of feeling the bed sink with his weight, she heard the crinkling of the map as he smoothed it out on the mattress.

He began talking to her, gesturing to the map. Skye's eyes opened wide, not knowing how she was supposed to react. His expression was clear that he wanted her to respond, but she had no idea what he had said or what she should say in return. He spoke again, this time more agitated, pointing again to the map. Skye looked down and realized he'd brought with him a map of Europe. *What?* she thought. *What does he want me to do with that map?*

The guy stood up and began to pace the room, ruffling his fingers through his hair. He was visibly upset about something, and Skye was becoming more and more nervous about the situation. *This guy could be a loose cannon, or he could be crazy. I don't want him to freak out on me. That'll only make the witch come in here and beat me when I'm so close to being done with this place.*

He suddenly stopped pacing and turned directly to her. He spoke again, this time slower and more pronounced, or so it seemed to Skye. It didn't matter, though, because she still had no way of knowing what the guy was saying. He made a slight grunt of frustration, which made Skye jump a bit, but even so, he didn't let up. He strode to her bed, got on his knees, and leaned into her so that his nose was almost touching hers. Very intensely this time, he spoke again right in her face, his dark green eyes staring deeply into hers. When he stopped talking, he remained close to her face, unwilling to budge until she gave him whatever it was he wanted.

She began shaking from his confrontation, feeling helplessly cornered. Not since she'd been here had she been face to face like this with anyone. She'd never allowed herself to make eye contact with a single one of those men. But now, she found her eyes glued to his, unable to break away from his passionate gaze. She felt as if he was prying into her soul, and more vulnerable than ever before.

Desperate for him to back off, her face trembled and her eyes filled with tears as she whispered, "What do you want from me?"

At her words, his eyes popped open and he stared at her in amazement as he gasped and sat back on his knees. A long moment passed. Only their breaths could be heard above the deep bass rhythm vibrating from the club below.

"Are you American?" he finally whispered...in English.

It was Skye's turn to gasp as she heard the language of her home spoken to her, by someone other than the witch, for the first time in months. Her hands went up to her face, and overwhelmed with emotion, she began to cry.

"Please, you tell me, are you American?" he whispered again.

With her face still buried in her hands, all Skye could do was nod her head and weep. She then pulled her knees up to her chest, wrapped her arms around her legs and bowed her body into a ball.

She could hear the young man folding the map, then standing himself up. He walked over to his backpack and put the map away. He then came back to her and knelt on the floor next to the bed.

"My name is Galen," he said in a very thick accent. "Sorry, my English, not so good, but enough for to talk. I promise I will not harm you. I want for to get you out of this terrible brothel."

With those words, Skye melted to her side on the mattress, uncontrollably weeping. She buried her face in her pillow to try and muffle her loud groans of emotional release.

"It's OK," Galen said softly. "You cry. I wait here until you ready to talk."

Just then, Galen thought he heard something just outside the bedroom door. He glanced over to Skye to see if she'd heard it, too, but she was still crying. Speeding over to the door, he pressed his ear against it to try and hear if someone was out there. The only sound he heard was the old woman's heels clicking down the hallway.

MOLLY VENZKE

LOTTIE & SCOTT

❧ 29 ❧

"Wil, don't you think you should try to sleep a little bit before we land in Greece?" Lottie asked her son. "If you start now, you'll still have two hours before we touch down."

Not looking up from his ipad, Wil said, "I'll sleep on the flight back."

"Wil, that's two days from now—"

Still engrossed in his computer, "Once the girls are safe, and we're all on our way home, I'll sleep."

"Wil—"

Finally meeting her eyes, "Please stop being 'mom' right now. I've got a mission to accomplish, and you've gotta know, this is how I roll." And he went back to his ipad, swiping from page to page and rehearsing his strategy.

Lottie stood still for a moment, wanting to say more, but instead she chose to edit herself and return to her seat. Scott, who was sitting opposite Wil, excused himself to get something to drink. He stopped by Lottie's seat and asked if he could get her a snack or a beverage. Keeping her gaze outside the airplane window, she said, "Not right now, Scott. Thank you very much."

Scott walked to the serving station and opened the small fridge, helping himself to a Coke and a single serving tray of fruit and cheese. He took his snack back to the seat across from Lottie, and sat down.

"Miss Charlotte, this jet is like nothing I've ever seen," Scott said. "Do you always travel in planes like these?"

"Oh, sugar, not *always*," she answered. And then she chuckled, "My daddy's jet is even larger than this one."

Scott laughed. "What in the world was it like growing up around so much money? Before today, I've only seen the view from a seat in coach."

"I don't know, honey. I can't really say what it's been like because I've never known anything other," she said. "But I will tell you this: it's times like these that I thank the good Lord in heaven that he's chosen to bless us." Her face became quite serious. "Scottie, I can't stop thinkin about what would've happened had Miss Aggie not come to find us. And then when we eventually *did* hear about the girls—once it was too late—how would we have felt that we had it in our power to help them, but were never given the chance? It makes me sick to my stomach just thinkin about it."

"Well, to be honest, ma'am, from my perspective of growin up in the inner-city projects, I've seen plenty of folks who have the money and *are* given the chance, and still don't do a single thing to help someone else in need."

Lottie looked at Scott for a moment. She smiled and said, "That's very true, Scott. And I'm ashamed to say that I'm sure my own family, as well as Richard and me, have seen those needs time and time again but chose to look the other way."

"Please, Miss Charlotte," Scott quickly replied. "You have to know that I wasn't referring that toward you guys at all. You're some of the most generous people I've ever met."

"Thank you, honey, but you've just known us for a few years. I'd be lyin if I said we've always acted the way we do today. In fact, when I look back, it's quite clear that Richard and I took very good care of ourselves, and of Wil, before we ever thought about helpin any of the folks around us. Why, it wasn't until we all experienced Katrina that Richard and I opened up our eyes to the people who needed help, and who were right under our noses. I mean, it's not like we were ignorant to them; we knew the needs were there, but...I don't know...we were too busy buildin our own deal. And even after the hurricane, while it might be true that we've given large amounts of money to help people, all of that was still only out of our abundance. It's not like any of that givin caused us worry about where our next meal was comin from.

"No...It's not until you meet someone like Miss Aggie that you come face to face with true generosity. I bet that woman has spent her whole life givin and servin and helpin people, even when it was her last roll of quarters. And no doubt, she'll keep on givin 'til her last dyin breath. That's just the kind of woman she is. And what makes her even more special is that she does the things she does, just because it's the right thing to do. It's not for any type of public recognition; you can tell she couldn't care less about anything like that. She'll just keep lovin on the folks around her, and in the end, at least in the big scheme of things, hardly anyone will ever know her name."

The two sat for a few minutes thinking about what had just been said. Scott broke the silence.

"Speaking of Miss Aggie, I haven't seen her for the last several hours. Where is she?"

"She's asleep in the cabin bedroom."

"What?" Scott asked. "This jet has a *bedroom*?"

"Didn't Wil show you around before we took off?"

"Hell no! Oh, pardon me, Miss Charlotte; I mean, heck no." Lottie waved her hand at him as if to say, 'Don't worry about it.' Scott continued, "Ma'am, you've seen him today; he's in ranger mode. Giving a tour of the aircraft is the last thing on his mind."

"Yes. Well, you see that door over there? That's a small cabin with a nice bed in it. After we ate, I urged Miss Aggie to go in there and sleep. The woman is simply exhausted, so much so, she isn't even aware how much. I'm glad she agreed, because it's goin on six solid hours that she's been in there sleepin. I'm sorry that boy of mine forgot his manners and didn't give you a chance to take a look around the jet."

Scott laughed at her comment. "I hate to break the news to you, Miss Charlotte, but your son's never been one to play host *or* to mind his manners when there's something important to be done."

"Well now, thank you Scott," she said, as she winked at him. "Now I'll go to my grave knowin I completely failed as a good Southern mama."

"Wow, I'm just putting my foot in my mouth every time I'm opening it, aren't I?"

"I'm just teasin you, sugar. Wil's just like his father; when there's a job at hand, he's all work and no play."

"And that's exactly why you don't need to worry about whether or not the guy gets any rest. I've operated with a lot of soldiers, and Wil's the best there is. I've seen him go 5 days straight on basically no sleep at all and still stay the sharpest man on the team. He's a beast when it comes to things like this."

"Thank you, Scott," said Lottie, managing a smile. "Even so, it's impossible for me to stop worryin. Especially after his last mission."

"Nothing about that day could've been prevented, ma'am. Those bastards came out of nowhere. I'm sure this won't be anything like that, not to mention that Wil has done an amazing amount of work in these last 24 hours to ensure that it won't be."

"I've barely gotten him to say two words about what his plan is once we touch down. Can you tell me anything? Anything at all? Like, how did your meetin go with the Trafficking Hope people in Baton Rouge? Did you get the information you needed? Were they able to help you get connected with that organization in Greece? Once we get there, do you know who you're lookin for? Where you're going? How you're gonna get find Skye?—"

"Whoa, whoa, whoa," said Scott, chuckling at her barrage of questions. "Slow down a minute, Miss Charlotte."

"I'm sorry, sugar. But my son hasn't told me a *thing*!"

"O.K. I'll do my best to let you in on what I know. You realize, I'll be staying with you and Miss Aggie, right? So Wil hasn't given me all the details of what he's planning, but here's what I've gathered so far: I was at the meeting with the team from Trafficking Hope. They were very knowledgeable about the entire issue, even about how much this kind of thing is going on right now in Louisiana. You'll be shocked to hear some of the stories they told us about little girls being trafficked right in New Orleans, but I won't go into any of that right now. I know Wil is planning on sharing all that with you once we get back to the States. He wants to connect you with the Trafficking Hope team because he said the work they are doing is right up your alley.

"Anyway, they hooked us up with A21, the organization we found on the internet the other night. Turns out, the two org's are very closely linked with each other, and they gave us the numbers we needed to contact the right people on their staff. The A21 guy there in Greece was able to shed light on how the sex industry is structured in Thessaloniki, and how to approach the people involved. We gave him the addresses we got from Jack's emails, and he told us the area Jack is targeting is primarily a part of the red light district that mostly services the Greeks.

"This was really good to know, because Wil probably would've just gone in there and tried to gather intelligence, not realizing that the fact he was American would deter anyone from talking to him. A lot of the brothels there turn away foreigners, and if you don't speak Greek, they usher you right on out. Now in the areas that are newer and more urban, this isn't the case, but where we think Elle is being sold, it is. That's where Wil's friend, Aeton, will be absolutely *key*. Remember, Aeton is the soldier he met when he was over for the Olympics in Greece. Honestly, I don't know what we'd've done without that contact. He's going to be our ticket in to those brothels."

"If that is true, then how did Jack get on the inside of their circle?" asked Lottie.

"We don't know for sure. His contact must either be Greek, or have some very good friends who are. We're not going to know for sure until we get Jack."

"And once we get him, he's gonna rot to death in a snake infested jail cell, right?"

"Let's hope so," said Scott. "Now...Once we touch down, I'll be taking you and Miss Aggie to the Electra Hotel, but Wil's gonna hit the ground running. Aeton'll get Wil from the airport, and it's possible that we won't see him again until our pick up time Friday afternoon. I'll be in touch with him via cell, and maybe even meeting him if he needs something, but you need to know that until he's got the girls in hand, you might not be seeing him."

Lottie sighed deeply. "Thank you for tellin me that. That's good information for me to have, for sure. Do you know *exactly* how he plans to rescue the girls? How is he gonna get Elle out of that auction? And how in the world is he goin to find Skye?"

"Miss Charlotte, a mission like this isn't that cut and dried. It'll be very organic, even from hour to hour, because while we have a great foundation of intelligence, there still are many variables at work. But no one thinks better on his feet than Wil. He's a genius.

And if Aeton is as good as Wil has said, then you've got a dream team going in after those girls."

Just then, Scott noticed Wil. He looked at Lottie and then nodded his head in the direction of Wil. She glanced over her shoulder at Wil's seat. She smiled when she saw that he'd set his ipad down on the table in front of him and reclined his chair. He was sleeping.

"Well, it looks like he obeyed you after all," Scott said in a low voice.

"Yes, but you'd better not tell him that," she answered. And as Scott stood up to return to his seat, she added, "And don't you dare wake him up!"

GALEN

✝ *30* ✝

HER NAME WAS SKYE.

Galen couldn't have been happier that he finally knew her name, and even better than that, she was an American! No doubt her government would work quickly to get her back home, once he was able to get her out of that terrible place and take her to the proper authorities. He smiled at the thought, as his taxi drove him to what he knew would be his last visit at the brothel. After all these nights, and so much of his money, he finally was going to be able to help her escape. His heart raced just picturing her running away from the brothel.

It will all be worth it, Galen thought. *All the risk, all the money I spent, and whatever backlash I get from my parents because of it. Every bit of it will be worth knowing she is safe. And that she will be from now on.*

The night before had not been easy. He understood why she would be so hesitant to trust anyone, but as the hours went by, he had started to worry that the morning would come before he'd convinced her to let him help her. It took much time and many gently spoken words for Skye to begin to open up. In fact, it wasn't until he began to explain his plan for her escape that she finally shared her story with him.

She had told him she didn't know exactly how long she'd been in the brothel, but her guess was less than one year, maybe as little as six months. She was from America, a state called Louisiana, and her father had brought her here and sold her. Her face had turned to hate as she mentioned her father. He'd told everyone that he was taking her to London to attend a special, advanced high school, but when they arrived in Greece, he'd made her take part in a beauty pageant. Only it wasn't a pageant at all; it was a place where people came to buy girls. After giving this information, Skye had closed back up, refusing to disclose anything else. But Galen could fill in the rest of the details on his own.

He'd told her she didn't need to talk anymore, and he offered her the food again. "Please eat," he'd urged her. "You need strength for tomorrow."

At last, she received the food, and when she had bit into the *spanakopites*, her face had lit up, almost to a smile. After her first taste, Skye didn't need any more encouragement to eat every last bit of the food Galen's mum had made. While she ate, he shared with her his plan for her escape.

He would bring his backpack again, only this time, it would be filled with an extra set of clothes, a pair of his sister's jeans, and a shirt that would be exactly the same as the one he'd be wearing. Once he got to her room, they'd wait a couple hours before they put the plan into action. Skye would put on the clothes, stuff her hair into his cap, take the orange backpack, and pose as him as she left the brothel.

He very clearly had described her exit, drawing out on a piece of paper exactly where she needed to go. She'd have to keep her head down, and walk quickly down the hallway, descend the red spiral staircase, pass through the strip club below and go out the door. Galen had taken Skye to her barred window and pointed out to her a large hedge of bushes by the sidewalk, a few short blocks up. He knew he needed to pick a hideout that could clearly be seen from Skye's window so that there would be no question about the exact location. Once she'd made it outside, she was to turn left, walk up two blocks, and crawl inside the bushes to wait until he met her.

Galen would watch from her window to make sure she made it to the hedge safely. Then, he would wait another hour or so to leave himself. He told Skye he'd stay until he was sure the old woman was working with another customer, and dart out then. He'd quickly run to the bushes, let her know he was there, and hail a cab. As soon as the cab stopped, Skye would come out of her hiding place, and they'd both ride safely to his house. Finally, once they were at Galen's home, she'd be able to telephone whomever she needed, and they'd begin the process of getting her home to America.

The look on Skye's face when he'd gotten to the end of his plan and had said "then you'll be on your way home to Louisiana," was indescribable. She looked almost angelic to Galen, as this was the first time he'd seen her face illuminated with such hope. Her expression faded quickly, however, as her own fear and doubts crept in.

Galen did his best to squelch her doubts. He'd taken her hands softly in his and whispered to her, "No fear. I help you get out. I promise to god." She'd nodded her head, and Galen could sense she really wanted to believe in him.

And he could relate with her, because he was working hard to believe in himself, too. He could feel his own uncertainties about what he was about to do. He was terrified at the thought of what would happen—to them both—if his plan did not work. What if the owner caught Skye as she tried to leave disguised? Or for some reason came back in the room to find only Galen? Or, what if Skye was not emotionally stable enough to handle the full exit? Would they beat her? Kill her? Kill him?

"Isn't this the place?" the taxi driver said loudly.

Galen hadn't even realized the car had stopped, or that the cabbie had been talking to him. He looked out the window and felt his stomach churn at the sight of the club. Part of him wished he'd never seen this place, never encountered this underworld, and never began to care so deeply for the young girl trapped inside.

"This is it," said Galen, as he paid the man his fare. He grabbed his backpack and stretched his legs out of the cab. "At least tonight'll be my last time ever to set foot inside a place like this."

He walked into the front doors and was surprised to see two different guards at the entrance. Because they didn't recognize him, they made him pay the fee before they allowed him to enter into the club. *It must be those other guys' day off,* he thought. *How lucky for us.*

These new guys totally won't notice that I'll be leaving this place twice tonight. And he interpreted it as a good sign that all would go well.

Galen looked at his watch and realized he was a bit earlier than usual, so he stood in the back of the club for a few moments. He didn't want to appear overly anxious to the old hag upstairs. Earlier that morning when he'd left, the woman had once again begun to grill him about when he'd be bringing his friends. Her comments were sharp and suspicious. He did his best to convince her that in just two nights, he would be accompanied by his entire lot of friends. He told her they'd all planned to stay for two nights straight, coming and going as much as they pleased, and with lots of money to waste. At his promises, she'd given him a strange look, and Galen couldn't read from it whether she was buying his lies or not.

Stop worrying about that old bitch, he tried to console himself. *Just get tonight over with and forget you ever met that fat ugly wench.*

He paced back and forth in the back of the crowd until finally, he couldn't wait anymore. He felt he might explode out of his skin if he stayed down here another minute. He darted through the room and as he climbed the red spiral staircase, he could feel heat rising in his face and neck. He stopped for a moment and took some deep breaths to try and slow down his heart rate.

As soon as he reached the top, the old woman was waiting for him. She smiled broadly at him and said, "Hello, Love! I see you just cannot get enough of my girl in there." Galen gave his best effort to smile back at her. "Really, Love," she continued. "I have much better girls than the one you seem so in love with. How about you add a little variety in your night and pick one of my other girls?"

Galen felt taunted by the hag. "Not tonight," he said. "Maybe tomorrow night, once I'm with all my friends, we'll be able to share notes with each other and change things up."

"I thought as much," she said. "You have your money?"

It wasn't until Galen reached out his hand to pass the money over to the woman that he realized how nervous he was. His hand was trembling as he placed the bills in her hand. He hoped she didn't notice, but she was far too keen to let it slip by.

"Ooooh!" she giggle-snorted. "Are you still nervous to see your little piece of a** in there? Look at you shaking like a leaf!"

"No, I'm not nervous," he snapped. "I've just had too much coffee today. Too many cups always makes my hands shake like that."

"Hmm," she said. "Follow me, Love."

Galen walked behind the short hobbling woman, wondering if on this particular night she was making the choice to walk extra slow down the narrow hallway, or if it simply felt that way. Galen couldn't wait for this night to be over.

The woman fumbled with her keys as she fingered through them to find the correct one for Skye's door.

"It's that one," Galen blurted out, pointing to the correct key.

The hag burst into laughter. "Ooooh! You're nervous *and* impatient tonight! Well, let's see if we can calm those nerves for you." And she unlocked Skye's door. She stood at the entrance as the door swung open, and as she gestured for him to go inside, she gave him a strange smirk.

Galen ignored her condescension and passed by her. Once inside, his eyes darted around the room. From the bed to the chair in the corner, to the sink, and back to the bed. The room was empty. Skye was gone.

He whirled around and demanded, "Where is she?"

The woman spoke back in her singsongy way, "I told you, you should've picked someone new tonight."

Galen's head felt like it was on fire. "Where is she?! What did you do with her, you old bitch?"

"Are you trying to threaten me, Love?" she seethed. "Trust me, I'm not a woman you're going to want to threaten." She narrowed her eyes at him. "I don't know who you think you are, you little s**t. Are you so stupid to think I couldn't see what was happening between you and that precious little whore of yours? Well, my Love, tonight you're going to wish you'd never laid eyes on her."

She moved into the room, leaving the door gaping open. But the space was instantly filled with the two large door guards, the ones who usually greeted Galen every night at the entrance. Apparently, it wasn't their night off, after all.

"Don't kill him," the woman said to the two men. "I don't want to have to cover that mess up. Just make it look like an everyday barroom brawl, and let this little boy know he'd better never set foot in this area of town again."

Panicking, Galen charged for the door. "Skye!" he yelled at the top of his lungs. "Skye!" And the men plowed into him like bags of cement. He felt a fist burrow deep into his gut and another slam into the side of his jaw. He could taste his own blood filling his mouth as another blow hit his ribs. He lost his breath and fell to the ground, his head forcefully hitting the concrete floor.

The men let up for just a moment as Galen opened his eyes and realized he was right next to Skye's bed. He looked under the cot to see if there was anything at all he could use to defend himself with. The only object he saw was a tiny silver chain. He reached out to grab it and realized it was a girl's charm bracelet.

He tried to stand up, but he only got to his hands and knees before the two men launched their second round of attacks. As they ruthlessly continued kicking him in the sides of his stomach and legs, Galen slipped out of consciousness.

WIL & AETON

❃ 31 ❃

BEFORE THE PLANE HAD COME TO A FULL STOP, Wil was already grabbing his duffel bag, gearing up to race as fast as he could through security. And the moment the stairs were in place outside the aircraft's exit, he was ready to go. He said a quick good-bye to Miss Aggie, bent down to kiss his mom on her head and tell her not to worry, and gave a final fist bump to Scott.

"I'll be in touch," he called over his shoulder as he left the plane, already calling Aeton on his cell. "Dude, you here yet?"

Aeton: Almost. I'm going to stay in my car because I don't want to take any chances toting guns through the airport.
Wil: Ha! That's right. We gotta remember we're civilians now.
Aeton: When you've gone through customs, go to baggage claim, and find the bridge marked "Beta." When you walk outside, I'll be in the beat-up black VW.
Wil: Cool. See you then. I'll text you when I'm almost there.
Aeton: Out.

As Wil stood in line at Customs, he thumbed through the pages of information he planned to review with Aeton once he got in the car. He'd already faxed everything to him, but he wanted to confirm that Aeton had had the time to thoroughly digest the details.

The information about Elle was cut and dry, at least as far as the time and location of the auction. At 1pm on Friday, the sale of the girls would begin, and because Elle was so young, Jack's contact had written she'd most certainly be early in the bidding. Since the youngest girls sell at the highest prices, the people who ran the auction wouldn't want the buyers to hold on to their cash, waiting until the end for the big ticket items to come out. The man had written that if Jack was lucky enough to have the youngest girl, which was very likely since Elle had just turned 10, then she'd probably win the highest bid of the night.

Upon reading these transcripts again, Wil wondered if he'd truly possess the restraint not to physically rip Jack to shreds for putting Elle in this type of situation. *Let's just hope I don't actually see that bastard face to face,* he thought.

It was Wil's turn at Customs. He slid the papers into his bag and walked up to the agent's station. Wil passed through without a hitch, and as he left the Customs area, he thought of how different things might've been had he not had a contact who already lived in Greece. *Thank god for Aeton. I'd really be taking my chances trying to get my weapons through airport security. I'm sure my dad would've figured something out, but that'd just taken more time, and we barely have enough of that as it is.*

He sent a text to Aeton and then checked his watch. Wednesday, 19:30. Less than 40 hours to rescue Elle. *But it's not Elle I'm worried about,* he thought. *We've already got that information. Skye on the other hand, I have absolutely no idea how we're going to find her in this short of a time frame.*

Wil realized he was almost running, but he didn't care; it helped him burn off some adrenaline. He located the bridge marked "Beta" and exited the airport. He looked around for a black VW, and heard a car horn to his far right. Aeton was standing next to the parked car, waving.

Wil had forgotten how tall Aeton was, and how much they looked alike. With Aeton's dark hair and green eyes, they could pass as brothers. He ran over to the car, and the two men greeted each other with a man-hug.

Wil: Dude! When you said look for the beat-up VW, you weren't kidding. Ha! We're going to look like circus freaks folding ourselves in and out of this tiny car.

Aeton: I know. But I had to borrow my brother's car because we just bought a new minivan, and the part of town we're going tonight isn't the safest. My wife will beat me if someone broke into it.

Wil: You bought a minivan? Serious?

Aeton: Hey, we got a baby now. We have to look the part.

Wil: *(as both were getting in the car)* Oh that's right, man, I'm sorry; I can't believe I forgot about the baby for a sec. You got pics?

Aeton: Of course. Just pick up my cell, and you can have a slideshow.

Wil: *(looking through the pictures)* Wow. She's a cutie. She must look like your wife.

Aeton: *(laughing)* Thanks, a**hole.

Wil: *(pulling the papers of information back out of his bag)* I hope you don't mind if we dive right in. Were you able to make sense out of all these pages I faxed earlier? And do you know exactly where we need to go tonight? I tried to Google Earth the street names mentioned in Jack's emails, but the images that came up seemed either really out of date, or not the right ones.

Aeton: Two things about where we're going: #1, it doesn't look like what you Americans might think a brothel district would look like. It's not Las Vegas. Thessaloniki does have places like that, but the area Jack's in is the older part of the red-light district. It looks more like a cross between a residential area and an industrial area. I had to read through those email copies twice, because I have to say, it's strange to me that your uncle would choose this place to make a deal. I'd think there'd be more money in the other parts of the city.

Wil: Yeah, well, that douche bag doesn't seem to be all that smart. From what we gathered, it appears this just happened to be where Jack's contact knew the right people in the biz.

Aeton: And that is *very* much how things work here; it's all about relationship and who you know, which brings me to #2: you're going to have to let me do *all* the talking...even if some of them can speak English. When I was down there last night poking around, I realized that the brothels and strip club owners are used to dealing with Greeks only.

Wil: Yeah...that's what a guy from that A21 org told me. What's that all about?

Aeton: It's just how things are here. Now, the gals walking the streets, I think they'll go with any guy, depending upon what their pimps have told them to do. But the actual establishments are fairly closed to foreigners. However, if I play it that you're my friend who I'm trying to show a good Greek time, I'm pretty sure we'll be fine, but you'll have to let me lead.

Wil: I'm good with that. So you checked it out last night?

Aeton: Yes. I walked around talking to some of the other customers down there who seemed to know what they were doing. Then, I went into a few clubs and sat at the bar, asking the bartenders where the best places were to find young girls. I got several leads.

Wil: Awesome. What about the auction? Were you able to get us into it, or are we gonna have to pull a Rambo?

Aeton: *(laughing)* Let's only use that as a last resort, ranger. We have a meeting in the late morning with a woman who owns the joint where the girls will be sold. Apparently this old lady is a major player in the whole brothel scene; she controls a lot of people, and almost everyone I talked to seemed to hate her, and fear her.

Wil: You're a rockstar! How'd you get all the way to the top so soon?

Aeton: You said money's not an issue, right?

Wil: Absolutely.

Aeton: That's how I did it. I promised we'd bring big money, but *only* if she'd meet with us.

Wil: Who were you talking to?

Aeton: One of her body guards. I got the right name from a bartender down the street. The guard wouldn't let me speak directly to her, but he called her on his cell while I was standing right there.

Wil: So, how much do we need for tomorrow?
Aeton: Six figures. Cash.
Wil: No problem. I'll text my dad and have him wire a quarter to a bank by our hotel.
Aeton: Make *sure* you have it in hand by our meeting tomorrow, or we might as will skip it. She's going to want to see for herself. There's no way we can build trust with her in such a short amount of time, but if we have enough cash right there, I'm pretty sure she'll let us into the auction.
Wil: *(As he was composing the text on his phone)* Do you think 250'll be enough?
Aeton: At least for our meeting, yes; as long as it's in euros. We'll have to watch for her response, try and read if she's impressed or not.
Wil: Done.

The two men rode in silence for a while as Wil finished his text. It burned Wil up on the inside to give such a large amount of money to anyone who would take part in this disgusting and corrupt industry. He'd much rather storm in there and kill the whole lot than hand over one red cent to that old woman, or any of the other brothel owners for that matter. And Wil hadn't hesitated to let his dad know how he felt, too. Before Wil had boarded the plane for Greece, he'd gone around and around with Richard about how much money he should allow himself to lose.

"Wil, it's *just* money," his dad had said. "Who cares how much it takes to get Skye and Elle back? I'd rather lose my whole fortune and have them home safe, than to keep the money and lose those girls!"

"Dad, I'm not saying we should jeopardize their safety," Wil had argued. "I'm just saying we shouldn't let those f***in bastards get any more money than they've already made off *all* the poor girls they've got locked up."

"You're missing the point, Wil. I don't care about the money, and I don't even care who ends up with it...as long as *we* end up with the girls."

"I don't understand how you can stand to see those people get rewarded for committing some of the worst crimes possible?!"

"I'm not going to argue about it anymore, son," Richard had said. "I want your word that you'll give them whatever amount they ask. Let's not make this situation harder on ourselves than it already is. What is the money for, if not to use it for something like this?"

Wil had finally conceded. "Alright, alright. You win. Besides, it's your money; you can give it to whomever you wish."

As Wil watched his phone, waiting for a text back from his dad, he shook his head, still feeling the sting of that argument. His idea of justice was to make a wrong thing right, and part of that was making the bad people pay for their actions...not reward them with riches. But he'd given his word, and that was that. Moreover, he knew he needed to focus himself in the moment at hand. He wondered if, after Aeton had spent the prior night scoping out the red-light district, his friend had come up with a feasible strategy for locating Skye.

"So, Aeton," Wil said. "After hanging out there last night, what is going to be the best way to locate Skye? Do you think we just need to go from brothel to brothel?"

Aeton didn't respond right away, and Wil wondered if he'd heard the question. There was a traffic light ahead that had just turned red and Aeton was slowing down the car. But once it had fully stopped, Aeton looked over at Wil. From the serious look on his face, Wil could see the question was heard; he simply wasn't sure how to answer it.

Looking back at the traffic light ahead of them, Aeton exhaled heavily. "Wil," he said. "You've got to know that she could be anywhere by now. One of the bartenders I talked to last night was bragging about how often the girls are rotated in and out. Depending upon what kind of brothel she's in, she could've even been sold again and moved out of the city, maybe even the country."

"Yeah, I know," Wil said. "The A21 guy told me the same thing, but we at least have to try our damnedest to find her. I can't go back to Miss Aggie, that black Cajun woman I told you about, and tell her Skye's lost without honestly being able to tell her we did our best."

"I'm up for whatever you need," Aeton said.

Wil: When I was talking with the A21 guy, he said that when you go into the brothels, they can show you upfront what girls they have. He said some places will line them up and have them walk past the guys in the lobby, and others will have a small book with pictures to choose from. Is that true?

Aeton: He'd know more than me. I've never been in one, other than last night.

Wil: If you don't have another plan, then, I suggest we systematically go from place to place and see if we can find her. What do you think?

Aeton: Let's do it. *Aeton slowed his driving.* We're here.

Wil: Really? This is it?

Aeton: I told you, it wouldn't be what you'd expect. Keep an eye out for a parking spot.

Wil was surprised to see the streets lined bumper to bumper with cars. They had to drive up and down several streets before they were fortunate and found an opening on the side of the road, just large enough for Aeton to squeeze his VW into. This spot seemed close to the main action, and they only got it because a car had just left the spot.

When Wil got out of the car, he almost tripped on what appeared to be a bum sleeping on the sidewalk, just next to where they'd parked. He was crumpled up in a ball, and it seemed odd to Wil that this would be the place a homeless person would pick to take a nap. It was totally random, not to mention, right in the middle of the sidewalk.

He had the thought to try and move the poor guy out of the pathway of people, but Wil wasn't sure what state he was in, or how he'd respond if he was awakened. He leaned down to get a closer look at him, but Wil couldn't see his face because it was covered up by his orange backpack.

"Come on, man," said Aeton, several steps down the sidewalk. "What's the hold up?"

"Right!" replied Wil. "I'm coming." He decided he couldn't afford any distractions, and he stepped over the guy to catch up to Aeton. Wil thought that if the guy was still there when they came back, maybe they could help him out then.

MOLLY VENZKE

SKYE

✤ *32* ✤

SKYE AWOKE TO A PITCH BLACK ROOM, her hands and feet bound as she lay on a rancid concrete floor. She tried to move, but the pain was too great. And when she opened her mouth to groan, she realized her lips were still gaff-taped shut. Then the incidences of the last several hours came back to her.

She began to cry, but the throbbing pain in her sides and back kept her from being able to release her full grief or to even take in a complete breath. In her mind, she prayed desperately that if there was a god, he'd prove himself once and for all by taking away her life this instant.

If only that Galen had never come, she thought. *Who did he think he was trying to be my savior? He only made things worse! If he hadn't come, I'd've been able to end all this and I'd be dead by now. This would've all been over. But now, I'm beaten up, tied up, and I can't even <u>try</u> to kill myself! I hate him for doing this to me!*

Skye tried to get her bearings, but the utter darkness of her cell hid everything. There were no windows, no lights, not even the tiniest of a crack to hint towards the presence of a door. And she could hear no sounds except her own breathing and the beating of her heart. She could not tell the size of the room, or the shape, or worse yet, if anyone else was in there with her. She shuddered at the thought.

Then a new thought relaxed her, causing her body to surrender onto the nauseating floor. *At least now I know this is the beginning of the end. Either they'll keep me here until they kill me, or they'll take me back to my room, and the second I get the chance, I'll kill myself. It might get worse before it gets better, but at least I know I only have a couple more days to endure this hell.*

As Skye lay there, she felt her wounds pulsing with terrible pain in tandem with her every heartbeat. The witch had beaten her harder than ever before as she lashed out with rage because of Skye's connection with Galen. The young girl still had no idea how the witch had figured out their plan, but however she did, she was unrelenting with her punishment.

Skye couldn't believe how stupid she'd been to believe that anything good could happen to her in a place like this. But there had been such hope and excitement in Galen's eyes that she'd let herself get swept away in it. For the first time since she'd been here, someone had looked into her eyes with what seemed to be genuine compassion, even love, and like a naive little girl, she'd fallen for it.

He'd told her she was beautiful and that she didn't belong in a place like this. He'd told her that he'd spent almost all his own money over the past several nights just to make sure she wouldn't have to degrade herself. He'd told her he was going to do everything in his power to get her out of the brothel. And she believed him.

How could I have been such a complete idiot? Why would someone I never met do this for me? Everything he told me was probably a great big lie. For all I know, the dude works for the witch, and she was just seeing if I would fall for the whole deal! How dumb could I be?!

Skye rehearsed the events of the past day. As Galen, or whatever his real name was, was leaving that morning, he'd looked back at Skye and given her a discreet smile. Skye had responded with an ever-so-slight nod, the tiniest gesture she could offer without the witch noticing. But the old woman had gotten a strange look on her face, and Skye had quickly dropped her gaze to her bed, fearing the woman had indeed seen their nonverbal communication. However, the witch was a master at hiding her thoughts, and Skye had no way to be certain.

The witch had begun talking loudly to Galen as she closed Skye's door and escorted him down the hallway, and as usual, Skye had no way to understand her foreign words. She sat on her bed, waiting for the witch to return, hoping that by whatever expression the old hag wore, she'd at least be able to tell if the woman suspected anything.

The moments had stretched long until finally, Skye could hear the echoing clicks of the witch's heels as she hobbled back toward her door. When she had entered, she wore her lipstick-smeared smile as she had approached her bed. Skye had let out a sigh of relief, thinking the woman was coming over to pat her head as she had done for the last several days. And the witch's hand had slowly risen for the pat, only at the last moment, her motion switched to a backhand as she'd violently slapped Skye across the face.

"You think me stupid?!" the witch had hissed. "You think you can fool me, you little whore?" Then she'd hit Skye again as the girl tried to curl up in a ball to protect herself. "What you and that boy up to? You tell me! What you and that boy up to?!"

But Skye could only curl tighter on her bed, knowing the witch was about to unleash the fullness of her anger.

"You stupid slut! You will pay for your betrayal." And the witch had disappeared from the room.

Skye had lain on her bed, trembling, as she imagined what horrid punishment the witch was going to impose. She braced herself, listening for the heel clicks to sound the witch's return.

The old woman had hobbled back in, holding a roll of gaff tape and a thick leather lash. She'd marched over to the bed, had dragged Skye by the hair onto the floor, and in what seemed like an instant, she'd taped her mouth shut and her wrists together. Then she'd jerked at Skye's feet and secured her legs at the ankles. Once completely bound, the witch began to mercilessly whip Skye with the leather lash. The floggings were so swift and strong as they had hit Skye's back and legs that it seemed impossible to have been coming from a single source. The pain was overwhelming, and Skye's cognizance was swallowed up by a sea of unbearable pain.

The next thing Skye knew, she'd woken up in this black room. She had no sense of how much time had passed, how long she'd be here, the extent of her wounds, or what kind of torture was still yet to come.

⚜

GALEN AND NIKKOS

✞ 33 ✞

GALEN OPENED HIS EYES, shocked to be laying outside on a sidewalk in the middle of the night. Even more surprising were the groups of people who were walking right past him, simply stepping over him when needed. As his eyes adjusted to his surroundings, he could feel his entire head pounding in pain. He tried to sit up, but the combination of the ache in his head and the stale taste of blood in his mouth sent a wave of nausea washing over him. Determined not to vomit, he laid back down for a moment to concentrate on his breathing and to try to spit out the blood from his mouth.

Slow, he thought. *I need to move very slowly. But I'm going to have to get off this sidewalk or someone's going to step on me.* In a cold sweat, he pushed his body as far as he could towards the far edge of the walkway. There he lay for several moments as he gathered his strength and began to assess his injuries.

He was able to move all of his limbs, so none of them had been broken; at least there was that. His teeth were intact, and he was able to move his jaw, but the awful taste in his mouth had to go. He remembered the small water bottle that he always kept in his backpack, and as he lifted his right hand to unzip the bag, he realized he was holding something.

He propped himself up on his left elbow to try and make out what was in his hand. He squinted his eyes to focus on the object, and saw it was a small, silver chain with three charms on it One was a silver heart, one was a birdcage, and one was a silver bird. *Oh my god, this must be Skye's.* His ribs were screaming and he couldn't sustain his position, so he laid back down on the ground. He recalled the moment in her room when he'd been knocked to the floor and had reached out under her bed to grab this bracelet. He didn't know what had compelled him to take it, but at this moment, he was so thankful that he had. The thought of Skye filled his heart with a mixture of fear and deep regret.

What must they have done to her? he thought, and he closed his eyes and began to cry. "Oh god..." he whispered. "What have I done? Skye, I'm so sorry...it's all my fault, Skye...I'm so sorry." He clutched the bracelet close to his lips and wept.

Several moments passed. *I never should've tried to do this on my own. I've got to get myself some help.* He pulled his backpack over to him and fished out his cell to call Nikkos. There was no answer, so Galen tried again.

"Hey, brother!" answered Nikkos. Galen could tell he was at a party. "Why are you calling me this late?"

"Nikkos," Galen's voice was hoarse. "Nikkos, I need your help."

"Speak up, brother, I can't hear you over the music!"

"Nikkos, listen to me," he said as loudly as he could. "I need your help. I need your help!"

"Hold on a minute," Nikkos said. Galen could hear Nikkos' cell rustling around as he was moving to a space where it was quieter. Galen heard a door shut, and the loud sounds turned to muffles. "Now, what did you say?"

"Nikkos, I need your help. Right now."

"Are you crying, brother?"

"No, but I've been beaten, and I can hardly move. I can't get home."

"What?!" Nikkos said, suddenly switching his tone. "Where are you? Who did this to you? I'm going to kill them!" Galen heard the door re-open and Nikkos yell, "George! George! Get your a** in here! Someone's mugged my brother!" And then back into his cell phone, "Galen, where are you? We're going to come there right now and pick you up."

"I'm not quite sure; as soon as I can stand up I'll call you back and give you street names. But if you just start driving to that place you took me on my birthday..." his voice trailed off as he tried to catch his breath.

"What have you gotten yourself into, brother?"

"Please. Just start your way over here, Nikkos. Please. I'll call you in a few minutes once I know exactly where I am."

"I'll be there in less than 30. I'm bringing George with me." And before Galen could argue, Nikkos had hung up.

He lay back on the sidewalk and breathed. His clothes were damp from his sweat, causing him to shiver. After resting a while, he managed to sit up. He still couldn't stand unaided, so he was forced to try and stop a pedestrian to ask what street he was on. None of the men who were walking by would so much as look at him.

Galen saw a woman walking in his direction, and from her attire, there was no doubt she was a prostitute. He debated with himself about asking this woman for help, but he figured he had no other choice. He called out to her as she was passing by.

"Please, miss," Galen said. "Please! Could you help me for just a moment?"

She stopped, and when she got a good look at him, she said, "What happened to you, honey? Are you alright?"

"I really don't want to bother you; this will just take a second. Someone's coming to pick me up, and I have no idea where I am. Can you please tell me what street this is? I need to call them back..." he was out of breath again and had to stop.

"Honey, you make the call and hand that phone over to me. I'll take care of whatever you need."

Galen was too weak at this point to allow his pride to refuse her help. He pressed the redial button and handed his cell over to the woman. As he lay his head back, trying to find the ability to take a deep breath, he heard her talking to Nikkos, giving him the exact street names and directions.

"And right now, he's sitting on the sidewalk," the woman said. "Look on your right for a silver Honda parked on the side, followed by an older black car; a VW, I think. (she looked closer at the car) Yeah, it's a black VW, and he's right there next to it. How long do you think you'll be?....OK, I'll stay with him as long as I can." She hung up the phone and handed it back to Galen.

"He'll be here soon," she said. "What in the hell happened to you?"

"Thank you," said Galen. "I really appreciate your help."

She squatted down next to him, and Galen was very impressed at her ability to balance herself steadily in such high heels.

"Honey, can I get you anything? A drink of some kind? You look terrible. Whoever did this to you did a real good job."

"Yeah, I can feel that. No, I don't need anything; my brother will be here in a minute. And you really don't have to wait here until he comes. *(pausing to take a breath)* The last thing I'd want is for you to get in trouble because you're sitting here with me."

"A few minutes won't hurt. Listen, honey, you just lay back and rest, and I'll stand here and act like I'm working. But really, I'll be watching after you until your ride gets here. OK?"

"OK," Galen said, smiling at her. "Thank you."

He closed his eyes and tried to breathe. He could hear the woman slowly walking back and forth, keeping a close distance to him. In a million years, Galen would've never imagined that the sound of a hooker's heels clicking along on a sidewalk could've brought him such a feeling of comfort.

Once Nikkos arrived and crouched down to him, Galen could see the worry on his brother's face.

"Do I look that bad?" Galen asked.

"You're going to be fine, brother." But Galen could definitely sense the uncertainty in Nikkos' voice. "Let's get you out of here."

Trying to get Galen into the car was a more difficult process than any of them had prepared for. His pain was so excruciating, he could barely be moved, let alone attempt to stand. Nikkos was certain several of Galen's ribs were broken, maybe even with internal bleeding.

Luckily, they had brought George's Suzuki Vitara, so they were able to put down the back seats in order to make room for Galen to lay down. Nikkos and George did their best to carry his dead weight as carefully as possible. However, when they rolled him into the car, Galen let out a loud cry.

"Just be thankful that I'd been drinking so much tonight," said Nikkos, attempting to keep the mood light. "Otherwise I'd never have asked George to drive. We'd be trying to squeeze you into my Jeep right now."

"Hey, it's a miracle I'd only just gotten to the party," added George. "Or else, I'd have been no better off than you, Nikkos."

Galen groaned in pain as they finished arranging his body in such a way to allow the car's back gate to shut.

"Thank you for coming," Galen said. "Now, I just want to get home and crash in my own bed for a couple days."

"Hell no, we're not going home!" said Nikkos. "We're taking you to the hospital."

"No—"

"If you could only see yourself right now, Galen; for chrissake, you just got the total s**t knocked out of you! You're lucky they didn't kill you and throw your body on the railroad tracks." He closed the back of the Suzuki and the guys climbed into the front seats.

"Let's take him to Saint Loukas Hospital on Panarama," said Nikkos as he shut his door.

"Got it," said George.

"Little brother, I'm not going to ask you anything about what happened tonight until after the hospital," Nikkos said over his shoulder. "I don't want to be guilty of lying to the doctors, or the police, if they need us to make a report. But you don't say a word to them, either; you let me do all the talking.

"George, our story will be this: Galen was walking around downtown, and some guys came out of nowhere, mugged him, and beat the s**t out of him. They threw him in the back of a van and tossed him out on the street where we picked him up. It's as simple as that. Got it?"

"Sounds good," said George.

"And that's our story for Mum and Pop, too; you hear me?" Nikkos said.

Galen grunted in response. At this point, he'd go along with just about anything Nikkos asked. He was miserable in the back of that car, as his entire body throbbed with every turn and bump the vehicle made. He tried to divert his attention away from his anguish, but the only person he saw when he closed his eyes was Skye. She's all he could think about. *Where did they take her? What are they doing to her? Damn that old bitch to hell for hurting her!* And the heartfelt pain of those images was far greater than what he was dealing with physically.

It's all my fault, he thought. *Whatever's happening to her right now is all my fault. Would she have been better off if I'd just have left her alone? But I sincerely believed my plan was going to work and that Skye was going to get out of that place. What does she think of me now? Does she hate me for what I've put her through?* That notion seared Galen's heart.

Galen felt helpless to do anything further to help his friend. And he wondered how he'd go on from here, knowing Skye was somewhere in the world thinking ill of him...maybe even wishing she'd never laid eyes on him.

WIL

❧ 34 ❧

Wɪʟ ᴡᴀs ᴅᴀᴢᴇᴅ as he walked into the Electra Hotel. After 10 hours straight of walking the streets of Thessaloniki, going from brothel to brothel, strip club to strip club, looking for any sign of Skye, Wil felt weary and defeated. He and Aeton had not so much as found the tiniest thread that might lead them to Skye's whereabouts. The magnitude of what they were attempting to accomplish in such a short amount of time was beginning to sink in, and Wil wondered if he was out of his league.

He walked all the way to one of the elevators before it dawned on him that he hadn't been inside this hotel. He was sharing a room with Scott, who'd already checked in, but Wil had yet to get a key. Shaking his head at his absentmindedness, he turned to go back to the front desk.

It was 05:45, and Wil couldn't wait to take a shower. Not so much because he was dirty; he looked pristine right now compared to how gross he'd get during some of his military operations. It was more that he wanted to wash his mind from all the filth he'd seen over the last several hours. During his years in the service, he never chose to join any of his fellow soldiers when on occasion they'd go looking to hook up with girls in seedy bars or strip joints. So, tonight was Wil's first experience "hooker-hopping" as one of his buddies used to call it. He remembered how he used to roll his eyes at his friend when he'd use that phrase; but now, the thought of those words made his stomach turn.

Many of the girls he met tonight appeared well under eighteen years of age, and all of them had a similar hollow look in their eyes. Even in the pornographic photos the brothel owners would show Aeton and Wil, behind the makeup and sexual poses, their "bedroom" eyes looked vacant. In several brothels, the owners would line up the girls before the men in the lobby, so each man could make his selection. Wil had felt himself ready to come undone. His impulse was to kick the s**t out of every single man in the place and to rescue all the girls to safety. And knowing he and Aeton had the ability to quickly accomplish these beatings only intensified his temptation to fight.

It was a huge concern for Wil that he was finding it difficult to keep his emotions in check. This was completely out of character for him, and he hated the unsteadiness he was feeling. Wil had always been lauded by both commanding and fellow officers of his ability to maintain his unwavering focus, no matter what the situation. Nothing *ever* shook Wil. But tonight had.

This sobered Wil, and he knew he had to get himself under control before his late morning meeting with the woman running the auction. She was supposed to be a sharp one, with a reputation of being able to sniff trouble a mile a way. He had to make sure he was on point during this meeting. So even though Wil normally never took breaks, he knew he needed one now.

He showed the receptionist his ID, and she handed him his key. Room 320. He thanked her and started again in the direction of the elevators.

This is my first time out on an intense mission since the explosion, he thought. *Have I lost what it takes, or am I just tired? Either way, now certainly isn't the time to doubt. I've got to do what it takes to keep my head in the game.*

He rode the elevator up to the third floor, found his room, and entered as quietly as possible. He didn't want to wake Scott, and more importantly, he didn't feel like talking about the night he'd just had. As soon as the door cracked open, Wil let out a sigh of disappointment. The room light was on.

Scott was sitting outside on the balcony, drinking a cup of coffee. At the sound of Wil's entrance, he quickly came to meet him. But Scott was an extremely perceptive man, and the moment they locked eyes, it was as if they had an entire conversation. Scott gave him a casual head-nod greeting and said matter-of-factly, "Your bag is over there. What time do you need to head out again?"

"Right now it's 05:50? I need to meet Aeton at 09:30, he's picking me up outside."

"Great. I was just about ready to go down, get more breakfast, and walk around a bit. So you can have the room to yourself. Just fyi, your mom and Miss Aggie's suite is right next to ours, and our rooms basically share a balcony. So only go out there when you're ready to chat."

Wil chuckled. "Got it. Thanks."

As he knelt down to put on his shoes, Scott said, "I'll text you around 09:00 to see if you need me to bring you back some food."

Scott grabbed his wallet and room key and strode to the door. Just as he'd opened it, Wil said, "Thanks, dude. I appreciate it."

"No prob, man." And he was gone.

Wil flopped himself down on his bed, set his watch for 08:30, and closed his eyes. A deep sleep was indeed waiting for him, but the mental journey to get there was not fun. As he drifted off, his mind turned into a cruel slideshow, fast-forwarding through all the hundreds of girls' faces he'd looked into throughout the last hours. Each girl's expression was more fearful than the one before, her eyes pleading with him to rescue her out of her torture. He wrestled with these images for quite a while until finally his fatigue took over and he fell asleep.

Wil sprang up in bed, his adrenaline already pumping. He felt sweat rolling down his chest and was sure he'd just had a nightmare, but he chose not to recall its details. Instead, he gathered his mind to focus on his whereabouts. Hotel. Greece. Skye. Elle. Meeting with Aeton.

He spun around to grab his watch, and just as he did, his 08:30 alarm sounded. He smiled at himself, knowing even with all that had happened in the last few days, his internal stopwatch was still spot on. This little sign of acuteness gave Wil the confidence he needed, that his ability to handle this mission was up to par.

He jumped out of bed, feeling as if his 2½ hour nap had actually been a full night's sleep. As he showered, he went through a mental check list: dress, coffee, eat, meet with Mom, get the money Dad wired, meet Aeton outside the lobby at 09:30, coffee again, meet auction lady, continue search for Skye.

As he dressed, he felt his stomach burning with hunger, and he wondered if Scott had any leftovers out on the balcony that he could scrounge. He walked out and found some cold, rubbery toast and a half pot of coffee. *This'll at least tide me over until I can get something decent,* he thought. He stuffed the bread into his mouth and for a moment forgot to chew when he looked up and saw the view before him. The sight of the bright aqua Mediterranean Sea was stunning.

"It's beautiful, isn't it?" he heard someone say behind him. He'd forgotten Scott's words about his mom's suite being next door. But Wil was glad to hear her comforting voice.

"It really is," answered Wil without turning around. "How come we never took a family vacation to Greece? This place is incredible."

"I don't know. But after this is all over, maybe we'll come back someday and take a cruise. *(she paused for a moment)* I wasn't expecting to see you until the Friday afternoon pick up. Is everything OK?"

"Oh, yeah," said Wil as he stuffed another piece of bread in his mouth. "I needed to pick up the cash Dad wired, so I figured I might as well grab a shower while I'm at it."

"I just got back from pickin up the money. And not to make you look cliche' or anything, but I wasn't sure how one carried around that much cash. So, I also bought a briefcase for you to carry it in." She disappeared inside her suite for a moment, and returned with a brown briefcase. She handed it to Wil.

"Thanks so much, Mom. This is great. Yeah, who carries a quarter of cash anymore? Unless you're a criminal or something. Anyway, Aeton and I decided we shouldn't carry it all in one place. He's picking up some cash belts for each of us to wear on our bodies, and also, I'll keep part of it in my leather laptop bag."

"Yes, of course," she said. "That makes total sense." After a long pause, she said, "Do you mind if I ask you about last night?"

CAGED

"No," Wil said, checking his watch. 08:52. "But unfortunately, I haven't much to tell you." He stretched his neck so he could glance into his mom's room to see if he Aggie was nearby. "Where's Miss Aggie?" he asked quietly.

"Right now, she's downstairs in the restaurant."

Wil looked directly into Lottie's eyes and said carefully, "Mom, I'm not gonna lie to you. Chances are very slim that we're going to find Skye. I wish I could tell you differently, but..." his voice trailed off for a moment. "Aeton and I went from place to place last night; I can't tell you how many girls we saw, never imagined there could be so many brothels in such a small radius. I mean, when I was in that meeting with Trafficking Hope, they told me what it was going to be like here, but I don't know, I guess I didn't believe them, or thought they were exaggerating...I don't know what I thought. But after last night, I finally got a scope of what we're *really* dealing with, and it's a way bigger machine than I'd realized, with many different levels, at that. Plus, these people are constantly moving the girls around, from brothel to brothel, even city to city.

"As far as Elle is concerned, we've got a specific time and address; as a matter of fact, in a few minutes, we're even meeting with the gal who's running the whole auction tomorrow afternoon. But to find Skye..." Wil just shook his head. "I think we need to prepare Miss Aggie about what she should and should not expect from this trip."

Lottie sat down in the balcony chair and looked out at the sea. Wil could see her eyes filling with tears. "Honey, you can only do what you can do. That's all we're askin. Let's focus on gettin Elle, and we'll do our best to locate Skye; but if we can't, well, we'll just have to come up with another plan of attack. As far as Miss Aggie is concerned, I'll talk with her today, when the time is right. We both are wantin to keep our minds occupied while we're waitin, so we're goin sight-seein to the White Tower and several of the Thessaloniki churches. I'm sure the right moment will come for me to tell her."

"Thanks, Mom." Wil's phone went off; it was a text from Scott. "Listen, I need to go downstairs and grab some food. I'll be in touch throughout the day with updates."

"Sure, sure. You go, honey," she said. Before she could add anything else, Wil was gone.

MOLLY VENZKE

ELLE

✦ *35* ✦

ELLE WAS SO DESPERATE to see someone she knew besides her dad, she felt as if her heart was moaning within her. She'd grown despondent over the last day and a half, unable to eat any of the food Jack brought to the hotel room. All she did was lie on her bed and try to sleep. She wasn't interested in reading, watching television, or talking; she simply tried to sleep the days away until she would see Skye.

And Jack didn't even seem to notice, or if he did, he certainly didn't show the least bit of concern. He only thought about himself, what he wanted to do, and where he wanted to go. Now, as Elle lie in her bed glaring over at the sleeping man who was supposed to be caring for her and spending time with her, she could only felt contempt.

Every day locked up in this hotel room is one less day I could be spending with Skye, she thought. *Why did we even leave Louisiana so early? Just so we could be here in time for that stupid contest? Couldn't we have just gotten here a couple days ago and done the pageant? Then I would've had way more time to be with Skye. Part of me wants to totally mess up tomorrow, just to get back at him for making me do all this junk over these last several days.*

But Elle wouldn't dare. She'd never done anything so rebellious, and who knows what her father would do to punish her. He might even make her go straight home without ever seeing her sister. While she couldn't wait to be home with her mom and MawMaw Aggie, she certainly didn't want to risk losing the chance to be with Skye.

A soft buzzing sound came from the small table separating hers and Jack's beds. It was his cell phone receiving a message of some sort. Elle wondered if maybe it was a text from her mom? She sat up in bed so that when Jack checked his phone, he'd see she was awake. But Jack didn't budge. He was asleep deeply enough that he hadn't even heard the vibration go off.

Elle could see the small message light pulsing on the side of Jack's phone. She was dying to know if the text was from her mom. For several minutes, she debated whether or not she should check it. Normally, Jack never let anyone else touch his cell, but Elle tried to justify this instance as being a special circumstance. What if it was an emergency? What if her mom needed something that Jack should know about...this very minute? Surely, he would understand why Elle took it upon herself to look.

Her rationalizations convinced her, and very quietly, she scooted to the edge of her bed, listening to make sure Jack was sound asleep. Holding her breath, she reached over to grab his phone and to slowly bring it back to her bed. She hid under the covers so the display light wouldn't shine too brightly.

As she touched the screen to illuminate it, Elle's heart sank. It wasn't a text from her mom; it was from a person called "stableboyz." Because of the name, she assumed, it was probably one of the guys Jack sold horses with. She touched the screen again to turn it off, but instead, she accidentally opened the text. It read: "talked w 1 of the buyers for 2morrow. he's real interested in ur mare. got a fetish for ginger hair. he's ready 2 pay big money. its lookin good 4 u!!"

Elle wondered what those words meant. She didn't know her dad was selling any horses while they were here on vacation. *That guy must work for my dad and is just giving him an update from home,* she thought.

The thought of home made her heart skip, and it occurred to her: *I have Dad's phone right here...I should try and call Mom!* Elle lost her breath for a second; she'd give anything to talk with her mom. *He's totally zonked out right now, so he won't hear me if I snuck into the bathroom and called her from in there. He'll never even know I did it until he gets the bill, and we'll probably be back home by then, and then I'll pay for the call myself with my piggy bank.*

She was so excited, she could hardly restrain from giggling. Once again, she checked to make sure Jack was asleep, and then attempting to be completely silent, Elle slid out of her bed and tip-toed to the bathroom. She closed the door, and sat down with her back against it. She didn't risk turning the bathroom light on, so she had to manage the call in the dark. It wasn't until she was scrolling down Jack's contacts, that she could see how shaky her hands were from nervousness. She found Macy's name and pressed 'send'.

As she listened to the phone ringing on the other end, her insides began to whirl, and she felt as though her heart would beat right out of her chest. After three rings, she heard her mom answer the phone, but before Macy had a chance to speak, Elle gushed.

"Oh Mama! Mama! I'm so glad you answered! I miss you so much, and wish you were here. We still haven't gotten to see Skye yet, and I miss you so much!"

"Hold on a minute, honey," an unfamiliar woman's voice said. "Who is this?"

Surprised to hear a voice other than Macy's, Elle wasn't sure what to say. She lifted the phone from her ear to make sure she'd pressed the correct contact. The screen said "Macy," but this person was definitely not her.

"Ummm..." said Elle. "I'm calling for Macy DuMonde. Can I talk to her please?"

"Listen, honey, can you tell me who you are?" the person asked.

"I'm Elle, her daughter. Can you please get my mama?"

There was a moment of delay before the woman said, "Elle, is this your daddy's phone?" Elle was afraid to answer. "Honey, is this your daddy's phone?" she asked again. "Can you please let me speak to your daddy?"

It was Elle's turn to pause as she tried to think of how to answer that question without telling the lady she'd snuck her father's phone in the middle of the night while he was sleeping.

"Can you please just get my mama?" Elle asked. "I really want to talk with her."

"Honey, your mama is...well...she can't talk right now; can you-"

"Why? What's the matter with her? Who is this?" Elle was getting more anxious by the second.

"Honey, this is Miss Lillie at the Maringouin Police Station." The woman was speaking very gently. "I really need to talk with your father, sweetie; we've been tryin to call him every day for almost a week now."

"Why?! What's happened to Mama? Is she alright?" Elle had completely forgotten to keep her voice down as she felt a panicky feeling rise within her. "Please, is Mama OK? Is she OK?"

Elle's body skimmed across the bathroom tiles as the door behind her aggressively swung open.

"Who in the hell are you talking to?!" Jack yelled in a raspy voice. He flipped on the light, and both of them squinted their eyes to adjust. "Is that my cell, you little brat?"

"Daddy, I'm so sorry! It's just that I was missing Mama so much, and I thought it would be OK if I called her for just a second. I was only going to talk with her for one tiny second, and you can totally take the money in my piggy bank to pay for it. But Mama didn't answer! The police station did!"

"Give me that phone," he whispered. And when Elle handed him the cell, he covered the speaker and added, "And get your a** back in bed before I beat it black and blue." He shoved her out of the bathroom, then slammed and locked the door.

Elle's concern for her mother overshadowed her fear of getting spanked, and she stood close to the door to overhear what was being said. Her dad's voice changed to a civil tone as he continued the call:

"Yes, this is Jack DuMonde.....Yes, I believe I have gotten your messages, but I'm out of the country, so the reception is very bad. The voice mails were breaking up and I couldn't make them out.....Can you tell me why you have my wife's cell phone?.....Why can't you just tell me over the phone?.....Yes, I understand that, but like I said, I'm out of the country at the moment, so I'd appreciate it if you just told me right now.....What?.....I'm sorry, but could you say that again?.....When did this happen?....."

Elle heard Jack unlocking the bathroom door, so she shot herself like a bullet into her bed. He came over to his suitcase and began looking for something. She could hear the sound of Miss Lillie's voice on the other end, but it was impossible to make out what her words were.

"Ummm..." Jack said. "I'm sure you can understand that I don't know what to say right now.....I'm sorry, I can't hear you.....What? Can you repeat that? You're breaking up....Hello?.....Hello, are you still there? There's only silence coming from your end..."

Elle wondered why Jack was saying that because she could plainly hear the sound of the woman's voice; maybe she couldn't decipher what Miss Lillie was saying, but Elle could certainly hear there wasn't silence.

"Hello?....I'm sorry, I think I've lost you.....Hello?" And with that, Jack not only ended the call, but he also turned off his phone altogether. He stopped ruffling through his bag and sat down on his bed.

"S**t!" he hissed. "S**t! S**t! S**t!" He got up to walk back into the bathroom and muttered under his breath, "Macy, your timing was always f***ing horrible." And he slammed the door behind him.

Elle lay terrified in her bed, and she began to feel like her world was crumbling apart.

❧{ 36 }❧

❧ WIL AND AETON ❧

WIL WAS STANDING OUTSIDE when Aeton pulled up to the entrance of the Electra Hotel. He ran over to the VW and knocked on the passenger window. Aeton stretched across the seat to unroll it.

"Hey, man," Wil said. "Did you get any sleep?"

"Only a bit." Aeton answered. "Honestly, I was a little disturbed by everything we saw last night."

"Me too, Bro. I wanna kill those bastards. You can just park the car here for a sec while we go in and figure out how to situate all the cash," Wil said. "Do you have the belts?"

"I've got them. Are you sure it's OK to park here?"

"Yeah, as long as it's only for a few minutes. I already checked with the front desk."

Aeton grabbed a small duffle bag from the back seat of the car and got out. As they entered the lobby, Aeton asked, "How did your dad get all that cash to you in such a short amount of time?"

"Who knows? It's my dad; he always can pull off stuff like that."

Aeton held up the bag that had the cash belts inside. "Where do you want to go to put these on?"

"You know what? I was thinking we could just use the bathroom down here, but now I'm thinking we'd better be safe and use my room," said Wil. "The stairs are right here; it'll be much faster to take these than wait for the elevator."

The young men bounded up the three flights of stairs to Wil's hotel room. Once inside, Wil flopped the briefcase down on the bed and opened it. The sight of its contents stopped Aeton in his tracks.

"Look at all that f***ing money!" Aeton whispered. He reached out to touch the piles of euros. "I've never seen that much cash in my life!"

"It is kind of weird to see it all in one place like that," Wil said matter-of-factly. And then he noticed Aeton, who seemed in a trance as he was unable to take his eyes off the money. "Bro," Wil said sharply. "What's wrong with you? Seriously, it's just money. Are you going to be OK, because we've got to keep our heads in the game."

Still staring at the money, Aeton said, "I'm sorry...it's just...I've never seen that much cash before."

"Look at me, Aeton," Wil directed. He waited until Aeton made eye contact. "It's *just* money. Think of your new baby girl, and what you would do if any of those people got a hold of her. You wouldn't think twice to pay this much money to get her back."

He shook his head and said. "You're right. I'm sorry. I just have never seen that much, or realized how much f***ing pull money has. I mean, I can literally *feel* the power coming off of it."

"Dude." Wil was annoyed.

Embarrassed, Aeton looked downward. "Right. You're right. I'm sorry."

"So, you're good?" Wil asked, not fully convinced. "You sure you're not gonna go all *Gollum* on me?"

Aeton laughed. "Yeah, man. I'm good."

"OK," said Wil, "Cause all I'm saying is, if I hear you start calling that money *"my precious,"* I swear, I'll kick your a**."

Aeton put his hand on Wil's shoulder, and looked him squarely in the eyes. "I'm over it. I promise, you can totally trust me."

Wil took a moment to assess his friend. "Alright. I believe you. Just keep your baby girl's face in the forefront of your mind if you feel yourself starting to slip."

"Man, if I do that, then I'm personally going to rip the balls off of every single one of them...and I'd do it very slowly. But I'm with you; I understand what you're getting at."

The men got to work separating the money, filling the pockets of the cash belts, and strapping them on their bodies. A portion of the money went across their chests, and another portion was belted around their thighs. The remainder went into a small, black leather laptop bag.

They checked themselves in a full-length mirror to make certain the money was hidden under their clothes. As they were leaving Wil's hotel room, Aeton's cell phone rang. Wil could hear a bit of confusion in Aeton's responses, but since he was speaking Greek, Wil didn't understand what was being said. They ran down the stairs to the lobby, and exited the hotel.

Aeton ended his call and said, "Well, there's been a slight change of plans."

Wil: What do you mean?
Aeton: Remember that bodyguard guy I told you about?
Wil: The one who's our 'in' with the gal holding the auction tomorrow?
Aeton: Yes. That was him on the phone. We're still meeting with the old woman, but the location has changed at the last minute.
Wil: Why?
Aeton: He wouldn't say anything except that she wanted us to meet her at one of her other strip clubs.
Wil: Hmm. Do you think we should be suspicious?
Aeton: Hell yes! I think we need to be suspicious of everything we're doing. These people sell *people* for a living. Who knows what else they're capable of?
Wil: Well, as long as we're not going to some old abandoned warehouse, I think we'll be OK. At least she didn't cancel completely.
Aeton: No, it's definitely not in a remote area, he gave me the address, and described the outside of the club.
Wil: You got your gun right?
Aeton: Gun*sss*, brother, as in more than one.
Wil: Yeah, me too. Just in case, we better make sure they're easily accessible.
Aeton: Roger that, as you Americans say.
Wil: Roger that.

❦ *SKYE* ❦

SKYE HEARD THE LOCKS RATTLING on the door. Someone was coming in. She began trembling with fear at the thought of what the next minutes might hold for her. She'd lost all concept of time in this pitch black cell, and she wondered how long she'd been lying on its cold, concrete floor.

The door cracked open, and from just that little bit of light, Skye's pupils burned as they quickly contracted. She squinted to see who, what, and how many were entering her room. She could tell by the outline of the person's body that it was the witch. Then suddenly, the old hag flung open the door, flooding the room with such a light that Skye was temporarily blinded. The witch giggle-snorted at her, as Skye blinked her eyes as fast as she could to try and see.

The witch walked over to her and ripped off the gaff tape from her mouth. Skye was sure some of her skin had ripped off with it.

"Oohh, my little slut," said the witch. "I hope your stay here has taught you something." She came very close to Skye's face. "You *never* try to disobey me. And you never *ever* try to run away. I was coming for to whip you more, but I decide to get rid of you instead."

Skye wondered by what means this ugly hag was going to kill her. She didn't care; finally, this all would be over. But unfortunately, death was not what the witch had in mind.

"Tomorrow, I sell you to the highest bidder. That way, you can be gone from here, and I make some money. We both get our way, ah? You lucky I don't kill you."

The witch began to uncoil the gaff tape that bound Skye's ankles, and once she'd finished, she wadded the tape in a ball and stuck it in her pocket. Towards the door, she yelled something in Greek, and immediately a woman shuffled in.

Skye deduced the woman to be in her 40s, but she couldn't see her face well enough to know for certain. The woman never took her eyes off the floor, and strips of her salt-and-pepper colored hair hung forward, shading her face. She wore a long moss-green sweater, brown leggings, and a pair of slippers. The witch spoke to her, giving commands, and the woman nodded her head in response.

"This is Dula, one of my servants. She will be with you until I get rid of you. I do not trust you to be alone. She will help clean your filth and get you ready for to sell. I warn you; don't get any more ideas about running. Dula is loyal to me; she will tell me, and I will beat you."

The witch spoke more directions to Dula, and then exited the room. Dula shuffled over to Skye and held out her hands, in a gesture for Skye to get up.

Skye attempted to sit up, but the pain from her whipping caused her to fall back and curl up on her side. Dula sat down on the floor, and without looking Skye in the face, she began undoing the gaff tape that held Skye's wrists together. Dula worked slowly and gently, seemingly to cause as little pain as possible.

Once Skye's hands were free, Dula put her arms underneath Skye's armpits and lifted her to a seated position. Skye groaned. Then, the woman wrapped Skye's arms around her shoulders and steadily helped Skye to stand. Skye was shocked at how this demure, shuffling woman could draw her up with such ease.

Dula kept Skye's right arm over her own shoulders and placed her left arm around Skye's waist. Side by side, the pair shuffled out of that horrid black room and into a narrow hallway. Skye breathed in what seemed like very fresh air, and thought she'd give almost anything for a drink of cold water.

At the end of this dim hallway was a door, which Dula unlocked with a single key. She slipped the key back into the pocket of her sweater, and opened the door. They shuffled in, and she turned on the light. The space looked very much like Skye's brothel bedroom, except this one had a small bathtub, and a wardrobe. In addition, this room appeared to be very lived in. The walls were decorated with city posters, a large bookcase filled with books stood in the corner, and the barred windowsill held several small potted plants.

Without looking up, Dula let go of Skye and pointed to her bed. Skye didn't need to be told twice; she was finding it quite painful to remain standing, and the bed appeared very soft and inviting. As she managed to move herself over and onto Dula's bed, she promised, *I'm still going to find a way to kill myself, but I need to rest here for a little bit. That'll help give me the strength to figure out a plan.*

Skye melted into the soft mattress. From the corner, she heard Dula starting to run a bath.

❦ *WIL AND AETON* ❦

"Are you sure this is the right place?" asked Wil as he scanned the front of the strip club that looked more like a prison. It was made of gray concrete, and some of the upper windows had bars on them. And it certainly didn't have the obvious neon signage that the New Orleans clubs had all along Bourbon Street.

"There's only one way to find out," Aeton said.

"We didn't come here last night when we were looking for Skye, did we?"

"We went to so many freakin places, Wil, I couldn't begin to remember them all. But look over there down by all the warehouses; do you see those railroad tracks? I don't remember coming near those...so my best guess would be that we did *not* make it here last night."

"It's hard to believe that after going all night hopping from brothel to brothel, there still are so many we have left to check. Although, as far as this place is concerned, it's probably a good thing. If the woman we're meeting was in this club last night, there's a very good chance she'd recognize us today."

"Yes," said Aeton. "You ready? I'm sure this is the street the guy gave me."

"Let's go."

"Remember, let me do *all* the talking."

"As far as she'll know, I'm a mute."

Aeton led the way as he opened the large black doors to the club. Directly inside was a small foyer inhabited by two brutish men. Behind them were two more doors that swung open into what Wil could only assume was the main hall of the strip club. Aeton stepped up and spoke to the men, and as their focus was on Aeton, Wil took the momentary opportunity to size them up.

They looked alike, almost like brothers, having the same build of about 6'5" and each weighing in over 300 lbs. One had his head completely shaved, and the other wore a buzz cut. The bald one had a cloudy eye, and by the way he looked around, Wil was sure he was partially, if not fully, blind in that eye. They kept their weapons strapped on opposite sides of their back, which caused Will to make a mental note that the bald guy was left-handed. Both of them wore pointy, metal-tipped cowboy boots.

Aeton was speaking to the man with the buzz cut, who must've been the leader of the pair, because the bald guy simply stood there, hands behind his back, chest jutted out. Wil thought he was obviously trying to look dominating, and he wished he could prove who was really the alpha dog by throwing the guy down on the floor and making him beg for his life.

After a few minutes, the main guy gave them entrance. When he lifted his hand to push open the strip club doors, Wil saw it was covered with terrible burn scars. But by no means was the brute trying to conceal his deformities because his fingers were littered with gold nugget rings.

These dudes ain't playin, thought Wil. *Even so, Aeton and I could take 'em down if we needed. No doubt about it.*

The lead guy escorted Aeton and Wil into the club and the other followed behind them. *This is so freakin surreal,* thought Wil. *What in the hell am I doing walking in between these two mutants with a quarter of a mill strapped to my body? Oh god, this better work.*

Once again, Wil focused his energy on scoping out the place, and from a quick scan, he spotted four alternative exits, in case of emergency, as well as several items lying about that could be used as weapons. The room was empty, save the stages, the tables and chairs, and the various alcohol stations. He heard someone approaching from the far right, an inconsistent rhythm of clicks from a pair of stilettos. From the way the two bodyguards stood at attention when they also heard the sounds, Wil assumed it was the woman who owned this joint.

The short, fat woman in high heels seemed to defy gravity as she quickly hobbled, yet at the same time, glided over to the group of men. She spoke in a sing-songy way to her guards, and when she got close to them, she patted them condescendingly on their chests. However, the moment she addressed Aeton, she instantly turned suspicious and cunning. Wil observed their interactions, making sure to remain completely poker-faced.

Aeton and the woman spoke for several minutes; but all the while, she kept looking over at Wil. She seemed to be bothered by him, so much so, she abruptly stopped talking to Aeton in order to hobble over to him. Wil upheld a neutral, yet unthreatened, posture as she scrutinized him up and down. Squinting her eyes, she stared at his face, as if she was trying to decide if she'd seen him before. She looked into his eyes and spoke directly to him.

Wil didn't understand a word she said, but he was not about to be the one to break eye contact; he simply waited for Aeton to interpret.

"She thinks you look familiar, and she's asking if you've ever met," Aeton said.

Wil shook his head 'no.' The woman paused for a moment, poring over his features, and then spoke something else in Greek.

Aeton said, "She's asking again if you're absolutely sure you've never met." Wil could tell she was trying to ascertain if he was lying, so he continued to look the old woman straight in her eyes, and once again, he shook his head. For what seemed like a full minute, she continued to examine Wil head to toe.

Then, as abruptly as she'd stopped talking to Aeton, she began chattering again, motioning for them to come and sit at a table. The three sat as Aeton and the woman continued negotiating, and the guards remained standing beside the table.

Aeton turned to Wil. "She wants to see the money."

Wil set the black leather laptop case on the table and unzipped it to show its contents. She pulled out a stack of euros and thumbed through it. Then both Aeton and Wil lifted their shirts to reveal their money belts. Aeton appeared to be informing her how much cash was being carried in each location, and how it all added up to $250,000. He pointed to his thigh and pulled his pant leg tight over the money belt so she could see it was full of cash, and then did the same to Wil's leg.

The old woman stood up, took a stack of the euros and tried to put it in her pocket. She appeared confused as to why the bills wouldn't fit. She reached her other hand around and stuck it in the pocket, and when she felt what was in there, she rolled her eyes and giggle-snorted. She dug out a ball of wadded-up gaff tape. Tossing it aside, she made a comment to the body guards, who in turn laughed with her.

Now able to stuff the stack of cash in her pocket, she made one final comment to Aeton and then hobbled away on her stilettos, returning from the hallway from whence she came.

"Let's go," Aeton whispered to Wil.

The two men stood up and headed straight for the club doors without so much as nodding to the body guards. Once they had exited the strip club, Aeton said, "We're in."

❦{ 37 }❧

❦ *AGGIE AND LOTTIE* ❦

THE WHITE TOWER WAS an astonishing experience for Aggie. Throughout her life, she'd never been much of a traveler, and certainly had never been a tourist outside the United States. Now, to be visiting what many considered to be one of the most beautiful regions in the world, Aggie could hardly believe her eyes. As she stood outside on the terrace, the White Tower's highest rooftop, it wasn't enough for her to simply see the panoramic view; she wanted to take it in with all her senses.

For moments, she'd close her eyes and smell the saltiness of the Aegean Sea, and then she'd focus on the sounds of the birds, and the fresh breeze running across her face. And when she'd reopen her eyes, she'd once again be taken aback at how incredibly gorgeous the scene was before her.

It was a very clear day, so she was able to see the entire city, as well as miles across the sea. The water was bluer than anything she'd ever witnessed, and the sky over Thessaloniki appeared to be several times larger than the one over Lafayette.

How dat? Aggie thought. *Dis da same sky dat covers my home, but how it look so much bigger?*

Lottie walked up close to Aggie and said, "It's just magnificent, isn't it?"

"*Choooh*, Miss Lottie, I ain't never seen anyting like dis. I wish Hal was here to see it."

"Did you and Hal travel much?"

"*Mais, non*, not all dat much. Dere was a time we used to drive all over da South to tailgate at LSU Tiger games. Ha! Dose were some a da funnest times we had together. Hal had *beaucoup* (many) football brothers like dat. And once, for our 20th anniversary, we drove all da way to see da Niagra Falls. But I never done nothin like dis. I'm sure dat's not how it was for you and Mr. DuMonde."

Lottie softly laughed. "Yes, Richard and I have seen quite a bit of the world. We've been very fortunate, Miss Aggie. But I will promise you this; once we get the girls home, and all this is behind us, we'd love for ya'll to travel with us whenever and wherever you like."

Aggie paused for a minute and then said, "I'm sorry, Miss Lottie, I don't know what to say. Both you and Mr. DuMonde already been so kind."

"Well, now," Lottie said as she slipped her arm through the crook of Aggie's arm. "Don't give us so much credit. It'll be purely selfish on our part! Now that we're family, we're goin to want to get to know ya'll much better and spend lots and lots of time with you and the girls."

The new friends walked side by side for a few moments, making their way to the other side of the terrace. This vantage point allowed them to see directly into the heart of the city.

"*J'ai gros couer*," Aggie whispered.

"What, sugar?"

"Oh. Dat's Cajun for: I feel like cryin," Aggie said softly as she gazed at Thessaloniki. "How can someting so beautiful be a place where dere's so much evil? *Le Bon Dieu* shouldn't let the two live side by side like dat." She took in a deep breath. "Somewhere out dere is my Elle and my Skye-girl. I can't wait to squeeze em and take em home."

"Miss Aggie..." Lottie waited to go on until Aggie made eye contact with her. "I don't think I've told you yet that Wil made it back to the hotel for a short time this mornin, and I had a chance to talk with him about what he'd seen last night."

"Does he know where Skye is yet?" Aggie asked.

"That's just it," Lottie said carefully. "Last night, Wil and his friend searched high and low throughout dozens and dozens of places. They must've seen hundreds of girls. Not only that, they also learned from some of the men that were there about how often the girls are rotated around...in the city, and even into other countries." She paused to determine if Aggie was catching on to what she was trying to communicate. Aggie seemed unmoved.

"What I'm wanting to say to you, honey," Lottie went on, "is that even though it's only been several months since she's been here, Skye could be anywhere by now. Anywhere. Some of those brothels move the girls in and out weekly. So, Miss Aggie, what I think you need to understand is that it is highly, *highly* unlikely that the boys are goin to find Skye in this visit."

Aggie's expression still didn't waver. In fact, the corners of her mouth turned upwards into a small confident smile as she said resolutely, "Dey gone find her."

"Of course, honey. Of course we'll find her. We will look high and low, and we'll never stop lookin until she's home safe. But on this particular visit...Miss Aggie, it's most likely not goin to happen."

Aggie stood firm. "Dey gone find her, Miss Lottie, and dat's just gone be da way it's gone be."

"Aggie, listen—"

"*Non, non,* you need to listen to me, *Sha,*" Aggie spoke with great love. "I understand what you tryin to tell me, but here's what you don't know. And dat's dat God is on my side. Dat may sound foolish to you, but I know da Good Lawd didn't bring me dis far to leave me now. I just know dat I *know* dat's da truth. He made da way for me to get to you, and he'll make da way for Wil to find my Skye. I don't care how it looks right now, Miss Lottie, but I *know* he gone do it."

By Lottie's expression, Aggie could tell she didn't believe her. "I'm tellin you, he gone do it. You just watch. I don't wanna hear another word bout it, Miss Lottie. *He gone do it,* and dat's just gone be da way it's gone be."

Lottie sighed. "Alright, Miss Aggie. Not another word."

✞ *GALEN AND NIKKOS* ✞

GALEN OPENED HIS EYES to a nurse hovering close to his face. Startled, he jumped to scoot back, only to find his attempt futile; he was lying in a bed. He whirled his head around in panic, attempting to figure out where he was, but it felt like his body weighed a thousand pounds, and his head even more.

"Shh, shh, shh!" said the nurse. "You're fine, Galen, you're fine. Just lie back and relax. You've had a bit of an accident, and you're in the Saint Loukas hospital, and you're going to be just fine."

"Brother, I'm here," said Nikkos.

At the sound of his older brother's voice, Galen relaxed his head and closed his eyes. "What happened to me, Nikkos?" Galen whispered.

"That story has yet to be told, brother; and I'm almost afraid to ask you any questions. Mum and Pop just left to get some food, though, so we've only got a little bit of time until they get back." Then Nikkos said to the nurse, "We're going to be fine here, miss. I'll call you if we need anything."

As the nurse was leaving, Galen asked his brother, "How long have I been in here?"

"Almost a full day. You got the s**t kicked out of you, remember? And then you called me to pick you up down in the red-light district. What in the hell were you doing there anyway?"

Galen's throat felt like sandpaper. "Is there any water? Can I have a drink of something?"

Nikkos grabbed a cup of water that was sitting on the table next to Galen's bed and held it up to his lips. Galen took a long, steady drink.

"Thanks, Nikkos." He stopped to take a few breaths and then asked, "What kind of drugs am I on; I feel like I've been buried in sand."

"They got you on some pretty heavy stuff, because otherwise, you'd be screaming from the pain." Nikkos chuckled a bit, but then quickly became very serious. "But I thank the universe you called me when you did, brother, because if you hadn't you could've died out there."

"What? Am I really that bad off?"

"You have a pretty serious concussion, but that's not the worst of it. Whoever beat you up did a great job on your ribs. You've got a few broken ones, and one of them even punctured your lung. When George and I found you, I knew it was bad, but it wasn't until we got to the hospital that I knew for sure. And then, you started going into shock seizures...which completely freaked us out. I thought you were going to die right there. The doctors say you're going to be fine, though; but you will be in this place for three or four more days. And then after that, they said it'll take a few months for you to feel like your old self again."

Galen tried to remember what had happened to him, but the last thing he could recall was going to Skye's room and finding her gone. Then the old woman had brought in her two thugs, and that was it. He had no recollection of anything from the point the bodyguards started beating him until just a few minutes ago when he woke up in this hospital.

The two brothers sat in silence for awhile.

Finally, Nikkos said, "Look, brother, I've just got to ask you what you were doing there. You've been so weird ever since I took you to get laid for your birthday, and honestly, I thought you hated me for it. But then, you f***ing call me from there to come and pick you up, and we find you almost unconscious being taken care of by a hooker-turned-guardian-angel. *And,* your backpack is filled with all sorts of interesting things...a pair of girl's jeans, including a pair of underpants, a shirt that is exactly the same one that you were wearing, a pair of girl's running shoes. And this—"

Nikkos stood up to pull something out of his pocket. "Who does this belong to?"

Galen lifted his head to get a better look at what Nikkos was holding. It was a small silver chain with some charms on it, and suddenly, he remembered the moment he'd found that broken bracelet under Skye's bed.

"Please," whispered Galen as he held out his hand. "Let me have that."

"First tell me who it belongs to."

Galen was too weak to hold the weight of his head any longer, so he dropped back onto his pillow.

"Alright, Nikkos," Galen said slowly. "Here it is, and if you laugh or make fun of me, I swear I'll never talk to you again." He stopped to wait for Nikkos' response.

"I promise I won't laugh," Nikkos said, and he scooted to the edge of his seat.

"The night you took me to that brothel, I met a girl named Skye. I didn't know her name at first, obviously, but she finally told it to me a couple days ago. Nikkos, the girl you paid for that night on my birthday? Did you know that she was only as old as our sister, Dimitra? My god, Nikkos, she was just a *girl*. And I never had sex with her, by the way, there's no way I could do that...especially after seeing that look on her face." He stopped to take some breaths. "She was kept in an awful room that had padlocks on the outside of it, there were even bars on her windows for chrissake! She most certainly was not there by choice. I tried to talk with her, to help her, but she wasn't Greek. And when I left that morning, I just couldn't walk away and pretend it never happened."

"Good god, Galen...what did you get yourself into?"

"For the next several nights, I went back there and bought her shift—just like you did—so that she wouldn't have to have sex with all those men. My plan was to have her tell me where she was from so I could help her escape."

"How in the hell did you pay for all that?!"

"I used my savings."

"Galen—"

"Look, Nikkos, if that was Dimitra in there, you'd've done the same thing! Skye may not be our sister, but think about it, she's *somebody's* sister. I finally got her to talk and found out she was American. Her father had brought her here and sold her to the brothels less than a year ago."

"What?" Nikkos said. "What kind of a bastard does that to his own flesh and blood?"

"So we had a plan, I had it all figured out, and last night I went there for the last time...only when I got there, that bitch who owns the place had somehow found out. Skye was gone, and who knows what they did to her. And...well...you can see what they did to me." Again, he stopped talking for a bit to take some breaths. His chin was trembling, and he tried to hide his emotions from his older brother.

"Anyway, I obviously f***ed everything up for her. I've totally let her down. And now I know that all hope is lost, and I'll never see her again, or even know if she ever escaped from that hell."

Galen gave up trying to cover his pain, and as he closed his eyes to catch his breath, tears ran down the sides of his face.

"Now please, Nikkos," he whispered. "Give me her bracelet."

Nikkos was at a loss for words. He leaned over to put the silver chain in Galen's hand, and as he did, he kissed him on top of his head. And then he said. "I could never laugh at you for doing something like that, little brother. My only hope is that one day I'll be half the man that you are."

MOLLY VENZKE

❦{ 38 }❦

✦ *ELLE* ✦

JACK HAD STAYED CLOSE TO THE HOTEL the entire day. This long in his presence made Elle very uncomfortable, especially since the incident last night with his cell phone. But he hadn't said a word to her about it, and Elle wasn't about to bring it up. Certainly, he hadn't forgotten, and Elle was concerned if she talked of it, she'd only bring punishment upon herself.

Plus, her dad was acting strange. All day he'd been very fidgety and nervous. He was smoking almost nonstop, in addition to carrying on several text conversations on his phone. A few times he needed to make or answer a call, and without fail, he'd leave the room to talk. Elle knew not to assume his exits were a courtesy towards her; she'd come to realize this past week that Jack never did anything as a courtesy towards anyone but himself. Most likely, he was hiding yet another part of himself from her.

She wondered how long Jack had been so detached from the family, not to mention, so deceptive. Had he been like this her whole life? She tried to remember back as far as she could to find even the faintest warm memory of her father. She replayed past birthdays and holidays and searched these mental pictures for images of a nice Jack. Was there a recollection of a daddy-daughter hug, a meaningful talk, or a bedtime story?

Nothing. Elle was shocked to discover that she couldn't think of one time where her father had initiated loving contact or communication. In fact, now that she had replayed these memories, she realized that *all* of them involving a hug or a fun conversation, she had been the one who had approached him. Her dad had never initiated the contact. And it was painful to accept that, in truth, he also had never really welcomed her affection; he'd simply tolerated it.

Had he been this way to Skye, too; or was his nastiness only directed toward her? Elle decided she'd surely talk to Skye about this when they were together. While she didn't wish for Skye to have also been the brunt of Jack's disapproval, Elle also would be crushed to find out her father's aversion was only for her. Either way, she wanted to know the truth. No longer was she afraid to voice her feelings about Jack's rejection to her sister, or her mother. In fact, Elle promised herself that as soon as she returned home, she would also share with Macy all of her new discoveries about Jack.

When we get back to Louisiana, I'm going to tell Mama everything, Elle thought. *How mean Daddy is, how selfish he is, and how we need to get Skye to come home. I want to see her more, but there is no way I'm taking another trip like this with my dad. Maybe MawMaw Aggie is right? Maybe we just need to move in with her?*

The image of home reminded Elle of her cell phone conversation with Miss Lillie the night before. She wondered for the millionth time why the Maringouin Police Department had her mom's cell. She couldn't come up with any good reason, and that made her feel sick to her stomach. To try and believe the best, she worked diligently to convince herself that probably her mom had simply lost it at Bobbens Supermarket, or even had just dropped it while getting gas at the Jr Food Mart. Both of those places were close to the police station, and someone could've found it and walked it right over there to turn it in.

However, Miss Lillie's voice seemed more concerned than just a lost-and-found item, and the memory of her tone worried Elle. She was certain Miss Lillie had given Jack all the details when he grabbed the phone away, and she ached to ask him about everything the woman had told him. But she couldn't muster up the courage. He hadn't spoken a word to her since then, hadn't even looked at her.

If it truly was something serious, Elle thought, *if something terrible had happened to Mama, then why would he have pretended to not hear Miss Lillie, and then hang up the phone on her? He wouldn't have done that. He would've needed to know all the details.* Even with these justifications, she still couldn't make the deep pit in her stomach go away.

Elle's only solace was that finally, she could stop counting days and begin to count the hours until she'd be with Skye. It was Thursday evening, the pageant was tomorrow at 1 pm, and by that evening, she'd finally be with Skye! *And if I do happen to win big prizes, like Daddy says I will, then maybe he'll at least be happy enough to tell me what Miss Lillie said. Or, maybe even let me call our home phone number to talk to Mama?*

Elle glanced over at Jack as he flipped from station to station on the TV. She sighed. *Fat chance that anything I do could ever make Daddy happy.*

She prayed tomorrow would come quickly.

❦ SKYE ❦

DULA HAD YET TO MAKE EYE CONTACT with Skye; nevertheless, she had diligently tended to her wounds all afternoon. She began by giving Skye the first bath she'd had since she'd been in Greece. While there had been times the witch had allowed Skye to shower in a tiny bathroom shared by all the girls, mostly she was left to wash herself from the miniature basin in her bedroom. Skye had forgotten how luxurious it felt to submerge her entire body in clean, warm water. Even the pain from her beating didn't overshadow how wonderful the bath had felt.

After the bath, Dula had walked a naked Skye back to the bed and made her lie on her belly. She then shuffled over to her sink and had begun mixing together a strange-smelling concoction. Watching from the bed, Skye had wondered what the woman was making as she meticulously added ingredients from many different glass containers, some holding oils, others herbs, and others pastes.

When Dula, with brew in hand, had scuffed her way back towards the bed, Skye had wondered if the woman was going to force her to eat whatever it was she'd just made. Instead, she had knelt beside Skye and began to gently rub the mixture onto the cuts and welts along her back and legs. At first, Dula's touch had been excruciating, and Skye had buried her face into the pillow and cried. But very soon, an icy, tingling sensation began to penetrate the pain, almost to the point of making it disappear altogether. Before she knew it, Skye had turned her cheek onto the tear-laden pillow and had fallen into a deep sleep.

Skye, just now awake, looked around the room. From the view of the sky through the barred window, she knew several hours had passed. It was early evening and the other woman was napping on the floor beside the bed where Skye lay. But the moment Skye moved on the squeaky mattress, Dula sat up and began to inspect Skye's back.

Her homemade ointment had turned into a crusty film causing Skye's back to itch like crazy. When she reached back to scratch it, however, the woman brushed her hand away and shook her head 'no.' Dula scurried over to her sink, wet a large sponge, and began wiping off the paste in small, circular motions.

Once she was finished mopping off the paste, she returned the sponge to the sink and brought over a tray of food. She motioned to Skye to prop herself up so she could eat. The plate held some rustic bread, a dozen or so large green olives, and a small wedge of cheese. Skye offered Dula to take her share of the food, but the woman simply shook her downcast face and pointed back at her to eat. As Skye bit off a piece of the bread, she hoped Dula was not eating because she'd already had her fill.

The woman was making another batch of the ointment, and Skye was glad for it. Whatever the potion was that Dula was mixing, Skye could tell it held definite healing qualities, along with temporary pain relief. She hoped Dula would not wait long to put more of the medicine on her skin because she could already feel the pain in her back and legs creeping back in.

The instant Skye put the last olive in her mouth, Dula shuffled over, removed the tray from the bed, and carried it back to the door. She motioned for Skye to lie back on her stomach so she could reapply her magic paste. This second application didn't sting as much as the first, and Skye wondered just who this woman was and how anyone in cahoots with that witch could seem so kind.

After covering Skye's back and legs with the medicine, Dula washed her hands and returned to the bed, this time with a stool and a hair brush. She picked up Skye's head and turned it so she was facing away from her, and she began brushing Skye's black, wavy hair.

Skye closed her eyes and sensed herself feeling something totally foreign: relaxation. Not since she'd left the States had she felt the least bit relaxed, and even more surprising to her, this feeling was intermingled with a tinge of safety. She believed this woman was not going to try and harm her in any way, and although Skye was keenly aware this would be an extremely brief moment in time, she allowed herself to revel in it.

❧ *AGGIE* ❧

AGGIE WAS DETERMINED TO FIND herself a church. *I know it's late,* she thought as she descended in the elevator towards the hotel lobby, *but I gots ta get myself onto some holy ground 'fore my mind explodes. And dis ol' Cajun Catholic don't even care if it's a cathedral. Choooh, we in Greece, surely dere's a Greek Orthodox church open some wheres.*

The elevator opened, and Aggie quickly walked to the concierge. He was a short man, only one or two inches taller than Aggie, and he wore a thick black mustache.

"Please, sir," Aggie said to him. "Could you tell me if dere's a church open anywhere around here?"

The concierge looked up from his newspaper and gave her a strange look. "A church? Ma'am, it's 8 o'clock, and all the city tours would have ended by now."

"*Non, non, non.* I'm not lookin for a tour. I'm lookin for a place to sit and pray."

"I'm sorry, madam, I don't understand." He said as he gave her a confused look. "Like I said, all the churches in the city would be closed by now for visitors. They'll re-open in the morning."

Aggie was not one to give up. "Sir, is dere any God-fearin folk on your staff? Anyone here dat goes to church? Can I talk with one a dem folks?"

The man seemed indignant at her request, and he smoothed down his mustache with his right hand before he answered her.

"Ma'am, I'm sorry I cannot help you. I am certain all the churches are closed for the evening." And he returned to his newspaper.

Aggie stood stubbornly at his desk for a moment, hoping her presence would redirect his attention. But he continued to ignore her, and acted like he was engrossed in his paper. She turned with a huff and walked over to one of the large leather chairs that was sprinkled throughout the lobby. She sat down to try and strategize a new plan. "Dis girl ain't givin up dat easy, Mr. Man-with-da-black-caterpillar-mustache," she mumbled under her breath. "Dere's gotta be a way for dis God-honorin ol' woman to find herself a church."

She wondered what would happen if she simply went outside the hotel, hailed a cab, and asked the driver to take her to a church. "Surely he'd know if dey's a Catholic church in dis city."

Aggie checked her purse to make sure she had plenty of euros in her wallet, and decided to risk trusting a foreign cabbie. As she walked past the concierge and out the front doors, she quietly prayed, "*Bon Dieu*, I'm trustin in you to go before me and lead me to da right taxi."

The winter evening had brought with it a chilly breeze, and Aggie pulled her scarf around her neck. She spotted a taxi waiting on the street, and approached the passenger door.

"Excuse me, do you speak English?" she asked.

"As sure as shootin!" the young man said.

Aggie almost fell backward from surprise. "Are you American?" she asked.

"Why, yes ma'am! I'm a thoroughbred Texan, and proud of it," he said with a broad smile.

Aggie quickly opened the car door and scooted into the back seat before anyone else could claim this cab.

"*Choooh*, you da *last* ting I expected to find here in a Greek taxi cab," Aggie said. "Why you so far from home, *Sha?*"

"Well, ma'am, I decided to take a year off and backpack through Europe, but after only a month here, I found myself totally smitten with the prettiest gal I've ever seen. So I got myself a job to support myself while I'm tryin to win over her parents, which ain't gonna be very easy. Where are you from?"

"I'm a Louisiana Cajun, to da bone, and my name's Miss Aggie," she said as she reached over the front seat to shake his hand.

"Nice to meet you, Miss Aggie. Where can I take you tonight?"

"I'm lookin to find me a Catholic Church. Not one dat's old and on da tourist route, but one dat's actually still workin and havin mass. Are dere Catholics here in Greece?"

"I'm not sure, ma'am, I've never had anyone ask me. But let me check my map." He typed "catholic church" into his GPS and waited for a result to come up. After several seconds, he said, "Yes, ma'am! There's an Immaculate Conception of Holy Mary on Fragon Street, just a little over a kilometer from here. You want me to take you there?"

Resisting the urge to stand up and hug the young man, Aggie wiggled a bit in her seat as she said, "*Oui, oui!* Take me dere as fast as you can, *Sha!*" And as the taxi pulled out into traffic, Aggie hoped the Catholic churches here in Greece were open to the public, like they were back in Lafayette.

In just under five minutes, the car stopped, and the young man announced, "This is it, Miss Aggie. When you get outta the car, just go down that little walkway, and you'll see it."

Aggie paid the fare, and added several euros for a tip.

"Thank you kindly, Miss Aggie. Now when you leave, you'll need to come back here to hail another cab. All you need to say is 'the Electra Hotel' and they'll know exactly how to get you back to your room."

"Tank you so much, *Sha!*" Aggie said as she crossed the street and headed in the direction the cabbie had sent her. Almost immediately, she saw the small cathedral and its dark wooden entry doors. She hastened her step to the entrance and took a deep breath as she lifted her hand to pull on the oblong, wooden door handles.

They were unlocked! Aggie spoke her thanks to her '*Bon Dieu*' and reverently entered the church. She dipped her right middle finger into the small dish of holy water, genuflected, and made the sign of the cross.

When she looked up and saw the two lines of dark, wooden pews separated by an aisle of red carpet, she felt a tangible wave of relief and peace. "Hal, you see dis?" she whispered. "Dis look like da Cathedral your mama used to go to. It's got da red carpet, da dark pews, and da giant statue of da Virgin Mother smack dab in da middle of da altar...just like your mama's church did."

She looked around, and besides herself, she found the place was vacant. "Nobody here but me and da Lawd," she said as she walked to the front of the sanctuary. "Dat's OK, cuz dat's all I need." And she knelt down in one of the front pews to bow her head and begin to pray.

"Lawd," she whispered, "You know why I'm here, so I'm not gone beat 'round da bush. You gotta show us where my Skye-girl is, and dat's just gone be da way it's gone be. She your Skye-girl, too, Lawd, so I know you ain't gone sit by and let her be in dis place no more. *Choooh*, I'll pray all night, if dat's what it takes, but you gotta show yo'self strong." Aggie's voice began to crack with emotion. "Dey say it's impossible for us to find her, but I know it ain't impossible for you, Lawd. You can see *'xactly* where she is, so you gotta show Wil how to get her out dis place."

Aggie bent forward and rested her forehead onto her folded hands. She couldn't hold her fear and anxiety back any longer, and she began to cry, her quiet moans echoing through the hollow archways of the sanctuary.

❧{ 39 }❧

❀ *WIL* ❀

Wɪʟ ᴡᴀʟᴋᴇᴅ ɪɴᴛᴏ ᴛʜᴇ ʜᴏᴛᴇʟ ᴇʟᴇᴄᴛʀᴀ exhausted and defeated. He and Aeton had spent another very long day and night scouring the city in search of Skye. For almost 14 hours straight, they'd gone from brothel to brothel, strip club to strip club, methodically checking off every street and every building they found to be a hub to buy sex. Unlike the first night they'd looked, this time they'd spent more time in each location, attempting to build relationships with both the owners and the 'johns', and when they felt it was safe, they'd even show a picture of Skye to the patron and ask if she looked familiar.

A little after midnight, they'd gotten excited because a bartender in one of the clubs claimed to have recognized the young girl. He was a frequent visitor of a small brothel several blocks from where he worked, and he thought the picture looked like one of the prostitutes there. Wil and Aeton had darted out of the club, almost sprinting their way towards the brothel the man had described.

When they arrived, they were taken into a tiny foyer, as the owner bartered with Aeton over fees. Wil was disgusted at how filthy the place was, and when he craned his neck to see past the owner, it was clear the girls' rooms were even dirtier. None of the rooms had doors, just curtains on rods, and each cubicle was only big enough to hold a mattress on the floor and something that resembled a roll of paper towels. And by the wads of paper in the corners, it looked like there weren't even trash cans in them, either. While Wil was eager to find Skye, he hoped she had not spent the last several months living in this horrific place.

In the end, after Aeton described what he wanted to buy, the owner called over his shoulder at one of the girls. When she emerged from her 'room,' Wil's heart skipped a beat when he saw her black hair curling at her shoulders. But when she come close and lifted her face, she was definitely not Skye.

Both of the young men left the brothel, unable to speak a word for several minutes about what they'd just seen. The girl's face had been recently beaten, and she barely looked twelve years old.

They searched for another two hours, until finally, they realized they'd hit every location they knew existed. Either they'd missed one of the brothels, or Skye was being hidden away, or she was no longer in Thessaloniki.

It was now 3:30 am. Aeton had just dropped Wil off at the Electra Hotel, and Wil was sitting for a moment in one of the lobby's leather armchairs. He didn't want to go up to his room just yet. Scott would be sleeping, and Wil wasn't ready to go to bed. He needed to process the events of this night, as well as think through the strategy for today's auction.

And then he thought of Miss Aggie. How was he going to tell her he had failed to find Skye? The mental picture of her reaction was unbearable for Wil to imagine. He leaned forward in his chair, closed his eyes, and attempted to remember every detail of the last two nights. Was there any clue he had missed? Had he overlooked any suspicious reaction from a brothel owner, or from one of the 'johns'? Was he absolutely certain that he would've been able to recognize Skye, even if he did see her? Over and over in his mind, and for quite some time, he sat in the lobby brooding these details.

Wil wasn't sure how long he'd sat there when he felt someone's hand gently patting his forearm. The feeling was so comforting that he didn't even jump, and when he opened his eyes, he saw the hand was a dark brown color. It was Miss Aggie. His first impulse was to put on a strong facade to face her, but her touch was drawing a completely different response from him. With every pat of her hand, she seemed to be chipping away his armor, leaving him utterly unable to hide his vulnerability. He was shocked at himself, as he'd never responded this way before, but he couldn't help himself. Leaning further forward, he buried his face in his hands and he wept. His behavior at this moment was exactly the opposite of how he'd been trained as a soldier to respond. But try as he may to stop, his tears continued as he grieved over all he had experienced over the last few days.

Feeling outside of himself, Wil was bewildered as he observed himself so freely expressing his range of emotions: sorrow for all those young girls trapped in such an appalling life, hatred toward the sect of humanity who chose to make a profit off these child slaves, and complete failure at his inability to succeed in his mission.

"You a great young man, Wil," Aggie said tenderly. "And I know you done all you can do."

"I'm so sorry, Miss Aggie," he whispered. "I've totally let you and my mom and dad down. I'm so, so sorry."

"Now you listen to Miss Aggie, *Sha*," she whispered back. "You ain't done nothin but make yo mama and daddy proud...and me, too."

"But I couldn't find her—"

"Dat's OK, Wil. 'Sides...dis ain't over yet."

"You don't understand, ma'am; We've looked *everywhere*, and she's nowhere to be found."

"*Mais non, non*. Not ever'where cause my Skye-girl is still out dere. But you mark my words, Wil; we gone find her."

"How? How do you think we're going to do that?"

Aggie waited to answer him until he looked up into her eyes. It took several moments, but at last he ran his hands over his face and turned to connect with her.

Wil was not expecting to see the expression on Aggie's face. He would've guessed she'd look worried, fearful, and at this hour of the morning, ragged. But that's not at all what he saw. Her face appeared to almost glow with confidence and a perfect peace. She was smiling at him as if she knew a deep secret of the universe he had yet to understand.

"Wil, you go on upstairs now, and you get yo'self to bed. You done all you can do, now it's time to let da Lawd do what he gone do."

He wanted to argue with her logic that sounded ridiculous, not to mention completely impossible, but he couldn't seem to make the words form on his tongue. He let out a deep sigh and decided that better than try to debate with this sweet woman would be to simply obey her and get some much needed sleep. He would be meeting with everyone at 10:30 am to review the plan of attack for Elle's rescue, and he wanted to be as mentally sharp as possible. He nodded his head and stood to go.

"You wait and see, *Sha*. It's all gone be OK," Aggie reassured him as he walked toward the elevators.

Wil could not fathom how, with the circumstances as they were, this woman could be so full of hope. As he pressed the button for the elevator, he looked back over his shoulder at Aggie. She was just outside the hotel, getting into a cab. And he speculated where in the world that Cajun woman could be going at 4 o'clock in the morning.

✦ *ELLE* ✦

ELLE HAD NO IDEA WHERE her dad could be this early in the morning. Normally at six o'clock, or at least since they'd been in Greece, Jack would be passed out in his hotel bed from a night of doing who-knows-what. But Elle didn't want to spend too much time thinking about her dad because that would only dampen her mood. Nothing was going to wreck this day, because today, she was *finally* going to get to see Skye.

Unable to contain her excitement, the young girl shoved off her blankets and started jumping on her bed. She didn't care that it was so early or that people might be trying to sleep in the room next door. She had to let out her pent up energy somehow, and since her dad wasn't anywhere to be found, she allowed herself to bounce as high as she could.

After several minutes, she collapsed onto her bed, heart racing and blood pumping. She giggled as she rolled back and forth on the mattress, saying in a high-pitched voice, "Today's the day to see sissy! Today's the day to see sissy!"

Now, the only obstacle between her and Skye was that weird beauty pageant. And Elle had decided, no matter how her dad had treated her since they'd been here, she was still going to do her best for him. She figured, the happier he was with her performance, the happier he'd be to drive Elle to Skye's school as soon as the contest was over. In fact, she was going to be the ideal angel today, obeying his every command, and even doing things before he had to tell her. This thought prompted her to start getting ready for the one o'clock pageant.

She hopped out of bed and ran to the closet. Pulling out her new pink dress, she carefully smoothed it across her bed hand-pressing any wrinkles. She stepped back to admire it and imagined how pretty she was going to look today; especially if, after she washed her red hair, she took the extra time to dry her curls to perfect ringlets.

Elle hummed to herself as she skipped into the bathroom and turned on the water for the shower. *I cannot wait to see Skye,* she thought happily. *This is going to be a great day, and there is absolutely nothing that could possibly ruin it!*

❦ SKYE ❦

SKYE TRIED HER BEST to slide out of the squeaky bed without waking Dula. The woman had cared so meticulously for Skye throughout the night, applying her healing balm every four hours, that she didn't have the heart to wake her. But Skye also had to go to the bathroom, and she'd already stayed in bed waiting for over an hour for Dula to get up.

Holding her breath while squirming off the mattress and onto the floor, Skye moved very slowly in order to keep the bed coils' squeaking to a minimum. She slid herself toward the concrete, and landed in a crawling position. Only then did she tried to stand.

Skye had to clap her hand over her mouth to keep from groaning from the pain. While her body felt significantly better than the day before, her back and legs were still very, very tender. She glanced back at Dula to see if the noise had awakened her, but the woman had not budged from her slumbering position.

Skye was thankful for Dula's ointment, whatever kind it was. Yesterday, she could only hunch over as she attempted to walk, but now as she tip-toed to the toilet in the corner of the room, she found herself able to stand up straight.

As she crossed the room, the image of a moving person to her right almost startled her to a scream. She spun her face toward it, only to see her own reflection in the mirror above the sink. Her appearance shocked her to stillness. This was the first time she'd seen a clear reflection of herself since she'd been in the brothel. While there had been a very small mirror in her own bedroom, it was so cloudy, Skye always thought it looked like she was seeing herself through dark billows of smoke.

Is that really me? she thought as she moved closer to the mirror. *I look so thin, and so...old. How long have I been here? Oh my god, that just can't be me. I mean, I know that's me looking back at myself, but I don't even recognize that girl.* As her fingers slowly reached toward the mirror to touch her face's reflection, tears began to fall down her cheeks, and for several moments, she gazed at her image, a shadow of her former self.

Skye felt someone looking at her. Instinctively, she turned to see that Dula was now awake, staring at her. And for the first time since they'd been in each other's presence, their eyes met. Skye saw her caretaker's light green eyes were also brimming with tears.

Perhaps the woman and the young girl were worlds apart, diverse in age, unique in culture, and speaking different languages, but in that moment of nonverbal communication, their souls shared a deep connection of emotional pain and discarded youth. Even if they had words they could've shared, none would have expressed their understanding of each other as completely as did this one instance of eye contact.

Dula's door jiggled, and the sound instantly broke their secret bond. Skye continued her path over to the toilet, and Dula resumed her downcast posture. As Skye relieved herself, the witch entered, carrying a small bag. Not immediately seeing Skye, she began darting her eyes around the room until she found her sitting on the toilet in the corner.

Skye seethed with hatred for this wretched old woman, and wished that before she killed herself, she'd somehow be able to find a way to send the witch straight to hell. And now, not just because of what she'd done to her, but also because of what she'd done to Dula, and the countless other girls who had come here before her.

The witch saw Skye's loathing, and she laughed heartily.

"You think you hate me now," she sing-songed to her. "Just wait for you to get new owner, and you beg me for to take you back. You've had it good here, Love, even had your own room. Ha! You'll be lucky for to be bought by someone who even give you a room. Now stand up for to see your back."

Skye stood up and took a few steps toward the witch before turning around. She felt the old woman's eyes scrutinizing her.

"Dula has done good, the marks not so bad anymore. And I have a pretty slip; long for to cover all the marks."

The witch pulled out a dark blue satin slip and tossed it onto Skye's right shoulder.

"Put it on and let me see," the old hag ordered.

When Skye lifted her arms to dress herself, the sharp pains in her back prevented her from fully raising them. But she'd already let the slip drop over her head, so she was caught inside the thin tube of material. Feeling trapped, vulnerable, and out of control, Skye began to wriggle wildly, almost losing her balance and falling to the floor.

The witch snapped her fingers, and Skye heard Dula shuffling quickly towards her. Dula caught the toppling Skye just in time, and after helping her regain her balance, she lifted Skye's arms straight enough to allow the slip to begin to fall into place. Dula gently tugged the slip all the way down Skye's body, smoothed out the wrinkles, and then shuffled back to her place on the bed.

"You stand back and let me see," the witch ordered. As Skye stood posing, the hobbling woman circled around her, viewing her from every angle.

"Good!" she said, happily clapping her hands in approval. "This dress covers all the marks on your back and legs." Then the witch became serious again, squinting her eyes threateningly at Skye. "Now, you listen, you little whore, when I come to get you, you obey me, or I beat you more. And when you go out for to be sold, you walk like you have no pain, or I whip you again, two times harder. You hear?"

Skye didn't answer.

The witch leaned into her face and lifted her hand to harshly jerk her hair. Skye's head whipped back from the pull.

"I said," she repeated forcefully, "you hear me?"

Skye nodded, and the witch let her go with a shove.

The woman turned to Dula and barked out several commands, to which, Dula simply nodded. Then she hobbled out of the room, locking the door after her.

Once again with her face downward, Dula led Skye back to the bed and made her sit down. She helped Skye lift her arms in order to slide off the dark blue slip, and motioned for her to lie on her belly. She hung the slip on a wall hook next to the bed, and shuffled over to her sink to begin mixing another batch of her medicinal paste.

As Skye listened to the clinks of Dula's glass vials, her mind settled into her only place of comfort: possible strategies for suicide.

❧{ 40 }❧

❀ WIL ❀

WIL PACED HIS HOTEL ROOM waiting for Aeton to arrive for their final meeting, the morning of the auction. Everyone besides Aeton was present: Scott, Lottie, and Aggie. The time was 10:35, five minutes past their original start time, and Wil hated when meetings began late.

"Chill, dude," Scott said. "I'm sure he'll be here any second."

Annoyed, Wil didn't acknowledge Scott. Instead, he opened the hotel room door and looked up and down the hallway to see if maybe Aeton was approaching.

"I'm going to try him again," Wil said, but as he picked up his cell to call, it rang.

"Where the hell are you?" Wil answered. "Everyone else is here waiting for you." He swung the door back open and stepped out into the hallway to talk with Aeton. Even so, the others could hear Wil's muffled voice as he spoke aggressively into his phone.

Scott sat down on the bed and smiled at Lottie and Aggie, who were sitting side by side on the hotel loveseat that was positioned against the wall between the bed and the sliding glass balcony doors.

"He always gets like this at crunch time," he said. "He doesn't settle for anything less than perfection."

"He's just like his father," said Lottie, trying to smile. She wanted to say something to lighten the mood, but her mind was blank. As usual, she sat properly with her hands folded in her lap, but also as usual when she was upset, her thumbs were at work nervously crossing over each other. Aggie slid her hand over to cover Lottie's hands, and whispered, "Ever'ting's gone be alright, *Sha*."

Lottie's only response was to nod her head and then turn to look out at the gorgeous view of the sea.

Separating the love seat and two leather club chairs was an oblong coffee table, and lying open on it were three street maps of Thessaloniki. The maps were marked up with a red sharpie, as Wil had drawn the route lines from their hotel to the auction site, and from the auction site to the airport. Earlier this morning, Scott had once again practiced the drive in order to ensure he had memorized each route perfectly.

Bursting back into the room, Wil said, "Aeton's still ten minutes away. There was an accident, and he's stuck in traffic."

"Wil, we have plenty of time before we have to start," said Scott. "And really, there's not much for us to talk about, anyway. It's cut and dry for me and the ladies, because all we have to do is wait in the SUV. Plus, I already know the route, I even drove it again early this morning while you were sleeping. We can just chill for a few minutes until he gets here."

"Nope. I'm not waiting for him." And Wil crossed the room to sit in one of the club chairs. He handed one of the maps to Scott, one to Lottie, and he kept the last one laid out on the coffee table.

"OK," Wil said. "It's about 10:38, and the auction starts at one. Aeton and I will be leaving around 11:30 to grab some food and then head over to the auction site, which is right here." He pointed to the red square he'd drawn on the map. "You guys need to be checked out of the hotel and parked in place no later than 12:45. When we met with that lady who is running the auction, she told Aeton the buying and selling will happen in two segments, each part taking anywhere between 15-30 minutes, depending upon how many girls are in each one.

"We think that Elle will be in the first group, and if that's so, then we'll be able to cash out during the break between the two auction segments. So, in actuality, if the auction starts on time and all goes well, we could be leaving the location as early as 1:30. I'll send Scott a text as soon as we are ready to exit. Ideally, you'll leave your parking spot, pull the SUV as close to the entrance as possible, and we'll load up directly from the site."

"How you gone get Elle to go with you?" asked Aggie. "She gone be scared stiff if you just lift her up and take her out."

"We have no other choice, Miss Aggie," Wil said.

"But what dem folks gone do if dey see you carryin a screamin young girl over yo shoulders? What if dey try to stop you?"

"We've thought of that," Wil said, "but on the other hand, if these people make their fortune by doing this kind of thing, I can't imagine it'll be the first time a young girl has resisted being taken away by someone she didn't know. I hate to say it, but I don't think the people there are going to care less if Elle goes kicking and screaming. To them, that's just an every day part of the business."

"Lawd, have mercy," Aggie whispered.

"And as soon as she gets to the car," Lottie said, "she'll see you, Miss Aggie. And you'll be able to get her calm in no time."

A moment passed while the team was processing the information. Then, Scott cleared his throat and said, "So I hate to be the wet blanket, but we haven't talked much about alternative outcomes. What if something goes wrong? What if you can't text us? Or someone outbids you? What's our plan B?"

"We haven't talked about it because there is no plan B," answered Wil. "Plan A is to get Elle, and as far as I'm concerned, failure is not an option. Done deal. That's why it's so important for you to park close enough to the venue that you have a good view of the front. From the moment you park, dude, you've got to keep a razor-sharp focus on that entrance; especially if the time keeps going by and you haven't heard from me.

"But make no mistake: no matter *what* it takes, I'm not leaving that place without Elle, and I mean, *no matter what it takes.* So you can assume that if I come running like a bat outta hell with a little red-haired girl on my shoulders, you best get ready to haul a** once we get in the car."

"You got it," said Scott.

"Good," Wil said and stood up from his chair. As he walked toward the door, he turned and asked, "Any other questions?"

"Nope," said Scott.

"Mom?"

Lottie shook her head.

"Miss Aggie?"

"When we gone talk about da plan for Skye?"

At that question, Wil sighed and dropped his head. A few moments of silence passed between them.

"I don't know how to answer that, Miss Aggie," Wil said softly. "How about we keep our focus on Elle right now? Let's get her back first, and then we'll strategize the next plan to find Skye."

"You right, Mr. Wil; but I want you to know dat I'm still expectin to get on dat plane with *both* dem girls. I don't know how da Lawd's gone do it, I just know he is. So please, all I'm askin is you keep dem eyes open for my Skye-girl."

"Yes, Miss Aggie."

Wil's cell phone rang.

"That's gonna be Aeton, I bet he's down at the entrance." Wil said. He answered his phone and said, "Hold up, Aeton." Then he looked up at the others in the room. "Is there anything else we need to cover before I leave?"

When no one spoke up, Wil said, "OK. I'll see you all in just a few hours, with Elle in hand. Let's roll."

He grabbed his black leather laptop bag that was still filled with cash, gave Scott a final fist-bump, and exited the room.

✣ *ELLE* ✣

ELLE WANTED TO SKIP down the sidewalk, she felt so much excitement about the day. But Jack had already yelled at her twice for skipping ahead of him. They had just gotten out of the taxi, and were walking to the building where the beauty pageant was going to be held. Elle felt like a shaken can of pop.

"Are you *sure* they're not going to want me to perform anything, Daddy? Most pageants have a talent portion. I'll totally do it, if that'll make me win." Elle was chattering a-mile-a-minute. "I could sing a song; me and Skye used to sing together all the time, and I know lots of songs. I don't even need a piano to play; I could sing without music."

"You won't need to sing," Jack replied.

"I'm just saying, I *could* if you need me to. Don't think that I can't do it, if the judges ask for something at the last minute.

Because I can. I'll totally do *whatever* you want me to do so I can win this pageant for you."

"You won't need to do anything but just stand there," he said as he stopped walking. "This is the place. Listen to me: I don't want you to say anything to anyone once we get inside here. You stand next to me until that woman takes you back into the waiting room. Don't talk to any of the adults, and when you are backstage waiting to go out, I don't want you to talk to any of the other girls who are back there, you hear me? Not even *one* of them."

"Why not? It will be boring back there to just sit—"

"I said what I said, Elle," he scolded harshly. "The other girls back there are *not* your friends. They're going to be wanting to win this thing too, so they might say bad stuff to scare you, or to try and make you not want to compete."

"Oh." Elle hadn't thought of that.

"So you keep your eyes to the ground, and your lips zipped, you hear me?"

"Yes, Daddy."

"Good. Now let's go inside."

Jack opened the big black doors, and they were greeted by two enormous men. Elle knew she was small for her age, but she still wondered if these men were giants of some kind. They were *huge*, and the top of her head didn't even come up to their hips! She couldn't help but stare.

Her dad whispered something to one of them, while Elle kept gazing at the other man, who was bald. She noticed he had one eye that looked very cloudy, just like her neighbor friend's cat did when it had gotten cataracts. She felt her dad tugging her out of the lobby and into the larger room, and she remained mesmerized at the giants until she was fully inside the theatre and the lobby doors had closed. She began to look around, but her dad hissed at her, "Stop it! I told you to keep your head down and your mouth shut!"

Elle tried her best to obey, but her curiosity kept getting the best of her. Whenever she'd think her dad was not looking, she'd glance up through the corners of her eyes to get a snapshot of her surroundings.

It was very dark in the room, much darker than it had been on the day they'd met up with the owner, when she'd shown Elle how to walk on the stage. Knowing she might get a slap if she looked up at the warehouse ceiling, Elle just assumed that all those fluorescent lights must've been turned off, leaving only the stage lights turned on.

She heard a familiar voice, and knew instantly that it was the interpreter who had been showing Jack around since they'd arrived. He and her dad talked in hushed tones, so she wasn't able to make out too much. She closed her eyes to focus in on their words, but it was no use; however, she did notice that all the voices in the room sounded like they were men's. That was not at all what Elle would've anticipated. Back home, pageants like these were usually judged by women.

There was one woman's voice that stuck out above the rest, a shrill, sing-songy sound, and it continued to grow louder as she approached Jack and Elle. The girl knew it was the lady who owned the theatre. Continuing to talk in her 'outside voice,' she briefly spoke with the interpreter, patted Elle on the head, and then clicked away from them to greet someone else.

"What did she say," asked Jack.

"She said it was good we were here so early, because you could walk around with her to let people get a good look at her before the deal," said the interpreter.

"Yeah, I'm not so sure I want to do that," Jack said. "It's pretty dark in here, and I can't make out the faces of people until I'm right up on them."

"Who cares? No one's going to know you, plus your chances to get a good—"

Jack cut him off, and pulled him away. The only words Elle heard before the two men were out of earshot was Jack telling him about a weird phone call he got from the police. Elle wondered if her dad was talking about the call from the Marigouin police, who had her mom's cell phone? Or if he was referring to something else?

❧ SKYE ❧

As DULA CAREFULLY APPLIED SKYE'S MAKEUP, Skye wondered how often the woman prepared the witch's girls to be sold. *I bet the reason she tries not to make eye contact with me is because it makes it easier on her,* thought Skye. *I get that. If she doesn't connect with the girl she's helping, then she won't get attached. I do the same thing. It's a different situation, but that's exactly why I try to never make eye contact with the men who come in my room. It helps me to pretend it's not real, that they're just robots or something.*

Skye shuddered at the thought of being forced to service men again. *I'll never know the truth about that Galen guy, whether he was working for the witch or really on my side, but at least he gave me a few nights of freedom. And now that I've had that, there's no way I'm going back. I pray to god the place I'm going has a sheet, or a rope, and something to hang it on.*

Dula stood back and checked Skye's face. Approving her work, she led Skye to stand before the mirror so she could look at herself. But Skye didn't want to look, or even care about her appearance. It didn't matter anymore.

She heard Dula sigh deeply. She shuffled over to her medicine cabinet and came back with something in her hand. When she offered its contents to the young girl, Skye saw it was two small white pills.

"For pain," she said. Her voice was so raspy, it was almost inaudible. "You take for pain."

Skye was dumbfounded Dula had just spoken to her in English.

"What?" Skye whispered. "Dula, do you speak English?"

The woman shook her head and waved her arms for Skye to stop talking as she swiftly scuffed over to the bed and sat down. Her hair covered her downcast face, hiding her expression.

"Dula!" Skye whispered a bit louder. "You've got to talk to me! Do you speak English? Where are you from? How long have you been here?"

But the woman was becoming extremely upset, rocking back and forth on the bed, and waving her hands for Skye to stop talking. Not saying another word, Skye went to sit next to her. She waited for several moments, until the woman calmed down.

"I'm sorry," Skye whispered very slowly. "I won't try to make you say anything else. But if you do understand me, I want to say thank you for all you've done for me. You didn't have to be so nice to me. And I'm sorry for whatever that witch has done to you."

Skye watched to see if Dula would give her any indication that she'd understood what she'd said. But all Dula offered her was complete stillness, so there was no way for Skye to know. She tried looking through Dula's veil of hair that hung around her face, but it was too thick. Skye had almost given up when she saw a tear fall onto one of Dula's hands which was now settled in her lap. Skye exhaled in gratitude, knowing her words had been understood.

The door swung open, and the witch hobbled in.

"Time for you to come with me," she ordered. "We go down, get in car, and go to other place. It's time for you to be sold."

Skye wished she could give Dula a hug before she left, but if the witch saw her do that, Dula would most certainly be beaten for it. Instead, she used her hands to push her from sitting on the bed to standing up, and when she did, she let her hand slip over and softly touch Dula on the outside of her thigh, slightly giving her a pat. She hoped Dula understood her subtle way of saying good-bye.

Skye, dressed in her dark blue slip, turned toward the witch and followed her out of the room, knowing she was on her way to be sold to the highest bidder.

❖{ 41 }❖

❀ WIL AND AETON ❀

"I CAN'T BELIEVE we're getting here so late," Wil said as he ran down the sidewalk. "*And* that the only parking place was a half mile away."

"For the last time, man, I'm *sorry*," Aeton said. "There was nothing I could do about that accident. Plus, it's only 12:45. We're going to get there in just a couple minutes, still almost 15 minutes before it starts."

"I realize that, but I wanted to be there by 12:30. We have no idea how long it will take for us to check in, or whatever we have to do, to get our auction number."

"We're going to be fine," Aeton said, trying to keep up. "You need to slow down. Don't you think it's going to look weird for us to walk in there sweaty and out of breath? I don't think we should look that over-anxious."

Wil slowed to a fast walking pace. "I don't know what you're talking about. *I'm* not the one who's getting out of breath."

"Shut up, a**hole. You know what I mean."

"Yeah," Wil said as he slowed even more. "You're right."

The pair walked two more blocks at a regular gait until they approached the warehouse. Stopping, Wil said, "OK. Anything we need to review?"

"Nope," said Aeton. "We've been over it, and we're good."

"We're not leaving here without the girl," Wil said.

"Got it."

"No matter *what.*"

"Got it."

"No, man, look at me," Wil said. "Even if for some crazy reason something happens to me. You've got to promise me that you'll follow through and get her out of here. *Nothing* is more important than the success of this mission."

"Wil, you have my word," Aeton said solemnly. "Getting her safely to the car will be my top priority."

"Good. Thanks for being my wingman on this," Wil said. "There's no way I could've done this without you."

"It's what we do," Aeton said matter-of-factly. "And you'd've done the same for me."

"Anytime. You ready?"

"As I'll ever be."

"Me too. Let's go in."

Aeton opened the door to find the two large body guards from the day before manning the entrance. He and the main guard exchanged a few sentences before they were given admittance.

"It's pretty cut and dry," Aeton whispered to Wil. "The bidding happens with just our hands. And the guy was careful to add that we could only pay in cash, and if we tried to screw them, we'd find ourselves at the bottom of the sea."

"That's an original threat," Wil whispered back, sarcastically.

"Yeah, well, they're not paid for their creativity."

Wil scanned the room. It was quite dark, as the only illumination originated from the stage lights, and those were at half-power. The stage was a "U" shape, and small round tables with four seats each were gathered inside the legs of the runway. Because the auction was about to start, most of the people had already taken their seats. With a quick calculation, Wil assessed there were 45-48 people, and from the look of the backs of their heads, almost all were male. In addition to the men sitting, the room was lined with a few dozen standing men, all large and obviously employed as body guards. From their apparent disunity, Wil assumed they were not all employed by the old woman who ran the place, but rather, had come individually with each bidder.

"I guess we forgot to bring our bouncer," whispered Aeton.

"What are you talking about? I thought you were it," Wil said.

"Riiight. Where do you want to sit? There's a table closer to the front, or one right in the back."

"Back, definitely. Let's remain as anonymous as possible."

As they quietly sat at the small table, Aeton whispered, "Trust me. After you drop a quarter of a mill in the auction, the *last* thing we're going to be is anonymous."

✦ *ELLE* ✦

THIS WAS NOT AT *ALL* what Elle was expecting. Sitting in the room behind the stage, she had no idea what to think about this beauty contest, or about the actual contestants. First of all, this backstage room was very cramped with people, and there were only a few chairs on which to sit. A musty smell clung to the air, reminding Elle of the time MawMaw Aggie's basement had flooded. And the feeling inside the room was not good; Elle didn't know exactly how to describe it, she just knew it wasn't good...even a bit scary.

Because she was one of the shortest girls in the room, she couldn't see every girl, but the contestants she did see were not happy to be there at all. In fact, there were a few girls who had been forcibly pushed into the room, and when they didn't obey the person who'd brought them, they got slapped in the face. And Elle thought it was odd that she was the only girl without a chaperone. Some of contestants were one-on-one with a chaperone, and some were five or six to their chaperone; either way, it looked to Elle like she was the only one without someone watching over her.

Elle also wondered why the other girls were dressed like they were. Many had on little dresses that looked more like the slips her mom wore underneath her clothes; and some of the slips were so short, Elle could see their lacy underpants. A few of the older girls had on what looked like a bra or a girdle, and underpants. And not one of the girls looked as young as she was. Scanning the room again, she began to feel very out-of-place, certainly far too little to be a contestant in this beauty pageant.

As each moment passed, she was becoming more and more nervous, and she wished there was someone for her to talk to. Elle didn't care anymore that she'd promised her dad not to speak to anyone; she felt if she could connect with just one person, it would keep her from getting sick. The only problem was, she couldn't hear anyone using English.

She started to slowly push her way around the room, hoping to find a friend to play with. Even if the girl didn't speak her language, maybe they could draw on something, or sit and play hand clapping games. No one seemed interested in her, though. The moment she'd get a girl to make eye contact with her, that girl's chaperone would either come and stand between them, or move the girl away from Elle.

Maybe Daddy was right, Elle thought. *Maybe these girls really are only out to win, and wouldn't be nice to me at all. At least the chaperones are acting that way.*

Elle spotted a girl with long black hair sitting by herself in the far corner of the room. She was wearing a dark blue slip, and she didn't have anyone watching over her. Elle couldn't tell how old the girl was because she was sitting on the floor facing the wall.

Maybe that girl will play with me, thought Elle. *She doesn't have any scary chaperone standing by her, ready to pounce on me.*

Suddenly, everything got quiet in the room, as someone in the front was ringing a bell. When Elle turned to look, it was the sing-songy lady standing on a chair talking to everyone. Elle couldn't understand her language, but it seemed like she was giving everyone instructions. As she was talking, the old woman saw Elle standing nearer to the back of the room. She stopped speaking, pointed directly at her, and waved emphatically for Elle to come back up to the front.

Elle was surprised how quickly the other people in the room were to obey the old woman's every command. Seeing her point to Elle, the crowd automatically parted, making a slight aisle for Elle to easily get back to the front of the room.

As Elle approached the sing-songy lady, the woman gave her a big lipstick-smeared smile, and said, "You stay up here. You number three for to go out on stage."

Elle's heart skipped a beat. The pageant was starting, and she was number three to go out! On one hand, she was ecstatic that she was close to the beginning, so that she could get this stupid contest over with. On the other hand, knowing that in just a couple minutes she was going to step out into the unknown made her want to throw up. She took some deep breaths and tried to calm her nerves.

❧ WIL AND AETON ❧

THE LIGHTS BEGAN TO DIM, indicating the start of the auction, and a single spot stayed on an area just right of center stage, where the old woman was standing. Speaking into a microphone, she began to give the rules for the auction. Aeton interpreted for Wil:

"There will be 35 girls in the auction today, and they'll be sold in two parts. The first eight girls are prime, as they are brand new and doctor certified as virgins. They'll come out one by one, and the woman will start the bidding. After they are sold, there will be a short break, during which the bidders who won any of the first eight must pay and take their girl. The next section of bidding will start on the remaining 27 girls. They will be sold in order, according to their age, youngest to oldest."

"To bid," Aeton continued, "you need to raise your hand and be acknowledged by the old woman. Once she does so, your bid is binding, and you can't retract it. If you win a bid, and you try to take it back, her guards won't let you leave until you've paid."

The woman was still talking as Aeton said, "And now she's just talking about once we get our merchandise, we need to leave quickly so that she can re-open for business."

"This is freakin surreal," said Wil.

"I know," said Aeton. "I can't believe how normal these people are acting, like we're all here just to buy a pair of shoes."

"Shh," said Wil. "It's starting."

The house lights went out, and the stage lights brightened to full strength. Some music with a dance beat started playing and the first girl emerged from the center stage door. Wearing a short, black satin slip and high black heels, she appeared disoriented and confused as she squinted her eyes and craned her neck to see the audience. However, the moment she stepped forward, a spotlight hit her, blinding her, and causing her steps to falter.

Wil's stomach churned at the sight of this young girl. Because of the bright make-up on her face, he couldn't predict an accurate age, but as she wobbled her way down one length of the runway, he knew she was young enough to have never worn heels this high. And, she obviously had no clue why she was here or of her impending fate. When the girl passed by groups of men, Wil noticed they began whispering to each other, probably creating strategy for their bidding.

Once the girl had returned to the center of the stage, the old woman motioned first for her to stand still, and then for the sound guy to turn down the music. Flashing a grotesque smile at the crowd, the woman raised her voice and began the bidding. Wil sat dumbfounded as the men went at it, hands lifting all over the place, and the old woman taunting them with higher and higher bid amounts. Wil and Aeton glanced at each other, nonverbally sharing the shock of what they were witnessing.

The bidding quickly soared to 70,000 euros, and then more than half the hands stopped participating. The woman was able to tease the last few bidders upwards, until finally, the girl closed at 95,000.

Wil observed the process. Just after the bidding ended, the man who had won the girl stood up just a bit from his chair to make himself known to the old woman, and her two guards. The young girl was told to return to the backstage room by using the same center stage door from which she'd entered.

Dear god, thought Wil. *I have got to keep my head on straight. Seeing this is so much worse than I could've ever imagined, and I seriously want to kill every god-damned person in this room! I hope Aeton was right, and that Elle is at the beginning of the line of girls. I'm not sure how long I'm going to be able to sit and watch this.*

❦ 42 ❧

✦ ELLE ✦

ELLE'S STOMACH WAS FLIP-FLOPPING inside of her. The second girl had gone out a few minutes ago, and with each passing moment, Elle knew her turn was inching closer. Every part of her wanted to run away, and if there had been someplace for her to go, she quite possibly would've given into the temptation. But there was nowhere to go except out on that stage, and her head was whirring with nervousness.

Thank goodness I'm not going to have to say anything or answer questions, like the pageants back home, she thought. *At least there's that. All I have to do is smile, walk up and down, and stand still til the fat sing-songy lady tells me to leave. All done. And then I can get out of this stupid place and go see Skye.*

Elle tried to breathe deeply, but her chest wouldn't stretch open enough. Then she realized it was because she was hugging herself so tightly. Forcing herself to drop her arms, she took some breaths, only to subconsciously fold her arms right back up.

The stage door opened into the room and the girl who'd gone before her exited the stage. Elle would have given anything for that girl to know English so she could've asked her what it was like, and she tried to read the girl's face for the information. But the girl looked just as scared and confused as Elle felt, which only intensified Elle's urge to throw up.

The contestant before her had left the stage door open, and Elle stood staring at it, frozen with fear. She imagined it to be a mouth of a gigantic lion, and if she stepped into it, surely she'd be eaten alive.

A woman behind her pushed her on her back, harshly whispering undecipherable words. When Elle turned to face her, the woman was speaking a foreign language, waving her arms for Elle to get out onstage.

Elle knew she had no choice. Her legs tingled with anxiety, and as she stepped up the stairs to make her entrance, her knees were vibrating and weak. She breathed in one last deep breath and stepped through the door.

The second she emerged onto the stage, a white spotlight blinded her eyes. The bright light was all she could see, and it disoriented her to the point she completely forgot what she was supposed to do. She felt panic rise in her chest, fully aware she had been instructed to do something once she got out here, but just what that something was, she could not remember. And so she stood inside the belly of that lion, paralyzed.

❧ WIL ❧

WIL WAS STUNNED WHEN ELLE APPEARED. Miss Aggie had told him she looked small for her age, even shown him pictures, but until he saw this young girl walk out, he hadn't imagined how little she actually was. Maybe it was the maturity of this situation that magnified her youth, or the vile humanity surrounding her that made her appear so pure and chaste. At first, all Wil could do was sit in his chair and stare at the child forced on parade.

And he wasn't alone.

The crowd had grown eerily silent, enthralled by this 10-year-old girl, who barely looked 8, as she fidgeted nervously onstage. The spotlight shone on her beautiful, long red ringlets, while her clean, un-made-up face glowed white. Unlike the two girls that had walked before her, Elle had not yet begun her puberty, and she looked almost doll-like in her pink satin dress.

However, the crowd's silence was only momentary, because when the old woman raised her hand to start the bidding, the room erupted with energy and sound. Every hand waved wildly, vying for the auctioneers attention. Men were shouting, as the testosterone levels spiked into overdrive.

Wil felt an anger burn within his chest like never before, as these wolves frothed at the mouth and fought to win the prize of this child. *This is humanity at its worst,* thought Wil. *And I don't think I would have believed that people could stoop so low, if I wasn't sitting here watching it.*

He felt Aeton punch his arm.

"Dude, aren't you going to bid?" he asked urgently.

Keeping his eyes glued on Elle, Wil answered, "Not until we get closer to the end."

By now, Elle's eyes had adjusted to the spotlight, and she appeared fully confused by the action of the crowd. Wil noticed she was scanning the people, searching for someone. It took a couple of times going over the people, but then he saw Elle's eyes fix on someone in the audience, and the connection seemed to make her relax. Wil followed her eyes to find out who was on the other end of her stare.

It was Jack. Wil's eyes widened at this man who was a mirror image of his own father.

Or was he? Wil's righteous father would never have had the expression on his face that Jack did right now. It was one of greed and smugness as he smiled and watched the sale of his own flesh and blood. The worst kind of sale, at that. This was an auction that would turn this precious, innocent child into a sex slave.

With hatred flaring, Wil used this emotion to sharpen his senses and focus his mind to the mission at hand. But not before he made a vow to himself that once he'd gotten Elle safely out of here, he'd hunt this man down and make him pay for his sins.

"Where's the bid?" Wil asked Aeton.

"175, and it's still rising rapidly. We're going all the way, right?"

"Absolutely. I had my dad wire an extra 50, so if we take away what that woman grabbed the other day when we met her, we can go as high as 290."

"Good, because I think we're going to need it."

Bidders were in a frenzy as the woman continued to raise the stakes. Realizing her command over the room, she took her time as she calmly sing-songed the bid amounts higher and higher. 190...200...210...225.

It wasn't until she hit 230,000 that a threshold was reached, and over half the room dropped out. 235...240... Several more gave up on the bidding. 245...

"OK," said Wil. "Get in there. Take your time, and go all the way. I don't want Jack to see me, so this is all you." Wil slouched a bit in his chair, and once again focused on Elle.

The woman called again for 245, and there seemed to be no takers...245...The energetic bidding had come to a close, and a silence blanketed the room.

Aeton lifted his hand, which made the woman giggle-snort with glee, and she quickly began to raise the bids again. Only one other man was still in it with Aeton, and he was bidding with a confident air.

250...255...260...265...

Aeton was starting to get nervous.

✦ ELLE ✦

ELLE HAD FINALLY LOCATED her daddy's face in the crowd, and his expression filled her with relief. He was smiling, and apparently very proud of how she was doing. This reassurance calmed her mind, and she suddenly remembered she was supposed to have been walking up and down the right and left runways. She wondered if she should start that now, or stay put?

It feels like forever that I've been standing here, she thought. *My turn must almost be over, so it's probably too late to walk. Besides, Daddy looks happy at how it's going, so I sure don't want to do anything to mess that up.*

She wished she could understand what was being said, and why the judges kept raising their hands to the fat lady. Or, why at first everyone was waving, and why now only a couple were. Were they voting or something? The format for this beauty pageant reminded Elle of the time she went with MawMaw Aggie to what she called an estate sale. The people there had numbers on little white ping-pong paddles, and they'd lift them up to try and buy the things they wanted.

Elle could see clearly now into the audience, and only two of the judges were still voting. One was a guy in the back of the room, too far away for her to see his face, and the other was a weird man she'd met a few days ago when her dad had made her hike all over the city to meet these judges. He was the creepy one who was eating huge green olives and who kept touching her hair. She shuddered at the thought of him.

Back and forth the two men waved, and Elle wished she could just leave the stage. There was nothing left for her to do, and she felt completely awkward standing here as the audience stared at her.

Suddenly, the room grew very quiet, and Elle noticed that the crowd was no longer looking at her. All eyes were now on the creepy man. Even the old lady was focused on him, seemingly waiting for a response from him. And the man did not look happy.

Elle wasn't sure what was happening, so she glanced over at her dad. He was still smiling, even broader than before, so she was relieved to know the lag in the voting was not because she'd done anything wrong.

The fat woman sing-songed a few more sentences to the man. His only response was to wave his hand and shake his head. She waited for a few seconds to speak again, while the tension in the room thickened.

The creepy man stretched up in his seat and craned his neck to try and see the other judge in the back who had been voting with him. Then Elle saw him swivel the opposite way to make eye-contact with a different person, who was standing to the side. Elle strained to see who it was, and recognized it was the enormous, hairy man who had greeted them in the hotel room the day Jack had introduced her to the creepy man.

The pair communicated nonverbally across the room, and after a few exchanges, the huge man shook his head 'no.' When the creepy man turned forward again, Elle noticed quite an angry expression on his face.

The fat woman must not have noticed his annoyance because she sing-songed again to him, which only served to make him even more irate. He emphatically shook his head, and in an outburst of emotion, he swiped his hand across his table, causing his glass to shatter on the floor. Elle nearly jumped out of her skin at the sound, and was surprised that the fat lady's reaction was only to burst into laughter.

The fat lady motioned to the judge in the back, causing the other judges in the room to shout a few comments at him as well. Then she turned to Elle and motioned for her to exit. Elle glanced over at her dad to make sure she should obey, and only after he nodded at her, did she turn and leave the floor.

As she returned to the backstage room, she thought, *Thank god that's over with; it was the weirdest beauty pageant I've ever seen. And why were they all yelling at the fat lady like that while I was out there? Well, at least I know that my dad looked happy about how everything went. Now all I have to do is wait back here for him to come and get me. Then we can get out of here!*

❧{ 43 }❧

❦ *AGGIE AND LOTTIE* ❦

THE ONLY SOUND INSIDE THE VAN was the movement of their bodies as they shifted in their seats, anxiously awaiting the text from Wil. Both Lottie and Aggie were sitting in the back of the minivan, and Scott was in the driver's seat. It had been over a half hour since they'd found their parking place, just one block from the auction venue, and in that span of time, not one word had been spoken.

All the luggage had been stored behind the third row seats, except several items Aggie had pulled from her suitcase to hold until the girls had made it safely to the van. For Elle, Aggie had a complete change of clothes, including socks and shoes, along with her favorite books and her beloved stuffed animal, a fuzzy white monkey. Refusing to give up hope for Skye's rescue, Aggie also had a set of clothes for her, plus the journal and ipod Skye kept at Aggie's house.

For the last several minutes, Aggie's eyes had been closed as she whispered inaudible prayers for her *Bon Dieu* to help Wil succeed in his mission...for *both* her girls. All the while, Lottie monitored the auction warehouse for any sign of Wil.

Scott's phone chimed, notifying him of a text. At the sound, Aggie let out a verbal gasp, as she felt her stomach jump up into her throat. Lottie hopped out of her seat and leaned in toward Scott.

"What is it?" Lottie asked. "What's happened?"

"Just a minute, ma'am," Scott said as he touched the screen of his phone. He quickly read the text and replied, "They got her."

Both Aggie and Lottie let out sighs of relief.

"Dey got her in dey hands?" Aggie asked. "So, are dey on dere way out da place?"

"Oh wait," said Scott, correcting himself. "I'm sorry. They got her in the auction, but they haven't made contact with her yet. Wil says there's going to be a break in about ten minutes; they'll pay for her then, and get the hell out. But all is going as planned."

"Tank da Lawd, tank da Lawd, tank da Lawd!" sang Aggie as she picked up Elle's shirt, laid it on her lap and started to press it flat with her hands. "Not too long now, li'l Ellie, and you be sittin right here in MawMaw Aggie's lap."

"Now we just have to believe those boys will get her out safe and sound," said Lottie as she settled back into her seat and refocused her eyes toward the auction venue.

"He gone do it; and dat's just gone be da way it's gone be."

❧ WIL AND AETON ❧

IT WASN'T UNTIL ELLE EXITED THE STAGE and the next girl walked out that Wil and Aeton felt the freedom to talk. With the music playing and the crowd focused on the next item up for bid, the young men assumed it was safe to scoot the backs of their chairs closer and communicate about what had just transpired.

"I was getting worried there for a minute," said Aeton. "If that guy in the front had raised the bid by just a few more thousand, we would've had to make a run for it."

"Yeah," answered Wil, still slouched in his chair. "And that probably would've been bloody. Did you see Jack up there?"

Aeton nodded. "And he saw me too. I can't wrap my mind around how satisfied with himself he looked as the bidding kept growing. And once the old lady up there pointed at me as the winner, that douche bag had the audacity to nod at me like he was giving me his approval! I wanted to grab him by his balls and beat the living s**t out of him."

"Dude, don't even get me started. It kills me he's finally getting his hands on my dad's money. He's gonna walk away with two hundred eighty-five thousand euros of it, for *selling* his own daughter. That's over four hundred and twenty thousand US dollars! I want to kill him."

"And if you give me the signal, I'll take care of that for you."

"No way. That pleasure will be all mine, in due time. Only, death is too easy of a sentence for him; I want him to rot his life away in a skanky prison cell...with a very large, gay cellmate."

The girl onstage had finished her walk on the runway, and the woman was about to start the bidding. Wil and Aeton sat back in their chairs, both anxious for the first phase of this auction to be done, so they could pick up Elle and make their way back to the car.

Wil watched as the bids rose for this innocent child, just 13 years old. She stood in the center of the stage chewing on the nail of her thumb. *This girl looks every bit as confused as Elle,* he thought, *not to mention the two girls before her. It's so clear to me that none of them know the truth about why they're here. I wonder what they've been told this event is to make them participate?*

The bidding closed and she was purchased for just under 85 thousand euros to a tall Slavic man wearing an extremely expensive three piece suit.

At the end of the day, Wil thought, *how many millions of dollars will exchange hands as these people buy and sell these thirty-five girls?*

The old woman waved her offstage, and the fifth girl came out. She looked Slavic, and was a bit older than the others; Wil estimated around 15 years old. She sold for 45 thousand euros, and was followed by two more girls of similar appearance. They both sold for just under 40 thousand euros.

The eighth and last girl in the first phase of the auction was Asian, and like Elle, she set the room ablaze with a bidding frenzy. The old woman upfront had stressed this girl was not only the sole Asian in the sale, but she also was the men's last chance of the day to buy themselves a certified virgin.

Wil felt his gut churning with anger as these savages shouted out their bids, fighting to 'one up' the other. In the end, she sold for 225 thousand euros to the same man who had almost won Elle. And then the sing-songy lady announced the end to the first phase of the auction.

Aeton translated to Wil the woman's next words of instruction: Those who had purchased any of the first eight girls were to meet her two enormous body guards at a small table, located against the wall on the right side of the warehouse. Once the money was exchanged for the girls, they were to remove their merchandise from the room before returning to their seats for the second half of the auction. Because this first portion of the auction had taken longer than expected, the second round would begin in only a few minutes.

"Let's put all the money in the leather bag," said Wil. "That way, you can go over there to pay, and I can hang back and watch your back. I don't want Jack to see me; I have no idea if he's been keeping up on my family, and we can't risk him recognizing me."

"Got it," said Aeton. "As soon as I get Elle in my hands, we'll move out."

"I'll send Scott the text right now so he can get the car ready," said Wil. "Let's get 'er done."

Before standing up, the men emptied their cash belts into the black leather bag, making sure they filled it with an accurate count of 285 thousand euros.

✣ SKYE ✣

SKYE WAS STILL THINKING OF DULA when she heard the commotion at the front of the room. While she was waiting backstage for her turn to be sold, she had been sitting in a corner, trying to dissociate from everyone else. She had no desire to relate with any of the other girls; her internal pain was so great, she couldn't bear to see the looks of confusion and despair on anyone else's face. But the screaming upfront made her turn her head.

There were two young girls, who looked like they could be related, weeping loudly and clinging to each other as the witch was trying to separate them. Though the girls were crying out in a foreign language, Skye didn't need anyone to interpret. These were obviously sisters, who had suddenly realized their fate, and were grasping on to their final moments together.

The witch called out to one of her helpers to aid in tearing the girls apart, which only escalated the girls' screaming. Skye's eyes filled with tears as she watched the witch resort to violence, slapping them until they finally released each other.

If that was me and Elle, I'd kill that witch before she took Elle away from me, thought Skye.

No sooner had that thought ran through her mind, that she noticed the back of a girl who had red hair like her sister's. The girl was wearing a pink satin dress, and had just stepped up the stairs with a few of the other girls to go back onstage. Skye blinked her eyes to clear her tears, so she could get a better look at the redhead. But before she could focus more accurately, the girl had exited the room.

Oh my god, thought Skye. *That couldn't have been Elle, could it?* She shook her head. *No. No, there's no way that was her. That's crazy. It just looked like her because I saw those sisters being torn apart, and was thinking about her, right? It was my imagination...it was only my imagination.*

Skye's stomach turned nauseated at the thought of Elle being in a place like this. Remembering the witch's threats about harming her family if Skye chose to disobey, she began to wonder if those threats were actually true. *Maybe killing myself isn't the best idea,* she thought. *I can't go on living in this hell...but if I do something drastic, what if the witch's people really do hunt down my family? What if they steal Elle and make her take my place?*

Skye's heart plummeted into despair. She could never let that happen to Elle. Her eyes filled with tears as she realized the grim conclusion: she had no way out.

MOLLY VENZKE

❧{ 44 }❧

JACK MET ELLE AT THE FRONT OF THE STAGE with a smile on his face. As soon as Elle saw her father, she ran to him.

"Did I do OK?" she asked. "Daddy, did I win? That was the weirdest beauty pageant I've ever seen! But did I do OK?"

"You did f***ing great," Jack replied.

"Did I win, then? Are you happy? Can we go see Skye now?"

"We can go, in just a minute," he said. "There's only one more thing I have to take care of before we go see Skye."

"Yea!" she said, jumping toward her dad so she could hug him. "I cannot wait to see sissy!"

"Calm down, girl!" Jack barked. "You're making a scene. Now listen to me. We're going to go over there, so we can get your prizes, and when we do, I think they're going to want to take you somewhere for pictures before we leave. There'll probably be one or two of the judges who'll ask you to go with them, and I want you to do it without saying a word."

"Where will he take me?" asked Elle.

"Just somewhere to take pictures, because you won 1st place."

"I did? I won 1st place?!" she shrieked, hugging her father once again.

"Stop it!" hissed Jack, as he held firmly onto both of Elle's shoulders in order to calm her down.

"Are you *sure* I won?" asked Elle, confused why her dad wasn't more excited. "What about all those other girls backstage? They haven't even been voted on yet."

"Don't worry about them; they're in a different contest. You want to see Skye, don't you?" Jack asked. Elle nodded emphatically. "OK, then," Jack continued, "you only have to do these very last photos, and you'll be on your way. You go with whoever takes you, and then he'll bring you right back to me, and we'll get in the car and go to visit Skye."

"OK, Daddy," Elle said. "Whatever you say."

She took her dad's hand as they walked through the many judges toward a table against one of the walls. The fat, sing-songy lady was standing behind the table, and in between two huge men. Several people had lined up in front of the table, and all the girls who'd been contestants with Elle were grouped to the side of it.

"You need to go stand there with the other girls," said Jack.

"Daddy, why is that girl crying so hard?" she asked, pointing at one of the young girls. "She was in the back screaming, and the fat, old lady actually hit her to make her stop!"

"Uhhh...she's probably just sad she didn't win."

Elle felt bad, if what her daddy had said was true. As she took her place in the group of girls, she wished she knew how to speak the other girl's language so she could maybe help her feel better.

Wil was just fifteen feet from his uncle, Jack, and he had to use every discipline to not confront him. He loathed this man, who appeared identical to his father, but who acted in every way repulsively opposite from him. Wil's heart beat firmly in his chest as he forced himself to keep his distance from Jack.

Aeton was fifth in line, and Wil observed the transactions going on so he could mentally calculate an exact exit time. The old woman was dealing with the money exchange. She talked to her two body guards as she received and counted the money, stashed it for the time being in an open safe, and made notes on a pad of paper. Once the client had fully paid, the woman would allow him to take his girl and exit the building. Since all the cash was going into the same place, Wil assumed the sellers would settle with the fat woman at the end of the auction.

After three people had gone through the process of check-out, the woman spoke a few words to her body guards and left them to finish the transactions. She quickly hobbled over to the stage and made an announcement on the microphone. Her words invoked the rest of the audience to once again take their seats. The second phase of the auction was about to begin.

Wil watched Elle as she stood quietly, unwittingly waiting for her buyer to steal her away. Next to the other seven girls, who were easily four to five inches taller than her, Elle looked so little. No wonder her bidding shot up so high, so quickly; she was the only one here who could fully satisfy the perversion of a pedophile. Wil was overcome with gratitude that Miss Aggie had searched out his family, and that they all were able to rescue Elle from the hands of such a wicked fate.

Aeton was up to the table.

Only a few more minutes and we'll be outta here, thought Wil, as he felt adrenaline shoot through his body.

The music from the stage began, signifying the reopening of the auction. Wil glanced over and saw a girl walking on the stage, but he quickly returned his focus to Elle, Aeton, and the money exchange.

The main bodyguard was counting the money, as Jack stood close by with an eagle-eye on his every move. Once the guard was satisfied with Aeton's amount, he nodded at Jack, who in turn, took Elle by the hand and walked her over to Aeton. Wil couldn't believe how smoothly this was transpiring, and he twisted his head away from Jack to avoid an encounter.

Jack whispered a few words to Elle and pointed to Aeton. Elle nodded to show she understood, she approached Aeton, and took his hand. Completely stone-faced, Aeton made eye contact with Wil, and then turned with Elle in hand to lead her out of the warehouse. Wil was a few steps ahead of them, and as he moved toward the warehouse entrance, he pressed send on a text to Scott that read: "Get ready. We're walking out now."

As Wil, Aeton and Elle walked calmly towards the exit, the music on the stage stopped playing, indicating the start of the bidding on the first girl of the auction's second phase.

Suddenly, Wil sensed Aeton and Elle, who'd been behind him, had stopped moving. Wil spun around to assess the situation, and found Elle frozen in her tracks, her eyes glued to the stage. Wil followed her gaze to see the old woman's hand in the air, about to signal the first bid, and standing next to her was a girl who looked identical to the pictures of Skye.

"Skyyyyyyye!" yelled Elle. "Skyyyyyyye!!"

The girl onstage, who had been staring vacantly at the floor, immediately snapped into focus. Her eyes madly scanned the room to find the source of the voice.

"Dear god," Wil said to Aeton. "That's Skye!"

"Skyyyyee!" Elle screamed again. "It's me, Elle!" She had released herself from Aeton's hand, and was now sprinting toward the stage.

Aeton was just as shocked as Wil. "What's the plan?" he asked Wil.

"You get Elle to the car!" Wil commanded. "That's your number one goal. I'll get Skye."

Skye was stunned. Was she hallucinating, or had she actually heard her sister's voice? Had that red-headed girl in the backroom behind the stage *really* been Elle? She ran to the front of the stage and knelt down to see below the bright spotlight beams.

"Elle?" Skye called. "Elle! Is that really you?"

Elle was trying to maneuver her way through the tightly packed tables and chairs. She called up to her sister, "Skye! I didn't know you were in the beauty contest too! Does Daddy know you're here?"

Wil took a second to evaluate the room. Aeton was just a few feet from Elle, but Jack was moving quickly toward her as well. The old woman had stepped forward and was grabbing Skye around her waist, attempting to pull her back to her auction position. Wil knew he needed to scatter everyone's attention.

Without thinking it through, he ran over to the table with the two body guards, where they had just purchased Elle. Determined to disable them, Wil jumped over their table, and plowed into the guard whom he knew was blind in one eye. He immediately jabbed that guard deeply into his good eye, blinding him at least temporarily. The large man dropped to his knees in pain, and Wil kicked him squarely in his temple, causing him to fall unconscious.

The other guard attacked Wil from behind, pounding his back with extreme force. Knocked into a ball, Wil was able to reach down and slip out the knife he had strapped to his ankle. He lunged it at the brute, and from the warm liquid he now felt on his hand, he knew he'd succeeded in making contact. With the full weight of the man collapsing on top of him, they both hit the concrete fast, and Wil had to wrestle himself free from underneath the enormous body. Unsure where he'd stabbed the man or how long the wound would keep him down, Wil knew he needed to move quickly to cause a distraction big enough to disrupt the entire room.

He darted to the open safe and began whipping out pile after pile of euros, flinging them all up into the air. Creating a massive whirlwind of bills, he shouted, "Money! Euros! Take your euros!"

The room exploded into action with sounds of tables and chairs scooting across the cement floor, and men yelling at each other. Wil could hear the sing-songy lady screaming into the microphone for people to remain calm and to go back to their seats.

Wil needed to make it to the front of the room to save Skye, but now he was hindered by the crowd of men, including Jack, who were dashing in his direction to get their hands on the whirling money. As fast as he could, he began to weave his way through the thick mob of treasure-hunters.

Aeton was only several feet away from Elle when he came face to face with the man who had bid against him in the auction. He was a slender man, in a sleek suit, and he pressed his chest against Aeton's.

"Did you really think I'd let you buy my little red-headed prize away from me?" he said in Greek.

Aeton was shocked this slight man would dare threaten him, as he was clearly physically dominant. Aeton laughed at his threat, but as he lifted his hand to knock the man away, he felt himself being picked up from behind, as if he weighed nothing at all, and thrown several feet to his left. Aeton's body was airborne for a full two seconds before it crashed on top of a table. He slid off the top of it with such velocity that he became entangled inside two rod iron chairs as he continued to slide across the concrete floor.

Elle had reached her sister who was crouching down at the edge of the stage. Her words began spilling out to her beloved sister, who appeared completely surprised to see her.

"Oh Skye! I can't believe you're here! I've been waiting so long to see you, and I've missed you tons and tons. Did you know I was coming to visit? Is this where your school is? I have so much to talk to you about. You look so different from that last—"

Skye cut her off. "Elle, stop talking. What are you doing here? Who brought you here?"

"Daddy did! He brought me—"

"Oh my god, oh my god," Skye said as she tried to jump down off the stage. "Listen to me, Elle. You've got to get out of here. No matter how you do it, you've *got* to get out of here! Do *not* trust Dad, what*ever* you do, do *not trust anything he tells you!!*"

The witch decided to give up screaming into the microphone and trying to maintain order, and she advanced toward Skye. Seeing the girl was trying to get down off the stage, the witch latched onto Skye's long hair to keep her up on the platform.

"Let go of her!" Elle shrieked at the old woman. "Skyyye!"

"You get backstage, you little slut!" the witch hissed to Skye. Skye was fighting to regain her balance, but the witch's grip on her hair was too strong.

"RUN, Ellie! Get OUT OF HERE!" Skye yelled.

"But Skyyye!" Elle screamed.

"NO!" ordered Skye. "Get the hell out of here!"

Elle had no clue where she was going to go, but from the look on her sister's face, she knew she needed to obey. She spun around with every intention of making her way to the outside doors, but she only took a few steps until she felt someone grab her. It was the creepy man, who had voted so strongly for her.

"You will come with me," he spoke English into her ear. "I take care of you from now on."

His voice sent a chill up and down Elle's spine, and she began to sense the gravity of danger she was in. She began to kick and scream as loudly as she could. The man's hand aggressively clasped over her mouth as he said, "You not fight. You fight, I beat you."

The terror in Elle overrode his warning, and she bit down as hard as she could on his perfectly manicured hand. He tried to pull his hand back, but Elle was in shock. She just kept clamping down on it. Not until she tasted his blood in her mouth did she realize what she was doing, and opened her jaw.

The man threw her to the ground as he yelled words at her she didn't understand, and then shot verbal orders to his enormous, hairy bodyguard. Elle noticed that he'd just used his brute strength to throw the man she'd been walking with over some tables. But now, his focus was directed upon her and she was his next victim. Knowing she'd have absolutely no chance freeing herself from the clutches of that ape, she stayed on her hands and knees and began scrambling under the tables and chairs toward the back exit.

"Something's not right," said Scott. "It's taking too long for them to get out of there."

"How do you know?" asked Lottie.

"Wil's last text said they were about to walk out, and that was minutes ago," Scott replied. "Something's happening in there."

"Oh Lawd, Lawd," whispered Aggie. "*Mon Dieu*, reach yo hand in dere and make da way for my girl!"

"What should we do?" asked Lottie. "Should we do anything?"

"No. Wil's orders were to stay put."

"But we can't just sit here..." said Lottie.

"We have no choice," answered Scott. "Keep a sharp lookout, but get ready to fly like a bat outta hell, if need be."

Wil scanned the room for Aeton and Elle. Neither could be found. *Did Aeton really get her out of here so quickly?* he wondered. *I've got to make my way to Skye.* He took a few steps, but then noticed an empty chair scooting slowly across the floor. Elle was hiding under it, crawling her way toward the door.

In an instant, Wil threw the chair aside and grabbed hold of Elle. She began screaming at the top of her lungs, "Skyyye! Help me Skyyye!!!"

Wil heard the subtle sound of a gun with a silencer going off. *Are they shooting at me?* he thought. He had to get her out of here *now*. Ducking his body over hers to protect her, Wil wrapped his arms tightly around Elle, picked up her light frame, and ran towards the exit. He didn't hear another gun shot, but seconds later, he did feel the burn of a bullet's contact as it pierced his left calf.

His adrenaline covered the pain as he ran through the double exit doors and was blinded by the bright sunlight. He shook his head violently to make his eyes adjust as quickly as possible. He heard a car horn to his left, and he began to run toward it. Eyes clear, Wil saw the blue minivan and waved an arm for them to come.

Elle felt one of the man's arms release its grip, and she used the opportunity to try to kick and wriggle free. Losing his balance, the man stumbled, allowing Elle to push herself away from him. She fell to the sidewalk. As soon as her feet hit the ground, she took off sprinting as fast as she could away from her captor. Elle had no idea where to go; all she knew is she had to find someplace to hide.

The car pulled up beside Wil.

"Do you see her? Go get her!" Wil ordered.

"Aren't you gonna get in?" yelled Scott.

"No, I've gotta go back in there and get Skye!"

"What?!" exclaimed Lottie.

"Skye's in there, too! Scott, GO! Get Elle before she gets away or something happens to her, and then make sure you come back around here to get me and Skye! We'll be coming back out in a few minutes."

When Wil stood up, he felt the pain of the bullet in his calf, but it only took a few steps for him to focus past it. He had to get back in there and rescue Skye.

Scott floored the gas to catch up with Elle.

"Just get close 'nough for me to talk with her," Aggie said.

"Yes," said Lottie. "If you pull ahead of her, Scottie, you could even stop the van, and Miss Aggie could get out. I'm sure once Elle sees her, she'll get in the car."

"Good plan," said Scott.

The van drove past Elle and stopped about a half a block ahead of her. Lottie swung open the side panel door, and helped Aggie jump down.

Aggie walked to the middle of the sidewalk and faced the oncoming Elle. The moment Elle saw Aggie, she stopped running.

"MawMaw?" she gasped, out of breath. "Is that really you?"

"It's yo MawMaw Aggie, chile, in da flesh. I come all dis way just to hug yo neck. Dat's how much I missed my sweet Ellie."

Elle ran toward Aggie and fell into her arms. They both began to cry.

"MawMaw, I was so scared! MawMaw, I don't even know how to tell you about it...I was so scared!"

"I know, honeychile, I know. But Aggie's here now. You safe, *Sha*. You safe." Aggie sat back on her heels and rocked her girl.

Elle shot up. "Skye!" she said. "MawMaw, Skye is in there, and there was this big fat woman who was pulling her by the hair! She's a mean, mean lady, who I saw hit some of the other girls in the beauty pageant. We've got to get her outta there!"

"I know, *Sha*." Aggie worked hard to keep her voice calm. "We gone get her out. You know dat man who just brought you out? Dat's Wil, and he a good boy. All dem others in dere, dey evil, but da one who carried you out, why, he was bringin you to MawMaw. And now, he gone go get Skye."

"Who is he?"

"*Mais*, we'll get into all dat later, Ellie. But right now, let's get back in da car so we can go get Skye, and den we *all* can go home. I even brought Mr. Monkey with me for you to play with."

Elle hugged Aggie tightly, and then they both got up and climbed into the van.

❧{ 45 }❧

Skye had to save Elle. As the witch was pulling her toward the backstage room, Skye could hear Elle's screams. She scratched at the witch's hands to try and get herself free, but it didn't work. However, her attempts did create a momentary lag in the tugging, just enough for Skye to look out over the chaotic crowd and see Elle being carried out the door.

I cannot let anyone do to her what's been done to me! Skye's mind screamed. *I've got to do something to protect her!*

The witch had forced her to wear high heels for this event, and because Skye was normally shut up in her room, she wasn't used to steadying herself on them. As a result, the old woman held the advantage as she jerked the young girl off the stage. However, just as the witch was about to push Skye through the backstage door, Skye found her balance and seized the opportunity. With all her might, she kicked the witch in the shin with the pointy toe of her shoe. The woman reeled back from the pain and let go of Skye's hair. Sensing the release, Skye took advantage of the witch's teetering, and like a football player, she put her head down and tackled the her. She struck the old woman with such force, they both careened off the stage.

Lucky for Skye, the witch fell first, providing an ample cushion for Skye's fall. As soon as the pair hit the ground, Skye popped up, potently kicked the witch one last time, and then headed for the main exits, hoping to catch up with the people who stole Elle.

Meanwhile, Wil, who'd just left Elle in the care of Aggie, now was running to the warehouse entrance to pull open the doors. But they wouldn't budge. Someone had locked the doors.

"Damn it!" he said as he yanked as hard as he could to move them. He drew his gun and shot at the locks, but the doors remained bolted tight. *That old woman and her crew must've locked everybody inside the warehouse to make sure none of that money escaped,* he thought. He stepped back to scan the premises, to find an alternate way into the building.

There were no windows on the face of the warehouse, so he knew he had to start circling the massive structure. Running full speed to the right, he turned away from the main road and inspected the building's side wall. Nothing. No windows, no fire escape, no exits.

He continued to the rear, and found a loading dock. He climbed up the short brick wall to a single door that stood next to the dock. He tugged on the handle, not surprised to find it locked. *This door looks like it hasn't been used in years,* he thought. *Surely a few shots will pop open that lock.* Once again, he pulled out his gun and fired strategically at the spots where he believed the locks were located.

He leaned in to try the door, and when he aggressively jerked on what remained of the handle, the door swung open so freely, he almost fell over. The room in which he entered was pitch black, but the light from the open door provided enough illumination to see. There were huge set pieces and wooden crates haphazardly stored throughout the room, and from the dust and cobwebs everywhere, along with the thick carpet of dirt on the concrete floor, Wil could tell no one had been in here for a long, long time. He quickly began darting through the maze of storage to find a way back into the main warehouse space so he could rescue Skye.

Skye was unable to see a clear pathway to the exit doors; too many people were yelling and fighting with each other, clogging her way. Deciding her fastest route would be around the crowd, she sprinted to the left.

She'd barely gotten speed when a man came out of nowhere, and she smacked right into him. When she looked up, she was shocked to find herself face to face with Jack.

An avalanche of emotion swept over her as she staggered back, eyes wide open, staring at her father.

"Hello, Skye," said Jack, and he opened his arms to her. "I'm so, so glad I've *finally* found you. You don't know how desperate both your mother and me have been to get you home."

Skye stood still, mouth agape.

"I know what it must've looked like, Skye, all those months ago when I first brought you here," he said. "But I promise you, honey, I had no idea what kind of place this was."

"Where's Elle?" Skye managed to say.

"Thank god, she's made it out safely, Skye," said Jack, "and I want you to know that I'm here to take you away from all of this. In fact, that's exactly why I'm here...to take you home."

Skye's mind was buzzing. Was this real? Was her father actually saying these words to her?

Jack extended his hand towards her. "Come on, Skye," he said urgently. "We've got to get out of here, before anyone finds us out. Come on, girl, let me protect you and get you outta this hellhole. Let me take you some place where you'll be safe."

"Where's Elle?" Skye asked again. "Why did you bring her here?"

"We both came here to get *you*, Skye, and now we've *got* to get out of here...Now! Come on, I'll explain all of it to you later."

Skye couldn't think. His words made no sense to her, but more than anything in the world, she wanted someone to protect her and to take her to a place where she'd be safe.

Wil felt as if something was magically leading him through the darkness, down hallways, and around corners, because in just a matter of a few minutes, he'd found his way back inside the large auction room. He emerged through a door on the side wall of the warehouse interior, just opposite where he and Aeton had paid for Elle. The stage was to his far left, and the exit door to his far right. And the entirety of the room was in utter chaos.

Wil sprinted toward the center of the room, and found Aeton trying to stand up.

"Bro, what happened to you?" asked Wil.

"It doesn't matter; I got thrown. Where's Elle?"

"I got her out, and I'm back to get Skye."

"Great. I'm with you. I'm limping, but I'm with you."

Wil noticed Aeton's left arm was not moving.

"What's up with your arm?"

"My shoulder's dislocated. Don't worry about it; I'm fine. Let's go get Skye."

Jack was becoming impatient with Skye. He shook his outstretched hand, gesturing her to grab hold of it. "Come on, Skye, take my hand. If you want to escape, *now* is the time!"

Skye knew what she needed to do, and she reached out to take her father's hand. He smiled at her, and he pulled her close to him.

"Good choice, Skye," her dad said.

With tears in her eyes, she looked up into his face and said, "I will never, *ever* go anywhere with you again." And with that, she unleashed her hatred upon this man who was supposed to be her father, supposed to love her, supposed to protect her.

She kneed him as hard as she could in his groin, crying as she watched him double over in pain. Rage filled her chest, and when he fell to his knees, she kicked him again and again and again. Everything in her wanted to kill him.

"There she is," said Wil, pointing. "There's Skye."

"Oh my god, she's pummeling Jack!" said Aeton.

"Good girl," said Wil. "But look over there. A couple of the old woman's thugs are coming to get her, can you see that?"

"Let's go!" said Aeton.

Wil darted over to Skye and pulled her off Jack. She was sobbing as she flailed about, trying with all her might to break free from Wil's grasp and to get back to beating her father.

Wil tightened his arms to restrain her and said in her ear, "Listen to me, Skye, we've got to get you out of here. My name is Wil, and you don't know me, but I promise you, I'm not here to hurt you. Aggie Prejean sent us; and she's waiting outside in a car for you. We've already rescued Elle, now all we need is you. Please, I'm begging you to trust me."

"MawMaw Aggie is here?" she asked.

"Yes, Skye," Wil answered softly. "Aggie is just outside that door." He directed her focus to the large exit doors. "Your MawMaw Aggie has clothes for you and everything else. Please, *please*, let me take you out of here."

Skye melted into his arms and began sobbing uncontrollably.

Wil hoisted her up and said to Aeton, "Let's roll!"

Seeing the witch's thugs closing in on them, they ran as fast as they could toward the entrance. They went through the doors to the small lobby, but found the doors to the outside were still locked tight with a horizontal steel bolt. And the bolt was stuck.

"Aeton, you've got to hold those lobby doors closed while I work with this bolt!" Wil carefully set Skye on the ground and said, "Don't worry, Skye, this'll just take a minute."

He tugged as hard as he could on the bolt, jiggling it back and forth to free the exits.

Aeton had discovered the top vertical bolts for the lobby doors and had fastened them, but the bodyguards were fiercely pounding on them threatening to rush in.

"Wil, you've got to hurry. These little locks aren't going to be able to keep them out much longer!"

"I've almost got it, man," yelled Wil, "Hold them back!"

With one last yank, Wil burst open the front doors, gathered Skye in his arms and ran outside. Immediately as the trio dashed out, Wil heard a car horn to his right, and he sprinted toward it.

The two body guards were shouting behind them, and Wil instinctively knew they were about to fire their weapons. He saw the minivan had stopped about thirty feet from where he was, panel door open wide.

"Skye, you're going to have to run to that blue minivan. Both Elle and Aggie are in there waiting for you!" As he set her down, he felt a familiar heat pierce his back. It was another bullet.

"GO! GO! GO!" he yelled to Skye as he spun around to return fire on his predators. Aeton had already taken one of the men out, and as Wil fell to the ground, he made a clean shot into the forehead of the second guard.

In the van, Lottie's face was filled with horror as she saw her son collapse to the ground. "Wil!" she screamed. "WIL!"

She lurched toward the open door, but Scott spun around, grabbed her arm and yanked her back into her seat.

"No, Miss Charlotte!" he said. "You can't go out there. Look over there! There's more guys with guns coming outta the warehouse.

"But—"

"No!" he shouted sternly. "They'll kill you!"

Four men, guns cocked, had emerged from the building. Once they saw Skye running to the van, they open fired. A bullet could be heard hitting the back of the vehicle.

"Get Skye in the van!" Wil shouted to Scott, "And then get the hell outta here! NOW!!"

Aeton and Wil began firing back at them.

Skye ran to the van that had already begun to move, and leaped into the open door. Aggie's arms were outstretched wide towards her, and Skye fell into her lap. As the van started to accelerate, she sank into the softness and safety of her wonderful, loving Aggie, and started to weep.

"Oh my Skye-girl, you safe," whispered Aggie as she stroked her hair and began to cry with her. "You safe, my girl, you safe. *Le Bon Dieu* brought you back to me, and you safe. Aggie's gone watch over you from now on, and nothin's ever gone hurt you again, *Sha*." Aggie bent over her and kissed her cheek. "I promise you, nobody's ever gone hurt you again."

As they sped away, Lottie helplessly watched through a blur of tears as the image of Wil lying on the pavement grew smaller and smaller. With each inch of distance, she could feel her heart ripping deeper, not knowing if she would ever see her only son alive again. And by now, dozens of people were spilling out of the warehouse's open doors, the sounds of approaching police sirens causing them all to run in every direction. Lottie looked back at Aggie joyfully hugging her girls. While it was a beautiful image, Lottie couldn't help but wonder how profoundly that image had just cost her.

Elle snuggled into the side of her MawMaw and sister.

"Oh Elle!" whispered Skye as she reach out towards her. "I'm so glad you are safe! You don't even know what you've just been saved from." Skye's arm hugged her sister. "Oh, my sissy, I missed you so much."

Elle was crying as she buried her face in Skye's lap.

"Tank you, Lawd, for bringing my girls back to me," Aggie whispered heavenward, and then she said to her granddaughters, "Yo MawMaw Aggie loves you both mo dan you could ever know, and you gone be safe and sound *and* taken care of from now on." Aggie's arms drew the girls even closer into her as she added, "And dat's just gone be da way it's gone be."

320

❧ THE END ❧

But the journey has just begun...

Caged is the first novel in the *Justice Trilogy*.
To read preview chapters of the second novel in this series,
please go to www.cagedthebook.org

MOLLY VENZKE

Now Is The Time

a message from the author

Creating something from nothing has always been a passion of mine. Especially if costumes were involved. When I was a little girl, I'd make my sister and brother put on variety shows under our carport in Belleville, Illinois. Convinced of its Broadway possibilities, we'd handwrite invitations for every house in the neighborhood and invite them to come share in our performances chocked full of magic tricks, choreography to Barry Manilow's *Copacabana*, and scenes with cameos played by Barbie and Stretch Armstrong. What's the craziest thing to me is that people came. And they paid the 10-cent ticket price.

As I grew up, my passion for creativity expressed itself through a career as a singer, actor and even playwright; however, deep inside, I always harbored a desire to go to the "Olympics of Writing" and actually complete a novel of my own. But I kept that ambition on the Someday shelf in my heart. Someday when I'm older...Someday when the kids are all in school...Someday when all my proverbial ducks were neatly in a row. (As if anything in my creative life had *ever* been neatly in a row.)

When I got the idea for *Caged*, it was a most inconvenient season in my life to write a novel. Impossible, really. My husband and I were on the tail-end of a transitional whirlwind; in a matter of just 4 years, we *both* quit our salaried positions to begin separate commission-based careers, *and* I gave birth to 3 gorgeous baby girls (Not all at once, mind you; they're all 21 months apart.) Our hands were more than full, and for me to commit to a project of this magnitude would be completely irresponsible. So onto the Someday shelf the idea went, along with all the other novel plots I currently have standing in line inside my head.

But *Caged* refused to mind its manners and keep in the queue. I couldn't stop thinking about the 27 million people throughout the world who are living their lives on earth today as modern-day slaves. Of these, several million are young girls and boys whose childhood innocence is raped from them as they are imprisoned in wretched and tortuous environments and are forced to engage in despicable sexual acts. Children bought and sold, beaten and starved, daily required to be participants in pornography and earn mandatory wages by having sex with dozens of men every single day. And if they refuse? Then, they'll be beaten and gang-raped *again*. The images haunted me.

People like Christine Caine, co-founder of the A21 Campaign, continued to open my eyes and heart to this injustice upon humanity. She travels around the world speaking about this, and as I listened to her teachings and podcasts, I found it impossible to turn a blind eye. Then, humanitarians like Lee and Laura Domingue, founders of Trafficking Hope, stretched open my eyelids even more as they helped me to understand the gravity of human trafficking as it happens every day in America.

What?! I remember thinking. *This kind of thing doesn't happen in the United States of America, the Land of the Free!* And I was mortified to discover how terribly wrong I was. In fact, every year in the US, 150,000 youth are thought to be trafficked into the sex trade, and my own city of Seattle is a major portal for it. I unearthed stats that proved SeaTac, WA (a city just 15 minutes from where I live) to be the #6 most popular city in the nation—some sources cite it as #3—for "Johns" to come to and engage in sex with children! Not only was it happening in my nation; it was happening right in my backyard...And I'm sorry if I'm the first person to break this news to you, but it is also happening in *your* backyard.

As a Christian, I believe in the scriptures that teach us how God hears the cries of the poor and afflicted. So if this is true, then as these millions of people cry out for someone to notice their suffering, what must this sound like in heaven? I couldn't stop imagining the intensity of what God must be hearing. Surely, their voices are breaking the heart of my heavenly Father, and He, in turn, must be calling out to His people to do something, anything, to administer His love and justice to these hurting people, to let them know they have not been forgotten. I knew I could no longer sit in my lovely, blessed life and continue to think, "Someone's really got to do something about that."

But what? Obviously, as a mom of 3 very young children, I couldn't physically become an active participant in the day-to-day needs to combat this injustice. And as I mentioned before, my husband and I were both in the process of building new careers, so giving large amounts of money to the organizations that are making huge impacts in this issue, was also not an option at that particular time. But I had to do *something*.

Meanwhile, *Caged* was relentlessly poking up in the corner of my mind, wildly waving its arms. "Pick me! Pick me!"

It's funny what compassion can do to a person. And when I say compassion, I'm not talking about the heavy feeling people get when they hear a sad story. That's not compassion, that's just a heavy feeling. I'm talking about the feeling that compels a person to *take action*. As compassion for these kids grew in my heart, I became restless to act, and this caused me to see things differently. Excuses were exchanged for strategies, and impossibilities for possibilities.

Caged came off the Someday shelf and was moved to the DO IT NOW shelf. My husband and I agreed in the vision for the project; I'd write *Caged* and we'd give 100% of the proceeds to two organizations we deeply believe in, two that have proven themselves to be amazing teams working (and succeeding) to bring justice in this arena: Trafficking Hope and the A21 Campaign. We shared this vision with Lee and Laura Domingue, founders of Trafficking Hope, and they generously offered to underwrite the production and publishing costs of this novel. One year later, under the umbrella of Trafficking Hope, the novel *Caged* was released onto the market.

I share this story, because if after reading *Caged* you too are filled with an urgent compassion to act, I want to encourage you...YOU can make a difference! If I can do it, you can do it. Please don't simply say to yourself, like I did for so long, "Someone really should do something about that" and go back to your safe and happy life. Because that someone is me. And that someone can be you, too. And the time is NOW.

But I am also aware that you might be like most people, and you have no idea *what* to do. I want to help you. You can join the army of people who are determined to turn the tides of this issue away from terror and bondage towards HOPE and freedom. Here is a list of several things you can do RIGHT NOW to help administer justice to these millions of people:

1. Pray. Everyone can pray. Pray for the victims to be found and rescued. Pray for their rehabilitation and restoration. Pray for the many people who are putting their own lives at risk to save these victims. Pray for their safety, their families' safety, and for them to have the wisdom to know exactly how to strategize and act. Pray for the resources of people and money to be given towards this issue. Pray. Even if you simply think of one girl and pray...pray.

2. Educate yourself. Spend some time on Google, and you'll find an abundance of information on human trafficking, along with all its horrid tentacles. Great resources for information include:
www.cagedthebook.org
www.traffickinghope.org
www.thea21campaign.org
www.sharedhope.org
www.polarisproject.org
www.sctnow.org
www.notforsalecampaign.org

3. Spread Awareness. Use this book as a launching point. Buy copies of *Caged* along with the signature charm bracelet, and give them to friends and family (remember, 100% of all proceeds go to help stop human trafficking). Facebook and twitter about *Caged*, and include the link to www.traffickinghope.org so your friends can buy their own copy. Host a book club with *Caged* as the novel; to make it easy, we've provided discussion questions for your club in the next few pages. Write a review for *Caged* on amazon.com, as well as for your local newspapers. Once you start talking to your family and friends, you will see just how unaware people are about this issue, especially with regards to its prevalence in their own communities. Awareness is crucial! Once people know the facts, they will be compelled to act.

4. TAKE ACTION

* Financially support anti-trafficking organizations that you trust, and that you can see are making a strong impact in the arena they are focused.

* Educate yourself about the legislation in your state and government. Write your local and state representatives and senators; tell them to vote for tougher laws to be passed, laws that protect the victims and prosecute the perpetrators.

* Host clothing and jewelry drives, and give all the nice items to a local organization that helps young girls who've been rescued.

* Host an awareness night at your church, school, club, etc. Invite speakers who are on the front lines of this issue and have them communicate the details about human trafficking: stats about your local city, how to recognize trafficking, and where to go to call for help.

* Host a 5k walk/run designed to bring awareness and raise funds to be given to support a great organization.

* Do SOMETHING

Human Trafficking is an enormous problem. Globally. Nationally. Regionally. Locally. I invite you to join the cause and become a 21st century abolitionist. It's going to take a worldwide army, all of us joining forces together, to bring an end to this present-day form of slavery. We must do all that we can to bring justice to these millions of young girls, and also young boys, because they cannot save themselves.
It is up to you and me

to **be their voice,**

to **be their rescue,**

to **be their freedom.**

MOLLY VENZKE

ACKNOWLEDGEMENTS

Thank you to my best friend, my biggest fan, and my partner in this dramatic improvisational adventure, otherwise known as life. You have unconditionally loved me to wholeness, and have applauded my creative gifts, even when I wanted to curse them. Without you, this book would never have made it into anyone's hands. I love you, Jay Venzke.

Thank you to my mom, Janice Olson, and my pastor, Wendy Treat. No one on earth has influenced and guided my life more than you. You both are extraordinary women of compassion, courage, wisdom, integrity and perseverance. Thank you for believing in me and for pioneering a path for me (and so many others) to follow.

Christine Caine, you are a modern-day William Wilberforce, and I stand in awe of your unapologetic tenacity to help others. Thank you for opening my eyes to see this issue.

Lee and Laura Domingue, this novel would have missed its window of opportunity had you not embraced the vision. Thank you for being authentic examples of generosity and compassion; you both truly are living epistles. To the Trafficking Hope team: Laura M., Donna, Alliece, Amanda, and Katherine, thank you for sharing your time, your stories, and your wisdom with me. You all helped make this book a reality.

Thank you Leah Ann Messer & Beaucoup Designs for handcrafting the *Caged* charm bracelet, and Latasha Haynes Photography for the book cover photos (front and back). Creative excellence should be ya'll's middle names. And Tash & Ike, you are the dynamic duo of photog... get ready, because LHP is about to be known as an industry leader.

Thank you to Floyd and Vee Domingue, you are the human encyclopedia of all things Cajun and Mardi Gras. *Laissez les bons temps rouler!* Your input was invaluable. And Martha Williams, thank you for helping me bring Aggie to life.

Special Thanks to the reading/editing team: Dick and Jan Olson, Tina Scott, Kerri Weems, Tasha Treat, KT Coronado, Amy Welsh, Sarah Rickel, Jamyrlyn "RUReady" Mallory, Martha Flora, Lisa Garrison, Latasha Haynes, Randy Lagerquist, Michelle Hillstrom, Jessica Montgomery, Fahren Johnson, Deborah Hunter, Anna Groves, Shuie Altizer, and especially for her guidance in the 11th hour, Lynette Clarke. All of your suggestions and support helped fuel the creative flow, especially when the muse seemed to be playing hide-n-seek with me. Finally, Jill Cooper: You were my midwife for this literary birth, never afraid to say the words of truth that helped stretch my vision...even during the difficult contractions. *sigh* The baby is here at last; so it's time to take off those nasty surgical gloves.

Book Club Discussion Questions

1. Did the format of this book bring you into an awareness of human trafficking? If so, what are your thoughts and feelings about this issue after reading *Caged?*

2. At the end of the book, the author lists many options of how her readers can help to fight against this horrific practice. With which option to help do you feel most comfortable?

3. With which characters' quality do you most identify? Aggie's faith? The DuMonde's compassion? Wil's determination to succeed? Galen's courage in stepping into the unknown?

4. In *Caged,* the author presents Jack and Richard as twins. What do you think happened to Jack and Richard that caused the differences in their lifestyles?

5. The book states, *"He (Galen) couldn't understand why a prostitute would allow herself to be locked inside a room, even if it was for her own protection."* Given the implications of a door locked from the outside, does this change your mind about a possible preconceived notion of prostitutes? What about the young girls who have found themselves caught up in the sex industry? Do you think these girls should be prosecuted as criminals or victims? Why?

6. Galen was suddenly exposed to an unknown evil...human trafficking. How aware do you think the world is of this present evil practice?

ABOUT THE AUTHOR

Molly Venzke is a freelance writer, speaker and actor. The idea for *Caged* was birthed from her passion to not only bring awareness about human trafficking and its prevalence in our everyday society, but also to help fund organizations that are on the front lines, fighting to end this modern-day slavery. *Caged* was produced under the umbrella of Trafficking Hope.com, and 100% of its proceeds will go towards these anti-trafficking organizations. This book is the first novel in the *Justice* Trilogy, and while she has ghostwritten many non-fiction books, this is the author's first novel. She resides in the Seattle area with her husband and children.

12642572R00218

Made in the USA
Lexington, KY
18 December 2011